Bloodheir

BY BRIAN RUCKLEY

The Godless World
Winterbirth
Bloodheir

BRIAN RUCKLEY

Bloodheir

THE GODLESS WORLD

BOOK TWO

www.orbitbooks.net

ORBIT

First published in Great Britain in 2008 by Orbit

A CIP catalogue record for this book
is available from the British Library.

HB ISBN 978-1-84149-438-8
C format ISBN 978-1-84149-698-6

Typeset in Garamond by M Rules
Printed and bound in Great Britain by
Clays Ltd, St Ives plc

Orbit
An imprint of
Little, Brown Book Group
100 Victoria Embankment
London EC4Y 0DY

An Hachette Livre UK Company
www.hachettelivre.co.uk

For Fleur
because she is wonderful

Acknowledgements

I am grateful to the many people who have contributed to getting this trilogy into print, and without whom it would never have happened, or would not have been as enjoyable a process when it did.

Tina, my agent, and Sacha who started it all.

Everyone at Orbit, on both sides of the Atlantic: I won't name names, because they all contribute and they all do so with good humour and dedication and no little talent.

My family, especially my parents whose support and encouragement have been constants since the first day I started making up stories.

My friends, especially Tom who seems to have bought more copies of my first book than anyone else on the planet.

And Fleur, for being entirely invaluable and irreplaceable.

WRECKING CAPE

TAN DIHRIN

DIN SIVE

BLOODS
OF THE
BLACK ROAD

VALE OF
STONES

Anduran

LANNIS-HAIG

ANLANE

Kolkyre

KILKRY-
HAIG

AYTH-
HAIG

Dun
Aygll

TARAL-
HAIG

Drandar

Vaymouth

HAIG

DARGANNAN-
HAIG

Hoke

TAL DYRE

Bay of
Gold

FREE COAST

DEEP ROVE

N

W   E

S

DORNACH
KINGSHIP

ADRAVANE
KINGSHIP

The
HAIG BLOODS

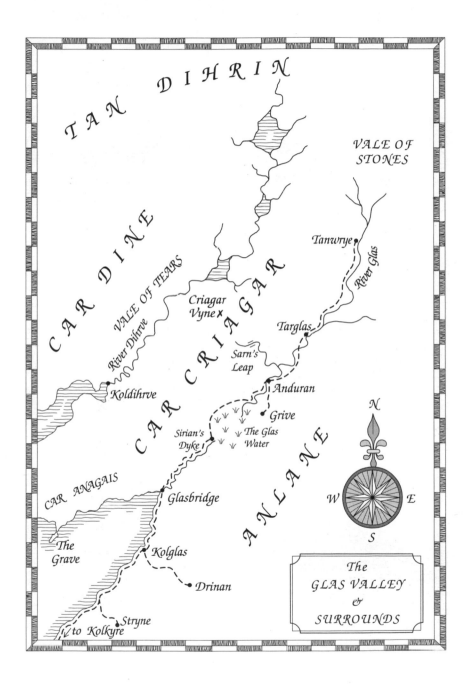

TAN DIHRIN

VALE OF STONES

CARDINE

VALE OF TEARS

River Dihrve

Criagar Vyne ✗

CAR CRIAGAR

Tanwrye

River Glas

Targlas

Sarn's Leap

Koldihrve

Anduran

Grive

Sirian's Dyke

The Glas Water

ANLANE

CAR ANAGAIS

Glasbridge

The Grave

Kolglas

Drinan

Stryne

to Kolkyre

N

W   E

S

The
GLAS VALLEY
&
SURROUNDS

to
Kolglas

Stryne

Hommen

*IL
ANARON*

Skeil
Anchor

In Cyr

KARKYRE

Hent

Kolkyre

Highfast

Anaron's
Bay

PEAKS

*VEILED
WOODS*

Donnish

Ive

River Kyre

*VARE
WASTE*

Stone

Kyresource
Lakes

Kilvale

to
Dun Aygll

N

W   E

S

*LANDS OF THE
KILKRY-HAIG
BLOOD*

Contents

What Has Gone Before

For years, an uneasy peace has held between the True Bloods and the followers of the Black Road, whose uncompromising creed of predestination long ago led to their exile into the north. The Lannis and Kilkry Bloods remain wary of the threat posed by the Black Road, but elsewhere in the domains of Gryvan oc Haig, the High Thane of the True Bloods, thoughts have turned to commerce and conquest in the far-distant south.

On the night of the annual festival of Winterbirth, sudden disaster engulfs the Lannis Blood. Their frontier stronghold of Tanwrye is besieged by one Black Road army; a second, impossibly, emerges from the vast forests of Anlane to assault their capital at Anduran. And Castle Kolglas, home to the Lannis Thane's nephew Orisian, is overrun by Inkallim, the dreaded elite warriors of the Black Road. Orisian sees his father slain, and his sister Anyara carried off into captivity along with his friend and mentor, the *na'kyrim* Inurian. Orisian himself barely escapes, fleeing into the wilderness with his bodyguard Rothe.

The Black Road invaders, led by Kanin and Wain nan Horin-Gyre, have forged an improbable and fragile alliance with the White Owl Kyrinin, mediated by a bitter *na'kyrim* named Aeglyss. With surprise on their side, and the fierce fatalism of their creed driving them on, they seize Anduran and slaughter the Lannis Thane and his family. Amidst the ruin, Inurian increasingly comes to fear that still greater danger lurks unrecognised, for he senses in Aeglyss both disfiguring anger and immense, as yet untapped, power.

Orisian receives unexpected aid from the Fox Kyrinin, and is soon reunited with Anyara and Inurian, who have made good their escape. But it is a joyless reunion: the enemy are in close pursuit and Inurian has been gravely wounded. As his strength fades, Inurian compels Orisian and the others to leave him behind.

Aeglyss confronts the dying Inurian, pleading for his aid and guidance, offering the chance of survival in exchange. Inurian refuses, and is slain by an enraged Aeglyss. Increasingly unstable, Aeglyss then finds himself rejected by the leaders of the Black Road as well. The alliance he built for them with the White Owls is repudiated by Kanin nan Horin-Gyre and Aeglyss is seized by the Kyrinin, required to answer for the failure of the promises he made.

Orisian and his companions find brief refuge in the mountainous Car Criagar with Yvane, another *na'kyrim*, but continuing pursuit drives them on and they make for Koldihrve, a remote town where they hope to find a ship to carry them south. In the course of their journey Orisian's interest in Ess'yr, the Kyrinin woman acting as both guide and guardian to him, grows. He comes to realise that she was Inurian's lover, but is nevertheless increasingly, though hesitantly, attracted to her himself.

Events are moving rapidly elsewhere, as the world slips towards chaos. The forces of the Black Road, led by Wain nan Horin-Gyre and by the implacable Inkallim Shraeve, continue their remorseless destruction of the Lannis Blood. In the far north, the secretive leaders of the Inkallim compete with the High Thane of Gyre himself for influence over this invasion that has achieved successes far beyond anyone's expectations; in the south, Gryvan oc Haig reluctantly and sluggishly assembles an army to march in support of Lannis, relying always upon the assurances of his infamous Chancellor, Mordyn Jerain, that events can be easily controlled.

Orisian and his companions escape on a ship even as Black Road warriors, with Kanin himself at their head, descend upon Koldihrve. They are carried to safety in Kolkyre, the capital of the Kilkry Blood. Meanwhile, the White Owl Kyrinin have made a fateful decision. Considering themselves betrayed, they crucify Aeglyss upon their ancient Breaking Stone. His agonies, though, lead not to death but to transformation. And in the moment of that transformation, *na'kyrim* everywhere – whether Yvane in Kolkyre's Tower of Thrones, or those hiding away in the fortress sanctuary of Highfast – sense the burgeoning of his terrible power; power that could have dire consequences for everyone in the Godless World.

Prologue

I will set the tale down here much as I had it from an old woman in Hoke, as she had it from her grandmother, and she from her grandmother before. I doubt there is anyone who has not heard it in one form or another. It is a good tale, but the wise will not take it as the truth, whole and entire. However flawed our understanding of the Anain may be, we can assume that they would not trouble to be so clear in the expression of their desire as this tale would have us believe. Nor does it seem likely that they would display even such brief patience as the story suggests. We lesser races, after all, must seem to them as slow and stilted and inconsequential as the mute and dull beasts of the field seem to us.

Tane, the Shining City, had fallen. The Kyrinin were undone, their lords and captains slain, their armies scattered to the winds. The streets were strewn with bodies and the drains overflowing with blood. The triumphant Huanin armies, marching under the argent stag-banner of the Alsire King, had broken down the walls and claimed the city as their own.

The conquering King stared out from the highest room of the Rose Citadel, in Tane's gilded heart, and he looked upon his work and was glad, for though he saw ruin and fire, still the city was the greatest in all the world and in it he would be the greatest King.

Now a tall tree grew in the courtyard outside that noble tower. The tree stretched a branch in through the window, and the branch twisted and cracked as it came. In the sound of its wooden bones breaking was a voice that spoke to the King.

"This city has run with blood, and the mind of the world is riven with pain and grief and fury. It is enough. Now we claim this place and will cleanse it and make it ours. You must take your armies away."

"I will not," the King replied, "for my warriors have given their lives to win this great city for me and it is to be the home and heart of my people."

At these words, the branch withdrew and the great tree was once more a tree, silent and still. The King summoned his servants and said to them, "Take your axes and cut down the tree in the court-yard, for I mislike its countenance. And when you have cut it down, burn the wood so that not a twig remains."

On the evening of the following day the King was again in that high chamber. Leaves blew in through the open window and spun upon the breeze and filled the room, and in the sighing of their dance was a voice that spoke to the King.

"This war of yours fouls the mind of the world. This city is filled with the cries of the dead and it is no place for the living. We will see an end to this war; we will take this city and still its tor-ment. Yours is the heart that will be broken if you do not depart from here with all your host, for this is a city of the dead and so it will remain."

But again the King shook his head. "If I leave as you request, all that has gone before — all the strife and the struggle that cast their dark pall over the land these last years — all this will be for nothing. I will not go, for all the lives that have been taken and all the loss that has been suffered were for the purpose of bringing me here."

And at these words of the King, the leaves that were in the room fell to the floor and spoke no more to him. The King summoned his servants and said to them, "Clear out these leaves and make a fire of them in the courtyard. When they are burned away to nothing, return and close this window up with shutters, and nail it fast. I dislike the breeze."

Now the King had a daughter, who was as bright in his eyes as the morning. On the third night the father and the daughter ate together in that highest chamber of the Rose Citadel, and made one another great promises for a glorious future.

But the Citadel shook in its stone bones, and the walls trembled. The shutters that had been fixed across the window were torn apart. Vines that grew without the Citadel came in like a thousand writhing snakes and they seized the King's daughter. They lifted her from the floor and coiled about her.

And the voice of the vines said, "Twice you have refused us, and thrice we will not allow. You will depart from this place on the morrow, or nothing of your happiness will remain unruined."

And the vines broke the neck of the King's child, and cracked her spine and snapped her arms and legs and cast her down on the cold stone floor at the King's feet.

As the heartbroken King's host departed the next morning, the ground shivered behind them and brought forth saplings: an ocean of trees sprang from the blood-fed loam and reached up towards the sun. When night fell and the King turned and looked back the way he had come, he saw not the great plain there had once been but a forest so vast that his eye could not track its limits. And of Tane, of the greatest and most wondrous city in all the world, there was no sign, for the forest had swallowed it and all its countless corpses.

Thus ended the War of the Tainted. Thus was born the Deep Rove, and men called it the Forest of the Dead and did not walk beneath its ill-rumoured canopy.

from Tales of the Anain
by Arvent of Dun Aygll

II

K'rina had been weeping intermittently for days. Her *na'kyrim* eyes, once so beautiful, were now red, veined and bleary. She did not sleep, took no food, hardly spoke. Her friends feared for her, but she did not respond to their efforts to help or comfort her.

She wandered amongst the pools and reed-beds that surrounded Dyrkyrnon. She squatted down beside stagnant ponds and peered blankly at the grey water. When wet fogs and drizzles drifted across the vast marshes she did not seem to notice, but allowed the moisture to settle on her hair and skin, mingling with her tears. Everywhere she went she was followed by two girls. They stayed a few paces behind her and did not intrude upon her grief-fuelled daze. They simply watched, and kept her from harm, and each night reported to the elders.

On the fourth evening K'rina did not return to her sleeping hut. Instead, she kept walking: out into the water-maze of the marshes, heading north-west. One of the attendant girls brought word to the village and the elders sent men to bring K'rina back. She did not struggle or protest. When they took hold of her she slumped into their arms and would say nothing.

In K'rina's sleeping hut, bathed in candlelight and the scent of soothing herbs, a tall *na'kyrim* knelt over the stricken woman. He pushed his fingers through her hair again and again, pressing each fingertip to her scalp. He whispered constantly in the tongue of the Heron Kyrinin. Black spiralling tattoos covered his face, even his closed eyelids. Beneath his firm touch K'rina was unresponsive. She did not weep, but her eyes were bleak and exhausted, as if they had not seen sleep for weeks. She stared up into the shadows that lurked against the hut's roof.

At length, the tall *na'kyrim* rocked back on his heels. He

regarded K'rina with a puzzled expression, then spread a woollen blanket over her and rose. He left, ducking his head to pass out into the wet night.

A cold rain was falling. The grass around the domed huts was sodden, the earth bloated with water. Paths of rush matting had been laid down. The man took only a few paces down one of these before he found his way blocked by a much shorter figure, cloaked in a too-large rain cape and leaning on a staff.

"It's wet," the tall man said. "Why aren't you inside, Arquan?"

"I will be soon enough. None of us would last long here if a little water pained us."

The tall man grunted in distant amusement and cast narrowed eyes up towards the sky. There was nothing to see: no stars, no moon, nothing but the darkness from which the remorseless rain fell.

"I wanted to hear how K'rina was," Arquan said from beneath the cowl of his cape. "Can you help her, Lacklaugh?"

The taller man stepped around Arquan and walked on.

"We shall all be meeting in the morning," he said as he went. "Why not wait until then?"

Arquan hurried after him, spilling rainwater from creases in his cape.

"I'd rather not. I'm sleeping badly, as all of us are: the nights are long and worrisome. I'd sooner talk than search in vain for rest. And you know K'rina has been a good friend to me."

"Come, then. I'll give you some shelter and something warm to drink. I can't offer anything to make your nights less worrisome, though."

Lacklaugh set out low stools for them to sit on and warmed wine beside the fire. Arquan, hunched up on one of the stools, rubbed his hands together and splayed them to soak up some of the fire's heat. Stumps were all that remained of the two smallest fingers on his left hand.

"I've always preferred frost and ice to these winter rains," he murmured.

"We'll be ice-bound soon enough," Lacklaugh grunted. He was scraping shavings from a block of hard cheese, delicately picking morsels from the knife's blade with his lips.

"Did K'rina have anything to say for herself, then?" Arquan asked. He helped himself to a cup of the dark red wine.

Lacklaugh mutely shook his head.

"Were you able to help her?"

"Not much." Lacklaugh unlaced his calf-length boots and pulled them from his feet. One had a long Kyrinin hunting knife scabbarded along its side – a legacy, like the tattoos that swirled across his face, of his youth, when each summer he had run with a Heron spear *a'an*. "She might sleep a little tonight, but what ails her is beyond my reach. I cannot even ease my own dreams, or still the itch of disquiet at the back of my own thoughts. How could I hope to heal her, when what she feels is so much more sharp-edged?"

"Yes," sighed Arquan. "And we know why it's she who suffers so much more than the rest of us, don't we?"

Lacklaugh shot him a grim glance. "Perhaps."

"Of course we do. She was the only one who loved – liked, even – that poisonous little wretch. She never forgave us for casting him out. It's been years, but I doubt there's been a day gone by when she's not thought of him, not grieved over his absence."

"No," Lacklaugh grunted. "She has carried a secret hope, all this time, that she would one day see Aeglyss again." He sighed, staring at the boot he still held in his hand. "She will go to him."

"What?"

"The intent, the desire, is clear in her mind. What is left of her mind, at least. She is on the brink of madness, I think. Ensnared. The . . . currents . . . in the Shared are far too strong for her."

"But why go to him?" cried Arquan in a mix of alarm, anger,

confusion. "What's been flowing in the Shared these last few days is . . . is corruption. Poison. Nothing you would want to draw nearer to."

Lacklaugh shrugged and tossed the boots to the foot of his sleeping mat. He swallowed down a great mouthful of the warmed wine. "We feel unease, we feel unbalanced by the taint leaking into our minds. But you said it yourself: she loved Aeglyss. She cared for him as a mother might. What she feels now is not the same as we do. She does not sense the wrongness or the danger of it all, only the pain, the suffering. His pain and suffering. She thinks of him as her child, and what mother could help but go to her child at the sound of his torment?"

"Well, we can't let her go," said Arquan.

Again, Lacklaugh shrugged. "Short of binding her hands and feet, keeping her under guard day and night, I doubt we can prevent it."

"Then we bind her. We guard her."

"Dyrkyrnon is not a gaol; we are not gaolers."

"Why not, if it's the only way to keep one of our own safe? She must emerge from this waking dream some time, and then she'll thank us. If Aeglyss is indeed at the root of this, there's nothing but harm can come of it."

"Oh, you will get no argument from me there. I said when we sent him away that he would bring nothing but misery wherever he went."

"I went deep – as deep as I dare – last night," growled Arquan. "You can't tell quite what's wrong, but everything feels out of kilter. And his presence is there, a shadow thrown across the Shared. Fouling it. All the old anger and contempt. The Shared reeks of it. But there's power, too, like the echoes of a great shout."

Lacklaugh sighed. "He was always strong, but to make himself felt all through the Shared like this . . . it defies understanding."

"Agreed. Something happened, clearly. We all felt the moment when something . . . broke. Whatever happened, he's not the Aeglyss we knew. Even then, when we cast him out, we were more than a little afraid of him, and of what he might do. Now . . ." Arquan shook his head as if shying away from the thought. "So what will you be saying to the rest of the elders tomorrow?" he asked.

"That I expect K'rina to keep trying to leave us, and that I see little sense in seeking to prevent her. If she stays here, she will only sink further and further into despair. She may harm herself, or someone else, in the end."

Arquan stared into his cup of wine.

"Trouble's even more likely to find her if she wanders off in search of Aeglyss," he said disconsolately.

Lacklaugh rose. He took a fishing spear from the wall and peered at its viciously barbed point.

"I need to replace the bindings on this," he muttered, and began searching around for some cord.

"This place hardens hearts," Arquan said, though without the accusation or reproach that the words implied.

"It does," agreed Lacklaugh as he sat back down and laid the spear across his knees. "Dyrkyrnon has never been a hotbed of soft hearts. But then, soft hearts are not what we have needed. If K'rina chooses to leave – however misguided the reasons for that choice – she puts herself beyond our protection. Our world is bounded by the pools, the mists. If we reach out beyond those limits, we invite the world to reach in. That is not what any of us would want."

"No."

"I still have friends amongst the Heron, though. I know young warriors who grow bored now that there is peace with the Hawk. No doubt they long for some kind of adventure. They might follow her – some of the way, at least. Guard her. Unless you want to volunteer as her guardian?"

"I'm an old man, and a coward." Arquan raised his left hand, showing the stubs of his two missing fingers. "I had my fill of the wide world long ago. It kept part of me so that I should not forget just how much it disliked me."

Lacklaugh did not look up. He was frowning in concentration as he wound the cord around the haft of his spear, binding the barbed bone point in place.

"I don't suppose there's any of us here who would leap at the chance to walk by her side," Arquan said. "Not at the best of times, and certainly not if Aeglyss is waiting at the end of whatever road she wants to follow. Perhaps your Heron friends are the best we can do."

"Perhaps they are," said Lacklaugh, grimacing as he pulled the cord tight. "You should not condemn yourself, or the rest of us, too harshly, though. If Aeglyss is indeed the cause of this . . . this sickening of the Shared, none of us here could offer K'rina much in the way of protection. None of us has that kind of strength, for all that we have the most potent *na'kyrim* outside Adravane amongst our number."

"We do," agreed Arquan glumly, then corrected himself at once. "We did. It appears the one we cast out can now lay claim to that dubious honour."

1

Kilkry-Haig

Put ten Kilkry men in a Kolkyre tavern, ply them with drink for a time, and you will hear ten different views on how it came to pass that their Blood meekly surrendered its authority to the Haig line. And there will be a seam of truth running through each one of those views, for no single blow broke the strength and will of the Kilkry Blood. Rather, it was an accumulation of wounds and ill fortune that undid their rule.

Some fifty years before, Kilkry had led the other Bloods to victory against Gyre and the Black Road cult. Their immense losses in battle, and through defection to the Black Road, had still not been entirely made good. And even as Kilkry laboured beneath those lingering wounds, Haig was rising to new heights of strength and prosperity. It had taken a century and a half, but the lands around Vaymouth – ruined during the Storm Years – were at last restored to the bountiful fertility that had seen them called The Verdant Shores in the days when they fed half the Aygll Kingship. The Thanes of the Haig Blood had grown rich, their armies numerous, their influence over the Taral and Ayth Bloods pervasive, on the back of those lands.

When the time came, the men of Kilkry, and of Lannis, would willingly have taken up arms, but Cannoch oc Kilkry could not bring himself to return the Bloods to the horrors of civil strife. He bent his knee, and with nothing more than that Haig became *highest of all the True Bloods. Hundreds – most likely thousands – would have died had Cannoch not humbled himself so, but you will find few people in the backstreets of Kolkyre prepared to thank him for it. The memory of better times suffuses this Blood, undimmed by the passage of time. Each generation is heir to the resentment and bitterness of the one before. These are people whose pride runs deep; they bred High Thanes once, and they are not likely to forget it.*

from Hallantyr's Sojourn

I

The *na'kyrim* lay curled on a pallet of interlaced hazel and juniper boughs inside the Voice's lodge. His knees were pressed up into his chest. His face rested in the sheltering cup of his hands. There was a pale, thin crust of vomit on the pallet by his head, and on his lips. There had been almost nothing in his stomach to come up, for he had hardly eaten since being brought down from the Breaking Stone. There were terrible wounds beneath the bindings on his wrists. The bandages were stained brown and earth-red by his blood.

He was alone in the hut save for a single Kyrinin woman: an aged, time-worn, herb-wise healer. Outside, on the threshold of the lodge, two warriors were squatting down on their haunches. Their purpose was not the imprisonment of the *na'kyrim* but his protection. Ever since Aeglyss had been taken down from the Breaking Stone and brought back here, there had been ill-tempered argument and dissent. This, the heart and home of the White Owl clan, the ancient *vo'an* around which its life turned, had been shaken. Children were kept out of sight while their parents met around the fires, arguing, accusing. Some wanted to kill the *na'kyrim*, to cut his throat and leave him for the eaters of the dead in the forest, as befitted an outsider, a betrayer. Others caught the scent of significance, of purpose. He had survived the Breaking Stone, and when he had been taken down from it and carried back to the *vo'an*, something else had come with him: something untouchable, invisible, unnamed. But it could be felt.

The *na'kyrim* woke. He blinked. The healer came and stood over him.

"You have not slept long," she said.

"I cannot rest. Whenever I close my eyes, my head is filled with a stench of malice and doubt. I'm surrounded by it here."

The healer's expression offered no denial. Aeglyss tried to raise himself up on his elbows, but failed. He slumped back with a hiss.

"You are weak," the healing woman murmured. "You need food, and water. And I cannot stop the weeping of your wounds. Your blood runs like a river. It is poisoned."

"You can't heal what ails me," Aeglyss said. "Can't even understand it. Your own blood is too pure for that. My wounds will look after themselves. Whatever it is that's in me, it's not poison. Not poison."

He grimaced and twisted his head as if afflicted by some blinding light.

"No, no," he gasped. His thin hands went to the sides of his head. New blood bloomed at his wrists, blushing through his bandages. The healing woman took a step backwards, away from him and towards the doorway that led out into the bright, safe world beyond. She could smell death here, in the air and the hides and the earth of the lodge. It should, perhaps, be burned when the *na'kyrim* was gone.

"Wait," Aeglyss snapped, reaching out to her, clawing the air. His eyes were pressed shut. "Do not leave me."

With a great effort he shifted to the edge of the pallet. He opened watery eyes, swung his feet out to rest on the ground.

"A passing moment only. It is so . . . so much, you see. You could not imagine. The Shared runs in me like . . . it boils."

"You are bleeding," the woman observed.

Aeglyss glanced at the bloodstained bindings and gave a faint shrug.

"Leave it. It's not . . . you must do something for me. Go to the Voice. Tell her I would talk with her."

The Voice of the White Owls was an old woman, silver-haired, stooped, slow. She wore the pale, speckled feathers of the owl around her neck. She leaned on a staff of oak. She whispered as she came, murmuring phrases that had been passed down over centuries as tools to focus and clear the mind. The healing woman followed in her footsteps.

They found the *na'kyrim* on his knees in the centre of the lodge, beside the ashen remains of the fire. He was flexing the fingers of his right hand, opening and closing them again and again. Both Voice and healer hesitated in the lodge's entrance, like deer catching danger on the wind.

"Do you mean to live or die?" the Voice asked.

Aeglyss looked up. At first his expression was blank, as if he did not recognise her, or did not speak the people's tongue. Then the clouds cleared from his eyes and he grimaced.

"Live. Help me up."

The Voice nodded to the healing woman, but she hesitated, reluctant.

"Help me up," rasped Aeglyss, and such was the weight of that command that even the Voice took a step forwards before she caught herself. The healing woman was faster, and more pliable. She went to the *na'kyrim*'s side, and he hauled himself up onto his feet, anchoring himself with handfuls of her clothes.

"Even after I have survived the Breaking Stone, there are those who would deny me my place here," said Aeglyss bitterly. "Do not imagine I am deaf, or blind, to it."

"Some are afraid," said the Voice. "Others are uncertain. Bad dreams assail us in the night since you returned. We are afflicted

by ill tempers, mistrust. The people fear that your presence dis-
colours their thoughts. They say you have clouded my
judgement; that you have done so before, and do so now. That
you betrayed us to your Huanin friends. They say we should take
the life that has been spared by the Breaking Stone. Others say it
is not for us to take a life that the Stone refuses."

"Bad dreams? Nothing that stalks this camp is anything more
than a faint echo of what burns inside my head. What you feel is a
breeze, a moth's flutter. I suffer the full storm, waking or sleeping."

Still he clung to the healer's shoulder, unable to support his
own weight. He was more than a head taller than the old woman,
but wasted and lean, like a sapling spindling its way up towards
distant light. She was steady beneath the burden.

"And I was the betrayed, not the betrayer," muttered Aeglyss.
"But you, Voice? What do you say? What conclusions have you
reached in all your pondering, your delay?"

"I have not decided," the Voice said carefully. "There has not
been enough talk. Not yet. You live, for now, and I . . ." she stumbled over her words, twitched her head in a kind of sudden
uncertainty that no Voice should every display ". . . there is no
decision yet. Until there is a decision, you cannot die. That must
be enough."

Aeglyss laughed. The healing woman started away from him,
alarmed at the raucous human sound. He held her there at his
side; leaned on her.

"Not enough. No. Never enough. Never . . ."

He swayed. His eyelids fluttered, his chin sank down towards
his chest. The healing woman, freed of some intangible restraint
that revealed itself only by its absence, darted away from him,
making for the protection of the Voice. Aeglyss staggered a few
steps to one side. The Voice watched impassively. The *na'kyrim*
steadied himself. His eyes opened, clear and sharp once more. He
lowered himself gingerly down onto the sleeping pallet, and
smiled ruefully at the two women.

"It will take time, for me to learn. To control this. I need one thing from you, though. Now, not later, not after any decisions. I will give the White Owls a gift of great strength in time, Voice, but first, you must do this one thing for me: send spear *a'ans* south. There is a woman, a Heron-born *na'kyrim*, who will come to me from out of the south. We – I – must have her."

The Voice was shaking her head. She tried to deny him. His brow furrowed. His mouth tightened. He held out his hands, palms up, towards her.

"You must do this one small thing for me, Voice," he whispered. Quite soft. Quite calm, but his voice was daggers in her ears, a cold compulsion in her heart. She nodded once and went, shivering, from the lodge, the healing woman close behind, casting fearful, awed glances back over her shoulder.

And in the lodge, Aeglyss the *na'kyrim* sank back on the pallet of juniper and hazel boughs. He held his arms flat at his sides, a little away from his body. His lips trembled now, in pain or fear or horror. The blood came freely from his wounds, saturating the cloth wrappings about his wrists, falling in viscous drips down amongst the twigs and fronds beneath him.

II

The road ran up from the south towards Kolkyre through flat farmlands. Inland, low hills filled the eastern horizon; to the west there was nothing but foaming waves rumbling on weed-strewn beaches and, far out beyond those breakers, the distant hump-backed mass of Il Anaron.

The High Thane's army snaked its way up the coast beneath wintry clouds. Aewult, the Haig Bloodheir, rode at the head of the column. The last of his ten thousand warriors were the better part of a day behind him, still straggling out of Donnish even as the Bloodheir came in sight of Kolkyre. His host had become a rough, ill-disciplined thing during the long march from Vay-mouth. There had been trouble in Donnish the night before: drunken warriors thieving from the townsfolk, then fighting with the hawkers and pedlars the army sucked to itself as a rotting corpse drew flies. There had been desertions, too. Many of the men in this army had only just returned from war against the rebellious Dargannan-Haig Blood. They had expected rest and revels, not another punishing march and the promise of battle against the Black Road.

The Bloodheir remained ignorant of most of the problems afflicting his army. Those who commanded his companies judged it wiser to manage the difficulties as best they could, rather than to risk the Bloodheir's ire by reporting them or – still worse – suggesting that he slow the remorseless pace of his advance. They all knew why Aewult drove onward so quickly, with so little regard for the cohesion of his forces. He hated the harsh realities of the campaign: the cold and the wet; the potholed roads; the hours in the saddle; the impoverished, dirty villages through which they passed. The Bloodheir wanted to win his victory and get back to his palace in Vaymouth as a matter of the utmost urgency.

So when the vanguard of the army of the True Bloods swept down the long, gentle slope that led to Kolkyre's southernmost gate, the Bloodheir himself was in its midst. His heralds blew horns and his bannermen snapped flags back and forth. The giants of his famous Palace Shield, haughty in their shimmering armour, let their horses run on and came hammering down the cobbled road like harbingers of glory.

Orisian oc Lannis-Haig stared up at the soaring spire of Kolkyre's Tower of Thrones, oblivious of the crowds gathered around him. A blustery wind was driving sheets of grey cloud eastwards off the sea. Seagulls were spinning about the Tower's summit, playing raucous games with the gale. They cut wild arcs and curves across the sky, screeching at one another as if in celebration. When Kilkry had been first among the Bloods, the Tower of Thrones was the axis around which the world turned. Now its austere grandeur remained but the worldly power of its inhabitants was more circumscribed.

Orisian forced his gaze back to the scene before him. He did not want to be here but in this, as in so much else, he seemed to have far fewer choices than once he did. The Tower stood atop a low, broad mound. A thick wall ran around the base of the mound, studded with gatehouses and small watchtowers. Between wall and Tower, on the slopes, a succession of Kilkry Thanes had created gardens. With Winterbirth gone, there was little by way of colour or greenery to show for all those years of effort, although the signs of meticulous husbandry were apparent. As Orisian looked around he saw not one rotting apple upon the lawns, not one fallen leaf marring the perfection of the flagstone paths.

The crowd now assembled on the grass was as well prepared as the gardens. Every tunic, every dress had been cleaned, every child firmly tutored in how to behave, every blade and shield polished to radiance. Lheanor oc Kilkry-Haig's entire household stood ready to greet the Haig Bloodheir and his mighty host.

Orisian, though he had insisted upon keeping to the outer fringes of this great welcoming party, still felt absurdly conspicuous. He was wearing borrowed clothes – the few fine vestments he once possessed had burned along with the rest of his life in Castle Kolglas – and they fitted imperfectly. He was flanked by Rothe, his shieldman, and by Taim Narran: two warriors who, Orisian imagined, made him look frail and only half-grown by comparison. None of which would have mattered, were it not for the fact that he felt curious eyes constantly upon him. He was, after all, the youngest Thane any of the Bloods had seen in many years.

"Lheanor looks a weary man," murmured Taim Narran.

Orisian watched the Kilkry-Haig Thane for a few moments. The old man did indeed have the air of one burdened by years.

He had a slight stoop, and all the majesty of his flowing, fur-trimmed robe only accentuated the pallor of his complexion. His long grey hair was limp. He and his wife Ilessa who stood beside him were quiet, still. All around them their attendants and officials held murmured conversations, adjusted their fine clothes, cast expectant glances in the direction of the Haig Bloodheir's approach. Lheanor and Ilessa did none of those things. They gazed off into the distance. They made no effort to hide the fact that their minds were elsewhere.

Orisian had seen this several times in the past few days. Every so often Lheanor or Ilessa – more often the Thane than his wife – would lose track of the world around them and drift away on some melancholic current of thought. The loss of their son Gerain had sorely wounded them. For Lheanor in particular, Orisian suspected, his son's death in battle against the Black Road had cut one of the moorings that bound him to the world. Orisian could understand that. He had seen more than enough loss of his own since Winterbirth to know what it could do to the heart, to the spirit.

An exuberant drumbeat rose up from somewhere in the streets. It ebbed and flowed, snatched to and fro on the sea wind. A ripple of anticipation spread through the crowd gathered by the Tower of Thrones.

"Aewult's Palace Shield," muttered Taim. "They have the drums specially made."

"Rumour has it they spend more time practising with their drums than with their swords," someone said behind Orisian.

He turned to find Roaric nan Kilkry-Haig standing there: Lheanor's one surviving son, now destined to succeed him as Thane. Orisian had met him once or twice when he was a child, though Roaric had never paid him much heed then. Now, the Kilkry-Haig Bloodheir was a brooding, intense presence. Wherever his eyes fell, they seemed to find fault and to gleam with accusatory anger.

"The Palace Shield certainly haven't fought any battles in my lifetime," Taim Narran said.

"They wouldn't want to mar the shine on their breastplates," said Roaric. He and Taim had an easy manner in one another's company. Orisian assumed that it sprang from their recent shared service in the war against Igryn oc Dargannan-Haig, and their shared anger and resentment at what they had seen – and suffered – there. A bitter kind of mutual sympathy seemed to lie at the root of it.

"How is your father?" Orisian asked the Bloodheir. "This must be hard for him."

Roaric glanced down at the ground.

"He presses on, as do we all," he said. "He blames himself for Gerain's death, and will not hear any argument. And now he must smile for Aewult, and pretend we are honoured to receive the High Thane's son."

"Honoured or not, we may need the swords he brings with him to drive the Black Road from our lands," murmured Taim.

"I don't think so," said Roaric, with a grimace. "And I don't believe you truly do either. Your lands – Orisian's lands – could be reclaimed by Lannis and Kilkry marching together. It hardly matters, though, which of us is right. It won't be you or me making the decision. Not now that Aewult's here. My father's a better man than me: I could find no words of welcome for that ill-born creature."

"It's one of the curses of being a Thane," said Rothe. "Having to wear one mask or another all the time."

Roaric nodded at Orisian's shieldman. Rothe's face was rather colourless, his skin a little slack in appearance. One arm and shoulder were bound up in a sling. There was a suggestion of weariness in his stance.

"You, Rothe Corlyn, look like a man who should be somewhere else," Roaric observed.

"Resting," agreed Orisian, "under the care of healers. I can't even make my own shieldman do as he is told."

"I've seen enough of healers these last few days," Rothe grumbled. "Good air will serve me just as well."

"How's the arm?" Roaric asked.

Rothe glanced at his bandaged limb. "Of little use – for the time being, anyway."

"And the shoulder?"

"Better than the arm. It'll take more than one Horin-Gyre crossbow bolt to put me down."

"Here he comes," said Taim Narran quietly.

The gates swept open and Aewult's Palace Shield rode in. They sat tall on massive warhorses, pennant-topped lances held erect. Their breastplates gleamed. Drummers rode with them, unleashing a flurry of beats and then falling silent as the shieldmen flanked the path up from the gate towards the Tower and the waiting crowds. Outside, beyond the encircling wall, there was a mounting tumult of hoofs and voices.

The Haig Bloodheir entered the gardens at a canter, wrestling to control his mount, the biggest horse that Orisian had ever seen. It tossed its head and strained at the reins as Aewult turned it in a tight circle. A dozen of his Shield fell in behind him and followed him up the path. There was a murmuring amongst the assembled dignitaries, whether of unease or admiration Orisian could not say. He saw one or two people at the front of the throng shuffling backwards, as if alarmed by these great horses and the men who rode them.

Aewult nan Haig rode to within a few paces of Lheanor and Ilessa. He towered over the old couple, his horse still unsettled. It was almost as if he expected the Thane of the Kilkry-Haig Blood to take hold of the animal's bridle so that he might dismount. Lheanor gazed silently up at the Bloodheir, his expression placid and empty.

"See who comes now," Taim Narran murmured to Orisian.

Looking back to the gate, Orisian witnessed an altogether more subdued entry. Riding a quiet bay horse, this newcomer had none of Aewult's crude energy or ostentation. He was poised, handsome and wore not armour but a luxuriant woollen cape decorated in red and gold. Instead of warriors he brought with him a band of well-dressed officials and attendants.

"Who is it?" Orisian asked, and guessed the answer in the same moment.

"The Shadowhand," Roaric said, his voice laden with contempt. "I didn't know we were to be cursed with his presence as well."

Mordyn Jerain, Chancellor to Gryvan oc Haig: Orisian knew of him only by rumour, and all those rumours said that he, more than any other, kept the Haig Blood secure in its mastery of all the others. Amongst those who resented Gryvan's rule, Mordyn Jerain was the man most often blamed for the worst of its excesses.

Seeing the famous Shadowhand for the first time, Orisian was struck by how unobtrusively he came riding up in Aewult's wake. There was no sign of arrogance; just a quiet man who looked around with a calm smile. His gaze met Orisian's and held it. Orisian could not imagine that the mighty Chancellor would know who he was by sight, yet there was a slight widening of that smile, a fractional inclination of the head. Orisian looked down at his feet.

"He's marked you already," Taim whispered. "He guesses who you are, by my presence at your side."

The notion that the Shadowhand should take an interest in him left Orisian craving nothing but anonymity and the insignificance that the last few weeks had stolen away from him.

Slightly too late, grooms had hurried to soothe Aewult's horse. The Bloodheir dismounted with a flourish. He hauled off his long leather gauntlets and took Lheanor oc Kilkry-Haig's hand in his own.

"How long do you suppose we have to stay?" Orisian wondered aloud. "Before we can leave without causing offence, I mean."

By the time the greetings and hollow pleasantries were done, and the Haig Bloodheir had been ushered into the Tower of Thrones, Orisian had slipped away with Rothe. He left Taim Narran to attend upon Lheanor oc Kilkry-Haig. Taim, Orisian knew, could represent the Lannis Blood amongst the great and the powerful more ably than he could himself. Neither Lheanor nor any of his family would be offended; if others felt differently, Orisian was not in the mood to care. At this moment, the mere thought of making the closer acquaintance of either Aewult or his father's Chancellor was almost horrifying to him. There were places he would much prefer to be.

One of them was the small house attached to the town garrison's barracks, just beyond the wall that ringed the Tower of Thrones and its gardens. Orisian approached it with a hurried, almost eager stride, a grumbling Rothe close behind him.

"They're not going anywhere," the shieldman muttered. "Do we have to rush so?"

"You confess you're too weary to keep up with me, then?" Orisian asked over his shoulder.

"No. It's my arm's a bit sorry for itself, not my legs."

There were Lannis guards posted outside the house. They snapped into alert postures as their young Thane drew near. Taim Narran had set them here at Orisian's request: two of his best men, survivors of the campaign against Igryn oc Dargannan-Haig and the carnage at An Caman fort.

"Any problems?" Orisian asked the guards.

"No, sire," replied one. "They've been quiet as the dead, and no one's tried to get in."

Orisian climbed the stairs quickly. He was aware of his own eagerness, and half of him thought it a touch childish, unworthy of a Thane. The other half of him savoured the pleasure of anticipation: it was something he felt little and seldom these days.

Ess'yr and Varryn were in the bedchamber at the top of the stairs. To Orisian's surprise, his sister Anyara was there as well.

"I heard the serving girls complaining that all the food they brought here was getting turned away," she explained, her brow bunched into a knot of irritation. She nodded in Varryn's direction. "He won't eat. It's like trying to deal with some sulking child."

Orisian glanced at the Kyrinin warrior. A sulking child was not the first image that sprang to mind. Varryn was seated cross-legged on the floor, where he and his sister, contemptuous of the soft beds, had slept since their confinement here. Even from that lowly position, Varryn's fierce presence was impressive. His long back was stiffly erect, his uniformly grey eyes staring at Orisian in that confidently passive way only Kyrinin could manage.

"The food's not to your liking?" Orisian asked.

"No," was all Varryn said.

His anger had been constant and consistent from the first moment they had all clambered aboard the Tal Dyreen ship that bore them away from Koldihrve. Its causes were many, Orisian suspected, but it had certainly not been blunted by the rigours of the voyage. Both Varryn and Ess'yr had suffered throughout from violent seasickness. Aboard the rocking deck of Edryn Delyne's vessel, Orisian had felt something new and unexpected towards them: pity. On land they'd seldom appeared anything other than capable – often intimidatingly so – but it had soon become clear that Kyrinin did not make good seafarers.

Turning to Ess'yr now, the sight of her still filled him with a kind of wonder. The pale delicacy of her features, the astonishing grace in her lean limbs, were there as they had always been; what was lacking, or at least diminished, was the utter ease with her surroundings that she had displayed in the forests of the Car Criagar and the Vale of Tears. Here, enclosed in a rather gloomy panelled bedchamber full of bulky furniture and embroidered bedding, she had the look of someone who knew she was out of place. For all that, she remained beautiful in Orisian's eyes. The blue, swirling tattoo on her face – far less intricate and detailed than the one that Varryn sported, but nevertheless striking – only served to accentuate the elegance of her lips, the clarity of her eyes.

"Have you refused the food as well?" Orisian asked her.

"Not all. But it is too wet, too lifeless. Too human." She said it without rancour, a mere statement of fact.

"Tell us what you would prefer and it will be provided," Orisian said.

"When do we leave?" Varryn demanded.

Orisian looked back to the warrior, determined to keep all sign of the weariness he felt out of his voice. This had been, from the instant his foot touched Kolkyre's quayside, the only thing Varryn would willingly talk about.

"You know you can leave whenever you want, and you know why it's difficult," he said. "We've offered you a boat and crew. Lheanor has, anyway."

An almost undetectable flick of Varryn's head and wrinkling of his nose betrayed his opinion of another seaborne venture.

"We will walk," the Kyrinin said in a tone that allowed no argument.

Orisian shrugged. "As you wish, but you know, too, what the chances of you reaching your lands are if you go alone. Lheanor can't even guarantee your safety on the street outside this house. If you thought you could do it, you'd have gone already."

Varryn sank into silence, glaring at the floorboards, and Orisian could see then what Anyara meant; perhaps more a truculent child than a sulking one, though. It pained him to see the steadfast warrior so disturbed. It made him feel guilty. He owed a great debt to these two Kyrinin, and so far had been unable to repay it as he should. Even so, since he had no easy answer to the constant complaints, they became tiring.

"If you won't go by boat, there's not much I can do yet," he said to Ess'yr. "You've refused Lheanor's offer of an escort to Kolglas. And even if you reached there, you'd still have to get through the Black Road army."

"We are Kyrinin," Ess'yr said quietly. "Huanin we do not know are not trusted."

"I know," Orisian sighed.

"We trust you. When will you go north?"

"Soon," said Orisian, and hoped it was true. "There is a great army here now. The Black Road will be defeated, and your way home will be opened. I will take you to Glasbridge myself. Soon."

"It must be soon. The enemy is on Fox land. Our spears are needed."

"We didn't want to come here any more than you did," Anyara muttered, ignoring Orisian's warning glare. "We'd be back in Kolglas now if that Tal Dyreen hadn't taken fright and shipped us down here instead."

Edryn Delyne, the captain who had given them passage away from Koldihrve, was long gone now, running across the west winds back towards the comforts of Tal Dyre. Their parting had not been on the best of terms. In the first day or two of the voyage he had exuded charm and solicitude. Everything changed once they encountered a boatload of fearful fishermen, who told Delyne that the Black Road had reached the sea and burned Glasbridge. He turned the ship towards Kolkyre and was deaf to all argument against his chosen course. Nothing, clearly, mattered to him save the safety of his precious ship and cargo. After that, Anyara had plagued him with accusations and invective, until Orisian had begun to worry for their safety.

"It doesn't matter how we ended up here," Orisian said firmly. "We're here now, and that's the end of it. It won't be for much longer. Ess'yr, tell me if you want anything. I'll get it for you if I can."

She regarded him for a few moments, and he felt a familiar

surge of pleasure and nervousness at being the object of that intense gaze.

"Water," she said at length. "Clean and fresh. They bring us wine. What good is wine?"

"Somebody'll have to find the cleanest of clean wells, if we're to get them the kind of water they're used to," Orisian mused as he made his way downstairs with Anyara and Rothe.

"Maybe so," said Rothe. "I'll sort out some proper food for them, though. I know what it is they're wanting: roast meat, nuts, dried fish, that kind of thing. I'll get the kitchen folk thinking straight about it."

Orisian smiled. His shieldman, once as suspicious and hostile towards Kyrinin as anyone else, had undergone a surprising transformation. He had fought alongside Varryn, and for a warrior that perhaps made all the difference.

"What about Yvane?" Anyara asked. "Is she any happier than they are?"

They stepped out onto the street, into the sharp, blustering breeze.

"Not that I've noticed," Orisian admitted. "She still hasn't come out of her room in the Tower, as far as I know. Now there's someone who really is sulking, I think."

* * *

As it sometimes did once Winterbirth was past, Kolkyre's air in the next dawn had the tang of the sea on it. A salty mist settled over the roofs and alleyways; all the timbers and the stones of the town were damp with it. The sailors and fishermen called it the *moir cest*, this breath of the sea that drifted in off Anaron's Bay, its name in the ancient language from which that of the Aygll Kingship, and later the Bloods, had grown. Its arrival in Kolkyre was held to be an ill omen for any undertaking. The longer the leaden fog persisted, the more downcast and querulous would the superstitious seamen who filled the dockside taverns become.

Such concerns did not deter Old Cailla as she made her careful way down towards the quayside, a long yoke across her shoulders. She knew without doubt that a body's fortune, whether good or ill, depended upon things other than the weather. She had lived more than three score years in Kolkyre, and seen the *moir cest* come and go hundreds of times. For the last thirty of those years, she had made this same journey every week, in rain and shine and storm alike: out from the servant's quarters in the grounds of the Tower of Thrones, around the edge of the garrison's barracks, then down the long straight slope of Sea Street towards the harbour. She had walked this way so often that she could have done it blind, let alone in a heavy mist.

At the foot of Sea Street she turned left and made her way along the row of inns, warehouses and workshops that lined the waterfront. The mist made everyone who was out and about keep their heads down and their voices low. There were oars rattling in a boat, invisible out on the water somewhere, and a few half-hearted shouts rang out. A handful of stallholders were setting out their wares on the quayside, but they did so in a subdued manner, as if they did not wish to disturb the melancholic fogs.

"It's a bad *moir cest*, eh, Cailla?" Merric called to her as she entered his shop.

The old woman swung her yoke off her shoulders and rested it against the doorpost. "I've seen worse and better."

"Well, so've I. I've seen more better than worse is all I'm saying."

"Fair enough. Perhaps you're right."

"Perhaps I am," Merric said, sounding pleased to have wrung this concession from her. "Look here, you'll have your pick of a good haul this morning."

He gestured at a row of pots set along a table. Every one of them was filled with shellfish, bathed in sea water. Cailla peered into each of the pots in turn.

"You've many guests up at the Tower now, eh?" Merric said. "They'll not have tasted the like of our Kolkyre shells down where they're from."

"That I wouldn't know," Old Cailla said. "All fresh, Merric?"

"I'd not try to pass anything but the freshest on you, you know that. You were buying from my father when I was still at my mother's breast. You'd sniff out a stale shell faster than I could myself, wouldn't you?"

Cailla grimaced at him: an indeterminate, gap-toothed expression that might have signified anything from disgust to amusement.

When she emerged a short while later, Cailla bore two lidded pots strung from her yoke. They swung heavily in time with her stride. A few steps from Merric's door, having felt the balance and sway of the pots, she paused. She knelt, lowering her burden to the ground, and made a few swift adjustments to the knots. Satisfied, she made to rise, one hand pushing against the cobbled surface of the path.

No one paid any great attention to Cailla on her weekly journey from the Tower to Merric's shop and back again. Had someone watched the old kitchen maid, they might have noted that every time, week after week and year upon year, she paused thus to adjust the balance of her yoke. Every time, she knelt in exactly the same place on the roadway, and rose with exactly the same touch of one hand to the cobblestones. They might note it, but would still have thought it nothing but the habit of a woman old enough that to change anything in her routine would be beyond her.

This time, there was a difference. No observer, however keen-eyed, could have caught it. Nevertheless, it was a difference profound enough to set Cailla's heart pounding in her chest as she made her slow way back up Sea Street. For the first time in several years, her finger had caught the edge of something nestled in the seam between two of the cobbles. A subtle flick had freed it and folded it up into the palm of her hand: a thin piece of wood into which was cut a single short line of script. Cailla had not looked at it. She did not need to. A brief examination with practised fingertips told her what the message was, and it bestowed upon her a great task in a worthy cause; the final shedding of the lie she had worn for a life all these years.

It was all the old woman could do not to laugh exultantly as she trudged on towards the mist-wrapped Tower of Thrones with her two heavy pots of shellfish.

III

"Allow me to offer this gift, Thane." Mordyn Jerain pressed a small bundle wrapped in the softest deer hide into Orisian's hands. "It is nothing much. Just a token of our High Thane's support for your cause. And of our sympathies."

"I am grateful," murmured Orisian as he fumbled with the folds of deerskin. The soft brown hide fell away to reveal a flat, round belt buckle of polished gold, twisted in mimicry of rope.

"It's a very fine piece," he said.

"Yes," agreed the Chancellor. "Made by one of Hoke's finest goldsmiths, we believe."

"Hoke," Orisian repeated.

"Indeed. It comes from Igryn oc Dargannan-Haig's own treasury."

"I see."

"You need not worry," said Mordyn, with a radiant smile. "Igryn has no further use for it."

"I imagine not," Orisian said. He, like everyone in Kolkyre, had heard of Igryn oc Dargannan-Haig's fate. The rebellious Thane, after his humiliating defeat at the hands of Gryvan oc Haig, had been blinded and taken in chains back to Vaymouth.

He languished there now, humbled along with the rest of his Blood. The belt buckle was what, then? Message? Threat?

The summons from the Shadowhand had been polite, deferential even, but it had been a summons nevertheless. It had come without further explanation, beyond a vaguely expressed desire to meet Orisian formally before the feast that Lheanor would be hosting in the Tower that evening. Orisian's nervousness had hardly been assuaged by Taim Narran's earnestly offered advice as they walked together towards the Steward's House where Mordyn had taken up residence.

"It's nothing more than that he wants to take your measure, I'm sure," the warrior had said. "He'll be pleasant most likely. Full of easy words. He's seldom short of them, from what I've seen. Most of what he says will be empty, though, or insincere, so pay it no heed."

Watching Mordyn now, Orisian detected no sign of either emptiness or insincerity. The man was relaxed, as apparently at ease as he might be if Orisian were an old friend.

"Let me offer you some wine," the Chancellor said, turning to a small table where a simple clay ewer stood.

"Only a little, thank you," Orisian said. He would have preferred none, but was fearful of giving offence, or betraying his nervousness.

"Let's sit." Mordyn nodded over his shoulder towards a pair of cushioned chairs. "I think you'll find the wine pleasing. It's one of the best out of Drandar: a gift to the High Thane from the Vintners. He allowed me to bring just a single vase with me." He handed Orisian a full goblet. "We can count ourselves greatly fortunate that it survived the journey. The roads are not as smooth as they might be in these parts."

Orisian took a cautious sip. No matter how good it might be – and it did indeed taste as smooth and rich as any wine he had ever come across – he had no intention of drinking more than that one mouthful.

"I cannot imagine how bitter your grief, your anger, must be," the Shadowhand sighed as he settled into the other chair. He shook his head sorrowfully. "That one so young should have to suffer such losses is most cruel. It is utterly undeserved."

"I have been taught not to wish for what cannot be."

"A valuable lesson," Mordyn said. "Much misery could be avoided in the world if it were more widely heeded. You've caused great excitement here."

"Not by choice."

"Of course. But a young man, come into a Thaneship in such . . . harsh circumstances. And bringing Kyrinin and *na'kyrim* to Kolkyre. Kyrinin, housed at the city's garrison! By choice or not, you've made yourself the subject of much gossip."

Perhaps it should be no surprise that the Chancellor knew about Ess'yr and Varryn, Orisian reflected, but it did unsettle him. The Shadowhand had barely settled into his chambers in Kolkyre, and already he knew things that Orisian would prefer he did not.

"You are, what – the seventh Thane of the Lannis Blood?" Mordyn said. The rapid shifts in the conversation left Orisian feeling slow-footed.

"Yes," he said quietly, realising he had raised the cup of wine to his lips again.

"You come after many great men. Croesan not the least of them, of course. Your uncle was a worthy successor to Sirian. Always firm in the defence of Lannis-Haig interests."

At the expense of proper deference to Gryvan oc Haig, Orisian guessed was the unspoken implication. He swallowed down another gulp of wine, hoping to quench the first flicker of anger in his breast. Silence, he had concluded, was much the wisest course here. The sooner it was all over, the better.

"A terrible blow, Croesan's loss," the Shadowhand said, with a sad shake of his head. "He would have been the very man to lead your people against the Black Road. The very man. It will be hard to measure up to his memory, but I am sure you will one day stand just as tall. We must ensure that you have the chance to grow, eh?"

The tone of Mordyn's words was convivial, yet Orisian had the nagging sense that the Chancellor was belittling him. He hoped that his face would not betray his mounting irritation. Mordyn dropped his voice to a conspiratorial murmur, so low that Orisian had to angle his head to catch it.

"You may find Aewult nan Haig somewhat overbearing – many do, I'm afraid – but he will not be here for long. Once he has restored your rightful lands to you, the Bloodheir will be gone in no time. And when you come to Vaymouth, you will find the High Thane much more . . . amenable. You've never been to Vaymouth, have you?"

"No." The Shadowhand's assumption that he would be making that journey had caught him unawares. It was not something to which he had given even a moment's thought.

"It's a wonderful city. Truly, you can't imagine until you have seen it. But then Taim Narran may have told you of it, since he's so recently passed through? How is he, by the way? When I spoke with him in Vaymouth he was very distressed. We'd only then heard the first rumours of the Black Road stirring, as I recall."

"He's well," Orisian said. "As well as any of us are, at least."

"Indeed. It's perhaps improper of me to say anything, but you may be well advised not to bring him to Vaymouth with you when you come. He and the High Thane did not part on the best of terms, you know. Taim Narran may be richly gifted in the matter of war – exceptionally so, by all account – but . . . well, you understand, I'm sure." Again, Mordyn smiled. It was an expression so winning, so open, that it elicited its pale reflection upon Orisian's lips before he could help himself. "Anyway, there's not one of us can say he is without fault. For all Aewult's failings, he knows how to lead an army. He will make short work of the Black Road, Thane, you need not concern yourself over that. We can leave that bloody business to those with more experience of such things than you or I."

"I don't mean to let others shoulder my burdens for me," Orisian said, the words sounding harder and angrier than he had intended.

The Chancellor shrugged. "Of course. But a wise man would never turn his back on good fortune. The High Thane has sent his own son – his Bloodheir, no less – to fight this battle on your behalf. You would not cast aside the cloak of his protection, would you?"

"No," said Orisian. No other answer was possible; even he, in his inexperience, knew that.

"No." Mordyn nodded. "Believe me, Thane, the wisest course here is to stand aside and let those with battle running through their veins resolve matters."

"My Blood fought alone until now," Orisian snapped, his self-control faltering. "Our . . . my people would not expect me to stand aside and let others finish the struggle."

"You think not?" The eyes above the smiling mouth were piercing and fixed. Orisian's anger melted away, replaced by unease. He wondered if he had crossed some invisible, and dangerous, boundary; and whether he had done it himself or been led there by the Shadowhand.

"Well, perhaps you are right," Mordyn murmured. "But Thanes must remember things that their people can sometimes forget, of course. The army Aewult has brought north is payment for an agreement his father made with your uncle. Gryvan protects those Bloods that have submitted to his own. A simple truth, best not forgotten."

The Chancellor reached for the wine ewer. "Let me fill your cup."

Orisian laid a hurried hand over the top of his goblet.

"No, thank you," he said. His mind was rattling around, fumbling for some kind of handhold.

"Does the wine not meet with your approval?"

"No, it's not that. It is as good as anything I've tasted. I'm tired, Chancellor, that's all."

"Ah. Well, these are trying times. The strongest of men would find it difficult, let alone someone of your youth. Perhaps you should consider excusing yourself from the feast tonight? I am sure Lheanor would understand; all of us would."

The concern on Mordyn's face was flawless. Whatever threat Orisian had seen there moments ago – or imagined he had seen – was utterly gone, replaced by simple sympathy. Sincere or not, it was utterly convincing and Orisian wondered at how easy it might be to be charmed by this man. Yet they said many men had died by his command, that every punishing tithe levied by the Haig Blood sprang from his greed, that he had turned the Ayth-Haig Thane into a helpless drunk, the better to subjugate his Blood.

"I could not do that, Chancellor," Orisian said.

Mordyn smiled and spread his hands. "No? Well, perhaps not. Ah, but we can dream, can we not? To be freed of the responsibilities that weigh down upon us? In my weak moments, I think of little else." He set his cup of wine down on the table. "Come, Thane. I'm keeping you from your preparations for the feast. Forgive my selfishness."

The Chancellor rose. Orisian, trying not to show the relief he felt, did likewise. He left clutching the golden belt buckle, feeling its weight in his hand like the greatest of burdens.

* * *

Lagair Haldyn, the High Thane's Steward in Kolkyre, was an indolent man. Mordyn Jerain knew this about him, just as he knew that he drank more than a wise man should, that he had a whore who would sometimes visit him when he travelled out of his wife's sight, that he had once conspired in the death of a grain merchant in Vaymouth. His less than appealing traits and habits were, though, balanced by two compensating qualities that predisposed him to serve the High Thane loyally: ambition and greed.

"He is only a child, Chancellor," the Steward was saying in that slovenly voice of his. "Since he turned up here he's shown no aptitude. It's as if he cannot believe he is Thane, as if he's afraid of the very idea. He won't present any problems."

"He is young," agreed Mordyn, "and it's true that he's come into this power long before he was ready for it. Still, there's a bit of fire in him. I stoked it up enough to catch sight of it. Not enough to sustain him in a battle of wills with us, though, I suspect."

He drained the last of the wine from his cup. It really was some of the very best wine to be had; quite wasted on Orisian oc Lannis-Haig. The ewer, still half full, stood on its little table. Lagair had been eyeing it greedily ever since he entered the room, but Mordyn had no intention of letting even one drop pass the man's lips.

"He will get good advice from Taim Narran if he pays heed," the Shadowhand said. "We would be wise to see if we can't prise the two of them apart, one way or another. And then there's Lheanor: he will look on Orisian with affection, no doubt."

Lagair grunted. "Lheanor has his own difficulties. I tell you, that man's on the edge of losing himself, just as Kennet nan Lannis-Haig did. He's got himself all twisted up, taking Gerain's death hard."

"Fine. A grief-crippled Lheanor makes for an impotent Kilkry Blood. But Orisian oc Lannis-Haig still merits a close watch. Whether he likes it or not, he's a potent figurehead for his Blood. All of this can yet end up very well for us, but not if we find ourselves burdened with an over-confident Lannis Blood, led by an ambitious young Thane."

"Very well. I still think you worry too much, though."

The Shadowhand shot Lagair a pointed glance and was rewarded with a flash of humility and nervousness in the Steward's face.

"Fortunately, what you think is of less import than what I choose to worry about," Mordyn said, articulating the words with precision.

The Steward smiled half-heartedly in agreement. Mordyn suspected that almost everything he did, even carousing with his whore, he did half-heartedly.

"If there's glory to be had here, it's Haig that must harvest it," the Chancellor mused.

That, he thought with a touch of despondency, meant Aewult nan Haig. There were few people he judged less worthy of glory, but the Bloodheir was here and he would have to serve. The Lannis-Haig Blood must be indebted to Haig for its salvation, thus Aewult must work that salvation.

"I will talk to Aewult," he continued. "We must ensure that Orisian stays here while we recover his homeland for him. And you, Steward: what is the state of your contacts here? Have you the means to set some rumours running in the backstreets and the markets?"

"If there is one thing I have learned in all my years," said Lagair with a self-satisfied smirk, "it is that no Steward worth his title should ever be without the means to stir up a rumour or two."

"Very well. Put it about that Orisian escaped the Black Road only because he fled and because he took sanctuary with woodwights and half-humans. And that he is too young and untried to save his Blood. All of those thoughts will already be rattling around somewhere in this rats' nest of a city. Feed them; encourage them."

Lagair nodded compliantly.

"Foolish of him to bring a *na'kyrim* here with him," Mordyn said.

"They've got her hidden away somewhere in the Tower, by all accounts. Lheanor's done everything he can to keep it quiet, the same way he's got those Kyrinin locked up out of sight. Word always gets out, though. It's no way for a new Thane to win favour, that's certain: consorting with halfbreeds and wights."

"I would be curious to see that *na'kyrim*, though," the Chancellor said, as much to himself as to the Steward. "I always found it . . . interesting that Kennet nan Lannis-Haig kept a *na'kyrim* counsellor. Such a thing might be useful, I suppose, if one could overcome the hostility of the common folk."

Lagair Haldyn snorted. "Not useful enough, given what befell Kennet."

"Well, it does not matter now. Do you know of a man called Ochan, by the way?"

"Ochan Lyre? The Cook, they call him, but I cannot guess what such as he would have done to merit your attention."

"If you cannot guess, better not to try. If there is one thing *I* have learned in all my years, Steward, which have been rather more demandingly spent than yours, it is that speculation quickly leads the unwary onto unsafe ground."

"Of course, Chancellor. Well . . . Ochan the Cook. A smuggler, by reputation, and a thief and a usurer."

"He is under someone's protection, then, if he has the reputation but hasn't been taken?"

The Steward shrugged. "He must have some arrangement, I imagine; with the Guard, most likely. Has the poor man incurred your displeasure in some way?"

"Not personally. But if he does not pay the tithes and taxes that he rightfully should . . . if the Kilkry-Haig Blood is incapable of controlling their own people, they should be encouraged towards a more stringent attitude. Can you make it happen? Can you unpick whatever protection he enjoys?"

Lagair pursed his lips in thought. It seemed an affected gesture to Mordyn, but he suppressed his impatience.

"I could," said the Steward. "Yes, I believe I could. A word in the right ear, you know. It may not be well received, of course. Interference seldom is, in these parts."

"Do it anyway. I want him gaoled. Or dead. Why is he called 'the Cook'?"

"Oh, a foolish story that he stewed and ate some rival long ago. No right-thinking man would give it any credence. You know how these thieves like to dress themselves in dark rumours."

"Yes," murmured the Shadowhand, thinking of Torquentine in Vaymouth: a shadow at the centre of a far more intricate web of rumour, but far too clever to let his name be widely known. Ochan the Cook would soon regret whatever he had done to draw Torquentine's attention. Though playing the role of Torquentine's vengeful messenger irked him, Mordyn was willing to see it through. It would be a profitable exchange of services, so long as Torquentine delivered on his promise to kill Gann nan Dargannan-Haig. And the Shadowhand had never been one to put pride above effectiveness.

"I will go and find the Bloodheir," Mordyn said, rising to his feet. "I should talk to him before the feast. He'll be in no mood to listen later on, and probably too drink-bruised to do so tomorrow."

He turned back after a few paces down the passage, and returned to the doorway. He was not surprised to find the High Thane's Steward leaning over the jug of wine, sniffing at it.

"Have one of your servants take that to my chambers, would you?" Mordyn said. "And get them to build up the fire there a bit more. I was cold last night."

The Chancellor was deep in thought as he headed for the Tower of Thrones. He was tired, for he had been sleeping badly ever since leaving Vaymouth. The chambers the Steward had provided for him here in Kolkyre were a very poor substitute for the comforts of his Palace of Red Stone. That, combined with the fact that he never slept easily while separated from his wife Tara, meant he suffered too many hours of wakefulness in the night. It did not help that he was, in any case, on edge.

Not the least of his concerns was his reliance on Aewult nan Haig. So far, the Bloodheir was irritating and offending various people without precipitating an irrecoverable breach. That could easily change. Every new day provided abundant opportunities for him to say or do something profoundly unhelpful. The sooner Aewult and his army were moved on, the better. The question thereafter would be whether he could manage the swift defeat of the Black Road.

All the signs, thankfully, were that the Black Road's forces in the Glas valley were too few to offer any serious resistance. Now that he was here in Kolkyre, where it began to be possible to sift fact from rumour, Mordyn was satisfied that Lannis-Haig had been undone by misfortune and by the cunning, rather than the numbers, of their enemies. The complicity of the White Owl Kyrinin, the ravages of the Heart Fever five years ago, a tendency to complacency in Croesan and his family: these were all it had taken to allow the Horin-Gyre Blood, alone, to bring Anduran down. They would be of little use against Aewult nan Haig's army.

The Shadowhand winced as flurries of sleety snow began to swirl around him. He had never much liked Kolkyre but at this time of year, when bitter winds came off the sea and every day seemed given over to fog or rain or sleet, it was particularly unpleasant. He folded his arms to protect his hands from the cold, and longed for the day when he would be on the road south once more. In Vaymouth now, Tara would be bathing, breathing the sweet clove-scented air she so loved; or perhaps hosting some gathering of the ladies of Gryvan's court, exquisitely garbed. Too far away, Mordyn thought, and too long to wait for our reunion. If Aewult did not win his victory quickly — insufferable as such a victory would no doubt make him — it would be a considerable time before the Chancellor forgave him.

IV

The hall of the Tower of Thrones was small but grand. It had room for no more than thirty or forty people, but on the night of the feast to welcome Aewult nan Haig, whatever the guests lacked in numbers was more than made up for by their grandeur. Lheanor oc Kilkry-Haig and his wife Ilessa sat at the high table. On their right hand was Aewult, then Orisian and Anyara. On the left sat Mordyn Jerain and the High Thane's Steward, Lagair. There should have been one other there. The rumour, already flying through the Tower's corridors, was that Roaric nan Kilkry-Haig had refused to share a table, or even a room, with the Haig Blood. Orisian, required to spend the evening at Aewult's elbow, almost wished he could have done likewise.

The long table that ran away down the length of the hall was filled with Lheanor's officials, the captains of the Haig army and the wealthiest merchants and Craftsmen of Kolkyre. It was not an admixture likely to produce high good humour, and so it proved. A kind of leaden, forced jollity arose, but it lacked conviction. The resentment and mistrust between the Haig and Kilkry Bloods were too deep-rooted to be wholly set aside for even a single night.

Musicians came and paraded up and down the hall. Falconers displayed Lheanor's finest hunting hawks. A trickster made coins disappear. None of it did much to ease the evening's latent tension. At length a storyteller was ushered in. As he bowed to Lheanor a hush fell across the room.

"In the Storm Years," the storyteller began, "not long after the Kingship fell, a man called Rase oc Rainur – tall and red and strong-handed – had a hall at Drinan, which was then but a village. In the summer, the people grazed their cattle far out through the forest. Now, there was a girl called Fianna, daughter of Evinn, who often stood watch over her father's cattle, taking only his two black dogs with her."

Aewult nan Haig leaned too close to Orisian, his breath heavy with wine and grease.

"I think I've heard this before," the Bloodheir said.

"It's a common tale here," Orisian replied. "It's called 'The Maid and the Woodwight'."

"A miserable one, isn't it? Doesn't everybody die?"

"Not quite everyone."

The storyteller pressed on, but he had clearly failed to catch the Bloodheir's attention. As a scattering of discussions resumed around the hall, Aewult turned his attention to Anyara.

"You've a very fair face, my lady." He flicked a wide grin at Orisian. "Has your sister given her affections to anyone, Thane?"

"My affections are my own," Anyara said, "and I don't give them away. I'm sure your own lady would say the same thing." She glanced pointedly at the beautiful young woman who sat amongst the Haig captains at the long table.

Orisian was not certain of her name – Ishbel, he thought – but it was already common knowledge in Kolkyre that she shared a bed with the Bloodheir. It was said that he had smuggled her all the way from Vaymouth in one of the supply wagons. Apparently Aewult's mother, Abeh oc Haig, had forbidden the liaison, as she disapproved of the woman's background or breeding. Whatever the truth of it, Orisian suspected it was not wise ground for Anyara to start digging in.

To his relief, Aewult appeared to be amused rather than annoyed.

"A pretty face but a pointed tongue, I see," the Bloodheir said through a mouthful of mutton. "You'll have to blunt that a bit if you want to marry her off, you know."

"I don't mean to marry her off," Orisian said quickly. He pressed forward against the table, hoping to put a barrier between Aewult and his sister. "How long do you expect to remain here in Kolkyre?"

"Keen to see us off to battle?" Aewult asked, with a smirk.

"You don't need to worry. We'll be on our way soon enough. We'll get your lands back for you, Thane, and sit you on your throne in Anduran. Believe me, I'll not spend a day more than I must up here. It's too cold and too wet."

"It'll get colder yet," Orisian said. "Our winters aren't really made for fighting."

"Ha! A bit of weather won't hinder us. I've an army here big enough to cut a path all the way to Kan Dredar if we needed to." The Bloodheir waved a bone from which he had picked all the meat, as if that somehow proved his point. "It'll be a massacre. You'll see. It's only Horin-Gyre that's come south, from the sound of it. Stupid, but then they're all a bit mad on the cold side of the Stone Vale, aren't they?"

"It was Inkallim and White Owls that attacked Kolglas at Winterbirth, not Horin-Gyre," Orisian muttered. There was a patronising, dismissive strand in Aewult's demeanour that annoyed him. Apart from anything else, it belittled the price that Croesan, Kennet and all the others had already paid for Horin-Gyre ambition.

The Bloodheir snorted, flourishing his empty goblet to attract the attention of a serving girl.

"There's not enough ravens or woodwights in all the world to trouble ten thousand determined men. Have you ever ridden to battle, Thane? Too young, I suppose. Have you even killed a man yet?"

Orisian could not help but look away. He remembered driving his knife into the chest of a fallen Tarbain warrior; remembered a torrent of blood that only grew in his memory. And the emptiness that came after that act, leaving unsated whatever hunger for revenge had preceded it.

Anyara was tearing at a slab of bread, concentrating with a fierce intensity that made Orisian glad he was seated between her and the Bloodheir.

Aewult drew his own conclusions from Orisian's silence.

"No, eh? Well, don't worry. You can rest here while we cleanse the Glas valley for you. You're the last of your Blood, Thane. There's no one to come after you. Can't risk anything unfortunate happening to you, can we? Haig warriors will do the dying that's needed to open the path back to your throne."

Orisian gazed at the storyteller, who was still manfully persisting in his efforts to make himself heard above the soft drone of conversation. Those last phrases had sounded glib, almost rehearsed, in Aewult's mouth, as if he was repeating a thought crafted by someone else. Orisian wondered whether Mordyn Jerain held even the Bloodheir's reins.

"There's been no shortage of dying already," he said.

"Maybe, but it's not gained you much, has it?" grunted Aewult. There was a blush in his cheeks, whether born of drink or heat or anger Orisian could not tell. But the Bloodheir's speech was losing its shape a little; his eyes were gleaming. He regarded Orisian with what seemed to be naked contempt.

"Those who've died did so fighting," Orisian snapped.

"Fighting and losing." Aewult's lips were stained red with wine. "Make no mistake, it'll take the strength of Haig to win you back your seat, Thane."

"At least you remember that my brother is Thane," Anyara hissed from beyond Orisian. "The way you talk, I'd thought you had forgotten. Bloodheir."

For once, Orisian hardly cared if Anyara wanted to pick a fight. His own jaw was tightening in anger, and a kind of furious shame burned in him: so little did Haig think of his Blood, and of him as its Thane, that he was treated as nothing more than a child. He was uncertain whether Aewult deliberately meant to goad him into some mistake or whether the Bloodheir simply did not care.

"Bloodheir to Gryvan," Aewult said, and grinned. He turned his attention to his plate, cutting into the joint of a chicken leg on his platter. His movements were crude and imprecise. The knife glanced off bone. "I speak with my father's authority. And I say Lannis stays behind when I march."

"We'll see," Orisian said. He turned to Anyara, urging her to silence with the slightest shake of his head.

The noise was so sudden and sharp that he started, almost lifting from his chair. Aewult had punched his knife into the table top and it stood there, trembling. The Bloodheir glared at Orisian.

"We'll see you do as the High Thane commands," he said. "That's what we'll see."

Lheanor had turned at the sound of blade splitting wood. Beyond the Thane, Orisian saw Mordyn Jerain leaning forward and looking down along the table. He thought he detected a momentary narrowing of the Shadowhand's eyes, a pinch of displeasure on his lips.

"I can't hear the tale with so much noise," Lheanor said, clear and strangely solemn. "It is almost done."

Slowly Aewult nan Haig sank back into his chair. He tugged the knife from the table and dropped it back onto his plate.

"Of course," he said, looking pointedly at the storyteller rather than at Lheanor. "Let's hear it."

The storyteller struggled on to the end of his tale amidst a taut silence. Once done, he retired with a look of undisguised relief on his face. There was some thin applause. The evening rolled uncomfortably on. Aewult nan Haig spoke not one more word to Orisian and Anyara. Before long, he abandoned the high table altogether. With a sour glance in Orisian's direction, he went down the hall and took the seat next to Ishbel for himself, leaving its evicted occupant to go in search of space elsewhere.

"Let's go," Anyara whispered to Orisian. "Tell Lheanor we want to call on Yvane, to see how she is. He won't mind that."

Orisian doubted whether Lheanor would mind if every single guest rose as one and left him alone in his hall. Ilessa oc Kilkry-Haig had been trying hard – keeping a smile on her face, laughing at whatever nothings the Shadowhand whispered to her – but her eyes betrayed the effort it took to maintain the appearance of pleasure, of levity. Apparently, it was an effort of which her husband was incapable.

Orisian looked from the Thane and his wife out over the rest of the gathering. Aewult was laughing at his own crude stories, Ishbel listening with rapt attention. Further down the table a Kolkyre merchant was arguing with some official who had travelled up from Vaymouth with the army. One of Aewult's warriors – perhaps from his Palace Shield, judging by his size – spilled a beaker of ale as he rose, swaying, from his seat. He was loudly extolling the virtues of Vaymouth's sword-makers.

"Yes," Orisian said to his sister. "We're not needed here."

They climbed into the higher reaches of the Tower of Thrones, ascending a narrow spiral staircase like those of Castle Kolglas. The stones in these walls were smoother, though, and of a hard rock that glistened as if wet beneath the light of the torches. For all the many hints of similarity – the smell of those torches, and of old wood; the way footsteps and voices shivered along the stonework – this place felt stranger and more ancient, in its bones, than the castle in the sea ever had. The Tower had, after all, been here since before the Gods abandoned the world. The Kilkry Thanes had only inherited it from its unknown makers.

A short passage led off the stairway to Yvane's room. An odd pair awaited Orisian and Anyara outside the door. Hammarn the *na'kyrim* was seated cross-legged on the cold flagstones, scratching away at a piece of wood with a tiny blade. Woodchips and shavings lay all around him. A young Lannis warrior was standing guard opposite Hammarn. He was watching the *na'kyrim* with an air of puzzled fascination, as if he had never seen anything quite so unusual as this white-haired, half-human old man.

At Orisian's approach, the guard straightened and stared ahead.

"Go and rest your legs," Orisian said to him. "Sit on the stairs a while, or find a window and get some air."

Hammarn scrambled to his feet as the guard moved away. He blew a little plume of wood dust from his carving and grinned first at Orisian, then at Anyara.

"How long have you been sitting out here?" she asked him.

Hammarn frowned. "A time, yes. Cold out, you know. All sorts of cold out there for the likes of me. Best place to be, I think." He jerked his head at the closed door. "Not very welcoming, though, these days. Bit cold in here, too."

Orisian rapped on the door.

"I am resting," Yvane shouted from within.

"Not true," whispered Hammarn. "She's not been sleeping, not restful at all. I know. She told me."

"Let us come and talk with you," Orisian said through the thick door. "You'd be doing us a favour. We need a hiding place to avoid a tiresome feast."

"Who's we?" Yvane asked, each word thick with suspicion.

"Me and Anyara. And Hammarn. Surely you don't mean to leave him sitting outside this door all night?"

There was an extended silence. Orisian shrugged at Anyara, noting the frown of irritation that had already settled on his sister's brow. He hoped that she and Yvane could resist the urge to set about one another, but even if they didn't it could hardly be more unpleasant than Aewult nan Haig's company.

"No one else, then," Yvane called by way of grudging permission.

Hammarn clapped Orisian roughly on the shoulder.

"Very persuasive," he grinned. "Always thought you stood most high in the lady's affections. Mind you . . . not sure she has affections, in truth."

Yvane was sitting in a broad bed, propped up against some voluminous pillows. She looked tired. Her eyes, almost as perfectly grey as a Kyrinin's, were sluggish. Her reddish brown hair had lost some of its former sheen.

Hammarn went straight to the side of her bed and held out the piece of wood he had been carving. Yvane had to reach clumsily across her body to take it: her nearer arm was still weak, having been skewered by a crossbow bolt during their escape from Koldihrve

"Made you a woodtwine, dear lady," said Hammarn. "Of Kulkain's first entry into Kolkyre as Thane, you'll see. He has Alban of Ist Norr in chains there, if you look close. Bit crude, perhaps. Not my finest."

"It's a welcome gift in any case, Hammarn," Yvane said. Orisian often thought she exhibited far more patience and gentleness in her dealings with Hammarn than with anyone else. It was almost as if she expended all her limited stores of those sentiments on the old *na'kyrim*, leaving none for anyone else.

"How are you feeling?" Orisian asked.

"How should I be feeling? I'm stuck at the top of a tower in Kolkyre – where they burned *na'kyrim*, by the way, before Grey Kulkain came to power. My right arm's all but useless because some madman, or madwoman for all I know, took it into their head to shoot me with a crossbow. And my head feels like it's full of woodpeckers, chipping away at the inside of my skull trying to get out."

"No better, then?" Anyara asked. Yvane scowled at her.

Orisian noted a tray of food lying apparently forgotten on a table by the shuttered window. He held a hand over the bowl of soup. It had gone cold.

"Don't tell me you're refusing food as well?" he said.

"I've no appetite," Yvane muttered.

"Nothing's changed?" Orisian asked, seating himself on the end of the bed. "In the Shared, I mean?"

"No." Yvane started to fold her arms, but winced and thought better of it. "No change."

"That's true, that's true," said Hammarn. "The taint can't enter this quiet head, can't stir the thoughts in this bucket." He rapped his knuckles against his forehead. "But even Hammarn can smell its stink."

"There you are, you see," said Yvane as if Hammarn's words explained everything. It took a long questioning look from Orisian to induce her to say anything more. "It's like a never-ending echo. That first night we spent in this town, the . . . the howl that filled the Shared, that woke me; it's the echo of that. Anger, pain, bitterness, all mixed up, all inside my head. And none of it mine."

"Not good, not good," murmured Hammarn. He was pacing up and down now, his hands clasped behind his back.

"Couldn't have put it better myself," Yvane said.

"Not yours," Anyara said. "His, then? Acglyss?"

"I've told you: I can't be certain."

"But you think it's him, don't you?" Anyara persisted. "Anger, pain, bitterness. That's how Inurian talked about what he saw inside Aeglyss."

Yvane sighed and looked down at Hammarn's woodtwine where it lay in her lap.

"I don't know," she said wearily. "I only glimpsed the edges of whatever it was that Inurian saw. But yes, it might be him. If it is . . . well, if he's still in league with the Black Road I think they might be in for a nasty surprise. It's frightening to think what it must be like inside his head now, if his is the sickness that's afflicting the Shared."

Hammarn had paused by the window, and pulled back one of the shutters.

"Look," he murmured. "Little fires."

Orisian joined him and looked down onto the dark gardens beneath them. A few torches were burning there, their bearers arrayed in a circle. In their orange light, two men, naked to the waist, were wrestling on the grass. Orisian could hear shouts of encouragement from the onlookers, made soft and faint by distance and the breeze.

It was probably Aewult's men, absenting themselves from the feast, hot with drink and the prospect of battle. They had an angry, arrogant hunger for revelry, the thousands of warriors the Bloodheir had brought north with him. They were barred from leaving their great camps outside the city except in small groups, but Orisian had already heard, from Rothe, rumours of thievery and drunkenness within Kolkyre. They took their mood from Aewult, perhaps, and there seemed to be nothing gentle in him.

"Lovely friends we have," Anyara said, looking over Orisian's shoulder.

"We can only hope our enemies justify our allies," Orisian murmured. He turned thoughtfully back towards Yvane.

"You can find out whether it's Aeglyss, can't you?" he asked her.

The *na'kyrim* winced. He could see that she knew what he meant, and that her reluctance was instinctive. Her hand rose defensively, unconsciously towards her injured shoulder.

"You've said that whatever's happening in the Shared is . . . dangerous," he persisted. "You've said it might be Aeglyss. Don't we need to know? He hounded Inurian to his death. He helped the Inkallim take Kolglas. He's our enemy. One of them, at least."

"You wouldn't ask that if you understood," Yvane said. "No reason why you should, of course. Last time I reached out through the Shared to Aeglyss, he drove me off. It . . . hurt."

"I know. But . . ." Orisian reached for words, finding nothing to quite express what he felt. "Something's changed. You've said it yourself. We – no – you might be the only person here who can say what it is."

"It's like an ocean, the Shared," Yvane said. She was unusually passive. Distant. "What's in it now is . . . poison. You're asking me to swim out into a poisoned sea; breathe its waters."

"Only to arm ourselves against our enemies. To know what we face. Aewult and his thousands of warriors: they think they're the answer to every question. They think nothing else matters. Maybe they're wrong."

"If I do it," muttered Yvane, recovering a touch of her customary bristle, "it'll be for me. It'll be because Inurian was a wise man who probably didn't deserve to die, and because he saw threat in Aeglyss. Not for Thanes or Bloodheirs or armies; not to help you Huanin kill each other in ever greater numbers."

"You will do it, then?" Anyara said, with a soft smile.

The three of them watched in silence while Yvane willed herself into slumber: Hammarn sitting nervously on the end of the bed, Orisian and Anyara leaning against the frame of the window. There was nothing obviously amiss with the sleep into which Yvane fell. Her face slackened, her eyelids trembled minutely. She looked gentle in her repose, as she never quite did when awake.

Orisian watched intently, aware that for all the apparent mundanity of the scene he was witnessing something remarkable. Yvane was right, of course, when she said he did not understand this. No human could. The Shared was the sole preserve of *na'kyrim*. He did not envy them that. Few of the mighty *na'kyrim* of legend, who wielded great powers drawn from the Shared, had profited by it in the end. While they lived, though, they had done enough harm to make those of his own time outcasts, feared and loathed as much for the mystery they embodied as for the mixed blood that ran in their veins. If the Shared was a gift, it came at a heavy price.

Yvane made soft sounds. Hammarn was growing nervous, fidgeting. The muffled noise of laughter and cheering rose up from outside. Neither Orisian nor Anyara looked round. Yvane held their attention.

Her head rolled slowly to one side. One of her hands opened, splaying itself out on the bed sheet. Hammarn stood up and edged closer to the window, though never taking his eyes off Yvane.

"Not sure," he whispered. "Not sure."

"Not sure of what?" Anyara asked.

The old *na'kyrim* shook his head sharply. "Feels . . . Not sure."

There was a tremor in Yvane's shoulders. Her breaths were coming faster and faster, turning into a faint panting.

"Is something wrong?" Orisian asked, pushing himself away from the wall. "Hammarn, is something wrong?" If Yvane came to harm in this endeavour, he knew that much of the blame would be his to bear.

Hammarn did not seem to have heard him.

"No," breathed Yvane. Her eyes were still closed, but her head was lifting now, coming away from the pillow. "That is not my name. I am not her."

"We should wake her," said Anyara, stepping towards the bed.

"No," snapped Yvane, much louder this time. Orisian could see the muscles in her pale neck, strung taut as a bowstring. Her hands were bunching into fists. A shiver ran down Orisian's spine.

Hammarn was sinking down to the floor, shaking. A faint moan escaped his lips.

Yvane pressed her head and shoulders back against the wall. Her eyes snapped open. Orisian saw alarm in them. He moved to go to her side, but before he had taken more than a couple of strides Hammarn was yelping and scrambling towards the corner of the room.

"He's here!" Hammarn cried. He twisted his head violently round and down, as if averting his eyes from some horrifying sight.

"Go," Yvane rasped. "Go." She was staring fixedly towards the door. Orisian and Anyara, standing side by side, looked that way. There was nothing: the plain wood of the door, the grey stonework of the walls. Nothing.

"I am not the one you seek," Yvane said.

Orisian's skin was crawling. The air was suddenly thick in his throat, the light fading around the edges of his vision. He put a hand on Anyara's arm, as much to stave off the dizzying sense of disorientation that beset him as anything. Shadows seemed to be . . . moving, shifting. He believed, in that moment, that there was something in the room with them. Something he could not see, or hear, but something that nevertheless had a weight, a presence.

"Leave me. Leave us." Yvane spat the words out. Fear and anger and insistence swelled her voice.

Anyara swayed against Orisian. He glanced at her, and saw beads of sweat on her brow, her eyelids sagging. He put an arm around her. Something unseen, intangible, was constricting his chest.

Then, without warning, it was gone. He breathed again, deeply. Anyara stiffened and straightened at his side. The tension ran out of Yvane's frame. Her shoulders sagged and she put her good hand to the side of her head, pressing briefly against her skull as if fighting off an ache.

"I will be listening to your suggestions with much less sympathy in future," the *na'kyrim* murmured.

"What happened?" Orisian asked.

"I turned stupid. That's what happened."

Hammarn unfolded himself out of the corner and hurried to Yvane's side. He regarded her with acute concern.

"Gone, though?" he whispered. "Gone? And you safe, lady? Safe and well."

Yvane smiled at him. Orisian noted the fragility of that smile; its weary, almost sad tone.

"He's gone, my friend," Yvane said, and turned to Orisian. "The Shared's a seething pit, and Aeglyss is the snake in its depths. I should have turned away, but . . . I was so close. I looked upon him. It might have been . . . I can't be sure. Perhaps there were Kyrinin there. He might be amongst the White Owls."

She closed her eyes, wrinkled her brow. The rawness of the memory was plain in her face.

"Whatever he's become, it's far beyond me. He had hold of me at once. But didn't know me." She grunted. "Thought I was someone else. And when I pulled away, came rushing back to myself, he followed. He couldn't do that before." She stared at Orisian. "He's learning new tricks."

"He didn't harm you, though," Orisian said quietly. "Did he?"

Yvane shook her head just once. "He's got ten – a hundred – times my strength in the Shared, but he doesn't know how to use it. Not yet. He's wild, half-mad. Still, I'll not be trying it again. Next time, I wouldn't get back; not unless he's the slowest learner the world has ever seen."

"At least we know it's him now," Anyara said. She spoke much more gently than was her wont, almost hesitant. "For sure, I mean. We – you – learned that much."

"That much, and a little more. He thought I was someone else, and when that thought was in him, I felt such . . . need. Such longing. There's someone he's searching for, someone he longs for, and her name is K'rina."

* * *

Ammen Lyre dar Kilkry-Haig had learned many things from his father, Ochan. He had learned that a clever man need not be subject to the same rules and restrictions as others; that the weak made themselves victims by virtue of their shortcomings; that a father might love daughters easily but would only love a son who fought for, and earned, that affection.

A year ago, not long after Ammen's thirteenth birthday, he had been cornered in a Kolkyre alleyway by two youths. They had good cause. While out that night carrying messages for Ochan, Ammen had found a man sprawled in the middle of a narrow, dark street. The reek of drink was as strong as he had ever smelled. Groping through the man's clothes, Ammen was disappointed to find not a single coin, but the sot did wear a fine little

knife on his belt, a blade with a horn handle and a decorated scabbard of good leather. Ammen unbuckled the belt and slid the
knife off, complete with sheath. As he straightened, glancing up
and down the silent street, the drunken man suddenly cried out
and grabbed at Ammen's sleeve.

Surprised rather than alarmed, Ammen tried to pull away, but
the man's grip was much stronger than seemed reasonable. He
rolled onto his side, shouting incoherently, pulling so hard at
Ammen's arm that the boy almost fell to his knees. Ammen
kicked him as hard as he could in the face. The man wailed and
relinquished his hold. Ammen wasted another moment in stamping ineffectually on his hand and then walked away. This was one
of the many small pieces of advice — all of it seeming the greatest, fiercest wisdom to Ammen — that his father had imparted: a
running man is more obvious than a painted dancing girl in a
room full of fishwives. So if you want to avoid notice, walk.

On that night a year ago, the advice had failed. Ammen had
covered less than two dozen paces before he'd heard angry shouts
behind him. Two young men had come out from one of the
shabby houses that lined the street, leaving its door open to spill
feeble lamplight into the night. One crouched by the drunken,
groaning figure on the ground; the other was staring after
Ammen. The two youths exchanged a few curt words — enough
to tell Ammen that the man he had robbed was their father — and
then the chase was on.

Ammen knew the streets around Kolkyre's harbour as well as
anyone. It was his father's territory, and thus his. But his pursuers
had longer legs, and they were driven by powerful indignation.
They ran him down in no time, and he turned at bay in a tight,
lightless alley that stank of fish guts. Afterwards, turning the
treasured memory of those moments over and over in his mind,
he was proud that even then, with the two burly youths bearing
down on him and shouting their fury in his face, he had not felt
fear. Their anger made them careless: in the deep darkness of that

alleyway they did not see Ammen draw their own father's knife from its scabbard. He slashed the first one across the face and was rewarded with a piercing howl of shock and the sight of his assailant reeling away. There was no time to savour the victory, for the second closed and Ammen took a stunning blow to his head. The crunching sound and the splash of blood over his lips told him that his nose was broken, but he was so dazed by the impact that he felt only a numbness that spread across his cheeks. He fell, and his attacker threw himself down on top of him, fumbling for the hand that held the knife. Ammen never could remember exactly what happened then, but he knew that he stabbed the young man more than once. He might not have killed him, for the blade was short and his strength faltering. It was enough, though. Ammen staggered to his feet and ran, rather unsteadily, for home.

Ochan's pleasure on hearing of the incident lit a glow of pride and joy in Ammen's heart.

"Keep that blade close by you," his father had laughed. "It'd be wrong to sell something that's served you so well. We'll call you Ammen Sharp now, shall we? The little boy who grew a tooth."

So Ammen became Ammen Sharp, and treasured the name. Having borne it for a year now, it felt as much his true name as any other. Only Ochan called him by it; his mother and sisters remained ignorant of its origins. Being a secret shared only by Ammen and his father, it had become that much more precious to the boy.

He was with Ochan, watching as his father sorted through a pile of trinkets, when his cousin Malachoir — one of the numerous distant relatives who served Ochan as thieves, runners, watchers, guards — poked his head nervously around the door. Ochan was engrossed, minutely examining each bauble and bracelet for any sign that it might have some true value.

Ammen had no idea where this little hoard had come from, and the question had not occurred to him. From his earliest years he had understood and accepted that goods and materials of every imaginable kind appeared in his father's possession and then, just as abruptly and inexplicably, disappeared once more.

Malachoir cleared his throat.

"What?" snapped Ochan without looking up. He disliked interruption.

"Urik's here," the cousin reported. "He wants to see you."

"What does that mudhead want?"

"He won't tell us. Says he needs to talk to you. Says there'll not be another chance if you won't talk to him now."

With a snarl of displeasure Ochan let a copper brooch fall from his hands.

"I pay that man so I never have to see him, not so that he can visit me in my house. It looks bad to have a Wardcaptain of the Guard showing up on my doorstep. Attracts attention."

"Well, he was hooded when he came. And he did come to the kitchen door, not—"

"Enough, enough," Ochan grunted. "Get him in here."

The man who entered was short and broad-shouldered, a stocky little bull. He wore a voluminous rain-cape that concealed any hint of his standing as a member of Kolkyre's Guard. Narrow, dark eyes darted from side to side as he edged into Ochan's presence.

"Look at that, look at that," said Ochan to his son. "Our very own Wardcaptain come to test our hospitality."

Ammen smiled, and then tried to fill the gaze he turned on Urik with suitable contempt. He knew this man was useful – important, even – to his father, but knew as well that he merited nothing in the way of respect.

"Don't puff yourself up too much, Ochan," Urik growled. "I've come here to warn you, not amuse you."

"Warn me? Warn me?" Ammen felt a shiver of anticipation at the tone in his father's voice. He knew it well. It presaged anger, danger, violence. When he was younger, Ammen had soon

learned its perilous implications. Urik evidently did not recognise it, or did not care.

"Yes, warn you," he snapped. "And I needn't have come, so
don't think you can—"

Ochan was up and out of his seat in a single smooth movement, lashing a long arm across the table to seize the collar of
Urik's cape. He pulled the Guardsman's face close to his own.

"I think I can do as I like in my own house, don't you, Urik?"

Urik hesitated for only a moment before nodding. Ochan
released him and sank back into his chair. He had knocked some
of his piled trinkets to the ground, and flicked a finger at them.

"Pick 'em up, boy," he said to Ammen, who obeyed at once,
going down beneath the table on his hands and knees.

"What is it you think you're warning me about, then?" he
heard his father asking.

"That your luck's run out, that's what. You've been named for
taking. The Guard'll be looking for you tomorrow. It'll be me, as
like as not."

"You?" roared Ochan. He sprang to his feet once more. His
chair tumbled backwards, one of the legs rapping Ammen's hip
as it went. "You? Is it that I'm not paying you enough, Urik? Is
that it? You've got yourself a hunger for more of my hard-won
coin. That's what this is about, is it?"

Ammen stuck his head up above the level of the table, not
wanting to miss such excitement. Urik had shrunk back towards
the door, holding up both his hands as if he could fend off
Ochan's anger.

"No, no," the Wardcaptain insisted. "It's nothing to do with
that. I don't want a thing more from you, Ochan. Not now, not
ever. You don't understand. This isn't us, it's not the Guard. The
word's come down from higher places, from the Tower of Thrones
itself. You're to be taken and there's nothing I can do to stop it.
Nothing."

"Then what use are you to me?" hissed Ochan as he edged

around the table. "I'll have back every coin I've passed into your stinking, fat little hands all these years."

"But I'm here, I'm here, aren't I? I'm here to give you the chance to disappear."

"Oh, yes, you'd like that, wouldn't you? If they take me, your name'll be the first to spill from these lips, Urik. You'll join me in whatever cell they've got in mind for me, or under the head-taker's axe."

"Ochan, please . . ." Ammen grinned to hear such a note of pleading in the voice of this man who held high office in the city's Guard. "Please don't think such things. I've taken my life in my hands just coming here to warn you. If I could turn them aside from your trail, don't you think I'd do it? Haven't I done it often enough before? No, this is beyond me, far beyond me. Your only chance is to take yourself off somewhere you'll not be found."

Ochan the Cook rushed forward and drove the Wardcaptain back against the wall. He pinned the small man's shoulders to the stone.

"It's the Shadowhand," Urik cried. "They say it's his command that you be taken. Sweet Gods, what could I do in the face of that? Nothing! Nothing!"

Ammen rose quietly to his feet. His father was silent and still, staring into Urik's fearful face. Ammen had heard of the Shadowhand, of course: the Tal Dyreen who whispered in the High Thane's ear.

Ochan released his grip on Urik's shoulders and stepped back, deep in thought. The Wardcaptain shook himself and resettled his cape about him.

"You must find a hiding place, Ochan. Take yourself away from here. You've family in Ive, haven't you? Or better yet, you could take to the Vare: no one would find you there."

"You want me to hide away amongst masterless men like some common cutpurse?" Ochan growled. "Don't insult me.

You must be wrong, anyway. Why would the Shadowhand care about me?"

"How would I know?" snapped Urik in exasperation. "I'm only telling you what I've been told. The order came through the High Thane's Steward, but I heard he used the Shadowhand's name to nail it in place. That's all I know, and if you've any sense it'll be enough. Disappear, for a while at least. Maybe the clouds will clear once all this trouble with the Black Road is done and the Shadowhand is back in Vaymouth."

"Get out," muttered Ochan, turning his back on the Wardcaptain. Urik did not hesitate to obey.

Ochan righted his chair and slumped back onto it, his eyes fixed on the knotted surface of the table. He ignored his son, and the heap of baubles that had so recently been the subject of such close scrutiny. Ammen drifted towards the door on soft feet.

"Time to visit your cousins in Skeil Anchor, perhaps," Ochan said quietly. "Better there than anywhere Urik might think of. But the Shadowhand can't truly be after my blood, can he? I can't have trodden on feet big enough to set him after me."

He beckoned Ammen closer. He draped a strong, long arm around the boy's shoulders.

"A miserable place, Skeil Anchor; wet and windy. But we'd not be looked for there. Not for a while, anyway. You'll come with me, boy."

Ammen grinned.

"But you tell everyone we're going to Ive," warned Ochan, jabbing a wet finger at him. "Your mother, your sisters, anyone who asks. You understand?"

Ammen nodded eagerly.

"The Shadowhand?" Ochan muttered. "Can't be right. I'll have that Urik's guts if he's lying about this. But then . . . there was . . . what was his name? Can't remember. The one I got Urik to pick up. He was from Vaymouth, wasn't he?" He looked up abruptly, his stare fixing on the wall in front of him. His arm fell away from Ochan's shoulder. "Gods, he couldn't have been Torquentine's man, could he? It couldn't be that fat slug who's . . ." He lapsed into a pensive silence.

"Are we going now?" Ammen asked cautiously.

"Tomorrow, early. There's one or two men I'll need to talk to before we go. No telling how long we might be gone. But we'll not stay here tonight. I know the watchmen on Polochain's warehouse by the quay. You head down there after dark. Tell them I sent you. I'll find you there, once I've done what needs doing."

Ammen Sharp packed a travelling bag, and while he did so a smile broke unbidden across his face again and again. Tomorrow he and his father would be on the road together. Ammen was pleased and proud: his sisters would never be invited to share in this part of Ochan's life. When his mother asked what was happening, Ammen told her they were going to Ive, and thought nothing of the lie.

He put his precious knife on his belt; crammed his wooden whistle into the pack, and his steel and flint, waterskin, stubby candles and the little crossbow he used to shoot seagulls from the rooftops.

It would be at least a full day's journey to Skeil Anchor, more likely two now that the nights were stretching. If he was lucky, there might be bad weather to delay them, force them to hole up in a wayside inn; give him more time to be alone with his father, his sole companion in adventure.

V

Glasbridge was a carcass of a town, its heart torn out by the flood waters of the Glas. The river had shrunk back into its old channel many days ago but there were still slicks of filthy water, knee-deep mud and piles of debris all through the once-busy streets. Most of the houses closest to the river had been cast down by the torrent; only a few that had been built of stone survived and even they were gutted and crumbling. The waves along the seafront lapped heavily, burdened by the flotsam that had been spewed out into the sea by the flood. And by bodies. Even now, the sea was still returning a few corpses each day to the city. They bobbed like bloated sacks along the harbour, pale and putrid.

Most of what the waters had not ruined, fire had claimed. Everywhere the black shells of buildings and their smoke-stained walls told a tale of destruction. The Black Road conquerors of Glasbridge had been too few in number to control the inferno once they had set it loose, and had been disinclined to make the effort. The town could be rebuilt if fate and fortune allowed them the opportunity. For now, all that mattered was that the remnants of the Lannis Blood's warriors could not gather here, and the other Haig Bloods could not use the harbour to bring spear-forested ships ashore.

Few people – the old, the very young, the sick and infirm – could be seen out on the ravaged streets, scrabbling amidst the rubble in search of food, clothing or lost relatives. They shared their search with the dogs and seagulls and crows that fought over every scrap of food. Many bodies were still hidden beneath the wreckage. Packs of dogs dug them out; they and the carrion birds and rats consumed them.

It was snowing as Kanin oc Horin-Gyre rode into Glasbridge. Big, fat flakes drifted like the seed-heads of countless winter flowers. They were blanketing the whole Glas valley, concealing its scars. Without any wind to drive them the flakes bobbed down in a lazy dance.

Kanin's horse trod carefully along the city street, stepping over the shattered remains of a trader's barrow. Like every one of the forty warriors who rode behind him, the Horin-Gyre Thane was hunched down against the weather. He wore a thick woollen cloak, looted from Koldihrve. The snow had piled up on his shoulders. Only his hands, protected by thick gauntlets, emerged from beneath the cloak to clutch the reins. The band of warriors came into Glasbridge silently. This had been the home of their Horin forebears before the Black Road's exile, yet they showed no jubilation at its recapture after so long. Kanin's mood defined that of those who followed him, and his had been grim for many days now.

The riders came to the place where a fine stone bridge had, until the town's ruin, vaulted across the broad channel of the Glas. Now only the stubs of the bridge remained, jutting out from either bank. The water flowing between those banks was turbid and dark. The river was still carrying vast amounts of soil that it had stripped from the fields upstream of Glasbridge. Workers had already thrown a makeshift crossing over it, laying rows of planks across a series of small, flat barges.

Half a dozen spearmen appeared from out of the snow. They challenged the riders. Kanin shrugged back the hood of his cloak, scattering snowflakes, and scowled at them.

"Do you not know your own Thane?" he growled.

The spearmen bowed their heads, begged forgiveness.

"Where is my sister?" Kanin asked.

Reunion with Wain lifted Kanin's spirits for a time at least. He embraced her, held her shoulders with his great gloved hands. Around them, in the yard of a wheelwright's abandoned work-shop, his weary band dismounted and stood by their horses. The thick snow was crusting the animals' manes.

"I'd not thought to see you for a time yet," Wain said to her brother.

"We rode hard," he replied, examining her features with a keen eye. "I looked for you at Sirian's Dyke. I did not think you would be camped in Glasbridge already."

Wain glanced away. "The Dyke was broken. That eased our path."

Kanin already knew the tale of the breaking of Sirian's Dyke, and the flood that had swept the road to Glasbridge clean of Lannis warriors and cracked open the town's defences; it had been on the lips of everyone they had met since they had descended out of the Car Criagar. He did not need to hear Wain say it to know that she resented the glory Shraeve and her Inkallim had won for themselves by destroying that great dam. Horin-Gyre and the Battle Inkall would never be the easiest of allies, and in the case of Wain and Shraeve mistrust was sharpened to active dislike.

"Let's get out of this," Kanin said, gesturing towards the snow-filled sky. "It's been snowing or raining on me from the moment I left Koldihrve. I've had enough of it."

"What happened, then?" Wain asked once they had settled in front of the fire in the absent wheelwright's house. "I know it cannot have been all that you hoped, or you'd have told me already."

A young girl – orphaned or abandoned in the chaos of Glasbridge's fall and now pressed into service by Wain – brought them bread and bowls of mutton stew. There were ugly burns on the backs of her hands, a legacy of the conflagration that had come after the flood. Kanin tore the bread into chunks and dipped them in the unappetising stew.

"We cornered the Lannis children in Koldihrve. The boy and the girl were both there. I had . . ." He stretched a hand out towards Wain, closing his fist on air. "I had him within my reach, as close as you are now. But they escaped us. A Tal Dyreen trading ship carried them away."

"You've got yourself a trophy, I see," Wain said with a nod at Kanin's brow.

The Thane put a hand to the long, half-healed cut there.

"A woodwight broke her bow on my head," he muttered. "I'd've had the Lannis-Haig brat otherwise. I was so close, Wain. So close." He shook his head.

"It's done," his sister said. "There's no point in regretting fate's path."

Kanin made a vague effort at a smile. Wain's resilience, her steadfast adherence to the creed, had always been a staff he could lean on. He knew she was right, and that he should mimic her calmness in the face of misfortune, but it had never come as easily to him. He had promised his father that the Lannis-Haig line would be extinguished. If fate would not permit him to fulfil that promise, he could not help but regret the fact.

"What of the White Owls?" Wain asked. "Cannek claims his Hunt Inkallim have seen bands of them coming back out of the Car Criagar these last few nights, crossing the valley."

Kanin shrugged. "I stayed clear of the wights as much as I could. They fought the Fox at Koldihrve. Won, I think, but I didn't linger. How do things stand here?"

"At our high tide. We've reached the outermost limit of what is possible. I've less than a thousand swords left."

Kanin rubbed his eyes. It had been far too long since he had slept properly. Even now, beside a vigorous fire, he could still feel the cold and damp of the Dihrve valley and the high Car Criagar in his limbs; in his heart, almost.

"No word from Tanwrye?"

"It is held against us still."

"And Ragnor oc Gyre has not seen fit to march to our aid?"

"There has been no reply to our messages."

"We're spent, then." Kanin set aside his bowl and stared at the dancing flames. "As you say, it's the high tide of our good fortune."

"Shraeve has set the townsfolk to building a ditch and dyke across the road from Kolglas."

Kanin grunted. "She thinks we can hold the road against all the armies of Kilkry-Haig? With a thousand swords?"

"Who knows what she thinks? She tells me nothing any more. It hardly matters. Fate has given us this much; no more or less." Wain's eyes, as she regarded her brother, were clear, placid. "It would not break my heart to come to the end of my Road here, like this. The Book of Lives has been as kind to us as we could have hoped, has it not? And we have followed the course it laid out for us willingly. Nothing more could be asked of us."

Kanin had wanted more. He had wanted their victories to be only the first, opening the way for all the armies of the other Bloods; he had wanted the Lannis line extinguished, in the name of his father. He had wanted to be able to die without regrets. Was that desire truly such a failing?

Wain put more wood on the fire: the spokes of a cartwheel that would never be made.

"I am minded to wait here," she said quietly. "Wait for our enemies to come and face us. I do not think we are fated, you and I, to limp back to Hakkan and die in our beds. If I'm right in that, I will die content."

Kanin stared at the orange heart of the fire. He had no great longing to see Hakkan again. It would be a poor kind of ending to struggle back across the Vale of Stones, defeated. More life would be no great boon after that.

"Yes," he murmured. "Content."

He wanted it to be true, but his heart remained uneasy.

The next morning was overcast. The snow had stopped in the night, and soon after dawn a thaw of sorts had begun. Kanin and Wain went out on the road south along the coast, at the head of thirty riders. Puddles lay all along the track. The sea lapped against the rocks and stony strands that lined the shore. Streams ran gurgling through culverts under the road, hastened by melt water.

They found Shraeve a little way outside Glasbridge. She and two dozen of her Inkallim were watching while enslaved towns-folk laboured. A ditch had been cut from the top of a shingle beach, across the road and on for two hundred or more paces inland to a rocky, wooded spur.

Running his eyes over the crowds of sullen labourers, and the low bund they were piling up with spoil from the ditch, Kanin recognised that Shraeve had chosen a good place for her works. Inland, low wooded hills and hummocks – outliers of the great mass of Anlane, further to the south – would hamper any marching army and provide ample opportunities for ambush. Anyone seeking to enter the Glas valley would have no choice but to attempt that rough ground or fight their way over Shraeve's barrier.

"It's as good a place as any to make a stand," Igris, leader of Kanin's Shield, muttered.

"It would be, if we had the strength to hold it," Kanin said, and nudged his horse on.

Shraeve herself was standing atop the rampart of sodden earth. She had her back to them as Kanin and his company drew near, her two sheathed swords crossed over her spine. He noticed that Wain drifted away, allowing her horse to slow and veer down onto the shore. Another sign, he assumed, that her patience with the ravens of the Battle was exhausted.

Shraeve turned. She looked down on Kanin with unreadable eyes.

"Welcome back, Thane."

"You have been busy," he said, encompassing the length of the embankment with a sweep of his arm.

She nodded. "We have many hands to put to the task, unwilling as they are."

"What will prevent them riding around your little wall, when they come?" he asked, indicating the wooded rising ground to the left. "It may be difficult for them, but we haven't the numbers to stop them."

"I will settle for making it difficult," Shraeve said, with a hint of contempt. "I expect nothing more than to make the attempt, and let fate decide. Have you come to tell me that is not enough for you? Do you mean to crawl back into the north?"

There was nothing new in her arrogance, Kanin thought – that was, after all, an attribute shared by every one of the Inkallim – but she had acquired a brazen, confrontational energy. Wain had warned him that since Anduran, Shraeve had been growing ever more assertive, more willing to challenge any authority that was not her own.

"No," he said, "that is not what I came to tell you, Shraeve."

He pointed at a nearby woman, struggling to carry a small collection of rocks cradled in her arms, slipping on the mud facing of the bank.

"These people are mine. Glasbridge is mine. These are Horin-Gyre lands, and this is a Horin-Gyre war, unless and until Ragnor oc Gyre claims it for his own. So, I thank you for your efforts in breaking this ground and raising this wall, but you may leave the task to us now. We will finish it. We will hold it."

Shraeve glared at him. She was fierce, this raven, but Kanin was resolute. If there was to be no glorious and lasting triumph in all of this, he could at least ensure that the glory of honest, faithful defeat belonged to Horin-Gyre. His Blood had earned that much.

The Inkallim sprang nimbly down from the bund and stood beside Kanin's horse. She clapped her hands together, shaking dirt from them; she must have been digging and building herself.

"As you wish. From the Children of the Hundred to the Horin-Gyre Blood, this ditch, this bank: a gift. Finish it quickly, Thane. The Hunt killed scouts creeping up from Kolglas in the night."

She waved an arm above her head and began walking back up the road towards Glasbridge. From all along the length of the embankment, the other Inkallim silently left their posts and began to follow her.

"At least you will not have to hold it for long," Shraeve called over her shoulder.

"What does that mean?" Kanin shouted after her as Wain rode up from the beach to his side.

"Have you not heard? Your messengers must be slow. The Battle is marching, coming to join you. The air about your head will be thick with ravens soon. We will see then, Kanin oc Horin-Gyre, whose war this is."

* * *

Stone walls ringed Tanwrye, and from them ramparts curved out across the southern entrance to the Stone Vale like the out-stretched fingers of a monitory hand. Their turrets, battlements and ditches blocked almost all the width of the pass. Tiny outlying forts studded the hillsides around, sentinels to watch over the track and the turbulent river that ran side by side out of the north. It was a formidable defence, and more than once it had proved itself against the Black Road. This time it was being tested to its limits. Most of the outer ramparts, and all of the isolated fortlets, had already fallen.

Iavin Helt dar Lannis-Haig was cold, down to the marrow of his bones. He had been at his post on the north tower of Tanwrye's wall since not long after nightfall. It had been snowing for most of that time. Winterbirth was long gone, and the peaks within sight of Tanwrye had been cloaked in their white winter vestments for days. Iavin hunched his shoulders, pushing the fur collar of his cape up around his ears. His hunger made it all worse. Staring out at the fires of the Black Road army, he could not help but wonder whether the besiegers fared as poorly as Tanwrye's defenders. By rights they should be even hungrier, colder and wearier than Iavin and his comrades, but in all the weeks of the siege there had been no sign of a weakening in the will of their enemy. Rather, it was Lannis-Haig hearts that were flagging.

The shortage of food was not the only thing grinding spirits down. Sickness was prowling the town, picking off the youngest and the oldest, the weak and the wounded. The youth who had shared Iavin's watch since the siege began had died just two nights gone. Firewood was running short. Families were burning their chairs, their bed frames and roof timbers in their hearths.

The hardships of the mind were just as severe as those of the body. More than a week ago, just out of bowshot but within clear sight of the walls, a company of Horin-Gyre warriors had erected two huge poles. Spiked atop them were two heads: the heads, if the shouts of the enemy were to be believed, of Croesan, Thane of the Lannis-Haig Blood, and his son Naradin. Iavin could not be certain if it was true – his eyesight was not sharp enough to recognise those crow-pecked features at such a distance – but most within Tanwrye were inclined to believe it. After all, if Croesan still lived, he would have brought an army to their relief by now.

Iavin brushed snowflakes from his collar. An old woman had given him gloves – gloves that had once belonged to the husband the Heart Fever took from her, as it had taken both of Iavin's parents – and without them he suspected his hands would have been too cold to hold his spear. He rolled his shoulders, trying to loosen the stiff muscles.

A point of light where there should have been none caught his eye. To the north, high up and far out in the heart of the Vale of Stones, a torch was burning. All else in that direction was utter darkness. There was no moonlight on this cloud-bound night. The yellowish fragment of fire bobbed like a solitary bright moth. Iavin blinked, suspicious that his cold and exhausted eyes were playing tricks. But the light remained, and one by one others appeared.

Iavin heard a muffled call from somewhere along the wall, and answering shouts. He was not imagining it, then. Others were seeing the same thing. Even as he watched, any last vestiges of doubt were dispelled. A long tongue of fire was slowly winding its way over a saddle in the pass. Scores of torches, carried by scores of hands, were coming south through the falling snow.

Horns sounded to call Tanwrye's captains to the walls. There were signs of movement amongst the besieging army, too. Figures passed to and fro in front of the campfires, orders were shouted. And the torches flowing out of the Vale of Stones were in the hundreds now. Iavin watched the fiery river in a kind of numb amazement. It was almost beautiful, this vision of light and fire in the winter's night; it would have been beautiful, had it not told him that death was coming for him, and for everyone in Tanwrye.

At dawn, they were still coming. Thousand upon thousand, company after company, the Black Road was flooding through the Vale of Stones. The rocky, snow-covered ground around Tanwrye was already thick with tents and with seething crowds. A constant rumble of noise drifted up and over the besieged town, like a never-ending peal of distant thunder.

Every warrior who could still walk had come to the walls to witness this gigantic assembly of their foe. Iavin Helt should have been resting by now, his watch long done, but nobody expected any rest today, unless it was the final, unending kind offered by the Sleeping Dark. He glanced down the line of grim-faced men that stretched along the top of the wall. There were not nearly enough of them to withstand the coming storm.

It was not only the number of these newly arrived foes that had stilled any hope in the hearts of Tanwrye's defenders, but their nature. Sometime in the night, amidst that river of blazing torches out of the Stone Vale, the Battle Inkall had arrived. So many of their great raven standards were now visible in the heart of the enemy camp that older, more experienced men than Iavin had shaken their heads in disbelief and despair. Tanwrye's garrison included some of the finest warriors the Lannis-Haig Blood could muster; not one of them thought himself a match for the ravens of the Battle Inkall.

Iavin's stomach was knotted and growling. He could not tell

whether it was hunger or fear. His throat felt tight, his mouth dry. His mind had emptied itself of thoughts, as if it too had been numbed by the night's awful cold. Hidden behind heavy clouds, the sun climbed the sky. The day grew no warmer, the light no less subdued. Eventually, in the late morning, surges of movement spread through the Black Road camp. Like some great beast bestirring itself, the army rumbled into motion.

The assault was controlled, precise and overwhelming. It rolled on through the afternoon. The few stretches of outlying wall and palisade that had still been held by Tanwrye's defenders were stormed one after another. A few survivors made it back to the main town walls; most of their comrades died at their posts.

Without pause, the Black Road host pressed closer and closer to the town. Beneath a sheltering cloud of crossbow bolts and arrows and stones, ladders were brought to the walls. So thick and relentless were the flights of missiles that those on the battlements who were not struck at once could only hunch down and press themselves against the stone, trying to ignore the cries and pleas of the less fortunate. Iavin, crouched low atop the tower, clenched his eyes shut. A hand was gripping his ankle. He knew it was an old man called Hergal, who had risen from his sickbed to come to the wall just that morning. He was already dead.

"Get up, get up!" someone was shouting.

It took a great effort of will, but Iavin opened his eyes and looked around.

Men were surging past him, going to meet a black-haired woman who was vaulting over the parapet. Her jerkin and breeches were dark leather, studded with metal. Iavin rose to his feet. It seemed absurd and impossible that the Inkallim – the infamous ravens of the Black Road – were here, within a few paces of where he stood. Hergal's dead hand fell away from his ankle.

The woman ducked inside the first warrior's blow, then drove upwards. She clamped one hand on his throat, stabbing her short sword into his stomach with the other. In a single movement she heaved the dying man backwards, knocking another warrior aside. She wrenched her sword free and spun to kick someone in the groin.

Iavin lunged at her with his spear. Her flank was exposed. He would strike her in the stomach, on the left side. He could see it happening, see her dying, in his mind's eye. Yet she rolled away and the spearpoint glanced off her hip bone. Somehow – Iavin could not understand how – she turned so quickly that she had hold of his spear before he could recover. She was far stronger than he had ever imagined a woman could be. He let go of the spear and fled as more dark-haired figures spilled over the wall.

He ran blindly down from the tower and into the town, without a single glance back. A captain he did not know was gathering men beside a well. He seized Iavin's arm, arresting his flight so abruptly that both of them almost fell.

"Stand your ground!" he shouted in Iavin's face. "Arm yourself!"

Iavin reeled, his mind still a blur of noise and images. Someone thrust a short sword into his hand and he stared down at it. There was blood already on the blade.

"With me," the captain was crying now, and Iavin was caught up in the rush and carried back towards the walls.

There was fighting on one of the ramps that slanted up to the battlements. No sign of Inkallim here, Iavin vaguely recognised as he pushed up with the others to join the fray. He fought against men who wore the ordinary woollen clothes of farmers or artisans, half of them armed with nothing more than clubs or small axes. The ramp was narrow, without the room for skill or precision. Iavin pushed and stabbed at whatever body appeared before him, concentrated only on not losing his footing on the incline. Time drifted.

There was a sharp blow on his head and for a moment he could see nothing. He could hear himself shouting, perhaps screaming, and felt some blade sliding across his arm and opening it. His sight leaked back as he was crushed against the low wall that bounded the ramp.

Then, "Back, back!" he heard.

The press of bodies shifted and swayed. Iavin was suddenly freed and he stumbled, slithering, down the ramp. He sprawled across a corpse and gagged at the corrupt stench of blood and opened guts. He scrambled to his feet and staggered off down the cobbled roadway. He was panting, heaving air into aching lungs. He could taste bile in the back of his mouth.

Iavin found himself in a small market square. He looked around. There were thirty or forty other warriors close by, some kneeling with spears and shields readied. A great block of sheds stood nearby. For the goats and sheep, Iavin remembered, that they bought and sold here. There was a massive stone-built hay barn, too. He was at the very heart of Tanwrye. There was nowhere else to fly to from here.

They came howling and boiling out from the side streets: Tarbain tribesmen, covered in bone and stone talismans. They swept up to the knot of Lannis-Haig warriors, flowed around it and embraced it like the flooding sea taking hold of a rocky outcrop. Iavin hacked and slashed. The clatter of weapons and stamping of feet, cries of horror and fury, all swelled and filled his ears. He felt blows against his arms and chest, flickers of pain carried away on the anger that seethed in him. Then on his side: a smack and a sudden numbness. He saw the blade darting back, saw a blur of his own blood. Darkness came rushing up, reached for him and flung its veil across his eyes.

Iavin still heard the terrible cacophony as he fell, but in a moment it too dissolved into the dark. His was only one amongst the many deaths on the day Tanwrye, the bastion so long believed to be impregnable, fell.

* * *

All through the *Antyryn Hyr*, the Thousand Tree-clad Valleys, the White Owls were moving. Messengers had gone out from the great *vo'an* at the heart of the forest, racing along the secret ways that Kyrinin feet had trodden for hundreds of years. From every one of the clan's winter camps, they had summoned a spear *a'an* to come. So the White Owls ran beneath the leafless canopy of Anlane and a cloud-thick sky. They came silent and swift to answer the Voice's call.

Five lifetimes ago, thousands of the White Owl had fought and died in the War of the Tainted. Only the Heron, Bull and Horse had fielded greater companies against the seething masses of humankind. The Huanin, who lived in a waking dream of their own splendour, might imagine that such strength was gone for ever. If so, they were misled by their own pride-fattened ignorance. The warband that had crossed into the Car Criagar to hunt Fox had been but a fraction of the clan's spears. The vast deeps of the Thousand Tree-Clad Valleys held numbers unguessed by the Huanin. Many hundreds of warriors were on the move as the winter deepened and the first full snows of the season began to fall.

Rumours ran with the spear *a'ans*, twisting and thickening, feeding off one another. There was a *na'kyrim*, it was said, child of a long-dead White Owl mother. A man who had been on the clan's Breaking Stone, the great boulder the Walking God had left behind, and – unthinkably, impossibly – had not died. Instead, the whisperers said, he had been changed. It was because of him, and because of what he had become, that the spears were now gathering.

The ground in front of the Voice's lodge was hard and bare, sculpted by the touch of thousands of feet over many years. Song staffs, entwined with skulls and feathers and ivy, stood there. The people gathered before them, facing the lodge. The woven *anhyne* looked on from one side. The smoke of the ever-burning *torkyr*, the constant flame of the clan, drifted from behind the lodge.

Not all had gathered outside the Voice's lodge, but many did. They came because they wanted to see and hear this *na'kyrim* who had stirred up such tumult; some because they thought this man must die before his presence caused more chaos, others because the scent of his power filled their hearts and minds with a febrile hope.

The *na'kyrim* lifted his head as he emerged from the lodge, casting his half-human eyes over the crowd. At the touch of that gaze, every man, woman and child felt a prickling of their skin, a drying in their throat. The *na'kyrim* was frail and drained, still ravaged by his long hours on the Breaking Stone, yet his presence was potent; arresting. It reached inside them, like an invisible hand.

He advanced slowly, carefully. The Voice came behind him. She walked with her head down.

Aeglyss took a great, deep breath as if flushing out his lungs with the clean air of the *vo'an*, the cleansing smoke of the *torkyr*. One of the *kakyrin*, the keepers of bones and stories and memories, stepped forwards from amongst the throng. He was an old man, the twofold *kin'thyn* tattoos on his face faded and weathered. His necklace of bone and owl feathers rustled as he walked. He stood in front of Aeglyss, but the *na'kyrim* ignored him.

"Is he not to be returned to the Breaking Stone, then?" the *kakyrin* enquired levelly. It was impossible to say whose answer he sought. He was examining Aeglyss through narrowed eyes.

"It's not . . . I can't be," Aeglyss murmured.

"Is he mind-sick?" the *kakyrin* asked.

"Perhaps," whispered the Voice. She took a few paces closer. "But it is a strange kind of mind-sickness. The Breaking Stone could not contain his spirit. Do you not feel it? He thickens the air with power. The White Owl have not had a child such as this in half a thousand years. Longer."

"He betrayed us before. Made false promises. His words, his

lies, they are more potent than anything you or I might utter. He can make nets out of words, to cast over our minds."

"He says he was the one betrayed, by the Huanin of the Road. He says the false promises he made were made at their behest, and that he thought them to be true when he spoke them. The thought is in my mind that I believe him in this, and it is my own thought, unsnared in any net of his making."

"You think he will give the clan back the strength it once had?"

"He may. We were mighty once, before the City fell. None then would have dared to steal our lands, fell our trees, drive our hunters from their summer grounds. We have been less than we were for a long time."

The *kakyrin* sniffed. "As has every people, of every land." He shook his head. His necklace rattled. "I see only a part-human whose mind has rotted."

Aeglyss cupped the old man's face in his hands. The *kakyrin* started backwards, but Aeglyss held him fast and the impulse to recoil seemed to fail almost before it had taken hold. The *kakyrin* began to groan. Aeglyss shook. His eyes rolled up slowly until the pupils were hidden.

"Do you see?" he rasped. "Do you see?"

The *kakyrin*'s legs went slack. He slumped, only Aeglyss's grip on his face keeping him from falling to the ground.

"Do you see?" Aeglyss demanded again, more distantly this time. The crowd of onlookers seethed; there were cries of anger, alarm.

"Release him," the Voice said to Aeglyss, putting a hand on his arm. She spoke the words not as a command but softly.

Aeglyss blinked and looked down at the old woman, then at the man. His hands fell back to his sides. The *kakyrin* slumped to his knees, and swayed there.

"Have you harmed him?" the Voice asked.

"No," breathed Aeglyss. "Not so much as you harmed me by

placing me on the Stone. But I have forgiven you. Forgiven all of you." He called it out loudly. "If I've been broken, it was only to be made afresh. Thus, I forgive you."

"All the world," the *kakyrin* was mumbling. "All the world."

A warrior stepped out from the crowd, his spear levelled at Aeglyss, dark intent fixed in his eyes. The *na'kyrim* held him with a flashing, savage glare.

"You are my mother's people," cried Aeglyss, and the warrior shrank from the cry. "You are my people. My heart beats in time with yours, and whatever mistakes there have been in the past are done with now. Forgiven, forgotten. I am not as I was, and the White Owls shall not be as they were. Together we shall make such a beginning as the world has never seen. All things can change. If I will it."

Children wailed in distant huts. The bravest of warriors felt tremors in their hands; the wisest of heads spun; the keenest of ears rang with endless echoes of anger and hunger.

"Have I not already given you the blood of the Fox to bathe your spears in? Has this not already been a bitter season for your enemies? More warriors now wear the *kin'thyn* than the clan has seen in a lifetime."

There were cries of assent, some dazed, some eager. There was weeping too, in the great crowd.

"If I will it," Aeglyss repeated, "all things can change. Let your will run with mine. I shall be the strength in your arms, the swiftness in your legs. You shall be the spear in my hands. I will bind the Huanin of the Road to us with bonds they cannot break; I will bend them until their arms serve our purposes. Long enough we have suffered. Long enough we have been less than we once were. Now all the world will be set into two camps: those who are friends to the White Owl and those who are enemies. And our enemies shall fall. They shall crumble. It is . . ."

He faltered, cast his stare up towards the flat sea of cloud. A thin, icy snow was beginning to fall. The *na'kyrim* sighed and fell to his knees. His head tipped back and he stared into the bleak, unbounded expanse of the sky.

"I shall be servant to all your hopes and dreams," he said quietly. "I shall make them real."

Though he spoke softly, all heard. And many felt belief unfolding itself in their hearts like a dark flower.

VI

The woman was holding something up to Orisian, but he could not quite see what it was. There were scabs on her face, whether from injury or disease he could not tell.

"Please take it, sire," the woman said. "It was my husband's. He died well, at Grive."

She was seated, with dozens of others, at the side of the road. It was a short street, in Kolkyre's northern quarter, lined with shacks and crude shelters. It had been largely uninhabited until recently, the refuge of just a few impoverished or sickly souls. Now new huts were springing up, made out of scavenged wood. Old, abandoned hovels were once again occupied. The recent arrivals had come out of the Glas valley. They were Orisian's people, fleeing all the way here to Kolkyre after the fall of Anduran and Glasbridge. Only those without friends or family, without the coin to buy better shelter, without a strong will or resilient hope, ended here on this squalid street.

Orisian took what the woman offered him. It was a simple leather skullcap. He pressed it back into her hands.

"Keep it. Please. I'm sure your husband would rather you kept it."

He walked on, with Taim and Rothe on either side of him.

"How many are there?" he asked Taim quietly.

"A hundred or so here. There're others who have found

themselves a better place in the city. These are the lost, the ones who escaped with nothing but the clothes on their backs."

A grubby little boy ran up and touched Orisian's leg before retreating back to his young mother's side.

"They've come a long way," Orisian murmured.

Taim nodded. "There's hundreds more at Kolglas, by all accounts, but there's not enough food there. And people are afraid the Black Road will take it, of course, so some have moved on to Stryne, to Hommen, even as far as here."

"They're getting food, aren't they?"

"Oh, yes. Lheanor's paid for some of it. He even sent wood-workers down here to help with the huts. The Woollers have been sending sacks of bread. They won't starve, Orisian."

"The only thing they need is their homes back," Rothe said. His anger was taut, a muscle beneath the skin of his words.

Up ahead, an old man was brandishing a stick at an overeager stray dog that nosed the sack beside him. The dog shrank back, baring its teeth. A younger man nearby threw a stone at it.

"Let's get back," Orisian said. "We're doing no good marching up and down in front of these people."

Rothe grunted. "I'd not be so sure about that. It won't feed them, but the sight of you might warm their hearts a little."

They walked back through busy, noisy streets, heading for the Tower of Thrones. Kolkyre's northern parts were where most of the artisans lived and their houses, workshops and stalls were everywhere. Little wagons full of timber blocked the narrow roads; beggars and hawkers harassed every passer-by.

Anger was seldom far away for Orisian, these last few days. Everything he saw, everything he heard, was a little coloured by it. He struggled to distinguish between the anger born of what the Horin-Gyre Blood had done to his people and that summoned up by the hostile, patronising games he feared Aewult and the Shadowhand were playing with him. He vaguely sensed, but could not disentangle, another strand that was turned inward: anger at what he feared might prove to be his own shortcomings and inadequacies; his inability to live up to the demands placed upon him.

"We serve no purpose, lingering here while half our Blood is unhomed and the other half is starving," he muttered.

A man pushing a barrow of charcoal came up behind them, shouting that they should move aside and let him pass. Rothe stopped and turned, glowering. The man almost slipped, hauling his barrow to a halt before it ran into the shieldman's shins. He spat out some harsh words, but bit his lip when Rothe took a step nearer to him.

Orisian pulled Rothe aside. "Let him pass. It's his street more than it's ours."

The man ran by them, weaving his way on through the crowds. There was an angry cry of pain as he scraped the barrow along someone's calf.

As they stood there for that moment, withdrawn to the edge of the street, Taim Narran surreptitiously touched Orisian's arm.

"There are two men, sire, some way behind us. Big. Leather jerkins. Do you see them?"

Orisian looked back the way they had come. He saw those that Taim meant easily enough: two burly men engaged in earnest conversation with a woman selling tallow candles through a window in the front of her house. He nodded.

"I saw at least one of them earlier, when we left the Tower," Taim said quietly. "Come, let's walk on."

He guided Orisian back into the flow of townsfolk. Rothe fell a few paces behind, shadowing the Thane and his Captain. Orisian noticed the shieldman carefully freeing his injured arm from its sling.

"They've followed us all the way up this street," Taim said. "Paused when we paused." He flicked a glance sideways, at a stall festooned with simple pots and jugs and beakers. "Moving again, now that we are."

"What do you suggest?" Orisian asked.

"Well, I may be seeing something that's not there. Even if I'm right, chances are they mean no immediate harm. In either case, we could ignore them for now; worry about it once you're safely back in the Tower."

Orisian sidestepped a little pile of horse dung. A mob of seagulls swept screaming low over the street in pursuit of one of their number that had snatched up some scrap of food. In the Car Criagar, and in distant Koldihrve, Orisian had thought that some kind of safety awaited them if only they could take to the sea and slip away to the south. Now, at the end of that journey, he found only more struggles, more uncertainties. Instead of becoming clearer, answers receded from him. And they would keep receding, he suspected, unless and until he found a way to chart his own course.

"Could they be Lheanor's men, watching over us?" he asked Taim.

"Unlikely, sire." The warrior sniffed. "He'd not set such a watch on you without letting us know, would he?"

"Then I want to know who they are, and what they intend. Now, before we get back to the Tower."

Taim beckoned Rothe without breaking his stride. The shieldman trotted up to join them.

"We'll turn along the next side street," Taim said quite casually. "You and Orisian press on down it, in clear sight. I'll hang back. Give the hounds sniffing our heels a surprise."

They took the next turning on their right. It was a narrow lane, though still busy. Some women and girls were hanging freshly dyed sheets out to dry. A pair of men were arguing over a cockerel that one of them held in his hands. Half a dozen children were throwing pebbles up onto a shingled roof, laughing at the rattle. Rothe led Orisian on at a slightly faster pace. Taim turned aside and Orisian lost sight of him.

"Best not to look back," Rothe muttered. "Don't want to give them any sign of what's happening."

"Can Taim manage two?"

"Oh, you needn't worry about that. They'll be sorry they woke up this morning."

Only a moment or two later, a flurry of footfalls, shouts and dull impacts burst out behind them and both Orisian and Rothe spun around. Taim was kneeling on one man who lay face down in the roadway. The second was hobbling off as fast as what looked to be a thoroughly deadened leg would allow.

The cockerel had escaped its owner in the excitement, and ran chattering off down the lane. Both the men who had been arguing over it set off in pursuit. The little gang of children had dropped their pebbles and were pointing excitedly at Taim and his captive.

"Could only hold one, sire," Taim said apologetically as Orisian and Rothe walked up to him.

"One's enough," Rothe said with feeling. "Let's turn him over."

They rolled the dazed man onto his back and Taim rested a swordpoint on his chest, pinning him to the cobbles. Rothe leaned down.

"Who are you, then?" he asked, and even to Orisian his voice sounded cold and threatening.

The prone man turned his face aside and maintained a stubborn silence. Taim tapped the man's chest with his blade.

"Now is not the moment for bravery. We are none of us here renowned for our patience. You'll come to no harm, if you but share your purpose with us."

"I'd no purpose but to be walking with a friend," the man spat a little indistinctly. He still seemed somewhat stunned, either by the unexpected course of events or by his fall to the ground. "We'd not thought to find bandits here. You've no right to set upon us."

Rothe straightened. He and Taim glanced at one another and Orisian saw some kind of understanding pass between the two warriors. Taim sheathed his sword. He kicked the man, without any great force, in the ribs.

"What's your name?" he asked.

"I'll not give my name to thieves."

Orisian caught a certain texture in the man's voice, an accent that was almost, but not quite, familiar.

"Stand up," Taim said wearily. He looked to Orisian. "We may as well send him on his way, sire. He'll tell us nothing beyond what he's already done just by opening his mouth."

Orisian nodded.

"Tell your master we don't like to be followed," Taim called after the man as he hurried, rather stiffly, away.

"Haig?" Orisian asked quietly.

Taim and Rothe both nodded.

"Nar Vay, I think," Taim said. "Somewhere close to the border with Ayth. But Haig, yes."

"Aewult, then. Or Mordyn Jerain."

"Or the Steward," Rothe suggested glumly. "Any one of them. All of them. It hardly matters which."

"No," agreed Orisian. "It doesn't. How many men have you got here, Taim? Seven hundred?"

If the warrior was surprised at the question, he hid it well. "About that. A handful under, perhaps, that are truly fit to march. If marching is what's in your thoughts, that is."

"So long as we're here, we're guests," Orisian said. "Beggars. Playthings for Haig. They mean to keep us here, rotting, while they settle affairs in the Glas valley. And what happens then? Aewult and the Shadowhand will make all our decisions for us if we let them."

"They wouldn't dare," Rothe growled.

"They might," Taim said.

"I just don't want to fail those people, homeless on that street back there. Or Croesan," Orisian sighed. Or my father, he could have added. Or Fariel, even. "Aewult might not be as clever as he thinks he is. He might not find it as easy as he expects to march all the way up to the Stone Vale. There are things . . ."

He left the thought unfinished. He had said nothing to anyone about what he and Anyara had witnessed in Yvane's chamber. In truth, they had seen nothing. Only felt, and heard what Yvane told them. He did not doubt that Aeglyss was a danger; others might not be so willing to trust the words of *na'kyrim*. He shrugged.

"It feels . . . if we were in Kolglas, we'd be on our own ground, if nothing else. Nobody could tell us what to do then. Nobody would find it so easy to set their spies on us."

"Aewult will be . . . upset, if we march without his approval," Taim observed.

"Can you move quickly, or quietly, enough to ensure he's got no chance of stopping you? That's all that would matter. Once you're on the road north, the way is clear."

Taim smiled. "I should think so. Certainly, I should imagine, with a little help from Lheanor and his people."

"I'll talk to the Thane," Orisian said. It eased him a little to make a choice, to set his feet on a path of his own choosing. Here in Kolkyre, he felt impotent and ringed about with uncertainty. Could it really be as easy as simply deciding to walk away from it?

"And another thing," he said. "I want Anyara to have a shield-man."

"A shieldman?" Taim echoed.

"The best man you have."

"That's . . . not usually done, sire."

"If it was, I wouldn't have to ask, would I? She's faced more danger than I have since Winterbirth. And she's all the family I have left. I want her to have a shieldman."

Taim bowed his head a fraction. "I will find someone."

Rothe took an almost sheepish step forwards, scratching absently at his beard in the way he always did when uncomfortable.

"You should have another shieldman of your own, Orisian," he said. "Several, in fact. We've been remiss not to take care of it sooner. Now you're Thane, and I'm broken-winged . . ."

"No," said Orisian, too quickly perhaps. "No more."

Rothe looked dismayed. Orisian touched him on his good arm.

"I don't need anyone but you, Rothe. You've served me better than my father could ever have asked of you. I won't have anyone else . . ."

He did not finish the thought. It might not be fitting, he imagined, for a Thane to show too much distaste for the sacrifice of others in his name. Already, on that torch-lit night of Winterbirth in Castle Kolglas, he had seen Kylane, his second shieldman, die in his defence: as hurtful a death, in some ways, as any there had been. Rothe had long ago made the promise to do likewise if needed, and Orisian would not shame him by trying to undo that, but he would permit no one else to shoulder the burden afresh.

He could see in Rothe's softening, sad expression that he did not need to explain his reasons. The man had been with him long enough to know something of how his mind worked.

"It's unwise," Taim Narran said. "However worthy Rothe might be, he cannot guard you always. You are Thane, as he says. You must allow us to see to your protection as . . ."

"No," Orisian insisted. He turned away. "Let's get back."

"It's all right, Taim," he heard Rothe saying with strained levity behind him. "These wounds are only grazes to the likes of me. I'll have shaken them off in another few days, then you'll see the Thane is still well-guarded."

As they drew near to the barracks, one of Taim's men, looking a little harassed, intercepted them.

"There was a messenger searching for you, sire. The, er, the guest in the Tower of Thrones wanted to see you. Urgent, I think."

"Yvane, you mean? Is that who you mean?" The guard nodded,

and Orisian frowned. "Well, call her by her name, then. There's no one to eavesdrop on us here."

A faint blush of colour spread in the guard's cheeks. Orisian at once regretted his sharp tone.

"What was it about, then?" he asked, calm this time. "I've other things to be doing at the moment."

"Don't know, sire. Seemed pressing, though. The messenger was . . . anxious."

"All right," Orisian said, struggling to conceal his disappointment. What he wanted to do now was see Ess'yr, and Varryn too. He wanted to see their pleasure at being given the chance to leave this place; reassure himself that Ess'yr – that both of them – would come with him. "Taim, we'll talk more later. Rothe and I will see what Yvane wants."

The *na'kyrim* was alone in her chambers, standing with her back to the window and her hands clasped behind her. As he entered, Orisian blinked. Some shadow or mote had passed across his right eye for a moment: a momentary blurring of his vision as if some invisible fingertip had pressed gently against his eyeball. It cleared.

"I don't have much time, Yvane. There's a lot happening now."

"Just you, Orisian, if you'd be so kind. This is only for you."

Orisian nodded to Rothe, whose indignation was undisguised. The shieldman opened his mouth to protest.

"It's fine, Rothe," Orisian said. "This won't take long."

Rothe went, closing the door behind him a little more firmly than was necessary.

"I don't think there's anything you could say to me that should be kept from Rothe," Orisian said, turning back to Yvane. Again, that irritation in his eye like the scratch of a wayward dust grain. He twitched his head, as if that might clear it. "He deserves better from you than . . ."

"It's my privacy that Yvane protects, not her own."

Orisian jumped sideways, almost exclaiming in surprise. Seated there, in a chair that a moment ago had been empty, was a *na'kyrim*: a short young man with his hands resting on his knees. His voice was soft, fluty.

"Don't worry," said Yvane before Orisian could speak, or call for Rothe. "He's no threat. This is Bannain, from Highfast."

Orisian took another step backwards, still unsettled. The man, he was sure, had not been there when he entered the room.

"How . . ." he began, but was not sure how to complete the question.

Bannain smiled in a detached kind of way, and flourished his long fingers.

"Mere trickery. I apologise if I startled you."

"Of course you startled me," snapped Orisian.

Yvane laid a hand on his arm, all the while frowning at Bannain as if in reprimand.

"He might be a little full of himself, Orisian, but he means no harm. Bannain has the knack of using the Shared in a very potent, but very narrow" – she emphasised that word – "way. It makes him well suited to certain tasks. He's been serving the Elect as a messenger for quite a few years."

Bannain folded his arms across his chest and stretched his legs out, resting the heel of one foot on the toe of the other.

"It's nothing too sinister," Yvane continued. "He just makes the eye . . . slide over him, if you like. He can only keep it up for a few moments, so he's not as clever as he thinks he is."

The younger *na'kyrim* smiled again. "All true. Again, I am sorry. I only wished to avoid the attention of anyone who came with you. Normally, none but Lheanor and one or two others know of my visits to Kolkyre. Of course, once I found out Yvane was here with news from the north I had to come and speak with her; and she in turn insists I tell my story to you as well."

"Your story?" Orisian asked warily.

"Bannain was sent here by the Council at Highfast to warn

Lheanor," Yvane explained. "I think you might want to hear what he has to say."

"All right, then. Tell me." Orisian could not quite shed his caution and mistrust. If Yvane said this man was safe, and had something useful to say, he believed her, but it did not mean he had to like Bannain's manner.

"Hard to explain, to one who is not *na'kyrim*," the young man said, "but Yvane claims you're more likely to grasp it than most. She's told you already about the canker that's appeared in the Shared?" His nose wrinkled in distaste as he asked the question.

"She has. And about its cause."

"Its cause. Indeed. You've met this man Aeglyss, I'm told."

"Not met. I've seen him, once. My sister was unlucky enough to spend more time in his company than me."

"Unlucky indeed, I imagine. We have one at Highfast – a woman from Dyrkyrnon – who knows Aeglyss of old, from when he was young. She has nothing good to say of him. She is certain that he is the source of the disturbances that now torment all waking *na'kyrim*. I gather Yvane here shares that certainty. But the real question is how did this happen? What does it signify?"

Bannain looked from Orisian to Yvane, his eyebrows raised like a tale-teller teasing his audience.

"Don't overdo it," growled Yvane. "Orisian is as much a Thane as Lheanor is, don't forget."

Bannain gave no sign of being abashed by the scolding.

"The Council at Highfast has given much thought to these matters," he continued, now setting his elbows on the arms of the chair and making a tent of his fingers. "This is as close to under-standing as they have come: on that night, the night none of us – none amongst the waking – is likely to forget, something hap-pened to this Aeglyss. Something that broke the barriers between his mind and the Shared.

"Precisely what it was hardly matters. The nub of things is this: Aeglyss has become something . . . new. Or very old, depending on how you look at it. There's been no *na'kyrim* who could cast such a long shadow in hundreds of years. The Shared has poured into him – and a little of him has leaked back into the Shared. He may be capable of remarkable things now.

"And thus the essence of the message Cerys had me bring to Lheanor: be careful. Be cautious. However things may seem to be now, it is the judgement of Highfast that the armies of the Black Road are not the most dangerous thing in the Glas valley."

Orisian stared at the young *na'kyrim*. "That much we already suspected."

"There's a little more," Yvane said, and looked pointedly at Bannain.

"A little, yes," he agreed. "Harder, though, to read its significance. There is a man at Highfast we call the Dreamer. He sleeps and speaks, now and again, of the currents flowing in the deepest Shared. Little of what he has said makes any sense, but some of it, some of it is very dark. It seems that the changes in the Shared have caught the attention of those best left undisturbed. The Dreamer whispers that the Anain are stirring."

"Well, that . . ." Orisian shut his mouth. He had no idea what he could sensibly say in response. The Anain – the race unlike any other, implacable, unknowable – were as far beyond his experience as anything could possibly be. To him, they were little more than creatures out of strange, usually fearful, stories; hardly more real than the wolfenkind who had disappeared from the world over a thousand years ago. He knew, having seen it with his own eyes and heard of it from Ess'yr, that they were more than that to the Kyrinin, but the knowledge had done nothing to blunt his own ignorance.

"The Anain have not roused themselves in a long time," Yvane murmured. "Not since they raised the Deep Rove, in fact: better than three centuries. All that time, they've taken no interest in what's happening. If they've shaken off their indifference now, there will be trouble."

Orisian raised his hands in exasperated helplessness.

"Not trouble I can do anything about, though." He looked questioningly first at Yvane and then at Bannain. "Aeglyss, the Shared: these things are far enough beyond my grasp already. But the Anain?"

"Beyond the grasp of any of us," conceded Bannain.

"But you do understand things that others might not," said Yvane, that blunt insistence Orisian knew so well creeping into her voice. "Your mind is a little less closed against all of this than most. You had Inurian at your side for all those years. You were there – you saw what happened – when I reached out to Aeglyss. This . . . this is moving beyond the understanding of . . . Huanin memories are too short. You all think you remember the likes of Minon or Orlane Kingbinder, but it's been centuries. You've all grown too used to knowing only *na'kyrim* like me and Bannain, with our silly, secret little talents. And the Anain: a hundred thousand swords would not suffice if they chose to wake from their slumber."

"I see that," said Orisian. "I do." And he did, at least in part. All those hours he had spent with Inurian, all his fascination for the Kyrinin, the days he had spent in a Fox *vo'an* and the *anhyne* he had seen there: these things told him that there was more to the world than the machinations of Thanes, strengths other than those that resided in swords and spears.

"Lheanor said the same thing," Bannain said. "He listened to what I had to tell him, and nodded, and said that he understood." The *na'kyrim* smiled ruefully and let his head tip to one side. "But he didn't really. He can't truly see how furious the coming storm might be. How could he? How could anyone but we *na'kyrim*? Aeglyss is becoming a fever in the Shared. And the Shared is . . . it is the thought of which we are all the expression. Huanin, Kyrinin, *na'kyrim*: all of us."

"Come to Highfast," Yvane said abruptly to Orisian. "Hammarn and I will be leaving tomorrow with Bannain. Come

and talk to the people there." She glanced at Bannain. "The
Council of Highfast is not famous for stirring itself in aid of
others, but they might. They might, if they believed you worthy
of that aid."

Orisian looked at her, and as he met her sharp, grey eyes he
could have been looking into the face of Inurian: Inurian, who in
the last few years had been the one person he had always felt he
could trust and be certain of. Though Yvane was far less gentle
and caring than Inurian had been, and Orisian had known her for
only a matter of weeks, he did trust her. She made a great show
of her indifference to the concerns of everyone else, but there were
signs, now and again, that that was more out of choice and habit
than nature.

"I'm going to Kolglas," Orisian murmured. Highfast: a secret
place, where Inurian had lived before he came to Kolglas. A year
ago, he would have leaped at the chance to visit such a mysterious place, to make that kind of contact with Inurian's history.
Now, nothing was so simple.

"There's one more thing you should know before you decide,"
Yvane said. She nodded to Bannain. He leaned forwards a little.

"A surprise to me. I thought nothing of it, until talking with
Yvane today. This woman – Eshenna – at Highfast, who knew
Aeglyss all those years ago. She has mentioned someone else, also
from Dyrkyrnon; has told the Council that there is some . . . some
bond between Aeglyss and a woman named K'rina."

Orisian recognised the name instantly. It was the name that
Yvane had teased out of the Shared, when she had struggled with
Aeglyss.

"I don't know whether it has any significance, but Eshenna,
just the day before I left Highfast, was claiming that this woman
K'rina was . . . moving. And rumours have reached us – faint,
unreliable little rumours – that there are White Owl bands on
the move too, in the western reaches of Anlane," said Bannain.

Orisian looked to Yvane. She shrugged and raised her eyebrows.

"I don't know. I've dug up as many answers as I can. Something's happening. What, I can't say. Perhaps Highfast can tell us."

"Is there a road from Highfast to Kolglas?" Orisian asked Bannain.

Bannain pursed his lips. "To call it a road might be to elevate it beyond its true worth," he said. "But there's a track — a good one — to Hent, and thence to the coast road at Hommen."

Orisian nodded. He wondered briefly, as he had done more than once in the last few days, what Croesan or Naradin, Kennet or Fariel would do. Any of those who should have been Thane before him, but for the blind savagery of chance and misfortune. Inurian would have chided him for letting such distractions intrude, he knew. Anyara might too, if she could see what thoughts murmured inside his head. And they were right enough. For good or ill, the decisions were his to make. Nothing, and no one, could relieve him of that.

* * *

The air inside the warehouse was laden with aromas: spice and fur, oil and timber all ran together to make the darkness heavy with strangeness. The roof timbers creaked in the night wind. Somewhere up there, in the shadowed intricacies of the beams and planking, there was the chatter of rats' claws.

Ammen Sharp cupped his hand around the tiny flame of a candle. The two men on watch outside had warned him not to make any light in here, fearful of a fire that could consume the whole building, but it was too dark and unfamiliar a place for him without it. He crept amongst the great towers of boxes and bundles, exploring the unearthly landscape of this treasure house. There were clay jars almost as tall as he was, their stoppers sealed with wax; crates stood one on top of another like cliffs; long rolls of fabric were piled up as if the trees of some soft forest had been harvested; strange powders and dusts covered the floor, releasing bursts of scent when his feet disturbed them.

For all his nervousness, Ammen found it exciting. Here, it seemed to him, was all the world, all its most distant and marvellous lands, collected together in this great stone ship of a building. Hidden away in here might be pots of carmine Nar Vay dyes, cloths from far-off Adravane, whale oils from the wave-lashed Bone Isles.

He clambered up over a mound of what he guessed were seal pelts, and onto a stack of crates. He squeezed into a space between two of them. He felt more secure now that he had a corner to call his own, hidden from view, and blew out the candle. He listened to the rats running, the faint knocking of anchored boats outside at the quay, the rattle of a loose shingle somewhere in the roof far above. He rested against one of the crates and imagined what it would be like on the road with his father, and in Skeil Anchor. People would know Ochan the Cook, he was sure. In the roadside inns and the fishing villages they would know Ochan, and they would see Ammen at his side and soon know him too.

A scraping sound disturbed his reverie. He shifted onto his knees and peered out over the bare expanse of stone floor towards the front of the warehouse. The little door by which the guards outside had let him in earlier was open once more, admitting a shaft of light from their lanterns. A thickset figure with a staff and a huge bag slung over his shoulders was stepping in. It was his father.

"Ammen," hissed Ochan. "Ammen Sharp. Where are you, boy?"

"Here," Ammen called, rising up and waving even though he was unsure whether his father would be able to see him.

"Quiet!" Ochan snapped. "Keep your voice down, you idiot."

The door closed behind him, and the warehouse's secretive gloom was restored. Ammen heard his father curse, and there was a thump as he dropped his bag to the ground.

"I can't see a thing in here," Ochan the Cook complained. "Have you got no light, boy?"

"They told me not to, but yes, I've got candles. I'll light one." He ducked down again, scrabbling about in search of the candle he had put out earlier. A splinter stabbed into one of his fingers and he gave a soft yelp.

"Oh, don't bother," Ochan muttered down below. "I'll get a lantern from the watchmen."

There was shouting then, and a sudden clatter of running feet.

Ammen sprang to his feet, but his father snapped, "Stay down, boy," and he did as he was told.

He heard the door smash open once more, saw sudden bursts of torchlight rushing across the walls, careening through the roof beams, as men came in out of the night.

"What do you want here, you little . . ." he heard Ochan rasping.

"Hold your tongue," came Urik's sharp, agitated voice.

Ammen Sharp could not resist the temptation to poke his head around the edge of his sheltering crate. To his horror, he saw his father facing half a dozen men, the squat shape of Urik the Wardcaptain to the fore. They all carried the iron-banded cudgels of the Guard; three of them held torches, the flames stretching out and crackling in the wind from the open door. Wild shadows spun crazily around the warehouse.

"I'll hold your tongue for you, if you come any closer," Ochan said, and Ammen clearly heard the danger, the threat in the words.

"Be still," cried Urik, raising his cudgel.

He sounded almost frantic to Ammen, on the verge of panic. This could not be what the Wardcaptain had wanted. He was surely too afraid of his own corruption being exposed to willingly allow Ochan to be cornered like this. Something must have gone wrong, Ammen thought as a cold, fearful anticipation ran through him.

"You've been followed half the day, Ochan Lyre," Urik was saying. "Don't think you can escape now."

"Escape? Escape?" Ochan's voice was rising, his anger with it. "And do they know about you, these thugs you've brought with you? Do they know—"

Urik howled and rushed forwards. Ochan was fast, though. He snapped the tip of his quarterstaff down and landed it square on Urik's forehead, sending the stocky little man staggering. Had it only been the two of them there in the warehouse, there would have been no doubt about the victor. But Urik was not alone. The other Guardsmen closed in on Ochan at once, cudgels flailing.

A cry lodged frozen in Ammen's throat as he watched the blows rain down. He wanted to leap out of his hiding place and fly to his father's aid, but his legs were locked as if his knees had rusted in place.

Ochan had gone down on his hands and knees. Urik stamped up to him, blood running in rivulets down his face.

"You bled me!" the Wardcaptain screeched. "You bled me!"

He hit Ochan once, hard, on the back of his head with his heavy iron-clad club. Ammen saw his father fall to the ground and knew in that instant, from the leaden slackness of his limbs, the wet limpness with which his head smacked onto the stone, that Ochan the Cook was dead.

The other Guardsmen restrained Urik, who was still shouting furiously. Ammen shrank back, trembling, into his little dark corner. He closed his eyes, held his hands to his face, pressing down on his mouth and the moans that were rising towards it. Lights were dancing inside his eyelids.

"Drag the body out," he heard someone say far, far away. "We'll get a wagon to take it."

And then, soon, they were gone and the door had closed behind them. And Ammen Sharp was alone with the dark, and his horror.

VII

"Aewult will not be happy when Taim marches," Lheanor oc Kilkry-Haig was saying softly. The Thane seldom spoke loudly these days. He sat in a capacious high-backed chair. He did not fill it as Orisian guessed he might once have done. Lheanor was hunched forwards a little, hands laid across one another in his lap, shoulders pinched in.

"No," Orisian acknowledged. "He might not. I don't want to cause trouble for you, but I may leave some behind me."

Lheanor's right hand stirred, the fingers fluttering as if to dismiss such a minor concern.

"A little more trouble will make no difference when there's so much of it already in the air. We've been told no Kilkry spears will be needed in the coming battles either, you know. Aewult wants our men scattered, sent home, even the ones Roaric brought back from the south. My son's . . . unhappy.

"And to bind the wound with salted bandages, I am requested – requested, mark you – to help in defraying the costs of this war, and that against Igryn. It's not the Chancellor himself who asks, of course. One of his scribblers, his counters, comes quietly and does the asking for him." Lheanor shook his head. "They'll not come knocking on the door of your treasury yet, Orisian. Not until you're back in Anduran. But knock they will, and stretch their greedy hands out."

"You'll give them what they want?" Orisian asked.

"Oh, yes. I bent the knee to the Haig Blood, as has every Thane of my line since Cannoch. And what's the value of an oath if we set it aside when the fulfilment of it becomes onerous, painful? The only other choice would, sooner or later, be war with Haig, and with Ayth and Taral. That way lies chaos: the very thing the Bloods were made to end. Anyway, it's not a war we could win."

The Kilkry Thane leaned sideways in his throne, looking past

Orisian to the ranks of his shieldmen arrayed along the far wall. Rothe was there too, standing tall and alert despite his still-bandaged arm.

"Let us walk in the gardens," Lheanor said as he rose, heavily, from his chair. "I find it does not help my mood to sit still for too long."

They went out into the chill air. Their guards followed behind, out of earshot but close. Orisian thought Lheanor would be cold, but the old man gave no sign of discomfort, as if the state of the world around him could no longer impinge on his thoughts. They set out along one of the garden's broad paths, curving away around the side of the hillock that supported the Tower.

"You're going to Highfast, then?" Lheanor said.

"Yes. I've seen – and heard – enough to make me think . . . I'm not sure. Perhaps armies are not the only kind of strength we need in this. But I'll stay there only briefly. I mean to meet Taim Narran at Kolglas. I'm told there's a good path from Highfast across the Peaks to Hent and then down to the coast."

"Good? I don't know. Passable, yes, if you don't wait too long, and if you've no wagons to haul. The Karkyre Peaks can be nasty in the winter." Lheanor flicked a glance at the sky. "Not quite yet, though, I suppose."

"What did you make of the word Bannain brought from Highfast? About Aeglyss, the Shared?" Orisian felt like a charlatan, pretending to discuss weighty matters with the Thane of a True Blood. He wondered if he would ever feel as though he belonged at the side of such a man.

Lheanor shrugged. "I worry about grain harvests, about tithes, about the Shadowhand's games. The worries of *na'kyrim* . . . well, some problems are best left to others. How can the likes of you and I oppose things that cannot be met with a blade, or an emissary, or cold coin? Don't mistake me, though: Cerys and her people at Highfast, they're a precious thing. Giving that place to the *na'kyrim* was not the least of Kulkain's wise deeds, not by a long way."

"Have you said anything about it – Bannain's message – to Aewult?"

"Ha! You really think the great warriors of Haig would care what a few *na'kyrim* think? Aewult would not listen to any counsel drawn from such a well. It would only feed his contempt for us, to learn that we gave it any credence ourselves. We have a few slender threads of tolerance left for the children of two races, your Blood and mine. But Haig? No. Even if they believed it . . . oh, there are old hatreds that could easily be stirred back into life. If people start to think there are *na'kyrim* mixed up in this war, how safe do you suppose any of them, anywhere, would be?"

"They took a risk, in sending Bannain to you," Orisian murmured.

"I like to think they trust me, as they have trusted my ancestors. Unfortunately, I fear they do not really understand how much power has leaked away from the Tower of Thrones."

Crows that had been strutting across the neat lawns in serried ranks flew off, cawing in irritation, as the two Thanes approached.

"They believe it's their garden more than mine," Lheanor said as he watched them go. "You're taking your Kyrinin with you, are you?"

"I am. They expect to be killing White Owls soon, and that . . . pleases them." He remembered well the smile that had burst from Ess'yr's flawless face at the news: a rare prize.

"I can't say I'll be sorry to see the back of them. I know they helped you, and that makes them friends of my Blood as much as yours, but word gets out, no matter how much care it's guarded with. There'd be a mob at the door demanding their deaths before too much longer."

"I know. I've brought more problems with me than I would have wished."

"Not you. Horin-Gyre. Haig. They're the ones who've crafted our troubles. And a foolish father, too ready to grant his son's desire for battle."

There was such a weight of sadness in Lheanor's voice that Orisian could almost feel its tug himself. He looked at the Thane of the Kilkry Blood and saw not a mighty leader but an old man, bowed by loss, beset by guilt.

"I wake up every day," Orisian said, "and . . . every morning I have to learn to believe it all over again: that they really are gone. A dozen times a day – no, more – I think of something I want to say to one of them, or ask. My father, my uncle, Inurian. My mother, even, and Fariel."

"There are a great many things I wish I could say to my son."

"You still have a son. Perhaps you should say them to him."

The Kilkry-Haig Thane glanced at him, and Orisian wondered if he should tread more carefully. But he did know something of this; in the matter of dead sons, of grieving fathers, he could claim some knowledge.

"I don't know you well, sire," he went on, "so you must tell me if I speak out of turn. My father lost a son, and I lost him because of that. Grief took him away from me before the Inkallim did."

"I walked here sometimes with Croesan, you know," Lheanor murmured. "And your father and mother once, perhaps more than once, years ago. We talked about . . . what?" A frown crumpled the old man's face, and then passed. "I'm not sure. Nothings, probably. For ones such as us, Thane, there are too few people in whose company we can be . . . idle. You come to treasure those you do have, and therefore are wounded by their passing."

Lheanor paused, looking down at the path on which they walked. One of the flat stones had lifted a little, disturbing the smooth surface.

"Look," Lheanor muttered. "The frost's got under that."

He made an irritated noise at the back of his throat and waved one of his shieldmen over. He pointed the stone out to the warrior.

"Find one of the gardeners and get them to relay that."

The man trotted off to carry out the command. Lheanor led Orisian on around the Tower of Thrones. They walked in a great, slow circle while overhead the clouds flowed in from the west.

"A man never speaks out of turn when he offers well-meant advice," Lheanor said. "My loss – my loss I find to be unbearable. Yet it is less than yours, and you remain unbowed by it. Unbroken. Thus it seems you are made of better stuff than me."

"No, that's not   " Orisian began, but Lheanor stilled him with an upraised hand.

"I envy you your youth. It's an armour against many things, youth. You refuse to play games with Aewult and the Shadowhand. I allow them to set fences about me, my Blood, my army. You do not. Whether what you intend is wise or not, I do not know; but I do know that I envy you the will to make the attempt."

The old Thane bent to snap a dead twig from a bush by the path. He pointed with it down towards a sweep of grass by the wall.

"I think I want to plant trees down there. Something that flowers in the spring, with white blossom, perhaps. My wife likes white blossom. That's one thing that does not change, isn't it? Whoever dies – even if we die ourselves – there is always another year to come. Every winter ends eventually."

He laid a hand on Orisian's shoulder.

"You do as you see fit, Thane. If you do not wish to follow at Haig's heels like some lady's tame dog, so be it. You will hear no complaint from the Kilkry Blood so long as I live, and none when Roaric is Thane after me, I think."

"There's one other thing I would ask of you," Orisian said.

"Ask it. If it's within my power, I'll grant it."

"Watch over Anyara for me. She's angry that I want her to stay behind, but I won't take her with me. I want her to be safe. I'd feel more sure of that knowing you – your family – are watching over her."

Lheanor smiled then, though the smile carried more regret than pleasure. "That is something I would willingly do even if you did not ask it of me. We will guard her as jealously as we would a daughter of our own. But do this for me in exchange, Orisian: do not give up your own life too easily. You go into danger, of one sort or another, and there are already too few good people left. Come and see, in years to come, whether the trees I plant have bloomed."

* * *

Jaen Narran was upset. She hid it, but the multitude of subtle signs did not escape Taim. Her lips were pressed tight together; she doled out the oatmeal gruel from the pot over the fire a little too fast, spilling wet lumps of it; she moved quickly from table to hearth and back again, taking small, sharp steps.

She would never shame him, and herself, by asking him to stay here with her. He would never embarrass them both by seeking to justify his return to the battlefield, so soon after he had come back from what they had both hoped would be his last such absence. She knew as well as he did that this was a battle that had to be fought, a call it would be unthinkable to refuse. And she knew that it would break his heart a little to leave her.

Taim stirred some salt into the grey sludge in his bowl. The quarters they had been given here in Kolkyre's barracks were good: spacious and warm and dry. They were better than those that the warriors who followed Taim enjoyed, crushed into halls meant for half their number. For the sake of his family, he accepted that he could not share his men's discomfort, but he could, and did, share their diet.

Jaen sat down on the other side of the rough table.

"I'll mend what I can tonight, then," she said. "There's still a lot of holes and tears I've not had time to make right yet. The rocks down south must be sharper than they are here."

"There're seamstresses here who can help."

Gobbets of gruel dripped from her spoon as Jaen held it poised halfway to her mouth. "I'll do it. I've been doing it for better than thirty years. I'll not stop now."

"No, I wouldn't want you to."

They ate in silence for a little while. The fire crackled. The wind was rising outside, blustering around the squat stone mass of the barracks.

"Where're the young ones?" Taim asked at length.

"Gone to the harbour. Achlinn's trying to find work on a fishing boat. Maira went with him, looking for word of friends."

Taim nodded. He was proud of his daughter, and of her husband too. Their flight with Jaen from Glasbridge had been so rushed that they had been able to bring almost nothing away with them. Most likely, they had no home to return to. In the face of all this, they showed nothing but determination.

Jaen was watching him, the way she did when she was pondering whether to say something. Taim raised his eyebrows questioningly.

"She'd want to tell you herself," Jaen murmured, "but perhaps the sooner you know, the better. Maira's with child."

Taim leaped to his feet so carelessly that his thighs cracked the edge of the table and set his bowl rocking.

"Truly? You're sure?"

Jaen smiled up at him, joyful and sad in the same moment. "Truly," she confirmed.

Taim came to her and threw his arms around her. She dropped her spoon.

"I didn't think it possible," he murmured in her ear.

"None of us did, did we?" said Jaen as she pushed him away so that she could rise. She cupped his face in her hands. "We thought the Fever'd barrened her, as it did others. But not so. You're to be a grandfather, Taim Narran."

The warrior laughed out loud and planted a firm kiss on his wife's forehead.

"Ha!" he cried to himself. "Ha!"

"So you see," Jaen said, sinking back into her seat, "you'll be needed home and safe at the end of all this. There's to be no doubts about it this time. No excuses, no delays. I want you at my side when our grandchild is born."

She gazed at him and Taim could feel her love, and his for her, in his chest like a beat, like another heart. Still so strong; as strong as it had ever been.

"I will be there," he said. "I will."

* * *

Old Cailla the kitchen maid had sharpened hundreds of knives in her life. No matter the purpose or value of the blade, she never did it with less than her full attention. In all things – choosing shellfish for the Thane's table, sharpening a knife, seasoning a soup – she was precise, thorough.

The particular knife on which she lavished all her care now was unremarkable, save in one respect: it belonged not to the kitchens of the Tower of Thrones, but to her alone. It had a short, thin blade set in a stubby wooden handle. Someone leaning over her shoulder and examining it might think it a peeling knife, or one for cutting fruit. In truth, it had never been used for any purpose. Aside from the very rare occasions on which she took it out to check its edge, and refresh it if needed, it never left its plain leather sheath.

She was alone in the cramped quarters she shared with three other maids. She sat on the edge of the wooden cot where she slept, working by the light of a single whale-oil lamp. The blade of the knife rasped over the stone that rested on her knees. Her fingers were not as straight and strong as they had once been, nor as dexterous or quick. Still, they were skilled. When she was done, the blade would have as sharp an edge as it could ever hold.

As she hunched over the whetstone, stroking the knife smoothly back and forth, Cailla's old, soft lips moved. They did so almost soundlessly, but not quite. Far too faint to be heard by any save the God for whom it was meant, she repeated over and over again a few short sentences: "My feet are on the Road. I go without fear. I know not pride."

2

Highfast

Next there is the mighty fortress Marain built amidst the Karkyre Peaks. No other Blood, nor even the Kingships of the far south, can claim such a stronghold as their own. The perdurable mountain itself, cut through by tunnels and chambers, is as much a part of the fastness as its walls and towers. Not Abremor, not the Red Hand of the Snake, not all the armies of Morvain's Revolt could breach its defences, though each tried. Whatever use my lord may find for this great place, it will not fail through want of strength.

What use that may be, I know not. The road this place was built to guard is a ruin, for since the great war against the Kyrinin none make the journey through the Peaks to Drandar. That way grew thick with bandits and with Snake raiders in the Storm Years. The cobblestones were torn up and used to build sheep pens, the drains clogged, the inns and way stations were burned or abandoned. Thus there is now no fit path beyond Highfast to either east or south, and none to the north save a mule-driver's track across the mountains to Hent. There was a village of quarrymen and drovers close by the castle once, but it is empty now. The airs here are cold and carry wild rains; the earth is thin, the rock is hard. It is a place fit only for the hardy or forgotten, for outcasts and exiles.

from A Survey of His Holdings
for Kulkain oc Kilkry *by*
Everrin Tosarch, Chancellor and Servant

I

Mar'athoin of the Heron Kyrinin sniffed at the feather. It had been tied to a twig on the stream-facing side of an alder tree. The path Mar'athoin and his two companions were following crossed the stream here, and the feather had been positioned so that no one – no Kyrinin, at least – could fail to see it as they made the crossing. It was a finger-feather, from the wing-tip of a forest hawk. A single thin strand of birch bark had been used to attach it.

Mar'athoin made a guttural coughing sound in the back of his throat. It brought the other two drifting out of the undergrowth. He nodded at the feather and his fellow warriors examined it closely.

"It must be *ettanaryn*, yes?" Mar'athoin said.

Cynyn, the youngest of the three by only a few days, straightened and ran a finger along his upper lip. It was a gesture copied from his elders, Mar'athoin knew. Cynyn no doubt thought it signified careful consideration of a problem. He had always been over-keen to credit anyone more than a few summers older than him with great wisdom.

"It must be," Cynyn pronounced.

Mar'athoin nodded. Like the other two, he had never seen Snake sign before, but there was nothing else this could be: *ettanaryn*, marking the furthermost extremity of the Snake clan's range. The Snake, like most of the northern clans, kept to old ways of summer wandering, winter gathering. Some *a'an* had set this marker here at the furthest point of their journeys back when the sun was high and the days long. Mar'athoin's own people, the Heron, were less wedded to the old cycle of *a'an* and *vo'an*, living as they did amidst the constant bounty of the marshes. Nevertheless, foraging bands did cover long distances in the height of summer, and they still sometimes left their own *ettanaryn*. Where the Snake used feathers, the Heron used split, notched bog-willow stakes.

Sithvyr leaned closer and sniffed at the feather as Mar'athoin had done.

"Not fresh," she observed. "There is no hand-scent on it."

"I thought the same," said Mar'athoin, relieved to be able to agree with her. He desired her, and would have been pained had she contradicted his own instincts.

"Should we make pause, then?" Cynyn asked.

"We should," Mar'athoin confirmed. He set out back across the stream. The other two followed him without comment. He was pleased with the way they had so readily accepted him as the leader of their little band. Before they had set out, seven nights ago now, it had not been certain whether he or Sithvyr would have the greater authority. Mar'athoin had hoped it would be him from the start. He had, after all, won his first *kin'thyn* in the fighting with the Hawk clan two summers gone – the youngest of the clan's warriors to have done so that year – and that was an honour Sithvyr could not yet boast.

"Lacklaugh would understand," Mar'athoin said as they retraced their steps a short way and squatted down to wait. "He carried spears with my father when they were younger. He knows our ways almost as well as we do."

He was almost certain he was right. Lacklaugh had urged them to keep a close watch on the other *na'kyrim*, the female whose mind was cracked, but he would understand the need to hesitate before crossing into Snake lands. It was an old rule, and not one to be lightly broken, that only a spear *a'an* offering battle would enter another clan's homelands without first pausing and reflecting on their action. So the three of them would wait here until the sun had turned another quarter of the sky in its endless journey. Only then would they follow the wandering *na'kyrim* woman into the lands of the Snake Kyrinin.

They went quickly through the evening, meaning to catch up with the *na'kyrim* before night fell. The darkness held no fears for them, but it would be harder to track her on a moonless night such as this promised to be. The forest path their quarry seemed to be following was far too obvious to be Kyrinin-made. Mar'athoin knew the Snake traded as well as fought with the Huanin lords to the south and west. It seemed likely to him that this was a traders' way; there were a few old and stale signs of horse or mule.

That she kept to such a clear trail made their task at once simple – the *na'kyrim* was clearly not trying to lose or conceal her-self – and potentially harder. She was more likely to wander into trouble if she kept to what must be a well-used route. Mar'athoin and his companions had promised Lacklaugh only that they would follow her as far as seemed fit to them, and guard her against harm only if they could do so without endangering them-selves or their people. Should the *na'kyrim* fall foul of the clan on whose domain she now trespassed, Mar'athoin could do nothing to protect her: the Heron had no quarrel with the Snake. Equally, if she stumbled across some rough Huanin trader who took against her, she would have to look after herself. Killing such a man within their territory, and without their permission, might well antagonise the Snake.

The trackway was running along the side of a steep valley. It was only lightly wooded, and great stretches of bog were visible beside the river below them. After the first day and night of their journey, they had settled – by silent consent – on what the Heron called their *trytavyr*: their way of going. Mar'athoin ran ahead of the others because his eyes and ears and nose were a fraction sharper than theirs. Next came Cynyn, keeping a good two dozen strides behind Mar'athoin so that he would have time to react to any signal. Last, close on Cynyn's heels, came Sithvyr. She had shown herself to be the fastest of all of them, at least over uneven ground. If Mar'athoin found trouble up ahead, she had the best chance of escaping to carry word back to their *vo'an* in the great marshes.

As they came to a thicker sweep of scrubby birch trees, and just as his instincts began to sing to Mar'athoin that the *na'kyrim* was close now, he threw himself into a crouch and snapped out a flat arm to halt the other two. Cynyn and Sithvyr grounded themselves silently. Mar'athoin remained motionless, his head bowed. It was not for him to speak first.

"You walk on land promised to others," came a gentle female voice from amongst the trees ahead. The Snake tongue was close cousin to that of the Heron; Mar'athoin had no difficulty in understanding it.

"This I know," he replied without looking up. "We made pause at your *ettanaryn*. We are Heron-born, and mean to pass only."

There was movement. A flock of little birds scattered, twittering in consternation. On the periphery of his vision, Mar'athoin detected two, perhaps three, figures drifting amongst the pale birches. There were at least four others, unseen, somewhere out there, if the scents and sounds on the breeze spoke truly to him.

"Where do you go?" the woman asked. Judging by her voice, she had moved closer.

"We seek a *na'kyrim*. We follow where she leads."

"Do you mean to bathe your spears?"

"No. We act on behalf of another, a Kyrinin-friend. He asked us to follow this one and see to her safety."

"Why? We have put our eyes on her, the one you seek. She is flawed. She speaks to the wind. She walks like a child, without care or sense. Do you mean to haul her out when she falls into a river, or catch her when she steps over a cliff?"

"If we can," replied Mar'athoin.

The unseen woman laughed. "Life must be good for the Heron. Your fowl-traps must be thick with birds, your smoking sheds full of fish and your borders empty of enemies, if you can send three on such a foolish errand."

"It is foolish," agreed Mar'athoin placidly.

"And what clan does she spring from, this half-human you trail? Whose fires does she call her own?"

"She was born of a Heron mother."

"Well, she rests up ahead. She made herself a bed of grass, in a bad place. She will be cold and wet in the morning. This night and two more, then she will be beyond our lands, if she keeps to this course. Keep to her track, do not stray, and you may pass with our goodwill. The Snake have no argument with the Heron."

"Nor the Heron with the Snake."

Mar'athin did not rise until he was sure all of the Snake had moved away. They would not go far, he knew. He brushed moss from his knees as Cynyn and Sithvyr came up to his shoulder.

"I counted six," Cynyn said.

Mar'athoin sniffed and strode on. "Eight."

They found K'rina huddled on the ground in the lee of a great rock. She had indeed torn up thick handfuls of grasses and rushes to make a bed of sorts for herself. She was already asleep, even though the sun had not yet touched the western horizon. Her slumber was punctuated by frequent mumbles and shivers.

The three Heron Kyrinin stood some distance downwind of her and watched. Remembering the words of the Snake woman, Mar'athoin felt a brief stirring of contempt for this useless *na'kyrim*. That her mind was misshapen, damaged, had been obvious from the start. It was only a matter of time before she fell victim to some misfortune. It was indeed foolish to waste time on her. But, he reminded himself, Lacklaugh had asked it as a favour. And if nothing else they would be able to return home and say they had made a good journey.

The question of just how far they would follow K'rina remained, though. Lacklaugh had not told them where she was going, if he even knew, but that she had some goal was beyond dispute: ever since she had left the marshes, her path had been straight, constant. Mar'athoin was not sure exactly what – or who – lay beyond Snake lands to the north or west. Huanin probably, he thought, and almost certainly the White Owls, though how far away they were he did not know. He had no desire to meet either of them. It might be that the time to turn back was drawing close.

He cast around for a suitable place to rest.

"I will be the first of my family to sleep on Snake ground," he said with a faint smile.

* * *

For the first time in what felt like weeks, the sun was shining on the Glas valley. A bright, sharp light bathed the fields. The ground was slick and soft, bloated with rain and melt-water. The herdsmen's trails and farm tracks that Wain nan Horin-Gyre chose to follow were muddy. Still, they were passable and better than the alternative: the main road up the valley, running on the northern bank of the river, had been almost obliterated when Sirian's Dyke broke. In places it was still ankle-deep in sucking, half-liquid silt that made travel both exhausting and slow. These fields south of the river had suffered less lasting damage. There was a slim chance that Wain and the hundred warriors at her back might even reach Grive by nightfall, having left Glasbridge before dawn. If not, there was no shortage of abandoned farmsteads to serve as overnight quarters.

Wain's horse was restless and irritable. Every so often it would bend its head back to snap at her knees. Her original mount – a fine animal, a sturdy survivor of the long march through Anlane all those weeks ago – had broken its leg during the furious assault on Glasbridge. This replacement was proving a disappointment. She and it had yet to find an accommodation with one another. Wain was minded to give it up and find a more amenable partner when they reached Anduran.

She felt less joyful or excited at the prospect of what awaited her in Anduran than she would have liked. This was, after all, what she and Kanin, and Angain their father, had hoped for all along: the Black Road was on the move, pouring through the hole Horin-Gyre had punched in the defences of the True Bloods. There was now at least a chance that everything they had gained might be held, that new and greater victories might yet be won for the creed. Puzzles remained, however, and they were troubling. By all accounts, it was not Ragnor oc Gyre's armies that had marched but the Battle Inkall, and thousands of the common folk. Where was the High Thane? Where were the other Bloods? Wain, and Kanin for that matter, would willingly have handed over leadership of this undertaking, and all the lands they had recovered, to Ragnor. The Thane of Thanes had a natural right to put himself at the head of this war. To surrender everything to Nyve's bloody ravens was not such an easy thought. Wain sighed and glanced up, narrowing her eyes against the piercing glare of the sun. There was no warmth in it.

She should not concern herself with what was yet to come, she knew. There remained much uncertainty about what she would actually find in Anduran, and until that uncertainty was dispelled there was nothing to be gained by stirring possibilities in her head. The only clear facts the messengers rushing to find her and Kanin in Glasbridge had been able to convey were that Tanwrye had at last fallen – and there was one piece of news, at least, that was nothing but good – and that the Children of the Hundred were leading a huge army down the valley, their van already taking up quarters in Anduran. Wain had left Glasbridge almost at once. Even so, she would not be the first to reach Anduran. Shraeve and her Inkallim were somewhere ahead, might even already be there.

Her horse nipped again at her leg, its teeth cracking together. She snapped the reins, flicking one towards its eye in discouragement. They were coming up to the edge of what had once been the Glas Water now. That great marshy lake had drained when Sirian's Dyke gave way, leaving a huge expanse of shrinking pools, rushes and sodden bare earth that lay like a dark sore across the centre of the valley. Somewhere out there the river had returned to its natural course, slumping back into the channel it had swollen out of when Sirian built his great dam. On a day as clear as this the eye could see far across the flat, treeless valley floor. And Wain's eye caught something unexpected.

Kan Avor was a black and grey mass out near the river, like the stump of some titanic fallen tree. The ruined city, freed from its watery bonds after more than a hundred years, had outlasted the dam built to drown it. Now, Wain saw dark strands of smoke strung out from amongst Kan Avor's ruins by the wind. Someone had lit fires there; someone had claimed the ancestral home of the Gyre Blood itself as their campsite. She turned her horse towards the dead city.

It was difficult going, their way constantly obstructed by stagnant pools and seemingly bottomless mud, but Wain picked out a winding path over ground that was almost solid. Here and there, exposed by the retreat of the Glas Water, bones jutted up out of the silt. The empty eye sockets of a half-buried skull stared at her. Many of the faithful had died on this ground, two and a half centuries ago.

The warriors behind her became widely separated. Most of them were on foot, and this was no place for marching. She ignored their difficulties. A score or so of riders kept up with her, including all six of her Shield, and that was enough. As they drew close to Kan Avor, its crumbling walls and shattered towers loomed over them. More grim than the sight of those walls themselves was the burden they bore. High up on what little remained of the city's great outer rampart hung bodies, dangling like the carcasses of slaughtered animals. Crows hopped along the top of the walls, calling to one another. The dead were not warriors. They bore the clothes of farmers or villagers.

Wain and her company rode on through the desolate outer parts of the city. The buildings here were poised halfway between being the work of men and of nature, so long had they been subject to the moulding of wind and water. Clumps of waterweeds were rotting in the streets. With each pace of their horses they came closer to the cluster of great buildings that had once dominated the city's heart, until at last they rode into the shadow of a derelict tower. It stood the height of six men above them, and in its heyday must have been much taller, for it had been decapitated by time. Rubble was strewn across the approach to the palace from which it rose. The base of the walls had a greenish-blackish tint where the water had lapped against them year after year. A statue lay half-shattered before the wide gateway. Since its descent from the heights above it had acquired a patina of moss and weed. The gates themselves were long gone, perhaps salvaged before Kan Avor was finally abandoned. The smoke of half a dozen fires rose from somewhere within.

Wain halted her horse beneath the arch of the gate, pausing there in the shadow to stare at the scene within the precincts of the collapsed palace. In a wide courtyard, amidst the mud and tumbled stones, arrayed around their fires, were fifty or more Kyrinin. Every pair of eyes, every grey gaze, was locked on her. There was a moment of perfect silence, save for the wind above them and the crackle of a fire above which a dog was spitted.

She looked back over her shoulder, mindful now of how few warriors were within easy reach of her call.

"The Bloodheir's sister."

A thrill of recognition ran through her at the sound of that voice, an instant shiver that carried a whole host of sentiments in its wake: anger, alarm, surprise . . . anticipation, was it? Excitement? She turned slowly – deliberately so – and saw Aeglyss rising from beside one of the fires. As he stood and languidly stretched his back, a cluster of Kyrinin close by him rose too.

Wain kept her eyes on the *na'kyrim*, gesturing for her Shield to draw up behind her.

"He is Thane now, halfbreed," she said. "Not Bloodheir any more."

Aeglyss nodded and ran both hands through his pale hair, pulling it back from his face. It was longer than it had been the last time Wain saw him. He held it there behind his head and then let it fall across his shoulders.

"Thane," he repeated, savouring the word as if it were a morsel of food. "Thane, then. It is, I suppose, in the nature of Bloodheirs to become Thanes sooner or later." He glanced at the dog roasting over the fire. "Can I offer you some meat, Thane's sister? We are not prepared for visitors, but what is mine is yours."

"I believe my brother made it clear to you that we had no wish to see you, or your friends, on our lands again." Wain nudged her horse a few paces into the courtyard, opening a space for her warriors to advance and spread themselves on her flanks. The animal was uneasy. Perhaps it had never smelled Kyrinin before.

"Did he?" Aeglyss murmured, with a little shrug of his shoulders. "I confess my memory is not all it was. I find myself much more drawn to the future now than to the past. Such a bitter thing, the past. So full of disappointments, don't you think?"

Wain's mind was racing. Aeglyss had disappeared some time ago, after Kanin had confronted him outside Anduran. The breach then had seemed irreversible; the breakdown of any alliance with the White Owls unquestionable. Yet here he was, the halfbreed her brother so detested, camped at the very heart, the home, of the Gyre Bloods with his little warband. And there were changes in him. His skin, always pallid, was now waxen. There were dark blotches pouched beneath his eyes, a wasted fragility about his frame. And yet his voice had a stronger spine of arrogance, a fuller, deeper timbre, than it did before. His gaze – those piercing, transfixing inhuman eyes – held Wain; she felt it on her skin, her body, like hands. Her heart was beating faster. A hollowness was in her stomach, almost fear, almost . . . something she could not quite name.

"Are you responsible for the dead on the walls?"

Aeglyss frowned, angled his head to squint up at her against the sharp light.

"Ah, not entirely. They didn't die by my hand, at least. White Owl spears did the deed. It can't trouble you, surely? They're nothing: Lannis strays, hiding away amongst these ruins when we arrived. I'd thought to find you and your brother here, not unhomed farmers."

"These are not your walls to decorate as you see fit. Kan Avor is the rightful possession of Ragnor oc Gyre. We hold it empty, ready for him to claim and occupy."

Aeglyss shrugged. "If you won't eat with me, you might at least dismount. We should talk, you and I. There are things you should know."

He held out his hands to her. She noticed for the first time that there were bandages around his wrists. And she felt as though those outstretched hands had taken hold of her, had laid themselves on her arms and were drawing her towards him: drawing her into a gentle, warm, firm embrace. To dispel the sensation, she kicked her horse forwards. It trotted to the edge of one of the fires, stirring up ash and dirt before it shied away from the flames. Every one of the Kyrinin had stood up now. They gathered beside and behind Aeglyss.

The *na'kyrim* laughed, and the laugh flowed over Wain like water. It was a living, liquid thing. An unnatural thing, she thought, not remotely human. Not remotely mirthful.

"I am so very tired of being refused," Aeglyss said. He hung his head, letting his arms fall back to his sides. "So long I had nothing else . . ." he jerked his head sideways, wincing, like a man beset by a stinging insect " . . . nothing else."

Wain glanced at the warriors who flanked her. On every face

she saw some intimation of the confusion, the disquiet, that writhed beneath. She knew it was in them because it was in her too; it was in the very walls of this decrepit courtyard. Aeglyss was breathing it out with the spent air from his lungs, breathing it over them.

"Get down," she heard him say, and her legs and arms were already obeying him. For a sluggish moment she was an observer, watching her body as it swung out of the saddle to the ground. She shook herself, and was standing there by her horse's head, holding its reins.

Aeglyss swayed a little. One of the Kyrinin beside him put a hand under the *na'kyrim*'s elbow until he had steadied himself. Wain considering climbing back onto her horse, but she feared how that might appear to the warriors she led. She kicked wet earth over the campfire burning by her feet. The flames hissed and died almost at once. The sunlight was strong here in the stone-enclosed space of the courtyard, undiluted by the wind. It was even a little warm on the side of her face. There was a stench on the air, of dank decay, rotten vegetation. She glared at Aeglyss.

"Oh," he said quietly. "I don't want to argue with you, Wain. You were always less cold than your brother. Life, possibilities, always burned more strongly in you. Even when you were children." He was looking at her out of the corner of his eye now, a harsh little smile curling his mouth. "Ha. Where did that come from, I wonder? There's so much that . . . comes to me now, and I don't know how, or why. I was always afraid of madness. Always. Is this it, do you think?"

"There's nothing new . . ." Wain began to say, but cut herself short as Aeglyss took a long stride forwards.

"No!" he cried. "Not madness. Just the woodworker, learning the use of a new tool; an archer learning the bend of a new bow. And no," softly now, soft in Wain's mind, "everything's new, that's what you should say. Nothing's the same, not ever. I'm not the same, Wain. This blunted blade you cast away has been sharpened. Do you doubt me?"

"I don't doubt that you are . . . different." And that much was true. His sheer presence, his mere proximity, set such thoughts and doubts crawling around in her mind, like ants nesting in the back of her skull. He had never had this kind of effect on her – on anyone, as far as she knew – before.

Some of her warriors had dismounted. Others were pressing in through the gateway behind her. They wanted to fight, she knew. They were afraid of Aeglyss, of this invisible cloud of potency that enveloped him. She had enough strength here, perhaps, to overcome the halfbreed and all his woodwights. If Kanin had been at her side, he would not have hesitated. And yet something in her quailed at the image of such slaughter, as if it would be a betrayal of a gift offered up to her by fate.

"No, you don't," Aeglyss said. "I can see it in you, I can smell it on you. You think there is something here."

He turned and pointed to one of the White Owl warriors: a muscular man with a mass of writhing lines tattooed on his face.

"See? The son of the Voice herself. He and his *a'an* – my spear *a'an* now. The White Owls accept me as one of their own. The whole clan is my spear *a'an*, my beloved people. But I am Horin-Gyre too, not just White Owl. By my father, I am of your Blood, Wain."

"That means nothing. What is it you want here? Have you come to offer us another alliance with your tame savages? You know the time for that has passed."

"Oh, I offer that. That, but much more." To her astonishment, Aeglyss knelt then, and bowed before her. It was so unexpected that she could only stand and stare at the crown of his head, the long hair that fell forwards and hid his face.

"I am become a new man," he murmured. "Servant of all desires. There are thousands coming. I can feel their footsteps in my mind, I can catch the scent of their ardour on the wind. War is to follow, war beyond all reason; unending, unmaking. And I will ride its currents like a bird on the storm. Let me bear us all up on my wings, Wain."

And in her heart then she felt a great hunger stir, a longing for the future and all its tumultuous possibilities. She saw the Black Road rushing like a living thing out from this shattered city and bearing them all on its broad back into a vast and endless plain, lit by a glorious fiery light, strewn with the corpses of the faithless. So, she wondered, is this how it is to be? Is this the shape of our fate? And a small, faint voice within her, not entirely her own, whispered, Yes, yes, this is how it is to be.

II

"Is it true?"

Aewult the Bloodheir was shouting at Anyara, his face so close to her own that she could smell the hot memory of his last meal. A blush of anger had coloured his rough, stubbled cheeks, a film of spittle coated the creases of his lips. His rage was clearly profound.

"Has your brother marched?" Aewult demanded. "Where are his warriors going? Kolglas?"

Anyara pulled her head back a fraction. However potent the Bloodheir's anger might be, she had her own stores of irritation to draw on. She planted a firm hand on his chest, applying just enough pressure to make sure that he noticed it. To her astonishment, and alarm, Aewult struck her arm aside.

Coinach was there at once, drawing her aside, putting himself between her and the Bloodheir. The shieldman stood tall, one hand on Anyara's arm, the other on the pommel of his sword. He and Aewult stared at one another, Aewult's eyes burning with indignation and threat, Coinach's cold and calm. At once horrified and excited, Anyara reached to pull her shieldman back, but another intervention came first.

"So long as you are under my roof, Bloodheir, you will not raise a hand against the sister of a Thane." Ilessa oc Kilkry-Haig's voice was imperious, all confidence and control.

It was enough to cut through Aewult's befuddling rage. He looked towards Lheanor's wife. Ilessa was seated at a broad table, papers scattered all over its surface. A gaggle of her Blood's officials – storesmen, oathmen – shared the table with her, every one of them staring at Aewult nan Haig. Anyara had been seated at that same table, discussing with Ilessa how best the Lannis folk who had fled into Kilkry lands might be fed and housed, when Aewult burst in. From the first moment of his furious entry, it had been as if he did not even see Ilessa or any of the others; his eyes – his demands and accusations – had been only for Anyara.

"I might raise a hand against that Thane himself, were he here," Aewult snarled, "but he isn't, is he? That's the point. And neither's his little army."

He did not sound at all repentant, but he did take a couple of paces back.

"I don't much care what the point is, or what dreadful wrong you think Orisian oc Lannis-Haig has done you," Ilessa said. "You are a guest here, and will conduct yourself accordingly. I would expect no less of even the Thane of Thanes, and your authority does not yet match your father's."

Aewult made a faint grunting noise and turned his attention back to Anyara. She was still half-shielded by Coinach, who appeared unwilling to rely solely on Ilessa's words to restrain the Bloodheir.

"You can tell your guard dog to stand aside, my lady," Aewult muttered. He did not deign to look at Coinach now. "If I caused you offence, I regret it, but I'll not have a shieldman putting himself in my face, certainly not a woman's shieldman."

There was such biting contempt in Aewult's tone that Anyara

understood for the first time just how difficult Coinach's new role might be for him. He was doing as his Thane commanded, yet there could be no glory – precious little credit, even – in being shieldman to a woman. He was more likely to harvest mockery than admiring glances.

She eased Coinach to one side, feeling his reluctance in the stiffness of his frame. She lifted her chin and met Aewult's gaze directly.

"I'll leave it to him to decide how best he should carry out his duties," she said.

"Ha!" Aewult slapped his thigh in sudden, harsh merriment. "You've enough bite about you that I wouldn't have thought you needed some boy-warrior to watch over you. Anyway, my question's still unanswered. Where's your brother? And what does Taim Narran intend to do with the men he's led out? Surely the Lannis Blood hasn't forgotten who commands this army, this campaign?"

"Oh, still your tongue, for everyone's sake," Ilessa snapped from the table. "Your tantrums will not win you any friends here."

"It's not friends I'm looking for," Aewult replied.

There is danger in all of this, Anyara thought. Haig thinks so little of us, and of Kilkry, that even the most trifling argument can be a fertile seedbed for strife. And this might not be the most trifling argument.

"Ah, so this is where everyone is."

Every head in the room turned to the doorway. Mordyn Jerain stood there, smiling as if in quiet satisfaction at solving some minor puzzle. His hands – smooth, elegant – were clasped in front of him. He wore a heavy coat of brushed velvet, a sheen of gold embroidery at the cuffs and hems and collar. A single long pace brought him into the room. That simple movement was enough for him to take possession of the space, make himself its focus.

"I thought I heard familiar voices," he murmured, looking from one face to the next. "From quite some little distance away, in fact."

"The Bloodheir was just expressing his disappointment at Orisian oc Lannis-Haig's absence," Ilessa said. Her voice, Anyara noted, was now utterly expressionless. There was no hint of the command she had used against Aewult.

Mordyn Jerain nodded thoughtfully, as if Ilessa's explanation satisfied every possible query he might have, and turned his dazzling smile on Anyara. She had to fold her arms to stop herself fidgeting with her dress. How foolish, she thought, to be so easily unsettled by this man's attention. She was not much given to discomfiture, yet all the Bloodheir's fury had not troubled her as much as the Shadowhand's clear, intelligent gaze.

"Disappointing, yes," Mordyn said. "A small misunderstanding, I'm sure. Your brother is brave, to strike out on his own when such danger is abroad. The Bloodheir is naturally concerned, as am I. As is everyone, no doubt. The Lannis-Haig Blood cannot afford any more misfortunes."

"Orisian can take care of himself," Anyara said as confidently as she could.

"I dare say he can."

"The question is not whether he can take of himself, but whether he remembers his duties and responsibilities," muttered Aewult nan Haig.

"Duties?" Anyara asked the Bloodheir, preferring the idea of more harsh words from him to that of more blandishments from Mordyn Jerain.

"To my father, and the True Bloods. If there are battles to be fought, I command the army that will fight them. Not your brother. Not Taim Narran."

The Chancellor held his hands up, still smiling equably. "Well, the battles are not here, and not yet. And it is up to a Thane how he conducts himself in time of war, of course. Orisian will learn how these things are done in time. Tell me, though, Anyara, it does seem strange that Taim Narran should have led your army off in one direction and your brother gone in another. If I understand rightly, Orisian left by the Kyre Gate, heading east. That's a strange way to make for Kolglas."

"Do leave the girl alone, Chancellor," said Ilessa before Anyara had time to respond. "She's tired and worried. We were discussing more important matters than her brother's whereabouts before we were interrupted."

"Of course. You must forgive us. Come, Bloodheir, let us leave these ladies to their deliberations."

* * *

Aewult nan Haig's anger was almost amusing, Mordyn Jerain reflected. It was built on foundations of disbelief: the Bloodheir was astonished that the child-Thane of the Lannis Blood would presume to leave Kolkyre without so much as a moment's discussion. One thing both Aewult and his brother Stravan had picked up from their mother was a pronounced, but sometimes shallow-rooted, sense of their own importance. Any sign that others did not share their own high opinion of themselves tended to cause great offence, and to Aewult's way of thinking what Orisian had done was no doubt tantamount to turning his back and walking away in the midst of a conversation.

Almost amusing, but not quite. Ilessa oc Kilkry-Haig had not been wrong to call it a disappointment. Everything had seemed to be coming together, but Orisian's sudden and unwonted display of independence had at a stroke unpicked some of the pattern that Mordyn was trying to weave. And now he had to deal with an angry Aewult.

All of the stairways in the Tower were narrow and cramped. Whatever forgotten people had built it, they had cared little for elegance or comfort. Aewult was distracted by his simmering fury and half-missed a step. He stumbled and might have pitched forwards down the stairwell if he had not fallen against Mordyn, and the Chancellor had not seized his arm. The Bloodheir threw his hand off as soon as he had recovered his balance.

"You're too gentle with them," Aewult muttered as they resumed their descent. Almost falling, and doing so in Mordyn's presence, would not help his mood.

"Hardly. I suspect Anyara nan Lannis-Haig is not the sort to crumble easily beneath threats or demands. I know Ilessa is not. You'd be better off finding a dog to beat if you want to disgorge your anger."

"Don't tell me what to do, Shadowhand. My father told me to listen to your advice, not take your orders."

"Well, my advice is not to waste your time on shouting at women. We have to make some quick decisions, and I've often found that's best done over a good meal. There's a fine roasted duck awaiting me – and you, if you're willing – in the Steward's House. Pallick had many faults, but he did at least have the sense to build and staff an excellent kitchen. Lagair's kept it going since he took the office over."

Aewult did not look enthusiastic, but he accepted the invitation. In the event, the promised duck was not yet ready. Lagair Haldyn's wife apologised effusively and disappeared to berate the cooks. The Steward himself was absent. He had taken some of the captains of Aewult's army hawking, if Mordyn remembered correctly. The Bloodheir planted himself in a chair by a fire and sat there in determined silence. Mordyn sat at a table and pretended to study some papers. He had already read them – he was consistently waking before dawn these days, and had many cold hours to occupy – but he judged it best to give Aewult's mood a chance to soften.

The Chancellor's mind wandered. It had always been a part of his nature to believe that everything mattered. The smallest of events, of details, could have some import when seen as a thread in the broader tapestry. That was partly his Tal Dyreen upbringing expressing itself: the island of his birth had always bred sharp minds and keen eyes. Had the Tal Dyreens been as collectively ambitious as they were greedy, that island could have been the world's great rising power, instead of the Haig Blood. Then, of course, Mordyn might not have been inclined to abandon his roots; he might now be a merchant prince himself, instead of Gryvan oc Haig's Shadowhand. But he was not. He served Gryvan because – he understood this about himself – he was drawn to power, to the mysterious, intangible process by which it was cultivated and used. He craved its proximity.

Equally mysterious, and what troubled him now, was the way in which power sometimes failed. By rights, the obvious power of the Haig Bloods should have been enough to deter foolhardy ventures on the part of the Black Road. Ragnor oc Gyre himself, Mordyn remained certain, had no wish to challenge Gryvan on the battlefield. Yet here they all were, fighting a war that no one except a few idiots in the Horin-Gyre Blood seemed to have wanted. And anyone as young and supposedly unsure of himself as Orisian oc Lannis-Haig should, by rights, be easy to control. Was it just childish arrogance, blind eagerness, that had led him to sneak out of Kolkyre like a common fugitive? Was he so unafraid of incurring Aewult's – or Gryvan's – displeasure, or did he simply not understand that he was doing so?

Most irritating of all was the possibility that Orisian knew exactly what he was doing, that he was deliberately trying to deprive the Haig Blood of its proper authority, trying to take away its victory. Perhaps the young Thane understood the importance of appearances. Or perhaps it was all Taim Narran's idea. It was not beyond possibility that he was the helmsman of Orisian's ship.

Aewult stirred at last. He took a log from the basket and threw it on the fire.

"Did Orisian really leave by the Kyre Gate, then?" the Bloodheir asked.

"Yes, I believe so."

"And Taim Narran went by the Skeil. Well, we know where he's going, at least: Kolglas. What's Orisian up to, though?"

Mordyn rose and went to stand nearer the fire. He flexed and massaged his hands, turning them in the warmth.

"Well, there are few possibilities if he's heading east. He could be making for Ive, but I cannot think of a single reason why he would be doing that. He might simply be playing some silly game of misdirection, I suppose. He could get to Kolglas eventually, crossing over the Karkyre Peaks, but it would seem a particularly arduous bit of subterfuge. There's always Highfast. Perhaps that's where he's going."

"Highfast? Why would he be interested in Highfast?"

Mordyn shook his head. "I have no idea. He does seem to have a liking for *na'kyrim*, though."

Aewult rubbed a hand over his unshaven chin. Mordyn could hear the rasp of the stubble. The Bloodheir was evidently too busy in the mornings to tend to his appearance. It was no great surprise, given that he shared his bed with that dancing girl he had brought up from Vaymouth.

"Well, Narran's only got a few hundred men," the Bloodheir muttered. "There can't be many more waiting for him at Kolglas. Whatever games they think they're playing, they still can't do much without us."

"That's probably true. You know more about the fighting of battles than I do, but still, it might be best if we don't allow them the chance to find out exactly what they can do."

Aewult curled a lip at the Chancellor. "Generous of you to admit even such slight imperfection in your wisdom. Don't imagine for a moment that I think it a sincere admission, though."

Mordyn silently reprimanded himself. He should exercise a little more restraint in his dealings with Aewult. The man was not entirely stupid, and offending him not entirely without its dangers. A little more carefully crafted flattery, a touch more convincing deference, would be wise. But the man was so wearing, so . . . unrewarding. And, Mordyn had to acknowledge, he was tired. How gleefully surprised his numerous detractors would be to discover the many fallibilities and shortcomings of the Shadowhand they so excoriated. If his abilities matched even a fraction of those the great mass of people ascribed to him, he would have been lord of all the world long ago. But he was, in the end, nothing more than a man like any other; today, a tired and frustrated man. He bowed his head just enough to give Aewult an impression of regret.

"There is still ample time for you to overtake Taim Narran, Bloodheir. You can be in Kolglas yourself before he has any opportunity to test the strength of the Black Road. Once you are there, he would not dare defy your command. If you tell him to retire from the field, or to go and stand garrison in some forest village, he would have to do it."

"So long as his Thane's not there, yes."

"Indeed. If you will allow me, I will see to Orisian oc Lannis-Haig myself. We – I – have underestimated that young man. Whether it is his stubbornness, his cunning or his stupidity that we have underestimated remains to be seen, but there is certainly something. I dislike my own mistakes more than any made by others, so I will give the correction of this one my closest attention."

He tossed another log onto the fire. The flames crackled over the bark, curling it and peeling it back from the pale wood beneath.

"Our lives will be much more tiring if we do not get the measure of him," he said. "We know the outcome of the present strife with the Black Road, after all: it is how things stand after your victory that will colour the next few years. And there are few things more troublesome than a Thane with a defiant streak."

"He'll have to learn the cost of defiance, then," muttered Aewult.

"The boy is young, inexperienced. I suspect I can turn him back, wherever he thinks he is going. Unless he is the slow one out of that family, he should be open to persuasion, especially if I can talk to him alone. But failing all else, yes, some blunt warnings – perhaps even a threat or two – should clarify for him the importance of retaining your goodwill, and that of your father. It is time, I think, to find out how this new Thane of Lannis responds to the crack of the whip."

* * *

Later, descending through the Tower of Thrones, Anyara stared at the back of her shieldman. Coinach was not overly tall, nor were his shoulders especially broad. Despite this, his was an impressive presence. He had a muscular bulk, and moved with the kind of restraint that Anyara associated with older, intensely capable men such as Taim Narran. For all his youth – he could not have been much more than twenty years old – he had an air of confidence. His face, though, was surprisingly gentle, for a warrior whom Taim had assured her was as skilled as any under his command.

Anyara still thought it foolish for Orisian to have forced a shieldman upon her, but the young man's company was not unpleasant. Which was just as well for Coinach, since Anyara might otherwise have vented some of her many frustrations on him. She had been aghast when Orisian had told her he meant to return to Kolglas without her.

She knew his reasons, of course; better, she believed, than Orisian knew them himself. Only someone who had experienced the utter, dismantling grief of profound loss could understand the fear it engendered: the fear of its repetition, a constant anticipation that the cruel world might at any moment inflict a still more excessive, wanton punishment. Orisian meant to fend off that possibility by keeping her out of harm's way. She understood that; understood the fear that haunted him. Almost every night, she experienced the consequences of loss herself. Her sleep was awash with evil dreams: dreams of darkness and fire and threat, dreams that had the same flavour as those she had suffered when the Heart Fever took possession of her. They had begun only after she had reached the comparative safety of Kolkyre, as if her mind, freed from the constant and immediate pressures of her captivity and then her flight to Koldihrve, had turned in on itself. Most mornings, Anyara woke drained, sometimes alarmed.

She had hidden it all from Orisian with meticulous care. She had no desire to add to his burdens, and therefore told him nothing of her dreams, or of the grief that was testing her inner defences to their limit. And she had not argued with him when he told her to remain here in the Tower of Thrones. Not for very long, at least. His face, as soon as she raised her voice, had betrayed the maelstrom of feelings that he could not express: regret, fear, guilt, love. But there had been an insistence there, too. She held her tongue. She allowed him to leave her behind, and hoped that doing so might ease his fears.

It left Anyara with a prodigious store of irritation and frustration, like a vat so full of vinegar that the acrid liquid trembled at the very lip, poised to spill forth at only the slightest nudge. Had Mordyn Jerain not arrived when he did, Aewult nan Haig might have been drenched. After the Chancellor and Bloodheir departed, she tried to return to her discussions with Ilessa oc Kilkry-Haig but found herself distracted by angry thoughts. The Thane's wife was understanding.

"Go," she said. "Take a walk in the gardens. The mind works poorly when the heart is so unsettled."

So Anyara followed Coinach down the long spiral staircase, and watched his shoulders, and his short, coarse hair. He fitted her image of what a young warrior should be like. She hoped, and assumed, that she would never have cause to discover whether his abilities matched that image.

A few steps out into the open air were enough to tell Anyara that the weather was not all it might have been. Desultory sleet had begun to fall, gobbets of slushy ice spitting down. She glanced up at the cloud-filled sky.

"Not fit for a stroll, really," she muttered.

"No," Coinach agreed.

Anyara sighed. She hated the idea of sitting around. Bitter experience had long ago taught her that inactivity only undermined her defences. Movement, occupation: these were the things that kept her beyond the reach of the past and of memories.

"You've orders to teach me how to fight, haven't you?" she asked Coinach.

"Yes, lady." The flicker of unease in his expression was tiny and faint, but Anyara noticed it. She let it pass.

"Let's begin that, then. So long as we can find somewhere sheltered."

"The barracks, lady. They have the training blades we would need there, too."

"Wooden?" she said with a trace of scorn. Coinach looked uncomfortable, perhaps even fearful of her displeasure, but he said nothing. There was an appealing boyishness about his expression, Anyara thought. He was, she reminded herself, not much older than her.

"Very well. Come, we can get rain capes from the guardroom. They keep them there for such moments."

The little room had been hollowed out of the thick wall of the Tower. Its walls were bare stone, and their smooth, hard surfaces were inflating the noise of the argument Anyara found in progress. A single guard, who obviously wished with all his heart that he was elsewhere, stood in the corner making a determined effort to go unnoticed. A maid, her cheek glowing from the aftermath of some recent blow, tears on her face, rushed out even as Anyara entered. The girl – who could not be more than fifteen or sixteen – brushed past, barely even noticing Anyara, and ran for the main stairway.

Ishbel, Aewult nan Haig's notorious companion, stood in the centre of the guardroom. She was shouting after the fleeing maidservant.

"The red one! With the black hood! The one you should have brought in the first place!"

She glanced at Anyara. Their eyes met for a moment, but Ishbel seemed not to recognise Anyara – or not to care. Her gaze snapped aside, still pursuing the maid.

"You'll not make me wear these rags!" Ishbel cried out.

"You struck the girl?" Anyara enquired softly.

That was enough to hold Ishbel's attention. She was truly beautiful, Anyara thought: flawless skin, sleek dark hair. Perfect, full cheeks that were suffused with a rosy blush of anger.

"She forgot my cape," Ishbel snapped. "Then thinks I should wear one of those." She gestured at the plain rain capes that hung on one wall of the guardroom. "Look at them!"

Anyara did as she was bid. "They seem fit for their purpose to me. I was seeking one myself." She smiled at the other woman, and not out of affection or politeness.

Ishbel glared at her. Anyara thought there was a moment of doubt, perhaps recognition, in there. Perhaps she knows who I am now, she thought.

"Not good enough for you?" she asked Ishbel sweetly. Out of the corner of her eye she noticed the guard hang his head and shrink still further back into the corner.

"I didn't come all this way to wander around this miserable city in the rain dressed like a fisherwoman."

"Oh. Why did you come all this way? To strike your servants? Or just to keep the Bloodheir's bed warm?" She heard Coinach groan behind her, and saw Ishbel open her mouth to respond. "I was always taught that the only people who struck their servants were those who deserved worse themselves," she said before either of them could interrupt her.

Such a twist of anger then disfigured Ishbel's fair face that Anyara imagined for a moment that she was about to be struck herself. She knew it was foolish – a thought that did not become the sister of a Thane – but she almost relished the prospect: it would, at least, offer a release for her caged frustrations. Surely no one could object if she struck back? Instead, Ishbel's face settled back into an expression of studied contempt.

"And I was taught that it's best to keep your nose out other people's affairs," she snapped.

Coinach pushed in front of Anyara, nodding almost respect-fully to Ishbel. He took one of the capes down from its hook.

"We have what we came for," he said to Anyara as he settled the cape on her shoulders and gently – so gently that it was little more than a suggestion in his hands – sought to turn her away. "It might be best to be on our way before the weather worsens."

Anyara allowed herself to be ushered out into the sleet. She paused outside the Tower, adjusting the cape and pulling up its hood.

"I didn't know it was a shieldman's task to guard me from the likes of her," she muttered.

"From whatever harm may threaten, I think, lady," the warrior said. "Whether self-inflicted or otherwise."

She tugged aside the edge of her hood in order to frown at him, but he was looking up at the sky.

"May even turn to snow soon," he mused. "Best to get down to the barracks."

He said it with an air of such casual observation that her irri-tation faded. It would not, after all, have been wise to stand there trading ever more barbed insults with Aewult's lover. The Haig Blood hardly needed more reasons to dislike her own.

"Come, then," she said as she set off down the path that curled away through the bleak gardens. "What will you be teaching me today?"

"We should start with the knife, I imagine. Always easy to carry a knife somewhere about you."

"A knife? That'll not help me much if some White Owl's trying to stick me with a spear, or some Inkallim's chopping me up with a sword."

She thought she heard Coinach sigh then. It was a faint, resigned sound. It made her smile, and she almost reached out to pat him encouragingly on the back.

"We'll make it a big knife, lady," he said. "The biggest we can find."

III

Urik the Wardcaptain was drunk when Ammen Sharp killed him. Falling-down, stupid drunk. Ammen would have made the attempt anyway, for he had no reserves of patience to draw upon, no caution left to soften his urgent hunger for revenge. That luck should so smile on him as to lead Urik into a tavern and keep him there long enough to render him defenceless only made Ammen more certain of the rightness of his course.

He had followed the Wardcaptain from the Guard House of Kolkyre's Harbour ward. The foulness of Urik's mood had been obvious from the first moment he stamped out into the evening. His path to the nearby tavern had been direct and determined. It was easy for Ammen to follow undetected. Sprawled flat on the roof, staring down at the door from which he expected his quarry to emerge, he had allowed himself to wonder briefly just how much trouble the Wardcaptain of the Guard was already in. His distress, his pressing need to drown it with ale, suggested that the bribes Urik had taken from Ammen's father had come to light, or were about to do so. Perhaps the Guard itself was close to turning on him; to sending him to the headtaker. In the end it mattered not at all, since Ammen Sharp meant to save them the trouble.

When the Wardcaptain came stumbling out onto the street below Ammen's rooftop perch he managed only a few strides before he fell on his face, into a puddle. As soon as he saw that, Ammen slithered back from the edge of the roof and lowered himself into the alley at the side of the tavern. Inside, he was urging Urik to rise, to gather himself enough to move on. Late as the hour was, and dark the night, there was still too many people abroad here. Even now, he could hear laughter out in the street, some little band mocking Urik's state. Ammen silently cursed whoever it was, hating them for interfering, for coming between him and the man who had killed his father. Soon enough the merry voices drifted away, and the only sounds he could hear were Urik coughing and spitting and the slopping of mud as he tried to rise. Ammen went out into the street. Urik was a stumbling shape reeling off down the long slope towards the sea. There was no sign of anyone else, but Ammen kept to the darkest places as he followed the Wardcaptain. It mattered greatly to him that he should not be caught, if only because he had other business to attend to once Urik was done with.

After Ammen had acquired his little knife a year ago, his father had told him often how to kill a man, demonstrating with sharp movements, clenched fists. Not the heart: too well-guarded by ribs. The throat, perhaps, or the groin, where the blood would pour like a fountain. With a bigger blade, you could try to open a man's guts or spear his liver, but Ammen's knife was too small for him to be sure of such a result. The throat might be the best, the surest, now that Urik was too drunk to resist.

Ammen had not had cause to use the knife in anger since that night a year ago in the darkened alley. For all his pride in bearing it, and in the manner of his winning it, he had never been one to seek out confrontation. His father had taught him that the best victory was the one gained before violence became necessary. In the long run, it was almost always better to use intimidation, bribery, deceit than your fists to bend a man to your will: their effects were, Ochan had always maintained, more reliable and long-lasting.

Urik had come to a halt. He was leaning against a stall, his feet sliding out from under him in small increments so that he sank slowly towards the ground. Ammen Sharp crouched down in the doorway of a basket-maker's shop. The darkness pooled there was deep enough to hide him from any casual eye. Glancing up and down the street, he saw no one. He could hear only distant voices; nothing of immediate concern. He watched Urik, wondering if the Wardcaptain had gone as far as he could go.

Ochan's insistence that violence was to be avoided had its exceptions, of course. Sometimes, Ammen had come to understand, there was no choice other than to unsheathe a blade or tighten a garrotte. If a man would not step aside, would not listen to reason or threat or the tempting song of coin, then his challenge must be answered in other ways. That was the nature of the world.

"There's none to look after us, boy," Ochan the Cook had muttered to his son once, while they stood together before the body of a man who had just been strangled on his orders. "Some folk say that when there were Gods in the world, everything was all light and warmth and loving. Everyone was kind and noble, and everything was all orderly and peaceable. Doubt it myself, but even if it's true that's not the world as it is now. That's not the world we live in."

He pointed at the sagging corpse in front of them. The man's hands and feet had been tied to the chair, his head hooded with a burlap sack. The knotted rope was still taut around his livid neck.

"We're not much more than dogs on two feet, boy, and don't you forget it. Sooner or later, you might have to fight for what you want. The ones who know how to fight come out on top, the ones who don't . . . well, there. You can see. They end up tied to chairs with bags over their heads."

Now, edging out from his hiding place into the street, Ammen Sharp knew that the world did not even adhere to the simple rules that his father had set out. Sometimes the ones who knew how to fight ended up dead anyway, their heads smashed in on the floor of someone else's warehouse. It was not only the Gods that had abandoned the world, but all sense, all justice. If even men such as Ochan, strong and powerful men who understood the pattern of things, could come to such an end, what was there left to believe in, to hope for? Not much. But there was revenge. Punishment.

Ammen edged up behind Urik. The Wardcaptain was retching. In a moment or two he would probably be on his knees, emptying his stomach. His entire attention, drunken and dislocated as it might be, was focused on the rebelliousness of his own body. Ammen took one last look up and down the length of the street: empty. Silent. He grasped Urik's greasy hair with his left hand, pulled the Wardcaptain's head up and back and stabbed him in the side of the neck.

Urik made a stupid, incoherent noise and tried to turn around. He was pawing the air. Ammen Sharp stabbed him again, and a made a couple of quick sawing motions with the blade. Blood was pulsing out in thick black splashes. That was enough to tell Ammen the wound would be fatal. He stamped hard on the back of Urik's knee, knocking him down. The Guardsman twisted as he fell and landed on his back, staring vacantly up into Ammen's face.

"For Ochan the Cook," Ammen hissed, and spat on the bridge of Urik's nose. He jammed the knife in again, into the front of Urik's throat. Part of him would have liked to stay, to watch the Wardcaptain's last breaths rattling bloodily out, but the pleasure of savouring those moments did not outweigh the risk of being caught. It would be ill-disciplined, silly, to ruin everything now by being captured.

Ammen Sharp ran this time. He went as fast as he could in the dark of the city's narrow ways, following one of the possible routes he had plotted in his mind during those long hours of waiting on the tavern's roof. He did not need the light of day, here amongst the alleys that had once been his father's domain. Down, down towards the harbour he ran, cutting this way and that, back and forth amongst the crowded ramshackle houses of poor fishermen and shore-scavengers. The bolt-hole he had found for himself, an abandoned kiln in a workshop long ago ruined by fire, awaited him: safe and secret. And as he ran, his mind raced too. He was done with Urik, but a further task remained to him. One more death was required in answer to what had happened in Polochain's warehouse, and he already knew it would be far more difficult to contrive than Urik's had been. It might even be beyond him; attempting it might achieve nothing but his own death. Nevertheless, he would try. It was the least his father deserved.

So, somehow, Ammen Sharp would find a way to kill the Shadowhand.

IV

"I heard you had a disagreement with Aewult's whore." Roaric nan Kilkry-Haig had an unpleasant, bitter smile on his face as he spoke.

Anyara avoided his gaze. "I thought she was a singer or something," she said.

"A dancer, once upon a time I think. Still, she loves his wealth, his glory, not him," Roaric said with a shrug. "Makes her something of a whore, doesn't it?"

Lheanor's son made Anyara uncomfortable. He meant well, she

knew. He thought himself a friend and ally of her Blood, and no doubt she could trust him in that. His anger was so raw, though, his character so veined with hostility, that it coloured his every conversation. Anyara suspected that what she saw in him was a distorted reflection of herself as she might have been, had she not learned to hold back bitterness and sorrow by strength of will. She found it ugly.

They rode together down towards the harbour. Coinach was, as always now, at Anyara's side. Roaric's Shield boasted half a dozen burly members, and they had taken the lead, barging a path through the crowds of Sea Street. A sealer's boat had arrived that morning, carrying sick and exhausted survivors of the fall of Glasbridge. Their own flimsy vessel had been driven ashore on Il Anaron's bleak northern coastline, after drifting, without stores of food or water, for a long time. Roaric meant to see to their care himself, and had invited Anyara to come with him.

"Anyway, I was pleased to hear you had put her in her place," the Bloodheir continued. "She imagines herself untouchable merely because she shares Aewult's bed. As if such things counted for anything here. She'd do well to learn a little discretion."

"I was told Aewult is leaving, in any case," said Anyara. She had no wish to dwell on her encounter with Ishbel. Even the memory of it made her angry, at both Ishbel and herself. It had been an act of weakness to so deliberately pick an argument with the woman.

"It's true," Roaric said, and his pleasure was obvious. "The advance companies of his army have already marched. He's out at the camp himself, trying to herd the rest into some kind of order. I've not seen such a mess of an army in a long time. At least Gryvan knows how to command a host. He didn't see fit to share that wisdom with his heir, apparently."

"I don't envy Taim Narran, when Aewult catches up with him."

Roaric laughed. "Oh, he can look after himself, your Captain.

I'd count myself lucky if I was half the man Taim is. If it's true, as I heard, that the Shadowhand has gone off on the trail of your brother, it's him you should be concerned for."

"Orisian can take care of himself as well," Anyara said, hoping it was true. The news that Mordyn Jerain had left at dawn, taking only a small company with him up the old Kyre road, had taken everyone by surprise. In truth, she suspected that Orisian would be distinctly unsettled should the Shadowhand catch up with him. "Some of my brother's companions would probably enjoy the opportunity to tell the Chancellor a thing or two, anyway."

The Bloodheir looked at her questioningly, and Anyara smiled.

"Yvane. I don't think you've met her."

Sea Street was broader and longer than any thoroughfare Anyara knew from the Glas valley. There were several grand houses — the homes of rich merchants and Craftsmen, she guessed — but much of its length was lined by shops and yards and stables. Though the day was cold and the air damp, the street was busy. She might be imagining it, but Anyara thought she could detect a certain boisterousness about the crowds that she had not seen before. Nobody here would mourn the departure of the Haig army. One of the Tower's maids had whispered to her as she prepared to ride out that, only last night, a Taral-Haig spearman who had got drunk in the wrong tavern had been badly beaten. He was found in an alleyway, battered, bruised and stripped naked. The maid had been simmering with excitement as she recounted the rumour.

The quayside itself was, if anything, even busier than Sea Street. Seagulls swept in tight circles above, at least as noisy as the humans below. Anyara had never seen so many vessels: the whole length of the waterfront was lined with everything from fat cargo ships to tiny rowboats. Life and trade continued here in all their variety, no matter what shadows threatened. The crowds were such that people pressed close to the horses. Anyara could sense how uneasy Coinach was becoming. If he was ashamed to have been given the task of standing as shieldman to a woman, it did not show. He was, Anyara was coming to recognise, almost obsessively alert to the slightest hint – invariably imagined, as far as she was concerned – of threat to her.

"The harbour master's taken your cast-ashores into his own house," Roaric told her. "They can't stay there, though. He doesn't have the space."

Anyara remembered that house from when she had arrived here with Orisian and the others: the first real warmth and welcome they had experienced since the night of Winterbirth.

"You can almost smell the relief that we're to see the back of Aewult and his army, can't you?" said Roaric, gazing out over the lively crowds. "The news has gone around the city faster than a plague of sneezes."

"It's good to see more happy faces," Anyara agreed. "I don't look forward to Aewult's return, though. It seems unlikely that he'll be any more pleasant once he's got a victory behind him."

"Oh, I don't think we'll see much of him after the fighting's done. He hates it here. He hates us. Even his desire to gloat, and to grind our faces into the dirt of his triumph, won't be enough to keep him here. That'll be a still happier day for us all, when we're watching his back disappear off down the road to Vaymouth."

"He'll be High Thane one day," Anyara said distantly. "My brother's master."

"Perhaps the Black Road will do us a favour and kill him," Roaric said with a grim smile. "Failing that, we can only wish his father a long life. And that's not something I've said before."

The people the harbour master had taken into his house were desperate folk: destitute, hungry, half of them sick. Anyara listened to their tales, and offered what comfort she could. She felt more anger than pity. Glasbridge had been a fine town, prosperous and bustling. The Black Road had ruined it, and all of the lives that

centred upon it, just as they had ruined so much else. In seeing
these shattered people, Anyara saw afresh all the loss and suffering that had been inflicted on her Blood; it was embodied in their
thin frames, in their fearful, exhausted faces.

She did not stay long. She promised them that they would be
helped, and fed, and have the attention of healers. Roaric assured
her they would be given shelter in Kolkyre's northern quarter,
where so many Lannis folk had already congregated. And then
she left, taking her anger and distress away lest it should show
itself too clearly. It would not help these people, she thought, to
see that the sister of their Thane was just as helplessly distraught
as they were.

Coinach escorted her back along the harbour and up Sea Street.
The Tower of Thrones stood ahead of them, like the last pillar of
some immense edifice long ago crumbled away.

"I'd hate to have to live all my life in a place like that," Anyara
said.

Coinach looked up at the soaring tower, but said nothing.

"It's too old, too . . . unlike everything else," Anyara went on.
"It feels cold to me."

"You miss your own home," Coinach said, turning his attention back to the crowds filling the street. "There's nothing
strange in that."

"I do miss it. I don't know how much of a home it'll be when
I return, though. The castle burned. My father – half the people
I knew – won't be there any more. Where's your home?"

"Now? I don't know. Wherever you go, my lady. I'm your
shieldman."

Anyara watched him for a moment or two. He did not look at
her, but at the dozens of faces that they passed. His eyes ranged
over the street scene like a hunter seeking birds in a field.

"Where did you leave from when you marched south with
Taim Narran, though?" she insisted.

"Anduran."

"Were your family still there? When the Black Road came, I mean."

Coinach shook his head, gave her a short, inexpressive glance. "I have no family to speak of, lady. My father died when I was very young, drowned on the river. My mother, and my sister, died of the Heart Fever."

"Oh."

They rode a little further in silence, ascending the long, slow rise of Sea Street. Two men were arguing, facing each other over a broken barrel from which a slick of some dark liquid had spread. They jabbed fingers at each other, spat accusations. Nobody paid them any attention. Anyara took her right hand from the reins and flexed it. There was a bruise across her knuckles. Coinach had taken his task of training her seriously, and it had not been an easy or painless experience.

"You'll have to stop calling me 'lady'," Anyara murmured. "It doesn't seem right, coming from someone who's going to be beating bruises into me with a training blade."

In the dimming light of that dusk, Anyara was on Kolkyre's northern wall, by the Skeil Gate, to see the last of Aewult nan Haig's army disappearing up the road that would lead them to Kolglas and beyond. The long column of supply wagons had been out of sight for some time. Now only the rearguard – a couple of hundred mounted Taral-Haig spearmen – could be seen, and they would soon vanish into the distant gloom.

"It's taken them all day to get themselves out of that camp," Lheanor oc Kilkry-Haig said at her side. "You'd think none of them know that the days grow shorter in winter."

"They'll have to stop for the night before they've even had a chance to get tired," Roaric agreed.

Seeing the Thane and his Bloodheir side by side, Anyara was struck by how alike they were in appearance. They were almost precisely the same height, and shared the same wide, firm stance.

Lheanor was an old man, Roaric still a relatively young one, but the likeness of their faces would have been enough to tell any observer that they were father and son.

"Aewult's a fool," Lheanor sighed. "Still, he should have four or five swords to match against each one of the Black Road's, so no doubt he'll have his victory."

"Unless Taim Narran has already won it by the time Aewult reaches Kolglas," Roaric said. His amusement at the thought was undisguised. Lheanor shot his son a vaguely disapproving glance. The Bloodheir did not seem to notice it.

"You should have more care what you wish for," the Thane said. "Or learn to read the currents rather better. If Orisian and Taim Narran cheat Aewult of his glory, we'll all pay a price, I can promise you. It's no part of the High Thane's intent – or that of the Shadowhand – that any Blood but Haig should come out of all this stronger than it went in."

"I know that well enough," Roaric muttered. He stared at his feet.

"Come," Lheanor said, turning to Anyara. "Let us retire to the Tower. This is one night at least when I mean to set aside worries about the past or the future. Whatever perils remain, today we are relieved of the burden of hosting uncomfortable guests. Those who remain are welcome, and we can feast amongst friends."

They walked together back towards the Tower of Thrones, the three of them surrounded by more than a score of shieldmen and attendants. The streets were emptying out with the approach of night, but those who were still abroad stood aside without protest as the Thane processed through his city. Lheanor walked slowly – whether through age or weariness, Anyara was not sure. She matched her pace to his. For all his talk of setting aside worries, his demeanour was not that of a man with a light heart.

"Do you really think there will be trouble, if Aewult feels my brother's cheated him of something?" Anyara asked him.

"There might be," Lheanor said softly. "It's not so much

Aewult's anger that concerns me, as what channel the Shadow-hand might dig for it. The Chancellor and the High Thane are not well known for resigning themselves to disappointment."

"You didn't tell Orisian to stay here, though, did you?"

"No. I'm an old man, and one with more than a trace of fear clouding his eyes. I have no right to try to dissuade a young Thane whose Blood is fighting for its life from whatever course of action he chooses. Anyway, we – your Blood and mine – have an army of quarrels with Haig already. One more will make little difference."

"He would have listened to your advice, I'm sure."

Lheanor gave her a kindly smile. "I did give him some, though not on the matter of staying here. But whatever the subject, he needs it less than he – or you – might imagine. He's no fool, your brother. He gave me some advice of his own, and it was welcome. And wise."

The Thane hung his head then, and watched the cobblestones flowing beneath his feet as he walked. He appeared disinclined to expand upon what had passed between him and Orisian. Anyara restrained her curiosity. She could not guess what advice her brother had seen fit to give this powerful old, man. But then, she reflected with a touch of sadness, Orisian was Thane now. He had ceased to be just her younger brother, who she could by turns tease and protect. Now, he stood at the head of the Blood. He could march away into strife and leave her behind; he could exchange advice with Lheanor oc Kilkry-Haig; he could choose to risk the enmity of the High Thane himself. Everything, all the world in all its smallest details, had changed since the night of Winterbirth. Even Orisian.

They followed the flagstone path up the mound, through the wintry gardens, and into the Tower of Thrones.

Lagair Haldyn sat with his wife, both of them sullen and uncommunicative. They formed a cold island in the lapping water of merriment, their eyes resolutely downcast. Roaric was glowering at the Steward.

"I don't know why they don't just leave, since they make their boredom so obvious," the Bloodheir muttered under his breath.

Anyara glanced over at Lagair. He had a slab of meat impaled on his knife, and took a bite from it as she watched. He caught her eye and flicked her an unconvincing smile before turning to his wife. An air of disapproval hung about the two of them, Anyara thought. Perhaps they were offended by the way the departure of the Haig army was being marked. If so, their stubbornly glum presence at this feast served as an effective reminder that Gryvan oc Haig was never truly absent; the High Thane's shadow was not removed merely because his warriors had marched on.

"I don't suppose they'll stay much longer," Anyara said to Roaric. "Just long enough to remind you they're still here."

"No, no," Lheanor was crying in exasperation. "I want wine, more wine."

A harassed girl, her efforts to fill the Thane's beaker with ale thus rebuffed, hurried away. She looked, to Anyara, as though she was close to tears. Lheanor rattled his empty cup on the table and cast about for someone who could give him what he wanted. Ilessa, his wife, laid a gently restraining hand on his arm. He calmed at once.

"Some sickness, a disturbance of the guts, has sent half the kitchen girls to their beds," he explained to Anyara. "We've had to borrow hands from everywhere else. There's stable boys carving meat and washerwomen baking bread. Most of them have no idea what they're doing."

Now that it was pointed out to her, Anyara could see that the servants rushing about the hall did not have the usual air of proficiency. She could see old women and red-faced men, boys carrying overladen plates. As she watched, two of them almost collided in their haste to keep the supply of food and drink flowing.

"It's bad luck to have so many fall sick," she murmured.

Lheanor grunted. "Life's way of reminding us that no day is ever so sunny that a little cloud may not appear. Still, it's no great trial. There'll be a few sore feet and aching backs by the end of the night, that's all."

Coinach was sitting at the near end of the table running down the length of the hall. Anyara watched him trying to fish something out of a flagon of ale that stood before him. He had half-risen from his bench, and wore a frown of concentration as he chased whatever had fallen in there with a finger. He looked, Anyara thought, like some ordinary village boy just then.

Someone further down the table was picking out a tune on a whistle. The melody danced its shrill way up and up, accompanied by shouts and laughs of encouragement, then collapsed in a flurry of missed notes. There was mocking applause.

"Ah, here we are," Lheanor said. An old woman – short and a little hunch-shouldered – had brought a jug of wine and was refilling his cup.

"Do you see, Anyara?" the Thane said with as broad a smile as Anyara had seen on him since she arrived in Kolkyre. "Us old folk have our uses still. It took an old, wise head to find me my wine. How long since you've served at table here, Cailla?"

The woman edged away from the table, clearly unwelcoming of such attention.

"Many years, sire. I keep to the kitchens these days."

"Yes. You served me when I first ate in this hall as Thane, though. I remember."

Cailla nodded and headed off with the empty jug. Someone set a fresh loaf of bread down on the table in front of Anyara and she caught the rich, hot smell of it. It was a smell she loved, but it carried some bitter memories with it now: the kitchens in Castle Kolglas, where rows of loaves would stand cooling; the hall there, where her father would never again feast as Lheanor did now. She was not even certain if that hall survived. Everyone said that the castle in the sea had burned, but how much of it was ruined she did not know.

Those thoughts occupied Anyara for a time. She ate sparingly, watching all that happened and feeling very much alone. She almost wished that she could sit alongside Coinach on the benches of the long table. However warm and welcoming Lheanor and the others might be, Coinach was the only one of her Blood who was here. No matter how little she knew of him, that one fact was enough to mean that they shared something important.

The meat and bread were cleared away. It was a messy, clumsy process, since so many of the servants were new to it. Eventually, though, the platters of sweet cakes and dried fruits, honey and oatbreads, began to emerge from the kitchens. The mood of the hall softened. Thoughts were drifting towards sleep. Anyara could feel weariness settling over her, and wondered whether tonight she might be granted a dreamless, gentle slumber.

She heard Lheanor make a contented, approving noise in his throat, and turned to look. Cailla, the aged kitchen maid, was leaning over the Thane's shoulder, setting down a bowl of stewed apples. She did it carefully, with a deftness that belied her years. Anyara's head began to turn away. Her eyes lingered for only an instant, but it was long enough to see – if not, at first, to understand – what happened next.

Cailla was straightening. Her right hand slipped smoothly beneath the cuff of her left sleeve and drew something out. Lheanor was glancing up at her, smiling, even as he reached for his cup of wine. The thing that Cailla was holding caught a spark of yellow light from the torches. She made a sudden movement. Lheanor jerked in his chair; his cup went flying. Roaric turned to look. Beyond the Thane, Anyara saw Ilessa's old, kind face as she too glanced round. Anyara was frozen, paralysed by incomprehension. Her mind stumbled over what her eyes told her. Ilessa's features were stretching themselves into a mask of horror.

Roaric was starting to move, surging up. Cailla was reaching, thrusting her knife at the Bloodheir's face. Roaric dodged the blow. Ilessa's mouth was open, screaming or wailing. Roaric bore Cailla backwards and down. Anyara's stare swung back onto Lheanor, and stayed there.

The grey-haired Thane of the Kilkry Blood was slumped limply, sinking. His head lolled to one side. He was looking at Anyara, his eyes quite still and clear. And his blood was pumping out of the wound in his neck, spilling on his shoulder and down his chest and onto the table, a terrible dark red flood that did not stop.

There was a cacophony then. An eruption of sound and movement that overwhelmed the senses. Within it, distinct amongst the welter of noise, Anyara could hear a rhythmic pulse, like the slow, wet beat of a drum. It was Roaric, hammering Cailla's head against the stone floor.

V

Anduran was seething, boiling with the masses of the Black Road. They had filled the half-ruined city, spilled out over the walls and sprawled across the surrounding fields. In their thousands, they swarmed like flies drawn to the remains of a great dead beast. Half the city had been burned, but even the gutted shells of buildings had been occupied if they offered so much as a fragment of shelter. Hundreds of tents had sprung up in the fields outside the walls. Every farmhouse within sight of the city had become the heart of a new canvas settlement; every barn held more men and women than horses.

Coming up towards the city from the direction of Grive, Wain nan Horin-Gyre was struck by the impression of disorder. She saw little sign of discipline or organisation. Most of the camps she passed had no banners to proclaim their Blood, no real warriors at all. The tents had been pitched apparently at random. She saw several that would be thrown down by the first severe wind; others that would soak their occupants in a finger's depth of water as soon as any heavy rains came. Dozens of campfires were burning, but there was no evidence that there had been much collection of firewood. People had gathered what they could from abandoned houses or the little clumps of trees and now preferred to savour the warmth rather than lay in the stocks to last them all through the night.

There were exceptions to the general air of carelessness. Wain led her warriors past one squat grey farmhouse that had been taken over by the Children of the Hundred. A raven-feathered banner was planted outside it. Smoke was rising from the chimney, and horses were being watered at a trough. A pair of Inkallim were standing outside sheds, guarding precious cattle to judge by the lowing that emanated from within. Their expressions blank, they watched Wain and her company pass.

She knew how strange – alarming even – her companions would appear to these observers. Aeglyss and his White Owls walked behind her own Horin-Gyre warriors. It was those Kyrinin that drew every eye as they came closer to Anduran itself, and Wain could see the hostility in every face. People came to the side of the road, scowling. She heard mutterings of contempt, anger. These were the ordinary folk of the creed, she reminded herself, drawn from all the Bloods of the Black Road: farmers, fishermen, hunters and craftsmen. Their faith was burning hot, or they would never have left their distant homes to come and fight here. And their hatred of woodwights was ingrained, unquestioning.

Wain turned her horse, ready to tell Aeglyss that his inhuman companions should wait out of sight. Even as she did so, someone threw a stone. It fell amongst the White Owl warriors. Another followed almost at once, and then a third. A thick crowd jostled itself closer on either side of the road, pressing up towards the fifty or so Kyrinin. There were angry shouts. The White Owls reacted quickly, silently. They backed into a tight clump, facing outwards, Aeglyss safe in its heart. Spearpoints bristled like the quills of a porcupine.

"Get back!" Wain cried as she urged her horse on, but the noise from the mob perhaps drowned her voice out.

A stout, pale man of middle years hacked at one of the Kyrinin spears with a little axe. The shaft of the spear dipped, swung and jabbed out in a single fluid movement. The point punched into the man's shoulder. He howled and stumbled back into the press of bodies.

"Scatter them," Wain shouted to her Shield, and drove her own horse into the midst of the crowd. She slipped one foot from a stirrup and kicked out. The warriors of her Shield, ploughing through the throng, were less restrained. She glimpsed swords rising and falling.

"They are under our protection," she cried at the backs of the fleeing figures that were suddenly all around.

She set her own warriors around the knot of Kyrinin: a wall of horseflesh and iron. Aeglyss looked up at her and smiled.

"A warm welcome," he murmured.

There was something so profoundly arrogant in the casual smile, the almost dismissive tone, that Wain's hand tightened on the reins. Even now, after hours of turning the question over in her mind, she did not understand what held her back. Why not reach down and strike this halfbreed creature? Why not just kill him and all his woodwights? And yet, and yet . . . There was a bright, fierce intensity in his half-human eyes. His air of powerful intent, firm will, was like a protective cloak thrown over his shoulders. When he made her the object of his full attention, when he held his penetrating gaze fast upon her, she could feel it on her, inside her. Sometimes, vanishingly faint, she thought she could hear, within her mind, the sound of what raged in him: a muted roar, as of an immense cataract muffled by distance.

However nagging her misgivings, however persistent the under-current of fear, when she looked at him she saw opportunity; possibility. He had served a purpose before, when he had opened the way through White Owl lands for the Horin-Gyre army. Now, clearly, he had changed. He had become . . . more. Therefore what greater purpose might he now serve, in the remorseless unveiling of fate's course?

"Wain?" Aeglyss said. "Are you all right?"

She shook herself, uncertain how much time she had lost to thought. Uncertain, for a moment, whether all of the thoughts that ran through her head were wholly her own. Was it her imag-ination, or did confusion, distraction, surround Aeglyss like a miasma of the mind?

"Your White Owls are liable to be cut to pieces before we reach the city," she said. "Send them away. They can surely find some woods to hide in until you return."

Aeglyss raised an eyebrow and looked at the Kyrinin warriors gathered around him.

"But this is my spear *a'an*, commanded by their Voice to remain at my side. It is no light duty. They take it most seriously."

"You're the one who claims to wield such great power," Wain muttered, hauling her horse around and away. "Persuade them to accept the parting. I can't protect them, or you, if they come further with us."

The scene inside Anduran was very different to that beyond the walls. The city had been claimed by the Inkallim, and by their quiet purposefulness. Riding through its streets, Wain saw more of the dour ravens than she had ever seen in one place before. The last time anything more than a handful of Battle Inkallim had taken the field had been precisely thirty-three years ago, when hundreds of them had marched with the army that Wain's doomed uncle had led through the Vale of Stones to die beneath the walls of Tanwrye. Marched, but not fought. The warriors of Horin-Gyre had been slaughtered while that company of Inkallim looked on. The cruel reversal fate had worked was not lost on Wain: her Blood's betrayers then might be its saviours now.

Aeglyss was walking a little way behind her. Wain's Shield rode, at her command, on either side of him; whether to protect him or her, she had not been sure even as she gave the order. In the halfbreed's footsteps came the one White Owl Kyrinin who had refused to be parted from him. It was the powerful, elaborately tattooed man that Aeglyss had identified as the son of the White Owl Voice. Hothyn, Wain now knew he was called. All of the other woodwights had departed, after an extended and – to Wain's ears rather agitated appeal from Aeglyss. She had sent a few of her own warriors to escort them, in the hope of preventing any further disturbances. Hothyn, though, had simply stood there, watching Aeglyss in silence.

"He will not go," Aeglyss said when Wain pressed the issue.

"You could make him, if you wanted to."

"I probably could. I'm not minded to do so."

It was typical of the halfbreed's manner, ever since Wain had found him at the ruins of Kan Avor: an easy arrogance, and a reticence about his intent and his standing with the woodwights. But she had consented to Hothyn's presence. She had seen enough to know that there might be bargaining to be done, here in Anduran. There was a question, unresolved, of control and influence. The Battle Inkall was clearly present in numbers, but where were the warriors of Gyre, and the other Bloods? Who commanded the masses of commonfolk? The army that their dead father had given to her and to Kanin to lead was now a broken, exhausted thing. If they hoped to make their voice heard in whatever was to follow, making it clear they still had hold of the White Owl Kyrinin would do no harm.

Wain left most of her warriors in the great square at Anduran's heart, and went on towards the castle with only her Shield, and with Aeglyss and Hothyn.

The courtyard of Castle Anduran was crowded. There were Gyre warriors scattered across it, tending to horses, cleaning weapons, or just sitting in silent groups on the cobbles. The figures that caught Wain's attention, though, were the Inkallim: twenty or thirty of them, standing by the front of the main keep. Shraeve was there, of course. She looked up as Wain drew near, staring, giving no sign of welcome.

Two men stood apart from the others, deep in conversation. One was clad in the dark leather of the Battle Inkall, his black-dyed hair hanging down over his shoulders. The other, older and broader, with a weather-roughened face and a rather battered chain-mail jerkin, had hide boots with long brown feathers sewn on at the calfs. Wain knew them both, though neither well, and their presence told her most of what she needed to know about how things stood, both here in Anduran and back beyond the Vale of Stones.

Fiallic, the Inkallim, was Banner-captain of the Battle. He was second only to Nyve in the hierarchy of that Inkall, and was assumed to be the First's most likely successor. It was said that he was the greatest warrior the Battle had produced in a hundred years. He had, if Wain remembered rightly, won the rank of Banner-captain in the shortest, most one-sided trial of combat the Battle had witnessed in half a century. The other man was Temegrin nan Gyre, a cousin of Ragnor's and Third Captain in the High Thane's standing army. He was widely called – at his own insistence – the Eagle, but his reputation hardly merited such a noble association. Wain had never heard of him winning any victory, save for the slaughter twenty years ago of some Tarbain villagers who had abandoned their homes and set out to march into the east rather than adopt the creed of the Black Road.

As she strode towards the two men, brushing past Shraeve without acknowledging her, Wain had to suppress a twinge of disappointment. If Temegrin was the best that Ragnor oc Gyre would offer in support of this war, the High Thane was making little effort to conceal his lack of enthusiasm. Unless the Eagle had been improbably elevated in status, he would be commanding at most a couple of thousand Gyre warriors: not much more than a token force. For the Banner-captain himself to be here, by contrast, spoke of total commitment on the part of the Battle. Such a divergence of intent between the Gyre Blood and the Inkallim did not bode well. And it did – as Shraeve had implied before she left Glasbridge – suggest that the ravens meant to make this war their own.

Temegrin glanced up as she drew near. He looked to be in poor humour.

"Greetings, lady," he rumbled.

She gave him a curt nod, then straightened her back and lifted her chin a fraction. She was almost as tall as Temegrin, and did not intend to appear anything other than his equal. In the last few weeks she had, she suspected, seen more fighting than he had in his whole life.

Fiallic the Inkallim faced her with a more welcoming expression. He had surprisingly gentle eyes. They gave a misleading impression of his nature, she was certain.

"Banner-captain," she said. "We never thought to see the Battle field such strength. I am pleased to find you here."

"I imagine you are," Fiallic said with a faint smile. "Shraeve tells me your own strength is all but spent."

"It is." Wain saw no point in denying it. "But we hold Glasbridge still. Much remains possible, if fate smiles upon us."

"Yes. Shraeve told me that as well."

"We'll save talk of what's possible for later," muttered Temegrin irritably. "We've enough to worry about in the now without turning to the hereafter. The High Thane's command was to raze Tanwrye, and that's done. I'll not consent to any discussion of further adventures until I know more of what we face."

"I doubt our enemies will grant us much time for discussion," said Fiallic in a soft voice.

"We expect an assault on Glasbridge at any time . . ." Wain began, but Temegrin cut her short, chopping the air with his hand.

"Enough. We'll not discuss this out in a courtyard for every ear to listen. And why is your brother not here, anyway? I'd thought he would be the one to deal with these matters."

Wain ignored the implied insult, shedding it with a twitch of her shoulders. "I share the burden of command with him. You can be assured that I speak with his authority as well as my own. And, as I said, there is likely to be bloodshed in the next few days. One of us had to remain."

Temegrin grunted, apparently unconvinced.

"I had heard your alliance with the White Owls was a thing of the past," murmured Fiallic.

Wain glanced at him, and found him looking beyond her. She turned her head, and saw Aeglyss and Hothyn standing there amidst her Shield. Many of the other warriors gathered in the courtyard were watching them, though the *na'kyrim* and Kyrinin themselves seemed unperturbed by this hostile attention. Aeglyss, Wain saw, had his eyes fixed upon her. She felt a tingle, like the brush of invisible fingertips, run down her neck.

Temegrin followed the line of Fiallic's gaze and made a thick, deep sound of disapproval.

"That alliance should be a thing of the past," the Eagle said. "What were you thinking, to bring a woodwight and a halfbreed here?"

Wain set her back to Aeglyss once more. Both Temegrin and Fiallic continued to stare at the silent *na'kyrim* and his inhuman companion. She wondered what they saw there. Did they, like her, feel Aeglyss's presence as an almost physical weight bearing down on their senses?

"That's another matter best discussed elsewhere," was all she said.

"Now, then," growled Temegrin. "Come."

He stamped up into the keep, his feet punishing the steps for his foul mood. Fiallic followed. Wain glanced at Aeglyss, and was caught on the hook of his eyes. Not so much as a tremor disturbed the immobility of his lips, yet she knew what he wanted; what he required of her. She gave a single, sharp nod to summon him and Hothyn after her.

"I didn't mean for these . . . these to join us," protested the Eagle as he, Wain and Fiallic settled into chairs around a fine circular table. The walls were partly panelled with dark wood. It might have been one of Croesan's private chambers once.

"You question their presence in my company," Wain muttered. "You can see for yourself. Judge for yourself." She could not keep a trace of irritation from her voice, though it was directed at herself as much as anyone. She should not have brought Aeglyss in here. It was the act of a fool, no better than jabbing a sleeping bear – or eagle – with a stick. Yet she had done it, and matters would fall out now as fate saw fit.

"I don't need to judge anything. A woodwight and a half-breed? They've no place in this room, and no place in the company of the faithful."

"Oh, that's an old song," whispered Aeglyss. He was standing behind Wain. She half-turned, meaning to tell him to be silent, but somehow the words stuck in her throat.

"You know . . ." the *na'kyrim* cocked his head as he spoke, his interest plainly caught by the thought he meant to express, "everything I see, everyone I meet, it seems to me that I have seen it, met them, before. I do not understand it, but everything, and everyone, tastes . . . familiar."

"I will not have our time wasted by some half-wight who—" Temegrin growled menacingly.

"You, for example," Aeglyss interrupted him. "The Eagle. I

know nothing of you, yet I know this: your heart does not burn
with hunger for the remade world. You find this world, this life,
more to your liking than one true to the creed should, perhaps."

Wain could clearly see the storm of fury that rose within
Temegrin. It blushed his cheeks, knotted his brow, bared his
teeth. But before that storm broke, Aeglyss laughed.

"Do you deny it?" he demanded of the Eagle through his
laughter, and the words were like corded whips that lashed from
him to Temegrin and coiled about the warrior's throat, his chest.
The air quivered at the sound of them and Wain flinched
despite herself. Even impassive Fiallic narrowed his eyes and
winced.

Temegrin was straining, yearning to pull back from whatever
it was that burned in the *na'kyrim*'s grey eyes. But he was held.
Beads of sweat were on his forehead. Wain could hear his teeth
grinding together. Her skin was crawling, her mouth dry. She felt
only the side eddies of whatever torrential flow Aeglyss had
turned upon Temegrin, yet her head spun, her mind tumbled out
of her grasp.

Then Aeglyss grunted and turned away, dropping his gaze to
the floor.

"No, you do not," he murmured.

Temegrin the Eagle slumped in his chair. His chest heaved – a
few wild breaths – and then slowed. He regained his composure.

"What . . . what monstrosity is this you've brought into our
midst, Wain?" he rasped.

"Wait," said Fiallic. His tone admitted no possibility of dissent
or disobedience. He was watching Aeglyss, though the *na'kyrim*
had drifted away from the table now, and was examining some
wooden panelling on the wall. "There will be no more talk, no
more discussion of any kind, in this room until the halfbreed has
removed himself. Or is removed. The wight, too."

And there, Wain thought, is the true face of the Banner-captain
of the Battle Inkall. There was more threat, more danger, in the

Inkallim's cold, level voice than Temegrin could ever imbue his bluster with.

Yet Aeglyss kept his back to them. It was if he had been struck deaf, or was some open-eyed sleepwalker. He laid his spidery fingers, with their long, clouded nails, on a dark, scratched panel, caressing it. Hothyn was staring at Wain. It was an empty gaze, without threat, without even comprehension as far as she could tell.

"Aeglyss," Wain said, and he straightened and turned to her. He regarded her with raised, questioning eyebrows, like some willing servant awaiting instruction.

"Leave us," she said. "Wait outside with my Shield."

He nodded, and left the room without a word. Hothyn went too: a great, lithe hound at the heels of his master, Wain thought. Only then, as it slowed, did she realise how fast her heart had been beating. Only as she unfolded her hand in her lap did she realise she had made a fist of it. She began to rub and turn the ring on her index finger.

"You will have to explain the company you keep," said Fiallic to her with an incongruous smile. "My ignorance of his kind is vast in its scale, but your halfbreed is . . . disturbing."

"My Blood was short of allies in this undertaking" – she shot a pointed glance in Temegrin's direction – "so we had to find them where we could. Through Aeglyss, we have bent the White Owls to the service of the Black Road. They have proved useful, and may do so again. Aeglyss has pledged hundreds of their spears to our cause. And you have seen for yourself that he has certain other talents. I cannot explain them, or him, but I am disinclined to set aside such possible advantage merely because you – any of us – find one man unsettling."

"I understand. But I was told your brother had already disavowed this alliance. Something has changed, apparently. Or is this a decision you have made without him?"

"Never mind disavowing," Temegrin snapped before Wain

could reply. "He attacked me. I'll see him dead for that. I want him . . ."

"I saw no attack," Fiallic murmured.

"What?" the Eagle cried. "The man's a . . . a mongrel. Unnatural! Not fit to serve the creed no matter what his uses. I will have—"

"You will have the wisdom to leave to the Lore the determination of what, or who, is fit to serve the creed," the Inkallim said flatly. "Theor sent Goedellin with us for just such purposes."

Temegrin's eyes narrowed, and Wain detected hatred in that fierce expression. The Eagle had been humiliated by Aeglyss. It left him with a blister of anger on his heart that might be dangerous. Anger, Wain had always been taught, was an emotion to be resisted. It could too easily become bitterness or resentment at fate's inevitable course.

"Goedellin?" she asked, eager to tease out the threads of power and influence, and to avoid discussion of Aeglyss if she could.

"An Inner Servant of the Lore," Fiallic said. "The First esteems him highly. He accompanied the Battle on our march, with a number of his colleagues."

Wain nodded. Whether Temegrin – or his distant master, Ragnor oc Gyre – liked it or not, the Inkallim meant to be masters of this war, then. The Battle would lay claim to its muscles, the Lore to its heart.

"The Lore has no place in the conduct of wars," Temegrin muttered, though his voice betrayed the fact that it was an old argument, already lost. "I carry the High Thane's authority here."

"You should spend more time amongst the host gathered outside this city," said Fiallic. "If you did, you would know that we none of us carry the authority that matters here. All those people out there follow the commands of their hearts, of their faith, not those of any captain. This is a righteous war. That is the only authority the thousands acknowledge; the only command that drives them."

Temegrin snorted in contempt. "You ravens, always spouting pieties. If there's no authority to be claimed, your own actions are a mystery. You think I don't know you've got your captains out there organising the commonfolk into companies? That you've been doing it ever since Tanwrye? Hundreds, isn't it? One Inkallim to command each hundred?"

Fiallic shrugged. "There must be some structure. I can spare the warriors to lead such companies; perhaps if Ragnor had given you more spears to bring south, you could have done the same."

Temegrin hammered the table with his fist. "Enough! I bear a warrant of authority from Ragnor oc Gyre, that he put into my hands himself. You will not mock that. And you will not question the High Thane's intent in my presence."

Fiallic scratched his cheek, meeting Temegrin's furious glare with calmness. The Inkallim pushed his chair back and rose. "I meant neither to mock nor question. You hear more than I speak. Perhaps this discussion is best postponed until a time when tempers run less hot. I imagine Wain would appreciate some food after her journey."

Wain got to her feet as quickly as she could without appearing over-eager. Though she was not hungry, she welcomed any excuse to leave the Eagle's company. It was, in any case, clear that whatever Temegrin might hope or imagine, the Children of the Hundred held the rudder of this war. Until she knew more of their intent, Wain would gladly postpone further argument.

Her Shield were waiting outside. Aeglyss and Hothyn were with them. The *na'kyrim* had sat down on the cobblestones, resting his back against the wall. His eyes were closed. Hothyn stood staring up at the castle's battlements, or perhaps at the clouds beyond.

"Come," Wain said. "There's food in the hall."

The hall in Castle Anduran's keep was in a state of some disorder. In one corner was a pile of wreckage – the shattered remains of tables – that was being used as firewood. Several of the windows had been smashed in during the final assault on the castle; blankets had been tied over them. One of the walls bore a great black smear of grimy soot. The few intact tables and benches were crowded, but most of the warriors in the hall were sitting on the floor. Some, Wain saw as she picked her way between them, were even asleep, curled up under jackets or capes. All of them looked to be of the Gyre Blood; there were certainly no Inkallim here, and none of the few Horin warriors she and her brother had left here as garrison.

Children hurried back and forth, carrying food and drink for the castle's new masters. They were orphans or captives, Wain guessed: Lannis waifs put to work. She looked about her while her Shield cleared some benches to make space for her. The Gyre warriors looked tired, lethargic. Perhaps Temegrin had imagined that whoever held this castle would hold the entire valley. If so, Fiallic's Inkallim were evidently out in the streets of the town and the fields beyond, proving him wrong.

The food the children brought for them was simple and sparse. Wain watched Aeglyss as she tore at a slab of almost stale bread. The *na'kyrim* seemed to have little appetite. Hothyn refused even to touch what was offered him. Dozens of stares were upon them, Wain knew, most of them no doubt hostile or suspicious. She did not care. Her Blood, not Gyre, had paid the death-price that fate demanded for this castle. She had been out there in the courtyard, sword in hand, to see the Lannis-Haig Thane cut down; she had herself slain his daughter-in-law and grandson high in this very keep. She had more right to sit and eat in this hall than any of the Eagle's lackeys.

She stared down at the surface of the table.

"You will not interfere in any discussion of mine again," she murmured.

Aeglyss glanced at her. "Will not? Am I one of your followers, then, Thane's sister? To be ordered this way and that at your whim?"

He spoke softly. As far as Wain could tell, no one – not even her Shield packed in along the opposite side of the table – would hear what they were saying. No one, she corrected herself, save perhaps Hothyn with his keen Kyrinin ears; but she had seen no sign that the woodwight understood the language of the Bloods.

"You think yourself more than that?" she muttered angrily.

Aeglyss pushed away the platter that had been placed before him.

"Whatever I'm following, it's no warrior maiden. And it won't be the ravens or Ragnor's tame eagle, either. You'll see. Your eyes will open."

"Your arrogance outruns your importance," Wain hissed, struggling to keep her voice down, "Already I regret not killing you at Kan Avor. Is that what you want?"

Only now did she look at the *na'kyrim*, fixing him with the glare that had cowed so many others before him. But he met her eyes with his own: grey, implacable. His slender hand slipped over hers, and though she meant to push him away, her arm was no longer subject to her will. There were shadows moving in his eyes, or perhaps behind them.

"Ignorance excuses all failings," he whispered, "in the greatest and most noble just as in the most lowly."

Wain could feel warmth inside her hand. It spread as if from some gentle ember buried deep in her flesh.

"You mistake past truths for those of the present, Thane's sister. It is easy to forgive, for you were not there when the world changed. You did not see me upon the Stone."

Heat tingled beneath the skin of her forearm, winding its tendrils over her muscles, crawling up and around her elbow. She imagined herself pulling away from this creature who wore the semblance of a man, yet she did not – could not – move. She was distantly aware of the drone of surrounding conversations, of the clatter of plates and tankards, but it was those stone-coloured eyes that seemed in that moment to contain all the world. And they held her, drew her close, even as her mind sought to deny them.

"I am a gift to you," Aeglyss said. "Call it fate if you like, or fortune, but never imagine that nothing has changed. You needn't fear men like Temegrin. Not now. He has been . . . exceeded. There is no strength – of arms, of will, of authority – that cannot be exceeded."

"I never feared him," murmured Wain. The sounds she made were so faint, more like breaths than words. The warmth was in her neck, blushing up, cupping her chin, reaching for her lips, her cheeks.

And then Aeglyss withdrew his hand from hers, and the warmth was gone. She fought a wave of dizziness. She could suddenly hear the babble of voices that filled the hall, feel the grain of the table top beneath her fingers. She brought her hands together, searching for the reassuring solidity of her rings. Aeglyss was looking over his shoulder now. Wain turned her head, and found Fiallic standing there.

"I thought we might have a quiet word," the Inkallim said. He was ignoring Aeglyss. The *na'kyrim* turned back to the table.

"If you wish," said Wain.

Fiallic gestured to the open door of the hall. "Will you walk with me? Just for a moment or two."

Wain hesitated, and silently cursed herself for doing so. She hated uncertainty, despised those who allowed it to gain a foothold in their thoughts, yet found herself more and more afflicted by it. She rose and strode away from the table, away from Aeglyss. Fiallic walked at her side.

"You seem distracted," the Inkallim said. "Does what you have found here in Anduran displease you?"

"I am fine," Wain snapped.

"Very well."

They threaded a path through the warriors scattered across the hall's floor. Gyre spearmen shuffled aside to let them pass, but did so grudgingly. Wain was tempted to kick one of them, or tread on a tardy hand.

Fiallic ushered her out into the courtyard. It was quieter now than it had been before. A wagon loaded with sacks of horse feed was rumbling in through the castle gate.

"You saw that Temegrin mislikes the path that fate is following," Fiallic said. He watched the wagon drawing to a halt. Men began to haul the sacks off.

"So much was obvious," Wain said.

"You are aware that the High Thane would not even have sent his Third Captain if the Battle Inkall had not marched to your aid? He made no move until the commonfolk began to follow us across the Stone Vale."

Wain had no intention of being drawn so easily into criticism of Ragnor oc Gyre. That a Banner-captain of the Battle should tread upon such ground was in itself worrying: it spoke of dangerous, unpredictable times.

"How many swords does Temegrin command?" she asked.

"A thousand and a half. Five hundred of them are Tarbains. Well-trained and disciplined, by the standards of Tarbains, but Tarbains nevertheless. It was we Inkallim, and the army of farmers and herdsmen and fishermen, that took Tanwrye, not the swords of Gyre."

Wain grunted non-committally.

"My advice to you would be to have a care in your dealings with the Eagle," Fiallic continued. "His master in Kan Dredar does not like this war. We do not know what orders Temegrin was given, but it is unlikely they were the same as those I received from the First of the Battle."

"And they were?" asked Wain. She strove to sound only mildly interested. There was something unsettling about one of the ravens being so forthcoming. She had never known there to be anything other than unity of purpose between the Inkallim and the Gyre Blood; not in her lifetime, at least.

"To pursue this conflict as far, and as fiercely, as fate will allow. To make myself an ally of your Blood. To oppose any effort – from whatever quarter – to deny the full expression of whatever outcome fate has in mind for us."

"And what outcome is it that you expect? What do the Children of the Hundred hope for?"

Fiallic smiled. The wagon, now empty, was being slowly wheeled around. The huge horse that drew it looked weary; its head was hanging low. Little birds were already dropping down from the battlements to scavenge feed that had leaked out from the sacks.

"I expect nothing," Fiallic said. "I wait to be shown what the Black Road has in store for us. We have the beast by the tail now. It will either turn upon us, and consume us, or drag us in its wake to glory."

"The beast?"

"War. There is no surer way to test fate."

"No," said Wain quietly.

"You should speak with Goedellin."

Wain hung her head for a moment. Those strange, intense moments with Aeglyss had left her inexplicably tired. Her arms and shoulders felt slack, lifeless; her thoughts were sluggish.

"Be assured that the Children of the Hundred are your friends," Fiallic said with measured precision. "The Horin-Gyre Blood has earned the gratitude of all in whom the faith burns brightly. If there are others whose gratitude is more . . . grudging, well, all the more reason to secure whatever bonds of friendship are offered. Goedellin represents the First of the Lore here. Whatever Temegrin may think, there is none more central to matters than Goedellin. There is none whose friendship could do more to secure your Blood's position."

"Very well. Very well."

VI

Goedellin, Inner Servant of the Lore Inkall, was not a man whose appearance put those meeting him for the first time at their ease. What little hair remained on his head was white and wispy; the scalp that showed beneath it was a tapestry of blotches, moles and blemishes. His lips were dark grey, veined with streaks of black: the legacy of the seerstem that some of the Lore used. His back was bent into a hook, pulling his shoulders and head down and forwards. Wain towered over him. Walking alongside him through the yard of what had been Anduran's gaol, she had to shorten her stride to little more than a shuffle to avoid leaving him behind. The Inkallim's legs were crooked, swaying out at the knees. He leaned on a thick, twisted stick.

"It was the house of the gaoler, I am told," Goedellin said as they drew near to the squat building.

"Yes," Wain murmured. "I think it was." She found Goedellin unsettling not so much in how he looked as in who he was. The Inner Servants of the Lore were its most senior and most respected members. Each one had spent years in the consideration of the creed, reflecting upon its meaning. They stood but a single step beneath the First himself in the hierarchy. For one such as Wain, wedded to the faith in heart and mind, Goedellin inspired a respectful, nervous awe that the bloodiest, most terrible of warriors could never have matched.

The door to the house opened as Goedellin stepped carefully up onto the threshold. A young Inkallim, perhaps a candidate for the Lore, ushered them inside. The interior was bare – looted, Wain suspected, when she and her brother had first overrun this city – but that austerity seemed fitting for the lodging of the Lore. The room Goedellin led her into still held a grand table – its surface now scarred, and notches cut into its edges – but the chairs clearly did not belong. They were simple, crude. Goedellin settled stiffly into one. He rested his walking stick against its arm, and indicated that Wain should sit opposite him.

"Fiallic advises me that I should not detain you for too long," the old man said. The tilt of his head made it hard to see his lips or eyes. Wain found herself staring at his scalp. "He tells me you will be eager to leave this place, and return to Glasbridge."

"My brother with be waiting for me, yes. There will be a great battle soon. I should be there."

"Of course. Your reputation is well known. They tell me you are a fierce young woman, Wain nan Horin-Gyre. But a faithful one, too."

"I hope to be."

"Well. Fiallic also told me you brought a halfbreed with you, who is already causing trouble."

"We sent him away. We tried to set him aside, and the wood-wights too. But fate has returned him to us. He brings the White Owls to fight for our cause; more than ever before. He says there are many hundreds of them, many hundreds, already moving through Anlane. It seems to me . . . or at least it did . . . I thought perhaps he would not have returned, despite all the obstacles, were he not fated to play a part in our struggle."

"It seems to you? You know, do you not, that the Lore frowns upon any suggestion that we can know in advance what course fate will follow?"

"I do. I pretend no knowledge of it. I speak only of a willingness to accept that fate may impose distasteful allies, whatever my personal preferences."

"That's a neat construction. It has a dutiful sound to it. Were you tutored in the creed by the Lore as a child?"

Wain nodded. "My father brought two Lore Inkallim to Hakkan when my brother and I were young. They remained only for a year or two." She felt now, facing this Inner Servant, much as she had then, listening in rapt wonder to the soft, firm voices of those tutors. The truth of what they had told her, all those years ago, had been so clear to her that it was like a blast of cold wind, scouring away dust from her child's heart.

"A good man, Angain," Goedellin mused. "Would that more of the Thanes did the same. It's rare for them to invite such tutors into their homes these days. Your Blood has long been an example that others might look to; a shame it has gone unregarded by those with the most to learn."

Wain hung her head and said nothing.

"You are uncertain now, of the halfbreed's place?" Goedellin asked her. "Of whether he is to be a part of all this?"

Wain nodded silently.

"So," the Inkallim sighed. "Whenever we come to a fork in the road, it looks like a choice. It feels like a decision. But these feelings, these choices that we imagine we could make, they are illusions. Choice and decision were taken from us. The Gods require of us that we learn to live without them; learn that some things are beyond our power to change. Such is the penance we must all do, in answer to the hubris of our forebears. You understand all of this, of course?"

"I do," Wain said.

"It is, in part, only a matter of perspective. A life can have but one path. We poor mortals see that path only when we stand at death's very portal, and can turn and look back down the road we have travelled. Then, and only then, we see the way we have come, unbranching, stretching back to the moment of our birth. The Black Road. However it might have appeared to us as we walked it, there were in truth no choices, no decisions. Only that one path, as the Hooded God read it in his book when we drew our first breath in this empty world."

Goedellin was watching her, pursing his dark-tinted lips. It seemed that he expected some kind of response.

"I understand this," Wain said. "I accepted it long ago."

"The creed rules your heart, and your mind?" Goedellin asked her. "Unreservedly? Certainly?"

"It does," she replied without hesitation.

Goedellin nodded: a gentle, kindly gesture. "And this *na'kyrim*? Is he a true adherent of the creed?"

Wain's hesitation was fleeting, but she saw in Goedellin's eyes that he noted it. "I believe he is," she said. She knew it sounded defensive. "I am not certain."

Again, Goedellin nodded. "You do well not to claim certainty. There's none of us, save the Last God himself, who can see into a heart and take the true measure of its devotion."

A sound outside caught his attention. He rose crookedly to his feet, and went with small, careful steps to the window. He beckoned Wain with a gnarled finger. Looking out, she saw twenty or thirty young children clustered in the yard. Many were crying, others were sullen and silent and fearful. Several shivered, clothed in thin garments that were no match for the wintry air. Battle Inkallim shepherded them across the cobblestones.

"A small part of the harvest," Goedellin murmured.

One of the children – a little girl – was jostled from behind and fell, cracking her knees. She wailed. One of the ravens reached down with a single hand and lifted her bodily to her feet, pushed her back in amongst the crowd of waifs.

"You're sending them north?" Wain asked.

"Of course. There is nothing for them here. Those that survive will be Children of the Hundred, one day. We do them a great service, though they may not know it for some time. And there will be losses to be made good. There will be gaps in the rank of the Battle to be filled before all this is done."

"You do mean to see this war fought, then," Wain murmured. "To its conclusion. Whatever that may be."

Goedellin shuffled back towards his chair. "We have three thousand of the Battle here. Such a force does not march lightly. They will not be returning to Kan Dredar until they have tested themselves fully against the Haig Bloods, and against fate."

Wain returned to her own seat.

"Your devotion to the creed is well known, of course," the Inkallim said as he settled back down. "My earlier question was not born of any doubt. How stands your brother in this regard? Do the fires of the faith burn as brightly in the new Thane of the Horin-Gyre Blood as they do in you? As they did in your father?"

"They do." Wain might have said no more than that, but her mind was caught up in this strange fancy that she was a child again, and Goedellin one of those old tutors who had so impressed her. Their wisdom, their sere gravity, had always compelled her to speak honestly. "Perhaps it takes more . . . effort on his part to hold firm to the creed. But he does hold firm."

"Do you understand why I make these enquiries, and ponder these matters?"

"I would not question the Lore's right to enquire as it sees fit in matters of the faith."

"No. I imagine you would not. Still, this is not solely a matter of the faith. The Lore, the Battle, the Hunt: all the Children of the Hundred are now engaged in this struggle that your Blood began. We are committed, to some extent. We will incur loss. We face risks, in terms of our standing, our relationship with the other Bloods. With Thanes."

"Your support for my Blood is a great gift. I – and my brother – know it."

"Well, there is the nub of things. Our support is for your Blood only insofar as it serves the larger purpose of supporting, of strengthening, the creed. So long as this war, and the survival of your Blood, offers some possibility of advancing the cause and the dominion of the Black Road, we Inkallim have little choice but to test the limitations that fate might set upon that advance." Goedellin glanced up from his hunched position, scouring Wain's face for some sign. "Do you think survival is too strong a word to use, perhaps?"

Outside, in the yard, a baby was crying now. It was a piercing sound, distracting. Wain hesitated. "I do not know. We have spent most of my Blood's fighting strength here. But it does not matter, in the end. If my Blood is fated to pass into extinction, so it must be. I know . . ." She faltered, fearful now that she might say the wrong thing. Yet the Inkallim's steady gaze struck her as more reassuring than threatening. "I know, or think I know, that our success has won us little affection from the Gyre Blood. The reasons why that should be so are obscure to me."

Goedellin grunted and lowered his eyes. "Our High Thane excels in matters of obscurity. Well. Your Blood will survive, if fate smiles upon us. Your brother might have made the shaping of such a smile a little easier, had he left an heir behind him, safe in your mother's care at Hakkan. No matter. We – the Inkallim – will stand shoulder to shoulder with you. For so long as it seems that such unity serves the cause of the Black Road, of course. Do you understand yet the import of what I said about choice? Its illusory nature?"

"I am not sure I do."

"There is little more to it than this: whatever choices we make – you about your *na'kyrim*, we Inkallim about the movement of armies – are predestined, their outcome already inscribed upon the pages of the Hooded God's book. The significance of any decision is not, therefore, in the decision itself, but in the thought that underlies it. The posture, if you like, of the mind that makes it. The correct posture is one that gives primacy to the advancement of the creed, and willingly accepts whatever consequences may flow from adhering to that principle."

"I understand that," Wain said, nodding. Goedellin was not looking at her, and could not see the gesture.

"Very well. The Firsts concluded that committing the strength of the Inkalls to this struggle offered at least the possibility of firming the Black Road's grip upon the world. Whether it does so or not, we will all live – or die – with the consequences of that commitment. We need ask ourselves only one question about this *na'kyrim* that so unsettles Fiallic, and so offends the noble Eagle.

Can he serve the creed? Does he offer the possibility of advancing our cause?"

"Yes," Wain said, and then, with greater certainty, "Yes."

Goedellin looked up at her and smiled blackly.

"Well, then," he said.

"Temegrin will not be happy. He wants Aeglyss dead."

"So Fiallic told me. No matter. The Eagle is timid. Those whose answer to the Black Road is timidity seldom prosper. You keep the halfbreed at your side. We will do what we can to dissuade Temegrin, and others if needed, from intemperate action."

Wain nodded. Goedellin coughed and hung his head, so that she could no longer see his eyes, or those stained lips.

"Go," the Inkallim muttered. "Take yourself back to Glasbridge, and your brother's side. The army is already starting to move. Our greatest victory in more than a century is mere days away. If fate favours us."

Wain gathered the few warriors of her Blood who remained in the city on the main square. She had them lay out their weapons and chain mail and shields on the ground. She and her Shield walked up and down the meagre ranks, heads down, eyes searching for any flaw. Wain found a mail shirt with broken links. She struck the man who owned it on the chest, staggering him a little.

"You're done here," she said as she walked. "We're done with this city. The newcomers can have it: Gyre, or the Battle, or the thousands who follow them. The battle's to the south now, and so is your Thane, so that's where we'll take ourselves. To Glasbridge. That's where your Blood makes its stand."

She kicked a battered shield with the toe of her boot. It skittered away over the cobbles.

"That'll split at the first blow. Find another. We'll stand against whatever marches up from the south. We'll hold it, and bleed it, and pin it there for this great army to come down upon it. And those of us who die will die in a great cause, and in a great victory."

The house where Wain and Kanin had taken quarters when they overran Anduran still stood, on the edge of the square. She wandered up its stairs, from room to room, while her warriors outside mounted up. There were memories here that had a warm, tempting texture to them: of their first, triumphant surge into this city, and of the dizzying sense that fate might lay out for them the richest of feasts. Wain knew that it was an indulgence to seek out those memories, and a failing to take comfort in them. In normal times, she would need no such recourse to the past. These were not normal times, though, and she felt almost a stranger in her own skull. She was unsettled. The certainties of life and of the world, usually so clear to her, had lost something of their sharpness. What reassurance her discussion with Goedellin had brought was a fragile thing, already fraying at the edges.

She stared, for a time, into a fireplace. There was only ash there now, and a few fragments of dead, charred wood.

A soft sound had her spinning on her heel, and reaching for her sword. Aeglyss was standing in the doorway, his hands clasped across his midriff.

"You should not be in here," Wain snapped.

"Why not?" the *na'kyrim* asked as he drifted into the room. "Is your solitude so precious to you?"

"Precious enough that I don't want it disturbed by you, half-breed." She strove to make her tone dismissive, contemptuous. It did not come easily, though.

Aeglyss smiled, and Wain had the lurching sense of her self splintering. It was as if two different beings, looking out through her eyes, saw two different things. That smile was at once leering and warming; the *na'kyrim*'s face was at once sickly and captivating; her throat tightened from both repulsion and anticipation. Was this madness?

Her vision blurred then, and the dim light that suffused the room dipped for an instant into a murky fog. She shook her head, and found Aeglyss close to her, almost touching. She stepped backwards from him, but he murmured "No," and followed her.

She tried to call for her Shield, but some invisible hand was pressed across her mouth, stilling all sound.

"It is your instincts you fight against, Thane's sister." He whispered the words, but they filled Wain's every sense, they were glowing and ringing and hot against her skin. "What I have become wakes something in you. Don't you see? You won't be the only one. When I reach out, when I drift, I can feel hopes and desires and hungers and hatreds all flocking about me. They cluster in my wake. Oh, I wish I could show you."

His mouth was close to her cheek. She could feel his breath, and smell his sweet, rotten exhalations.

"Let me show you. Open yourself to me." His hands, like spiders: one on her shoulder, the other cupping her breast, pressing the rings of her mail shirt against her. "Please."

The strands of her resistance were thinning. They would have parted, she distantly knew, had Aeglyss himself not faltered then. A spasm deformed his face, baring his teeth like a snarl. His hands jerked, perhaps bruising her in the instant before they splayed themselves open and fell away. Trembling, released, she pushed him and he staggered backwards.

"Help me," he gasped. "They're coming for me. Can you smell it? The leaves, the forest?"

He reeled sideways, thumping into the wall. Wain edged towards the open door, horrified but still feeling the residue of a shaming desire.

Aeglyss sagged. "No. No." He sank down on to his haunches, pressed against the wall, like a child making himself small, trying to hide. "You'll not have me. I'm too . . ."

Wain turned away. Her head was heavy, resistant to the movement. She took a step, and then another, and her legs were sluggish. She had to force her way out of the room against the reluctance of her own body.

"Wain," Aeglyss said behind her, and she could not help but look back at him. He was still crouched down there, in the crease between wall and floor, staring up at her. "I have terrible enemies," he murmured. "The great beasts of the Shared would turn upon me. But you are not my enemy. You know it, in your heart. And I am not yours. Please. I am the greatest friend fate will ever grant you, and your cause."

Perhaps. She was not certain whether she spoke it aloud, or only thought it deep in the turbulence this *na'kyrim* spun her mind into. Perhaps. I cannot think clearly. I cannot tell. Not any more. She walked out and descended into the more comprehensible company of her warriors.

VII

Something had died, up amongst the rocks. An eagle clambered into the sky as soon as Orisian and his company came in sight, its huge wings hauling it up and away from the hidden corpse. The ravens were more determined, or more hungry perhaps. They hopped and croaked amongst the boulders without regard to the column of riders passing on the road below.

Orisian had fifty men with him, all of them veterans of the war against Igryn oc Dargannan-Haig. The road they followed was an old one, a trading route from the days of the Kingship. Neglect had crumbled away some of its fabric, but it remained a good surface. It had carried them up the northern bank of the River Kyre, through the flat coastal farmlands and on into the rolling pasture-draped hills where the Kilkry Blood bred its famous horses and grazed its innumerable cattle. Now those hills were becoming mountains. The road ran along a terrace cut into a steep, bare slope above the river. The Kyre, down there in the huge gutter it had carved for itself, rushed between great boulders, rumbling as it foamed, milky, through rapids.

They had been climbing for some time. If he twisted and craned his neck, Orisian could still just make out the sea far behind them: a vast grey slab across the western horizon. Looking ahead, on up the road, there was nothing but the long bleak valley of the Kyre, driving into the heart of the Karkyre Peaks. Somewhere in those mountains, Orisian knew, was Highfast, and he hoped it would offer something by way of warmth or comfort. The Karkyre Peaks were no loftier than the Car Criagar, but they were, if anything, still more unwelcoming. There was almost no vegetation, even on these lower slopes. A few stunted and ragged bushes hung on amongst the stones, and there were scattered patches of wiry, sparse grass; apart from that, it was a world of bare rock, scree and stone-dust. Ahead, a score of jagged pinnacles dominated the skyline, sharp-backed ridges splaying out from them. The mountains of the Car Criagar were massive, old, broad-shouldered; these Karkyre Peaks were like serrated blades newly stabbed up from out of the earth.

The desolation, and perhaps the leaden quality of the light, worked on the minds of Orisian and all his companions. There was no talking. The only sounds were the persistent flat roar of the river below, the clatter of hoofs and the occasional eerie cries of ravens. Ess'yr, Varryn, Yvane and Hammarn had all refused to ride. They walked in the midst of the column of horsemen. The two Kyrinin were cowled, the better to conceal themselves from the curious — and potentially hostile — eyes of observers. Orisian was surprised at how much human life there was along this road, even now that they had reached such barren terrain. In the last day they had passed a dozen hamlets or solitary huts. The inhabitants were uniformly silent and hard-eyed, watching them pass from the shadows of doorways, as if they resented this disturbance of their solitude.

Rounding a turn, Orisian's eye was caught by a strange structure a short way above the road. It looked as though someone had tried to build a squat house out of great flat-sided boulders, only to be defeated by the sheer mass of their intended materials. Even at this distance, writing and symbols were faintly visible, cut into the weathered face of the rocks.

"What's that?" Orisian asked.

Bannain, riding just ahead on a short-legged mountain pony, glanced up.

"It's Morvain's tomb. He died here, retreating from Highfast after the failure of his siege. Looted out long ago. There's nothing left within. So I'm told, anyway."

"I'm surprised the Aygll Kings let it stand."

"Well, it was in the last days of their rule. It was Lerr, the Boy King, that Morvain rebelled against, and he'd already lost his grip on most of these lands. The child was dead himself within a year or two of Morvain's death."

"Hard times," Rothe muttered from behind them.

"Yes," acknowledged Bannain, then shrugged and gave his reins a casual shake. "No more so than these, though. This world's not given to resting easy."

They rode on. The road became ever more like a broad ledge cut into the side of a cliff. Walls of bare rock loomed above them. Below, a smaller river flowed into the Kyre: a tumultuous confluence that had fashioned a bowl in which to seethe. The road swung north and followed the lesser tributary up into the mountains.

Orisian rode beside Ess'yr. She was walking well, with no obvious sign of the broken ribs that had hampered her since their descent from the Car Criagar. Her face was hidden from him, lost in the depths of her capacious hood.

"I don't much like this place," Orisian said. "Not enough trees."

She said nothing for a few paces, then: "No. Not enough. It is said the God Who Laughed never walked this land, because its edges hurt his feet."

"A wise god. We'll not be here long, I hope. A day or two,

perhaps, and then on to Kolglas. You'll be able to see my home."

"I have seen it. From across the water. Close enough. And Inurian told me of it; the castle in the sea, he called it."

"Yes," murmured Orisian. "The castle in the sea." What made him imagine that this woman would care what place he called home? She was a creature of the forest and the hills, her heart as unmoved by castles and stone walls as anyone's could ever be. And she had been lover to a *na'kyrim*; a man as gentle and wise as any Orisian had ever known. There was nothing he could offer her that would compare with the memory of Inurian, or make good his absence. Still, he longed for her goodwill. He lacked the tools to secure it, but that did not blunt the desire.

"I owe you a bow," he said to her.

That made Ess'yr glance at him, a quick tip of her head sideways and up. He glimpsed her cheek, the thin line of her lips.

"I should have thought of it sooner," he said. "You broke it saving me from the Horin-Gyre Bloodheir; broke it on his face. If you hadn't, I might not be here now. I would have got you another one in Kolkyre if I'd thought of it."

He caught a grunt – possibly contemptuous – from Varryn's direction. Ess'yr's brother was walking a few paces behind them. It was easy to forget how acute a Kyrinin's hearing was. Ess'yr turned her eyes back to the road and the hood once more hid her face.

"I do not need a Huanin bow," she said. "I will have another in time. It will be a Fox bow, made on Fox lands."

"Or a White Owl bow, from a dead hand," said Varryn, just loud enough for Orisian to hear. He glanced back over his shoulder, unable to disguise his irritation. He did not want Varryn eavesdropping on every word he uttered to Ess'yr.

"You'll have your chance for revenge soon," he said.

"Not revenge," Ess'yr said. "Balance. The enemy have killed many Fox. Therefore many of the enemy must die."

"I don't know if it works, that kind of balancing."

"There is no other kind."

Dusk came on quickly. Ravens were flocking in the darkening sky, tumbling around the peaks, plummeting in to ledges on the cliff faces. Their harsh cries carried a long way. The little river – now far below them – disappeared into the gloom that settled across the valley floor. Its voice, by turns hissing and chattering as it churned its way down out of the mountains, could still be heard, though. Somewhere high up on the other side of the valley, rocks came loose and tumbled, rattling, over scree.

Orisian was starting to become concerned, fearing a night to be spent under the cold stars, when distant points of light came into view ahead. Bannain had assured them that they would reach shelter before nightfall, but only now was Orisian able to wholly believe it.

The inn was like no other he had seen before. As they drew closer, he struggled to tell where the disordered, boulder-strewn mountainside ended and the building began. It was clear that the inn had once been a huge structure with workshops and stables and cottages built around and onto it. Most of them had collapsed into rubble and ruin, crumbling back into the rock of which they had been made. Amidst this wreckage, the inn itself still stood. Slate tiles had slipped off part of its roof, and lay in a grey pile at the roadside. Oil lamps burned in some of the windows; others were dark and shuttered.

Torcaill, the man Taim Narran had assigned to lead Orisian's escort, brought them to a halt a little way short of the inn.

"I'll send a few men in first, sire," he said to Orisian. "It will not take long."

Orisian almost told him to forego such precautions. What possible danger could there be here, in this forgotten and abandoned place? But Torcaill took his responsibilities seriously, and Orisian

had no wish to belittle that. He nodded in assent. Torcaill led half
a dozen men on to the inn.

"What's he up to?" Yvane asked. The *na'kyrim* had come up to
stand beside Orisian's horse, her hand resting on its neck. The
animal looked round at her, but found her uninteresting and
hung its head in a vain search for grass.

"Just having a look before we go in," Orisian said.

Yvane grunted. "Does he fear some mountain goat waits
within to stick you with its horns? No . . . wait, perhaps it's lurking under one of the beds, ready to nip at your ankles?"

"You're in a lively mood," Orisian observed, looking down at
her.

"No, I'm not. I'm exhausted. It makes me light-headed, all
this walking."

"Ride, then. You've been offered a share of a horse's back more
than once."

"She's worried she'll fall off and crack her head," Rothe suggested, easing his horse past them.

Yvane glared after the shieldman as he drew up in front of the
inn and dismounted a little stiffly. He stretched, digging his fingers into the small of his back. The light falling from the
windows was bright now, the surrounding mountains almost
wholly lost in darkness. There were clouds enough to hide the
moon. Orisian shivered and puffed out his cheeks. The muffled
sound of boots thumping on stairs and floorboards came from the
inn. Rothe stood in the doorway and peered inside. After a
moment or two, he stepped back to allow Torcaill to emerge. The
warrior waved.

"Looks like you'll get a good night's rest, anyway," Orisian said
to Yvane. "Plenty more walking tomorrow, I expect, so no doubt
you'll need it."

"Not so much," Yvane muttered dolefully. "Highfast's not far
now."

"You're not looking forward to it."

The *na'kyrim* glanced up at him, and then away. It was a self-effacing, hesitant sort of movement; not what Orisian associated with Yvane at all. He almost felt sorry for her, but suspected that she would not welcome such a sentiment.

"Not greatly," she acknowledged. "Too late for changing minds, though."

The innkeeper who greeted them within was tall and thin, narrow eyes peering out from beneath bushy eyebrows. He gave no sign of pleasure at this unexpected glut of customers.

"There's beds for an even dozen of you," he said in the thick, lethargic accent of the Peaks. "The rest'll be bedding down in the ruins. And I've not enough food for so many. Most'll be feeding yourselves, too."

"That's fine," Orisian said, paying little attention. He went back outside, peered around in the darkness. He searched amongst the indistinct crowd of men and horses. He wanted to ask Ess'yr if she and Varryn would sleep inside. But the Kyrinin had already separated themselves from the others. They were slipping away, sinking into the night, moving into the thicket of broken walls and fallen roofs behind the inn. He stared after them even when the darkness had taken them from him.

"Is there broth?"

Orisian turned around. Old Hammarn was there, his hands clasped together.

"Always good after a long journey," the *na'kyrim* said. "And before, too."

"Come," Orisian smiled. "Let's go and see what we can find."

They reached Highfast the next day, amidst sleet and gusting winds. The great fortress loomed out of the belligerent sky, stark and grey and hard. It stood on a pinnacle of rock, capping the peak with a carapace of battlements and turrets. The road swept up to it around the exposed haunches of another, loftier mountain, and then threw a side-branch across a narrow stone bridge to the gates.

The wind roared at them and lashed them with waves of wet snow as they crossed that bridge. Orisian looked only briefly to the side. The dizzying drop and the dark rock slopes far below resolved him to lock his eyes upon the gates ahead. They were tall and narrow. Their wood was scarred and pitted and cracked; the skin of their iron banding was split and rusted. Above them, Highfast's fortifications soared. Walls and towers were crowded thickly onto their precarious perch, so that it seemed half a dozen castles had been crammed and folded into one.

Bannain, riding at the head of the column with Torcaill, shouted something up at the turrets flanking the gate. The words were snatched away by the wind and Orisian did not hear them. There was no obvious response. Orisian pressed his chin into his chest and hunched his shoulders. He was wondering whether to dismount and put his horse between him and the wind when the gates opened. Torcaill led them in.

They rode through a tunnel. A few men with lanterns baffled against the wind lined the way, watching the band of riders with clear suspicion and puzzlement. Hoofs rang on the smooth stone floor and the echoes raced back and forth along the passage like a peal of harsh, tuneless bells. There was another gate, creaking back on ancient hinges, and then they emerged into a small courtyard.

It felt as if they were at the bottom of a great pit. On every side walls thrust up, climbing higher than anything made by men that Orisian had ever seen, save perhaps the Tower of Thrones itself. In places cliffs and boulders had been incorporated into the body of the castle, so that stonework flowed around outcroppings of the jagged pinnacle. There was a keep that seemed to have been built onto the face of a crag. No lights showed at its windows, despite the day's gloom. The rushing clouds above looked very distant.

Orisian gazed around in wonder. He had not expected Highfast to be such a strange and massive beast. He had never seen, or heard of, its like. Except, perhaps, for Criagar Vyne. That ruined city in the Car Criagar must once have had something of the same bleak magnificence, the same deep-rooted defiance of mountain and elements. But Criagar Vyne was empty; defeated. People still lived here in Highfast, still sheltered in its towering protection.

A short man, rotund but wearing a warrior's jerkin and sword, came out from a doorway and conferred with Torcaill. They both turned and looked in Orisian's direction. He swung himself out of the saddle and walked forwards, Rothe following close behind.

"I am Herraic Crenn dar Kilkry-Haig, sire," the short warrior said, dipping his head respectfully. "Captain of Highfast. It is an honour to have such visitors. I fear we're not well enough provisioned to offer you the hospitality you deserve."

The man sounded nervous to Orisian. "We don't need much other than a fire and some food. We'll be moving on in a day or two."

He ducked and winced as cold water, shed in fat droplets from some protrusion on the walls far above, spattered down onto the back of his neck.

"Come, come," Herraic said quickly. "Let's get a roof over your head. My men will stable your horses and get your escort into the barracks. We've room enough for them, I think. Half my men are out chasing rumours of wights in the forest east of here. They'll likely not be back for days."

Torcaill went to see to the settling of his men; Rothe, Ess'yr, Varryn and the two *na'kyrim* followed Orisian. The passageways through which Herraic and Bannain led them were narrow and rough-cut. They curved and twisted, rose and fell, in a way that left Orisian disorientated. And no matter how deep they went into the rock, there was still a breeze on his face; cold, wet air still stirred, tugging at the flames of the torches that Herraic and his men carried. The sound of the wind was distant but always present, a low tone at the edge of his hearing.

They emerged in a gloomy, low-ceilinged chamber. There were slitted windows in the far wall, admitting a little muted daylight. Other than that, the only illumination was from a brazier in which charcoal glowed, throwing off so much heat that it was almost shocking after the long hours on the road. Orisian and the others clustered around, spreading their hands towards the brazier. Hammarn chuckled to himself in pleasure at the warmth. A pair of serving boys came with jugs of tepid wine to share out. Bannain the *na'kyrim* murmured something to Herraic and disappeared through a narrow portal without waiting for an answer. Herraic himself edged diffidently closer to Orisian.

"You're here for the *na'kyrim*, are you, lord?"

Orisian nodded.

"There's no other reason for anyone to come, of course," the Captain of Highfast murmured. "Not to say that many come to see Cerys and the rest either, mind you. Is there . . . should I know what brings you?"

Orisian hesitated. He had no real reason to be anything other than open with this man, yet found himself cautious. If whatever messengers Lheanor had sent ahead had been reticent, there was no need to undo that restraint. "Nothing of great consequence. I am heading for Kolglas, and wanted to speak with the *na'kyrim* here on my way. That's all."

"Ah, yes. Of course. Well, we will offer what comfort we can."

"I didn't mean to be a burden. There're not as many of you here as I expected."

Herraic gave a soft, wry laugh. "Not many. The loneliest posting, this. The garrison's only two dozen here, sire. No need for any more. No one to man the walls against, you see."

"It must be strange, so few of you in such a huge fortress."

"Oh, it suits some better than others, that's true. It must have been quite a place, once. Filled with noise and bustle, hundreds of people. The road went from here all the way to Drandar, you know. The richest road in all the Kingship, some say. Enough wagons on it every day to carry all the wealth of a King. That's what I heard." He gave an almost apologetic smile, a little shrug. "Now . . . well, you see for yourself. There's no road, no riches. It's just where folk like me get washed up."

"And the *na'kyrim*? How many of them?"

The question clearly caught Herraic unawares, though he tried to hide it.

"I couldn't say with certainty, sire. We see little of one another. They have the lower chambers, cut into the rock itself, and a few rooms high in the keep. Highfast is so large that . . . well, I meet with the Elect once or twice a month. Other than that . . ." He gave a faint shrug. His unease at the thought of those meetings with the Elect was evident.

Orisian knew well enough, from Inurian's residence in Kolglas, that even sharing a roof for years was not enough to make some people comfortable with *na'kyrim*. No matter how self-evidently close the bonds between Inurian and Kennet, Orisian's father, had become, there had been those who never reconciled themselves to the presence of a *na'kyrim* in the castle.

"You might want to give some thought to the lodging of those Kyrinin you brought with you, sire," Herraic whispered, leaning close to Orisian. "It would be best if they took shelter amongst the *na'kyrim* while you're here. There might be some . . . well, some unrest amongst my men if we quarter them with the garrison."

Orisian looked across to Ess'yr and Varryn. They were both watching the Captain of Highfast. Ess'yr's face was as placid, as calm, as always, but he could not help wondering whether somewhere beneath that fair exterior, lit orange by the radiant charcoal, anger and resentment lurked. She and her brother had saved his life more than once, yet still met with nothing but suspicion and hostility wherever they went in his company. Perhaps they expected nothing more; perhaps it was only Orisian who felt wounded on their behalf by such things.

"I don't think you could whisper quietly enough to keep what you say from their ears, you know," he murmured to Herraic.

The stocky warrior glanced in the direction of the two Kyrinin. They stared back. The tattoos on Varryn's face had a savage look to them in that light.

"No," Herraic muttered, nodding to Orisian. "No, of course. Still, you might want to think on it."

"I will."

Bannain reappeared in the doorway.

"Come, Thane," the *na'kyrim* said. "The hidden Highfast awaits you."

VIII

They went deeper, along narrow, rough-hewn passageways, down dark stairwells. There was a door, massive and thick, that took them into a wider corridor where there were oil lamps and a paved floor. And then Orisian saw something that brought him to a halt: a child. She was running towards them, smiling. She came on light, quick feet, arms outstretched and trailing the fine sleeves of an old, faded dress. A *na'kyrim* child; a pale, almost luminous presence amidst the shadows and weight of the fortress.

Orisian stopped so abruptly that Yvane walked into his back. She grunted in irritation and looked over his shoulder.

"What's the matter?" she demanded.

"Nothing. It's just . . . I've never seen one before."

"One? The child? Ha! Did you imagine we sprang into being already haggard and aged?"

Orisian shook his head. He watched the young girl. She had wrapped her arms around Bannain's thigh and grinned up at him as he ran a hand over her hair.

"It's not surprising she's the first you've seen," Yvane said, more gentle now. "Too many walls between Huanin and Kyrinin these days. Half the babies that do get themselves born are probably killed as soon as they've drawn breath, still wrapped in their swaddling cloths. That's the world we've all made for ourselves. That's why, whatever its faults, I'd not unmake Highfast. There's few enough places that girl could find safety: here, Koldihrve, Dyrkyrnon, one or two others."

"How many children are there here?"

"I don't know. When I left? Only three or four. We're a rare breed, and growing rarer."

The girl walked with them to the end of the corridor. She held Bannain's hand. He halted outside a door and knelt to whisper something to her. She laughed and nodded, and then darted into the room beyond when Bannain held the door open for her.

"Our herald will announce our arrival," he said with a smile.

Within, half a dozen *na'kyrim* were waiting. All were dressed alike in plain robes; all had the same still, erect posture. The little girl had run to the side of a woman who wore a crude, thick iron chain around her neck. The child spoke a few soft and excited words, then moved to stand apart, an expression of shy anticipation on her face. The woman took in Orisian and his motley companions with a single sweeping gaze. Orisian drew breath to speak, but she settled her cold attention upon Bannain.

"You left alone," she said, "yet return with a multitude."

To Orisian's ears, her tone was level, impassive. It appeared that Bannain detected more pointed sentiments, for his shoulders sagged a little and he stepped forwards with none of the brashness that Orisian had come to expect of him.

"It seemed wise, Elect. It seemed prudent."

"Prudent," the Elect repeated. Her eyes were on Orisian now. "You are the Thane of the Lannis-Haig Blood?"

"Yes." His voice came out with less authority than he would have liked. "I was told I might find good counsel here," he went on with what he hoped was more firmness, "but if we are not welcome, we will not trouble you. There are other places I should be."

"You are not unwelcome," the woman said, though her tone hardly lent credence to the words. She signalled Bannain to stand amongst the little group of *na'kyrim* gathered around her, and he obeyed without hesitation. "I am Cerys, Elect of the Council of Highfast. You, Thane, I now know. And Yvane, of course. Who else has Bannain brought with him?"

"Rothe, my shieldman. Ess'yr and Varryn, of the Fox. And Hammarn, who came with us from Koldihrve."

It was only Hammarn, Orisian noted, who seemed to earn some softening of the Elect's demeanour. She nodded in the old man's direction, to his embarrassment. He smiled, then frowned, then took on an empty, wide-eyed expression as if he had no idea what to do with his face.

"You have strange travelling companions, for a Thane of the Haig Bloods," Cerys observed with a hint of a narrow smile.

"So I've been told before."

It took Orisian a moment to realise that what he felt – a nagging sourness of the moment – was the crumbling of unacknowledged hopes. He had, without recognising it in himself, hoped he might find Inurian here: an echo of the warmth and understanding that he remembered. Ever since he had discovered that Highfast had once been Inurian's home, he had vaguely imagined it to be a place of welcome and safety; a place suffused with all those things he had lost since Winterbirth, and since Inurian's death. He felt, as those imaginings withered away, sadder and more like a child than he had done in a long time. He blinked at Cerys, and did not know what more to say.

"And what are these matters on which you seek our counsel, Thane?" she asked him softly.

"He came to speak of Aeglyss, Cerys," Yvane said before Orisian could reply. "He's as close to a friend as you'll find outside the Tower of Thrones, and he'll hear more of what you've got to say than Lheanor would."

Slowly, deliberately the Elect turned her head to meet Yvane's gaze with her own. To Orisian's surprise, and unease, it was Yvane who looked away first.

"We did not expect to see you here again, Yvane. How many years have you been gone?"

"I told him he would be welcome here, even if I was not," Yvane said. Still she kept her eyes down. "I'd rather you didn't make me a liar."

"Your preferences, and your reputation, are not our first concern here," Cerys said.

"Elect," Orisian said, a touch more sharply than he intended, "I came here because of what Bannain told me in Kolkyre. I wanted to learn what you know of Aeglyss, because he stands among enemies who have killed my family and my friends, and because *na'kyrim* whom I trust – Yvane, and Inurian too – judged him a danger to me and to my people. If you are willing to talk to me, I will listen. If you are not, tell me now so that I can go where I am needed."

Cerys regarded him in silence for a moment or two. Rothe was glowering at her. The Elect's hand had gone to the chain around her neck, her elegant fingers brushing the dark metal.

"Has Herraic given you chambers above?" she asked.

"He's looking after the warriors who came with me. I would be grateful if we" – he glanced around, including Rothe, Ess'yr and the others – "could be found somewhere to rest here, with you."

"Of course," the Elect said, with a subtle nod. "We will find room for you. I don't suppose Herraic particularly wants *na'kyrim* or Kyrinin taking up room in his keep. I'll send him a message that we'll take care of you. Bannain will show you where to go. You can rest a little; we'll have some food brought to you. Then I will talk with you, Thane, and we will see what help we might be to one another."

There were no windows in the chamber that Bannain found for them. The walls were damp, and every crevice seemed to have a spider's web woven into it. It was as much cave as room. A dozen simple beds lined one wall. Rothe prodded one of the thin mattresses after Bannain had left them. It looked as smooth as a bag of hazelnuts.

"Straw," the shieldman concluded. "Doesn't smell too good."

"It'll do," Orisian said. "We'll not be more than one night here, with any luck."

He sat on one of the beds, but promptly rose and moved further away from the oil lamp Bannain had left. The orange flame at its wick was giving off tendrils of noisome black smoke.

"I'm sure there'd be room for you with Torcaill and the rest," Rothe muttered as Orisian tested another bed. "Herraic'd find better quarters for a Thane than this."

Orisian glanced at Ess'yr and Varryn. The two Kyrinin were silently and methodically bedding down at the far end of the chamber. As always, they ignored the beds and made camp on the floor.

"No, Rothe. This'll do. One night; that's all."

Rothe looked disappointed, but stretched himself out on his bed. He winced as he folded his injured arm across his lap.

"You might get some help for that here, you know," Yvane observed. "Amonyn, one of the Council: he's a gifted healer. It works better when the wound's fresh, mind you, but he can fashion more mending out of the Shared than—"

"There's no need for that," Rothe said hurriedly. "It's well on the way to healing itself. I don't need that kind of help."

Yvane shrugged and sat down opposite Orisian.

"I thought we might have a warmer welcome," he said to her.

Yvane raised her fine eyebrows. "That was not so cold, by the standards of this place. Believe me, short of being *na'kyrim* yourself, you could not hope for much more. You're a stranger, come to them in fraught times. It's frightening for them. Don't forget, there's not many here have seen as much of the world as Inurian did, or as I have. They're not used to outsiders. They hate any disturbance of the tight little circles they walk in here. Round and round and—"

"Frightening?" Orisian interrupted her.

"Of course they're frightened," Yvane said, and Orisian wondered if that was truly a hint of scorn he heard in her voice; and whether it was meant for him or for the *na'kyrim* of Highfast. "Do I need to list the reasons for you? There's war, and not far away. Armies are marching hither and thither, none of them – whatever cause they fight for – filled with friends of *na'kyrim*. You turn up here with more warriors than have visited in however many years: a Thane, and one they've had no chance to take the measure of.

"Worse than all that, there's Aeglyss. Everyone here is sick. You shouldn't forget that, even if you can't understand it, can't feel it. I'm sick. His malice taints the Shared, and everyone here can feel it, every hour of every day. I'm tired before I get out of bed in the morning, because from the first instant of wakefulness I can hear his strength rumbling in the back of my mind. You folk with your pure blood, the gates of your minds are shut against the Shared; barred and bolted. Us poor *na'kyrim*, we're open. There's nothing between us and him. And he's a horror, believe me."

Orisian regarded her thoughtfully for a moment or two. She was afraid, he realised. What she described might or might not be true of Cerys and the others here in Highfast, but it was certainly true of Yvane herself. For days now, she had been on edge, and fear was part of what had put her there.

"I do believe you," he said, hanging his head.

"Good." She said it softly, almost gently.

Behind her, Hammarn was laying out half-finished woodtwines on the bed. He hummed to himself as he did so, nodding in agreement with some silent internal statement. Yvane glanced at him and smiled sadly.

"*Na'kyrim* are no more perfect than anyone else. But we are different. There are kinds of understanding here that you'll not find anywhere else. There is wisdom, if you can dig it out. You believed in Inurian, didn't you? Trusted him?"

Orisian nodded.

"Remember that. What you believed in is here too, even if it's not as obvious as it was in him. If you want to understand what Aeglyss means, this is the only place you might find an answer."

"I know. I wouldn't be here if I didn't know that."

Two young *na'kyrim* brought platters of simple food. They were nervous. They averted their eyes, and watched the floor.

"I was told to wait," one of them said. "When you have eaten, I am to escort the Thane to the library. The Elect will see him there. Just the Thane. No one else."

The smell was powerful, and instantly recognisable: the dry, dense admixture of parchment, bindings and dust. Orisian knew it from Inurian's room in Castle Kolglas, this aroma of books and manuscripts. Here in Highfast's Scribing Hall it was far stronger, far more pervasive, as if it had accumulated in layers in the air over all the years since the *na'kyrim* had first come here. The ceiling of the hall was high, yet the smell filled the cavernous space.

The far wall of the great chamber was natural stone, smoothed and polished by human hands but still part of the fabric of the peak on which Highfast stood. Small windows had been cut high up and they shed a muted light on the racks and shelves of books, scrolls and manuscripts. There were balconies on the wall opposite them, with dark tunnels burrowing back into the heart of the mountain. A few *na'kyrim* sat at tables, most of them writing, one or two simply reading from massive tomes. None of them looked up at Cerys and Orisian's entry.

"This is the main reason for our presence here," said the Elect. "The reason why Grey Kulkain granted our kind leave to make this our refuge."

Orisian looked around. He could hear the scratch of quills on parchment, the creak of some heavy leather-bound book being opened.

"We gather what writings we can," Cerys continued. "Copy those that are fading or damaged. We seek to learn from the collected wisdom of those who created the books, of course, but our most important duty is preservation." She picked up a slim, worn volume from a shelf and turned it in her hands, showing Orisian the wear and splits in its binding. "Knowledge is a fragile thing. Almost nothing remains of the Second Age of the world. Even the early parts of the Third are misty. The War of the Tainted and the Storm Years were enough to cost us a great deal: our histories, our memories of the Kingships and of what came before them are poor."

"I've never seen so many books," Orisian said.

"Nowhere else in the world are so many gathered together, I think." Cerys regarded him sternly. "Can you read?"

"Yes. Well enough."

"That's good. I imagine Inurian saw to that. A Thane should be able to read. There've been some who couldn't. Tavan, your uncle's father, was one, I believe. And if Thanes can't read, what's the point of all this?" The Elect gestured at the studious *na'kyrim* at their tables.

"If you rely only on Thanes to read your books and learn the lessons of the past, you might be disappointed by the results," Orisian murmured.

Cerys sniffed in sad amusement. "So young, and already so harsh in his judgement of his peers."

Orisian shrugged, unsure whether she was mocking him. With Cerys, he sensed none of the undercurrent of concern, even affection, that sometimes leavened Yvane's brusqueness. The Elect seemed far more distant, far more removed from passion or emotion. If his suspicion that Herraic Crenn did not relish his regular meetings with this woman was correct, Orisian had some sympathy with the man.

"Where I come from, people rely on the Thane, the Blood," he said, "but they rely on themselves too. And you won't find much affection there for the Thanes of Haig, or Ayth or Taral. Certainly no faith in their wisdom."

Cerys grunted and carefully replaced the book she had been holding in its place on the shelf.

"I imagine you're right. I don't know the Glas valley myself, though I've read Hallantyr's writings. He travelled quite widely, you know, eighty years ago or thereabouts. Through Kilkry lands, up the Glas, into the Car Criagar. He wrote of it well, and perceptively I thought." She glanced at Orisian. "There is some creation here, you see, not just copying. Hallantyr is not the only one of Highfast's people to have told new tales, recorded new insights. Yvane has probably told you otherwise. Her . . . frustrations coloured her view of us."

"I don't remember her saying much about it. She told me I should come here, so perhaps her opinion of you isn't as harsh as you think."

"Oh, I doubt she has changed so very much. Opinions seldom change a great deal once deep foundations have been laid."

Orisian went on between the ranks of tables. He found himself walking softly, unwilling to disturb the place's restful peace. Over the shoulder of one of the scribes, he glimpsed elegant script trailing from a quill, colonising blank parchment. The *na'kyrim* appeared unaware of Orisian's presence, her labour absorbing all of her attention. The writing was in a language that Orisian did not recognise. He drifted back towards the Elect.

"Did Inurian work here?" he asked her quietly.

She nodded. "Often. Somewhere here you could find his words, preserved."

"Why did he leave Highfast? I would have thought . . . it seems the kind of place he would have liked."

Orisian caught a brief flicker of emotion in the Elect's face: a stifled wince of sadness. She was not entirely empty of feeling, then.

"He did like it," Cerys said. "But he had his curiosities. He was less . . . wary of the world than most of us here are." She lapsed into silence, gazing up at the distant little windows. They were darkening now, as night drew near.

"And Yvane? Why did she leave?" Orisian asked.

Cerys blinked, turned her grey eyes to him for only a moment before looking away.

"Have you asked her that?"

"No. Not really."

"Best to do so, rather than seeking the answer from others."

Orisian folded his arms across his chest.

"What wisdom is there here that I can draw on, then?" he asked. "What can I learn from all of this that will help me?"

"If you're to learn anything it'll be from those of us who have done the reading already. And, perhaps, from the mind of one who sleeps in the Great Keep."

"Why show me this, then?"

Cerys smiled, and her calculating eyes narrowed. "Because you are a Thane. A Thane who knew and, I think, loved Inurian. You are to be one of the rulers of the world – whatever's left for you to rule over once all this is done – and this place needs the affection of rulers. Your father . . . he was a good man, you know. He sent us a gift each year, to help clothe and feed us. To keep our work here alive."

Orisian looked out over the ranks of tables. He had not known that about his father. Just one more of the many things he seemed to be learning, too late, about people he had thought he knew. One of the *na'kyrim* scribes had set aside his book and fallen asleep, his head resting on the back of his crossed hands.

"That's for later," he murmured. "Another time. Now there is a war to be fought. And I was told that I might learn things here – things about the *na'kyrim* who aids my enemies – that would help me in that."

Cerys regarded her feet, poking out from beneath the hem of her long robe, for a pensive moment and then turned on her heel.

"Very well. It's late, Thane. You must be tired. I know I am. Rest now, and in the morning you will meet the Dreamer. That's where the answer to some of your questions lies."

IX

Ammen Sharp hated the mountains. He hated the unruly horse he rode, and the bitter rain that fell upon him. He hated his rumbling hunger. It had been so long since he had slept that his head felt as though it was stuffed with feathers. The place where the dog had bitten his leg throbbed. But still he rode on, wrestling with his recalcitrant mount, hoping that soon, somehow, this would all be over.

Word that the Shadowhand had left Kolkyre spread so quickly around the city, riding a wave of relief, that Ammen Sharp had known of it within hours. He soon learned that Mordyn Jerain had gone east, accompanied by only a few warriors. Ammen did not care where the Chancellor was going, or why. He knew precious little of what roads led where, or which towns lay in which direction. The sum of his understanding resided in the names that Kolkyre's three gates bore: the road from the Skeil Gate went to Skeil Anchor, that from the Donnish Gate to Donnish and that from the Kyre Gate, by which the Shadowhand had departed . . . well, that went up the Kyre River. Where it ended did not matter to Ammen. His sole concern was whether he could follow the Chancellor.

At first, when he heard that the Shadowhand was gone, he had been seized by panic. It seemed that he had lost whatever slender chance there had been of avenging his father's death. To his shame, he had cried briefly, huddled inside the crumbling kiln he had taken as his hiding place, clutching his knees to his chest. He cursed himself for a fool, a child, and a weakling. Anger dried up his tears.

Once he thought about it with a cooler head, he knew what he needed: a horse. He was a bad rider but he could probably stay in a saddle for a trot, perhaps even a canter. Ochan had thought a son of his should know at least that much. He had said more than once that a man never knew when a horse might be just the thing he needed to put his troubles behind him. Ammen saw the sense in that, as he did in everything his father had said, though he had never seen Ochan in a saddle himself.

He considered stealing a mount inside the city but quickly discounted the idea. From the moment the recent flood of strangers – warriors from every Blood, pedlars, thieves, dispossessed farmers and woodsmen from the Glas valley – had started lapping around Kolkyre's walls anyone with anything worth protecting had been buying themselves guards. Every stable he could think of was almost certain to be protected. The city's gates were, in any case, choked with attentive sentries these days, and Ammen knew he did not have the look of the rightful owner of a riding horse. He must, he reasoned, leave on foot, and find the mount he needed beyond the walls.

Hours later, trudging down a muddy track in the near-dark of a cold evening, he had doubted his choice. He was already tired, even then, and those open spaces had made him feel vulnerable and exposed. He missed the sheltering presence of buildings, alleys and crowds. There were too many noises that he did not recognise, out here amongst the fields and ditches and copses: animal sounds, the creaking of branches or rustling of leaves. And smells: the stink of manure, the wet, green scent of weed-choked field drains.

But fortune had smiled upon Ammen in the night, and he found a solitary horse shut up in a big shed. A dog had come at him, and torn his leggings and gashed his leg. He had killed it with his knife. There had been shouts behind him as he rode away into the darkness, but no pursuit. He almost killed himself without the aid of any irate farmer, since the saddle he had hurriedly flung across the horse's back was not properly fastened and the stirrups were far too long for him. When he finally found the courage to stop and dismount so that he could try to rearrange everything, he almost lost the horse. It took all his strength to hold it. Since that terrifying moment he had stayed astride the animal, ignoring the agonised protest of his muscles.

So now he rode on, beyond exhaustion, up and up into higher, bleaker territories. The rain had soaked him so thoroughly that he expected at any moment to start shivering. The pack on his back felt so heavy it could have been filled with lead, even though there was little in there now save his water skin and little crossbow. The hard stone surface of the road seemed a huge distance below him, and he began to worry about falling off and breaking some bone. Ammen did not know how much further he could go. The only thing that kept him moving onwards was the knowledge that he was on the right track. He had spoken to an old man, thick-accented and suspicious in the doorway of his stone hut, and learned that a party of Haig men had ridden this way.

The rain stopped and the sky cleared as night began to fall. For a multitude of reasons, he did not dare to stop: he would fall still further behind the Shadowhand, his horse would run away as soon as he was off its back, he would fall asleep by the roadside and freeze or be killed by some cutpurse. Held erect only by stubbornness, he remained in the saddle and hoped for a moonlit night. He got it.

Some indeterminate time after the last wink of the sun had been snuffed out on the western horizon, and cold moonlight had turned all the world to shades of grey, he saw the light of windows and torches ahead. So fearful was he now of any encounter with another living thing that he kicked his reluctant mount into a trot so that he might pass by quickly. As he did so, clattering up the road, he saw a clutch of houses on the bare slope above the road, and amongst them an inn. There was a stable block, with guards outside it, and another pair of warriors loitering at the door of the inn. Staring back over his shoulder as he rode away from the hamlet, Ammen discovered his mind to be briefly alive once more. It could only be the Chancellor and his escort, he thought.

Dawn found him slumped over the neck of his horse. The animal stood at the edge of the road, tearing at some spiky grass. Ammen Sharp jerked into wakefulness, almost crying out at the stiff agonies that beset his back and legs. The horse barely stirred beneath him. It was at least as drained as he was. Horrified at his lapse, Ammen looked this way and that. Dawn had only just broken. The light was insipid, and he was deep in the shadow of the mountains to the east. He could remember little of his ride through the night, other than the single bright moment of his discovery of the Shadowhand's party. He could not even be sure how far ahead of them he was.

He did not get much further. The pain in his bone and muscle was too great, the fog in his head too obscuring. He lacked the strength to keep fighting against the horse's desire to stop. Each time it came to a listless halt, it took still more savage work with his heels to force it into motion again. At the point when he was on the verge of surrender, undone by both the animal's weakness and his own, Ammen looked up and saw the ruin of some hut or storehouse a short way up the slope above the road. It was like no building he had ever seen, with huge slabs of flat stone that bore some kind of writing, but it was close, and it was a hiding place.

Groaning at the effort, Ammen swung one leg up and across the horse's haunches and stumbled to the ground. He almost fell. His legs had forgotten how to bear him. As soon as his foot touched the ground, the place where the dog had bitten him flared into protest. The horse turned its head to stare at him and he was afraid that it would kick him. He slapped its rump as hard as he could and it trotted on up the road, the stirrups flapping at its side.

Even the short climb up to the little ruin cost Ammen every sliver of his remaining strength. He slumped down amidst the pile of rocks and wept, out of desolate, despairing fatigue.

* * *

Mordyn Jerain rode the stone track to Highfast in silence. He ignored – often did not even see – the fields and farms and villages, the hills and scree slopes, that passed by. He felt, now and again, the edge of the wind or the chill spray of a shower, but would only tug the hood of his cape a little lower, hunch his shoulders, and then forget the weather once more. His mind was busy. He thought of his precious Tara and his Palace of Red Stone; he wondered what strange sights and people might await him in the castle of the *na'kyrim* to which he travelled; he gnawed away at the question of how best to bring Orisian oc Lannis-Haig to heel; he sketched out, somewhat despondently, a number of ways in which Aewult might mishandle the recovery of the Glas valley.

He and his dozen guards maintained a steady but slow pace. They stopped twice at wayside inns to pass the night. On both occasions, a couple of the guards raced ahead to have the inns cleared and rooms prepared. The Chancellor noted, but found uninteresting, the mixture of awe and antipathy with which the innkeepers and their staff regarded him. He had one of his guards taste all the food that was served before he allowed any of it to pass his own lips. He slept badly, disturbed by uneven mattresses, the creeping of rats in the roof, the pattering of rain. Once, on the second night, he was even woken, after he had finally fallen asleep, by the clatter of some horse trotting by outside in the darkness.

Early on the third and last day of the journey they passed by

the tomb of Morvain. A crude and unimpressive memorial to that
infamous rebel's life and death, Mordyn thought, but still it was
the first thing he had seen since leaving Kolkyre that caught his
interest. The tomb's roof had fallen in. The Chancellor reined in
his horse and looked about him. He took in the bleak, bare walls
of the valley, the foaming river rushing over boulders down
below. It was an austere resting place for the corpse of one supposedly so vital, so vigorous.

Morvain had, in the Shadowhand's view, died a foolish, pointless death. The rebel had driven his army to the brink of
starvation maintaining his unsuccessful siege of Highfast. Finally
admitting defeat and leading them back down this road, he had
been thrown by his horse and soon died of his injuries. All in the
cause of rebelling against a Kingship that was already failing, and
of besieging a castle that was not only famously impregnable but
also, by then, unimportant. There could be few more pointed
illustrations of the need to choose one's battles with care.

Mordyn could see that there were inscriptions on some of the
jumbled rocks of the tomb. He was almost tempted to dismount
and clamber up there to see what they said. It would be fitting if
they were homilies on the fate awaiting those whose ambition
outran their judgement, but that seemed more than a little
unlikely.

The Shadowhand turned away. One of his escort was pointing
up the track. Frowning, Mordyn looked, and saw a single riderless horse standing dejectedly in the road some way ahead.

He lifted a heel to nudge his own horse onwards. Before he
could jab it back into the animal's flank, one of his guards was
shouting.

"There's someone up there."

"What's that?" another of the warriors called out.

Several of them kicked at their mounts, moving closer to
Mordyn.

He looked back up at the tomb. It was almost impossible to

make anything out clearly, but there did seem to be someone rising amidst the rocks: an indistinct, slight figure with something in its hands. The Shadowhand frowned. There was a crack and something was in the air, darting down. The sun came out. Its glare filled his eyes.

Mordyn felt an impact on his head and the world was suddenly smeared, blotched with black and dark red patches. Then he was seeing the sky, seeing the great sheet of cloud that was sliding away from the sun and leaving blue in its wake. He hit the ground and darkness enfolded him.

X

Tyn the Dreamer was a disturbing sight. He looked like a corpse. There was a faint acrid, sickly smell in the room, hovering on the edge of Orisian's senses and whispering of death to him. Tyn's silver hair – sparse but long – was splayed lifelessly across his pillow. His face looked like a skull overlaid with a thin white gauze. There was nothing to say the man was alive save the intermittent feeble rise and fall of his chest beneath the sheets.

Cerys and the other half-dozen *na'kyrim* who accompanied her and Orisian had a quiet, reserved demeanour, as if they were in the presence of some dead, mourned lord. Orisian looked around the small gathering – Cerys had not deigned to tell him the names of these people – and saw sorrow and awe together in their expressions. Turning back to Tyn, he wondered how old the man was. To judge by his emaciated appearance and his discoloured, fragile skin, he might have been over a century, but Orisian knew better than to make assumptions in the strange world of the *na'kyrim*.

"He has weakened a good deal, these last few days," Cerys murmured. "His body is failing, and not even Amonyn can do anything to halt its decline."

"Is he dying?" Orisian asked quietly.

"Perhaps. We do not know. Tyn long ago passed beyond our understanding. You are looking at something – at a man – unique in all the world. His mind travels parts of the Shared we could not follow him into, even before the recent . . . changes made it such a turbulent place."

Cerys leaned over the Dreamer, angling her head so that her ear hovered over his lips. "He chose this," she said, "but when he made his choice, the Shared was a wonder; a benign ocean to be explored. Some of us here envied him greatly, for his ability to give himself up to it so completely. Now, though . . . the ocean he travels has turned against him. Against us all."

One of the other *na'kyrim*, a tall and striking man, more power-fully built than any other of his kind that Orisian had seen, laid a hand on the Elect's back. It looked to Orisian like comfort. Cerys gave no sign that she felt the touch. She straightened.

"Even if we were deaf to the troubles in the Shared, Thane, we would still know that things had gone awry." She extended a long, languid finger towards the Dreamer. "Tyn's rest was once peaceful. Now it cannot even be called rest. He suffers, and his suffering spills over, in his tormented mutterings, his decaying body. He is quiet now, but often he is gripped by spasms. Sometimes he cries out: not words at all, just cries of horror. The change began on that night when we all sensed . . . whatever it was we sensed."

"Aeglyss," Orisian said.

"Yes," one of the other *na'kyrim* said quickly, before Cerys could reply. Orisian looked at her, and saw a young woman with fierce, clear grey eyes. Her features were unremarkable, more humanlike than those of most of her colleagues. Even her skin, though pale, had a certain warm health to it that most *na'kyrim* lacked. Orisian's mind made a swift connection.

"You know him? Aeglyss, I mean. Bannain said there was someone here who knew him long ago, in Dyrkyrnon."

The young woman made to speak, but Cerys held a hand out, stilling her. Orisian saw plainly enough that obedience to the gesture required an effort of self-control.

"This is Eshenna," the Elect said. "She came to us only a few years ago. And before that, yes, she lived in Dyrkyrnon. As did Aeglyss for a time, apparently. When he was a child."

"I did not know him well," Eshenna said, her gaze fixed on Orisian, "but well enough to recognise his presence in the Shared."

"And you know this woman K'rina?" Orisian asked.

"We will talk of Aeglyss later," the Elect said quietly. She was watching the Dreamer now. "There was another reason I wanted you to see Tyn; other news, that has come from his lips, drifting up out of whatever depths he is now lost in." She turned back to Orisian. "He speaks, you see. Our Dreamer speaks."

Orisian glanced back to the Dreamer. Tyn's cheek was twitching, his lips trembling. One of the *na'kyrim* – the man who had comforted Cerys before – sat on the edge of the bed and pressed his palm to the sleeper's forehead. His fingernails, Orisian saw, were as white as any Kyrinin's.

"Yes, I know he speaks," Orisian said. He tried to keep his voice level, calm. It was unsettling to be the object of so many pairs of intent, inhuman eyes, to be beneath the strange weight of their attention. And a vague frustration was building in him. He wanted to speak of Aeglyss now, not later. He had slept badly in the dank dormitory down in the guts of Highfast. Lying awake in the darkness, hearing the drip of water, the scurry of rats, his restless mind had turned from one image to another, and then another, without pause: Inurian, Ess'yr, Kennet. Dawn had found him still tired, and uneasy; doubtful of himself, and of Highfast.

"These days, much of what Tyn says is garbled," Cerys said. "It makes little sense, though it is all shot through with fear, and with distress. Until recently, we had scribes at his bedside all the time to record whatever they could. We had to remove them.

They were becoming . . . sick. Whatever corruption Aeglyss is spreading through the Shared is stronger here. Poor Tyn is a wick, through which it rises and leaks out."

"What is it that you want me to hear, then?" asked Orisian. The desire to leave this small, oppressive room with its decay-tinged air was growing strong within him. Rothe was awaiting him outside; fretting, no doubt, at being refused permission to accompany his charge into this chamber.

"Amongst those fragments Tyn has spoken that make any sense, much concerns the Anain. It accords with what some of us have suspected. They are stirring, Thane. They rouse themselves, and turn their attention outward, as they have not done for centuries."

She watched Orisian intently, searching for some reaction; all of them did. Rather than look back into those penetrating eyes, Orisian stared at Tyn's pallid face.

"Bannain said as much," he murmured.

"The Anain answer to no law but their own," Cerys said. "The rest of us – Huanin, Kyrinin, Saolin, *na'kyrim* – we are like bubbles of air that rise out the Shared, spin about on its surface. The Anain, they are the currents that move it; they are its ebb and flow. If they wake, if they . . . exert themselves, we will all be as powerless as the meekest lamb."

"I understand that. As I can do nothing to prevent it, it seems pointless to fret over it."

"Then you do not fully understand," Cerys said gravely. Orisian thought there was perhaps a trace of disappointment in her voice, but it was so faint that he could not be sure. "The attention of the Anain has been drawn by what happened to Aeglyss, by what he has become. We are all but certain of that. His power, his pain and anger, foul the Shared. That must be to the Anain as it would be to us if the air we breathe, the water we drink, the blood in our veins, were all corrupted. To know their intent or purposes is beyond us, but we fear they rise in order to oppose and destroy Aeglyss."

"Fear?" Orisian echoed. "He's as much to blame for the death of my father as anyone. He imprisoned my sister. Killed Inurian, we think. I do not fear his destruction."

"You should fear the means of it, if that means is the Anain," Cerys snapped. Orisian blinked in surprise at the sudden sharpness of her tone, and the way her words rang in his ears. There was a shivering down his spine, and a tingling in his scalp. For a moment, he was aware of nothing but the Elect's cold, hard face looming large in his vision. She was not human, he reminded himself; and not all *na'kyrim* were as restrained and gentle in their capacities as Inurian had been. He almost took a step backwards, giving in to the thrill of fear that jolted his heart, but he held himself firm.

"Last time the Anain rose," Cerys continued, more levelly, "they turned back armies, drowned a city beneath a sea of trees. They care nothing for our concerns, Thane, and we know next to nothing of theirs. They might raise another Deep Rove over your whole Glas valley. They might slaughter every *na'kyrim* in the world, all in the name of just one whose life offends them."

Orisian drew a deep breath down into his chest. His heartbeat slowed a little.

"You're afraid," he said quietly, facing Cerys. "Yvane told me as much."

He saw the Elect's jaw tighten, and fear fluttered again in his stomach, but he pressed on. "She said you – and her, and all *na'kyrim* – are afraid of Aeglyss, and of what he might do. There's more, though, isn't there? You're afraid of what might happen because of him, too. It might be the Anain, it might be Gryvan oc Haig, when he finds out there's a powerful *na'kyrim* who has sided with the Black Road."

No one replied for what seemed like a long time. Cerys had taken hold of the chain she wore around her neck. She stared at Orisian for a moment, then closed her eyes.

"Yvane ever thought in such ruts," someone said – Orisian was not sure who, though the voice was male.

Cerys smiled briefly, sadly.

"Will you come with me, Thane? Being in this room gives me a cruel headache. Perhaps fresher air is what we need."

He followed her willingly, glad to leave the tight confines of the Dreamer's chamber. Rothe's relief when he saw them emerge was evident. The big shieldman fell in close behind Orisian, who gave him a reassuring smile. The Elect made no protest at Rothe's presence.

He expected that Cerys would lead them back down, through the huge keep and into the passages and chambers cut into the rock of the mountain like the tracks of maggots in an apple. Instead, they climbed. A stone spiral of steps carried them up and disgorged them, unexpectedly, onto the keep's roof.

The wind blasted away all memory of the airless chamber where Tyn lay. It tugged at Orisian's hair and jacket, snapped the Elect's long, heavy dress about her legs. Orisian closed one eye and twisted his head away from the gale. Clouds were surging along overhead, layer upon layer of them flowing across the sky, a turbulent flood of vapours and mists. The convolutions and complexities of Highfast tumbled away beneath them: walls and buildings and battlements spilling down from the keep to crowd the peak.

Cerys, though, led them around the low crenellations to the keep's eastern edge. Holding her hair back from her face, she glanced at Orisian and then gestured out into the void. He leaned cautiously out and looked down. The sheer wall towered over a deep and wild gorge. The cliff faces beneath were precipitous; impregnable. Further out, ranks of jagged, craggy summits jostled to fill the horizon. Pennants of cloud, or perhaps powdery snow, were streaming out from the highest of them: fierce winter flags. Orisian could see not a single tree, no sign of life at all, save one. A great flock of crows was jousting with the wind beneath him. The black birds flashed to and fro, spinning and sweeping in the gale that roared down the gorge. They were like dark flecks of ash flung into the air by a furious fire. Some of them appeared to be disappearing into – and others emerging from – openings in the cliff far below.

Rothe, at Orisian's side, looked over the battlements, but shrank back almost at once. He gently pulled his Thane back, too.

"Inurian had a crow," Orisian said – loudly, against the wind – to Cerys.

The Elect nodded. "Many of us do, here. It's a tradition, all the way back to Lorryn." It seemed to Orisian that she did not need to shout as he did. Her voice reached him despite the raging air all about them. She looked out, let her gaze swing over the mountains and up to the seething clouds.

"This an old place, Thane; an ancient place, ringed about by ancient fears. It's a fitting home for *na'kyrim*, don't you think?" When Orisian said nothing, she looked at him. "I think you are a little disappointed with what you have found here."

It did not sound to Orisian like a question, so he did not reply. The Elect seemed neither angry nor offended.

"Any who choose to live in a place as hard as this must have something to fear, you might think; something driving them, nipping at their heels. And not just here. Where else can you find my kind? Dyrkyrnon, where dry land's rarer than a wise Thane; Koldihrve, out on the edge of everything. We are afraid. Of course we are. *Na'kyrim* know fear as well as we know our own shadows. Come."

She led them into the lee of a turret at the corner of the roof. It took the edge off the cold, though the wind still howled, scouring the stone of the keep.

"In Inurian," Cerys said, "you knew the best of us. He was master of his fear. Or rather, his curiosity mastered his fear, and him. He was, in the end, more interested in what lay beyond these walls than whatever safety might be found within. We who remain sequestered here are not the same as he was. You might think that a failing, but we cannot be other than we are. Other than the world has made us."

"I would not ask you to be," Orisian cried into the gale.

"Whether malice moves her tongue or not, Yvane is right. We are all afraid of Aeglyss, and of what his presence in the world might presage. If men decide that *na'kyrim* are once again a danger, there are too few of us, and we are too feeble, to do anything other than die meekly or flee. If the Anain decide they mislike the course of events, there's no one who could obstruct their will, no matter how strange or heartless its exercising. And if Aeglyss can master the possibilities of what he is becoming, rather than being destroyed by them, we might all be wading through the blood of the slaughtered before long. Do you know what is truly different about him, Thane? Do you understand why we – and you – should find him worthy of our fear?"

Orisian waited for her to give him the answer.

"Because he is an old thing," the Elect shouted above the wind's roar. "Something none of us have seen in our lifetimes. He is a *na'kyrim* so potent, so immersed in the Shared, that he, perhaps alone amongst us all, need not be afraid. Think! What kind of monstrosity must he be, for the Anain themselves to take notice of him? He may not have realised it himself yet, may not have understood what he is, but all of us here can feel it, in our hearts and in our minds. He is the first of our kind in more than three hundred years who might make himself the father of fear, rather than its child."

She held out a hand towards him. He hesitated for only the briefest of moments, then reached out and grasped it. The Elect's eyes narrowed a fraction; her lips tightened. Orisian felt a faint and distant flutter of warmth run across the palm of his hand.

"You feel that?" Cerys asked him.

"Something."

She released him. "You – your race – might be deaf and blind to the Shared, but that does not mean you are beyond its reach. If you were, I could not make you feel even that faint touch. There will be many, not just *na'kyrim*, whose sleep is disturbed by bad dreams now. There will be many whose minds become tinged with an anger not entirely their own.

"No creature whose head holds thoughts is truly separate from the Shared. Some believe it is the very stuff of which your mind is made. That is the country over which Aeglyss casts his shadow. That is where the Anain are rising." She sighed. "It is not only us poor *na'kyrim* who have things to fear in these times, Thane. Aeglyss is poisoning the well from which we all draw our thoughts, our desires. We *na'kyrim* are just the first to catch the taste of it."

On that wind-battered rooftop, with dark clouds rushing overhead and the cries of crows echoing in the bleak gorge, Orisian had a momentary sense of the world as a savagely hostile place. Cerys spoke of things he barely understood, yet for that moment he did not doubt that she was right. Terrible darkness could descend. It was possible, in a world such as this, for horror to be piled upon horror; for even the suffering he had already witnessed to be exceeded. He looked away from the *na'kyrim*'s earnest face. Rothe was standing close by, watching in silence. Orisian shivered.

"Can you tell me how to oppose him, then?" he asked Cerys.

"Only in part," the Elect said. "Perhaps by warning you of the dangers, we can arm you against them in some small way. And there is Eshenna. Talk with her. She believes . . . I cannot say whether she is right or not, but she believes there is something that might be done; chinks in Aeglyss's armour."

Orisian nodded.

"You may find her more like the Inurian you remember," Cerys observed as she led him back towards the stairwell. "She is not yet beset by fear, nor bereft of curiosity about the world. But remember that she is young, by our reckoning. Impetuous. And she remembers Aeglyss. Her thinking is coloured by that."

Highfast sank into another winter twilight as if it was going home, returning to the stuff of which it was made. The gale subsided, clouds congregated and breathed a fine mist across the fortress. Darkness mustered around the turrets and battlements, drifted down the flanks of the towers, pooled in its deep courtyards. The last few crows called out as they descended invisibly out of the night sky towards their roost.

Orisian, Rothe and Yvane walked in silence through the labyrinth of sombre passageways. A torch-bearer lit their way, chasing the shadows ahead of them. In their wake, the dark swept back in, tumbling always at Orisian's heels.

Their guide pushed open a door for them and stood to one side. "I'll wait out here, to light your way back," he said.

Within, they found Eshenna alone in a long, narrow dormitory. She sat on one of the beds, hands resting in her lap. In the tinted light of a single oil lamp, she might almost pass for human, Orisian thought. She stood when he entered, nodded. She looked nervous. He gestured for her to sit down again. He and Yvane sat on the bed opposite her. Rothe waited near to the door.

Orisian did not know whether bringing Yvane had been wise, but he wanted her help in navigating these waters. There was too much here that was unfamiliar and unknown. Yvane was no replacement for Inurian, but she was the closest thing he had to an interpreter.

"You know Aeglyss?" he asked Eshenna, and she nodded gravely.

"I wake every morning with the taste of anger in my mouth, the sound of hatred ringing in my ears. If I close my eyes now, I can feel his bile seeping into my mind. I know Aeglyss. I know this is him."

"Tell me who he is," Orisian said.

"He was a savage child." Eshenna spoke with feeling. "Not in deeds, so much, but in words, and in instincts. Spiteful. He suffered a great deal before he reached Dyrkyrnon. Many of us did, but most overcame those memories, or learned to live with them. He . . . treasured them, almost. He could not separate himself from what had happened to him, what had happened to his parents. The past weighed heavily on him.

"He told us that his father was a warrior of the Black Road, and that the White Owls killed him for loving a Kyrinin woman. His mother died, frozen or starved, on the northern edge of the marshes. She had fled from the clan with Aeglyss when they decided to kill him too. So he told the story, at least."

"But he didn't stay in Dyrkyrnon," Orisian said.

"He did for some years, but he was cast out. He inflicted many small cruelties, and some not so small. A girl . . ." Eshenna winced at the memory. "One girl in particular, Aeglyss desired. She was cold to him, as many of us were, but her coldness pained him in a different way. Much sharper. He would not – could not, I suppose – accept it, or ignore it. It ate away at him. One day he was found, alone in the marsh, crouching by a pool, staring down into the water. He was watching the girl. She was in there, under the surface, on her back. Mouth open. Drowning, without struggling.

"They hauled her out, and managed to save her. Aeglyss never said anything about it, not a word. The girl claimed not to remember what had happened. Whether that was true or not, she was never happy again; she never slept well, or laughed without a shadow in her voice. Everyone knew Aeglyss had . . . made it happen. Even then, the Shared had woken in him more strongly than some of us could understand. Everyone was afraid of what he might do, so they cast him out."

"Would have spared us all some trouble if they'd just killed him," muttered Yvane.

"I think there were some who wanted to. But he was sent away. No one in Dyrkyrnon ever heard of him again, as far as I know."

"Until now, I imagine," Yvane grunted. "I dare say he's back on their minds now."

Eshenna nodded. "They'll not act against him, though, if they can help it. Dyrkyrnon's like Highfast in that: they want no dealings with the wider world, in case it should decide to have dealings with them."

"Well, *I'll* act against him," said Orisian. "Everyone tells me he's a terrible danger, and I believe it, but no one's told me yet what I can do about it. Cerys said you might."

"Perhaps." She glanced from Orisian to Yvane and back again. "There was a woman at Dyrkyrnon – K'rina – who took Aeglyss as her ward, when he first came there. She raised him, and loved him despite all his faults. For some of our kind, you know, our childlessness is a great sorrow. So it was for K'rina. She took Aeglyss as her child. It broke her heart when he was cast out."

She hesitated.

"And . . . ?" Orisian prompted her.

"I know K'rina well. I cared for her, for a time, after Aeglyss left. Now, she is moving. She has left Dyrkyrnon, Thane. She is going to Aeglyss."

"You're certain of that?" Yvane asked quietly.

"It is part of my waking into the Shared. I can sometimes follow the trails left in it by the passage of familiar minds, sometimes trace the outline of distant thoughts. Just as I know, without doubt, that it is Aeglyss whose stench now fouls everything, so I know that K'rina has heard his cry, and will go to him. And he seeks her; longs for her."

Eshenna's confidence was forceful, and convincing, but it still left Orisian uncertain. He glanced at Yvane, whose expression was grave and thoughtful.

Eshenna leaned forwards a little. "It's a slender hope, but better than no hope at all. The last time I sought her, I could not draw near, so violent were the powers churning about her. She is important. To Aeglyss certainly, perhaps therefore to us. So I thought . . ."

Her voice trailed away. She was watching Orisian expectantly, hopefully.

"What is it you're suggesting, then?" he asked her. "That we take her?"

"Yes. She was the only one who could ever talk to him. When he was enraged, she could calm him. She could scold him without earning his hatred. She was the only one – the only one alive – whom he ever loved, as far as I know. He needs her. So take her, and hold her. Make her our ally, not his. Use her against him."

Orisian stared down at the floor. There were dark stains in the seams between the flat stones: mould, or some kind of rot. The stones themselves had a dull gleam, polished by the usage of centuries. He longed for certainty, for clarity. He longed for the lost days when his choices bore consequences of no more weight than parchment. And he longed for the time before this bitter, cruel strand entered his thoughts; the strand that wondered if this woman K'rina could be used to hurt Aeglyss. He looked at Yvane. She was watching Eshenna, but clearly sensed Orisian's gaze.

"Perhaps," she breathed, reluctant and heavy-hearted. "There is no *na'kyrim* in the world, that I know of, who could match what Aeglyss is becoming. None who could force his submission. You need more subtle weapons to oppose him, I think. Perhaps, if he remembers this woman . . . if he is vulnerable to her . . . she might be a wedge to open up some crack in him." She shrugged. "If you hold something precious to your enemy, it gives you some power over him. Isn't that the way these things work?"

Orisian stood up and went to the shuttered window. He could hear the night breezes rubbing themselves over the rock of Highfast. Putting a hand against the ancient wood of the shutters, he could feel the cold of the darkness without.

"Where is she?" he asked without looking round. "Do you know?"

"Less than two days away, I think," Eshenna said. "East of here, a little south. He'll have her soon, if nothing is done."

"Close, then," said Orisian softly. He was not sure, but he thought he could hear rain falling.

"Yes. I believe so."

Orisian turned about and regarded the two *na'kyrim* women.

"You would come, if I went to find this woman? Both of you? I would need you, Eshenna, to find her."

"Of course." He could see her eagerness, even though she kept it on a short leash. As Cerys had said, this one was not yet afraid, not yet finished with the world outside.

"I suppose so," muttered Yvane. "Not much to keep me here. Hammarn'll stay, though. He likes it. Found his home, I think."

Orisian was already making for the door. "I need to talk to Herraic. I'll send word, Eshenna, when I know what is to happen."

Orisian's mind was in turmoil as he followed his torch-bearing guide. Rothe, striding along at his side, looked worried.

"You mean to chase after this woman, then?" the shieldman asked.

"Maybe. If Aeglyss wants her . . . needs her, even. Maybe."

"The battle might be done, before we reach Kolglas," Rothe muttered. He sounded disappointed; worried.

"It might. But this need only take us a handful of days. What if they're right, Rothe? What if Aeglyss is really our greatest enemy?" Orisian came to an abrupt halt and turned, taking hold of Rothe's arms, staring into the big man's face. "Inurian feared him. Yvane, all of them here. They all say the same. And I never knew Inurian to be wrong about someone, Rothe. Never."

He wanted – needed – Rothe's support. It was, in fact, almost approval that he sought here. No Thane should require such a thing from a shieldman, but perhaps he could seek it from a true friend, one he trusted more than anyone else.

"I'm no use to Taim Narran, no use to anyone, on a battlefield, Rothe. Do you understand? He's what our Blood needs there. But

I'm here, and this is something I can do. Something that might be important. More important, even."

Rothe did not look wholly convinced. But he nodded, just once, and that was enough.

They found Herraic deep in conversation with two of his men, outside their barracks. The portly Captain of Highfast had the jittery air of a man besieged by events. He drew Orisian aside as soon as they walked up.

"Thane, Thane. Good. I hoped to speak with you this evening. Some surprising news, I've had."

"In a moment," Orisian said. "Will you answer me a question first?"

"Of course."

"You told me when I arrived here that half your men had gone eastwards. Rumours of Kyrinin, you said?"

Herraic nodded, clearly puzzled that the activities of his tiny garrison should be of interest to a Thane.

"Yes, sire. There're a handful of woodsmen and hunters in the forests to the east of the Peaks. Word came from one or two of them that there had been signs of wights moving. A couple of trappers have even gone missing, supposedly." He shrugged. "Not seen White Owls on our borders for many years. Still, people said there were warbands moving south. I'd've thought there would have been more trouble reported if it was true, but It seemed best to look into it, foolish though it sounds."

"Warbands," Orisian repeated.

"It will turn out to be nothing, sire. I'm sure of it."

"No," Orisian murmured. "I don't think it will. I think Eshenna's right. It's K'rina. They're coming for her. Why would he want her so badly?"

Herraic looked puzzled. He spread his hands, displaying his incomprehension. Orisian ignored the gesture.

"I think we'll be leaving you, Captain." He turned to Rothe. "Find Torcaill. Get everyone ready."

The shieldman went without hesitation, and without demur. Herraic stared in confusion after him. There was something rather plaintive in his expression, Orisian thought.

"You will?" the Captain said. "Oh. I don't suppose . . . I've had word, you see. That's what I wanted to talk to you about: can't say I understand how or why, but the Shadowhand — sorry, the Haig Chancellor — is on his way."

Orisian's heart sank. His mind went blank, leaving him to stare dumbly at the Captain of Highfast.

"Injured," Herraic continued. He was clasping his hands, squeezing them together nervously. He had angled his head a little, widened his eyes, like a supplicant seeking some favour. "Quite gravely injured, it would seem. I'm not sure what happened: some boy loosed a crossbow bolt at him, from the sound of it. Unfortunately, the Chancellor's guards killed the child, so we'll likely never know why. But could he have been coming to see you, sire? That's what I wondered. I thought perhaps . . ."

"No," said Orisian firmly. "Mordyn Jerain has no business with me that I know of. You must forgive me, Captain, but I cannot stay. I have duties elsewhere. I leave tonight. As soon as our horses can be readied."

The downcast expression that settled upon Herraic's face at that made Orisian feel a twinge of guilt. The poor man's quiet, settled world was being shaken to bits. But it would take more than that to induce Orisian to wait placidly for Mordyn Jerain to appear. Whatever freedom of action Orisian had won for himself by leaving Kolkyre was unlikely to survive the Shadowhand's presence.

He went quickly, wholly possessed now by the desire to be gone from this place. As he walked, he heard some of Herraic's warriors talking excitedly in the doorway of their kitchens.

"The Shadowhand's coming," one was saying, his voice all awe and trepidation. "The Shadowhand's coming."

XI

Sirian's Dyke was a changed village. The last time Wain had been here, she had witnessed the destruction by Shraeve and her Inkallim of the great dam that gave the place its name. Parts of that dam still stood, but they were now only pointless reminders of the hubris of a long-dead Thane. The Glas Water, the marshy lake the dam had retained in order to drown Kan Avor, was gone. The river now flowed unimpeded. Its banks were indistinct: huge expanses of waterlogged mud and debris laid down in the flood of the dam's breaking.

The village itself had lost its purpose in the moment of the dam's ruin. Its people had, for years, been employed in the main-tenance of the dyke and in serving the needs of travellers on the road from Anduran to Glasbridge. The dyke was gone, and there were no travellers on the road, only warriors. Bereft of purpose, Sirian's Dyke was now bereft too of its inhabitants. Not a single man, woman or child of the Lannis Blood remained. Those who had not been killed when the Black Road first overran the village, or had not fled of their own accord, had been dispersed: the adults pressed into service in Anduran or Glasbridge, the children most likely seized by the Inkallim and sent north.

In place of the original villagers, Sirian's Dyke now housed a few Inkallim and the dozens of eager followers they had gathered to themselves. They were only passing through, making for the battle everyone knew was imminent, at Glasbridge or beyond. Fiallic was taking the bulk of the army along the southern side of the valley, intending to fall upon the flank or rear of any force that marched against Glasbridge. Those, like Wain, who had chosen to follow the road down the river's northern bank faced a more trying journey. Beyond Sirian's Dyke, she knew, the way through the flood-wrecked landscape would be difficult. But it would take her back to Kanin's side, and that was where she meant to stand and fight. It had, too, the advantage of keeping

Aeglyss and his Kyrinin away from the great mass of the faithful, and from the wrath of Temegrin the Eagle.

Satisfied that her horse was suitably settled for the night, Wain backed out of the stall, slapping the beast's haunches as she went. The gesture was part irritation and part grudging respect for the animal's obstinacy; it had been stubborn and obstreperous all day. It looked back at her with what she suspected was contempt.

In the yard outside, her warriors were making arrangements for their own horses, tying them to a long rope stretched along the side of the stable block. Beyond them, out in the damp dusk where the village gave way to open fields and copses, Wain could see the indistinct shapes of the White Owls, pitching their own camp. Aeglyss would be with them. His mood had been foul ever since Anduran, his presence so brooding and surly that it had unsettled everyone, including Wain. He had not uttered a single word to her – or to anyone, as far as she could tell – for more than a day. Sometimes when she looked at the halfbreed, she felt as though she was looking upon the greatest hope for their cause. Sometimes she was only afraid.

The inn was already crowded. Thirty or forty commoners of the Gaven-Gyre Blood had taken it over. Wain had her warriors turn them out. She meant to shut herself away in a room, and sleep for as long as her restless mind and body would permit. Such was her hope, but nothing came of it. Her thoughts were too turbulent to submit to slumber. She lay in the darkness with her eyes open for a while, then rose and pulled on her boots and jerkin and leggings, and went out into the yard.

It was a still night, and quiet, but it spoke to her of a change in the weather. She had grown up in Castle Hakkan, where every winter brought intensive tuition in the art of reading the air and the wind and the sky. Snow was coming, she thought. That would be a good thing. No one chose to fight in this season willingly, but if it must be done, it would surely favour the cause of the Black Road. The enemy they were to face could not know winter quite as intimately as did the Gyre Bloods.

The guards attending to the horses noticed her presence and busied themselves, taking on an air of exaggerated alertness. She gazed up. The clouds that would bring the snow were not here yet. The night sky glittered with innumerable stars, strewn across the firmament like grains of luminous sand. The moon was bright. Wain's breath plumed mistily upwards and dispersed onto the chill air. A fox barked once, out near the river. Drunken laughter, good-humoured, was drifting out from one of the cottages. Then she heard another sound, at first unclear. She turned. It was Kyrinin voices, high and sharp on the clear air, but meaningless to her. For a moment she imagined it to be an argument amongst dogs, a dispute amongst birds. Then she caught the tone of alarm, the anger and fear that animated the incomprehensible words.

Wain hesitated. She did not know quite what held her back. It was an imprecise trepidation. She shook it off and strode out into the moon-washed field. A handful of warriors straggled after her. The White Owl camp was in tumult. Some of the Kyrinin warriors had already scattered out from amongst the crude tents and now stood some distance away, staring back, taut like dogs sensing danger but not yet understanding it. A knot of White Owls remained at the centre of the encampment, milling about in a way she had never seen amongst Kyrinin before. Some were shouting, their voices strained. None seemed even to notice Wain's arrival.

She pushed her way through, and still none of the Kyrinin paid her any heed. Their attention was fixed upon the small patch of ground they had encircled. Aeglyss was lying there, half-curled on his side, one arm stretched out. His hand shook, jerking back and forth over the grass. His eyes were clamped shut. A low groan forced its way out between his teeth. Wain took a step forwards, intending to lift him bodily, but stopped short. Even in the flattening, colourless moonlight, and with the flickering shadows cast by small campfires, it was clear that something was wrong.

Aeglyss lay on a great disc of dead grass: a near-perfect circle much paler than the rest of the field. Within that circle, the grass was not only dead but unnaturally long, sprawling in great matted swathes. It was as if a great clump of whip-like stalks had come surging up out of the ground, and then died back in almost the same instant. And as her eyes picked out more detail, Wain saw that there were tendrils of now-dead and brittle grass wrapped around the wrist of the *na'kyrim*'s outstretched arm; another hung about his neck like some rustic ornament, a third spiralled around his leg. There was soil smeared across his face and through his hair. A slick of blood, black by the light of the moon, had spread from the wound in his wrist. He jerked convulsively. There was a strange, warm smell on the night air that Wain could not place. It was redolent of ploughed fields, wet logs. It did not belong.

The White Owls were agitated, yapping and whining at each other. Wain saw Hothyn — the one she took to be the closest thing these savages had to a leader — standing opposite her, staring down at the *na'kyrim*. For once, his face had an almost human animation. She saw horrified fascination. Whatever had happened here, it had produced something more complicated than simple fear amongst those who witnessed it. The Kyrinin seemed paralysed by bewilderment.

"The *na'kyrim*'s sick. Get him indoors," Wain said to her own warriors as they pushed up behind her.

They did as she commanded. The Kyrinin raised no objection, as she had half-expected they might. They watched as a couple of Wain's Shield lifted Aeglyss between them. Strands of grass came with him, reluctant to release their grip. The warriors carried him back towards the inn. Wain followed, and a few paces behind her Hothyn came like an attentive, watchful hound.

"I can find no wound, other than scratches, save those he already bore," the healer sighed as she washed the *na'kyrim*'s blood from her hands. "Those holes in his wrists have opened up again. I have given him fresh bandages. That's all I can do for him."

The young woman shrugged. She seemed to Wain to be inexperienced, unsure of her knowledge and skills, but she was the best they had been able to find amongst the companies in Sirian's Dyke. It took no great talent, in any case, to see that what afflicted Aeglyss was not merely to do with his body.

He was calmer now, but occasional tremors still shook his arms. His lips trembled. Sometimes he groaned or muttered barely audible nonsense. He had twice slipped into fraught laughter: a harsh, angry kind of cackle. Wain wondered if his mind had finally broken. The thought that, after all that had happened, this man might now betray her hopes by succumbing to madness made her angry.

The healer glanced nervously at Hothyn. The Kyrinin stood silently in the corner, as he had done throughout her examination of Aeglyss. His inhuman eyes never left the *na'kyrim*, never acknowledged the existence of anything save that gaunt form prostrate on the bed.

"Get out," Wain said irritably to the younger woman. She bowed her head and left.

Aeglyss was murmuring again. Wain leaned over, straining to catch some of the words, but it was not even a human tongue he spoke in. Some woodwight cant, perhaps. His breath stank, an exhalation of decay, as if his flesh was rotting somewhere on the inside. Wain grimaced, and saw then that his eyes, so close to her own, were open: chips of grey stone, now shot with a net of red lines, like a myriad of tiny fissures exposing the meat that lay beneath their surface. She jerked her head away, repelled by such proximity.

"What's wrong with you?" she asked.

Aeglyss smiled feebly. "Nothing. I thrive."

Wain snorted.

"You shouldn't mock," Aeglyss rasped. "It reveals the depths of your ignorance. I grow stronger."

He laughed, but it was too much for him. The sound contorted itself into a wheezing cough that rocked his shoulders. Spittle flecked his chin. Wain turned away in disgust. Hothyn, she saw, remained fixated upon Aeglyss. The Kyrinin stood quite still, wide-eyed.

"I still live," Aeglyss snapped. "They came for me, in their fear. They meant to quiet me, and silence me, and break me. Ha! They did not know! I still live, and they fled away, through the . . ."

His words collapsed into another fit of coughing. Wain looked back to him.

"You're ranting," she muttered. "Are you mad, then?"

"No. Not mad." He sounded angry. "This isn't madness, you stupid . . . Not madness. I don't know what it is. I don't know." And as quickly as that, the anger was gone and what she saw in his face, and heard in his voice, was fear, confusion. Almost child-like; a sickening feebleness.

"I don't understand," he murmured. "What do the Anain care for me? What offence have I given to them? I've done nothing . . . yet they come and tear at my mind, try to snuff me out. They think they are the masters of everything. Or perhaps they don't think at all. Perhaps . . . ah, what does it matter? I am beyond them. Even them."

Wain had the impression that he had lapsed into some inward-looking reverie, but then his head lolled to one side and he stared straight at her.

"Do you hear me, Thane's sister? I am beyond even them, the awful Anain. They cannot conquer me. What wondrous monster must I be, then?"

"I do not know," Wain said. Pressure was building at her temples, a hot, hurtful beat in the bone of her skull. Somehow, she could still smell Aeglyss's foul breath. It crowded her nostrils and writhed at the back of her mouth, down her throat. It was vile, but seemed no more terrible than the dead touch of his eyes on her skin. The room had become terribly oppressive. The air gave her no nourishment.

"You should rest," she said, and left. She could hear Aeglyss laughing as she descended, and just as the sickly sound followed her, so she carried the stench of him with her, and the echo of his ferocity in her mind.

She demanded wine, and drank it thirstily. She had one of her Shield stoke up the fire and pile logs onto it until the flames leaped. Still she felt cold, beyond the reach of warmth.

The sound of horses outside stirred her out of her distraction. Shod hoofs were ringing on the cobbles of the yard. Voices were raised. She threw open the door of the inn and glared out, ready to vent her unease upon any convenient victim. The light that flooded out around her as she stood in the doorway illuminated thirty or more mounted figures, but Wain held her tongue. They were Inkallim, stern and haughty. Shraeve was at their head, and she stared down from her lofty position with an expression of arrogant amusement.

"I thought you would be back in Glasbridge by now," the Inkallim said.

"And I thought you'd be riding with Fiallic and his host. He's your master, isn't he?"

"Fate's my master, as it is yours. The approaches to Glasbridge must be held, if that host is to find its way to our enemy's flank. That's where the matter will be most bloodily decided, so that's where we will stand." Shraeve swung out of the saddle and dropped to the ground. "And, anyway, I was curious. I heard much that was interesting regarding your tame halfbreed, while I was in Anduran. It seems a good deal has changed since you and I were last in this dismal little village."

"It's none of your concern," Wain snapped. "Those who bear more authority than you amongst the Children have spoken with me about Aeglyss. You'll find quarters for your people amongst the cottages, if that's what you seek. There's no other room to spare."

"You should learn to distinguish more precisely between your friends and your enemies, my lady," Shraeve said with a contemptuous smile. "We ravens are your Blood's closest allies now, whether you like it or not." She led her horse away along the track towards the dark rows of hovels that ran down to the river. As one, the rest of the Inkallim silently dismounted and followed. Wain watched them go, wrestling to contain her shapeless, saturating anger, and then turned back into the inn and shut the door behind her.

The night sank to its coldest depths. Wain lay unsleeping in her chamber. A square of moonlight fell through the window and onto the bed sheets, like a gossamer-thin silvered scarf laid out there. She stared up at the rough wooden beams of the ceiling. Sleep had always been a problem for her when her mind was active. This was different, though. Whenever she tried to constrain her thoughts, they bounded away from her as if stung by the smack of a carter's whip. And always they turned and turned about the subject of Aeglyss.

For a time she wished Kanin was there, then thought better of it. Her brother loathed the *na'kyrim* too much to see clearly. He was limited by that. His convictions had always been flawed by a seam of restraint. Kanin's passion, his faith, could only carry him so far; it was never unconditional. She loved her brother for that failing, the sliver of difference between them that made him who he was. But still it was a difference; it meant there was a part of her he would never quite comprehend.

Wain had never yet found a boundary she would hesitate to cross if the Black Road led her that way. Was that why she felt this aching hunger in her chest? Something in her had stirred and glimpsed a far horizon that promised much. Whatever it was, Aeglyss had woken it. Yet he had woken revulsion in her too.

The shadows shifted. The dark pools in the room flowed and parted and Aeglyss was standing by her bed. He was reaching out a single thin hand towards her. She opened her mouth to cry out, commanded her body to strike out at him, yet she made no sound or movement. Fear rattled in her head, but it was short-lived. Something else displaced it; something still and soft that settled over her. Aeglyss took a step closer. He leaned into the shaft of moonlight. It put a bar of light along his cheekbone. Wain lay quite still, yet she felt as if every muscle in her body was quivering in urgent terror. New thoughts were laying themselves down in her mind, crossing the gap between Aeglyss and her like silent whispers. They were not hers, yet alike enough to her own that she could not turn them away.

"Have you ever been refused, Thane's sister?" he was asking her. "In anything?"

His voice was a living thing that cased itself up against her skin, curled around her shoulders and throat and touched itself against her lips.

"I have grown so weary of it, you see," Aeglyss murmured, and he was close to her. She felt his hand on her breast, gentle. She felt him in her head, and she could not tell what was him and what her.

"All my life I have been denied by those who thought themselves my betters," he whispered. "Not any more. Not in anything. I am learning, slowly. Each day I see afresh what is possible, each day I grow. I can turn back the Anain themselves; I can taste thoughts in minds half a world away; I can hear my mother, can call her . . . no, no. Not my mother."

He blinked and shook his head, wincing. For a moment, Wain recovered herself and drew breath to cry out. Then the *na'kyrim*'s eyes were on her once again and his hand was clamped over her mouth. Her sense of herself flickered and receded as smoothly and steadily as a soft tide.

"Hush, hush. This isn't for anyone but you and I. This is to be love. Only that, for ever. It's what you want, if you'll but listen to your own desires. I'll show you the way. We'll go together."

As he lifted the sheets away, some silent part of Wain cried out one last time in horror and fear. It was a vanishing, vanquished part, and soon it was gone altogether.

Aeglyss stood in the milky early-morning light, talking intently with Hothyn and half a dozen more White Owls. Wain looked down upon him from the window of her room in the inn. She could see him clearly, below in the yard, yet he was there in the window with her too. He was entwined about her thoughts like ivy on a tree. She would never be without him now.

She was aware that the sensations coursing through her, the certainties fortifying themselves within her head, were not her own. It seemed unimportant; just as unimportant as the faint, faint voice of guilt that survived somewhere inside her. That voice murmured of betrayal. She had betrayed her brother. How, she could not understand. The accusatory voice spoke in a language that she did not comprehend, though she knew that once – before last night – it had been the tongue of her own thoughts. She found it easy to disregard even that strangeness. The Black Road followed whatever course it must, and never had she felt her feet, and all the world's, to be more firmly upon it.

She had been awake, in the small hours of the night, when Aeglyss was restlessly turning in his sleep. Moonlight lit the trails of tears on his face. He had wept and cursed without waking and she had heard the torment in his voice.

In the dawn, while he still slept, she had lain beside him and watched him. His face was at peace, by then. His eyes were moving beneath their lids, his breathing was heavy and slow. There was nothing left of the repulsion she had once felt at his inhuman features. It was a distant memory, the legacy of a different person. Instead, she saw a rigorous beauty in the way his bones shaped his skin and in the graceful white-nailed fingers lying upon the sheet.

He had passed in an instant from seemingly deep sleep to wakefulness. His grey eyes flicked open and met her own with a clear, alert gaze. A thrill of fear ran through her in that instant, as if she was a child caught observing some forbidden scene. He said nothing. He barely acknowledged her, in fact, beyond that first, piercing stare. He rose, doused his head and face with cold water and dressed.

Wain had sat naked on the bed and watched him moving about the room. She did not need him to speak to her. He was there, already, behind her eyes. Only when he was about to leave had he looked at her. He regarded her dispassionately. He crossed to her and turned her so that he could see the marks he had left on her back.

"Someone told me once that I had a dog's heart," he said. For some reason that made him laugh, bitter and pained. "But he underestimated me. I've a bit of the wolf in me, at least, from the look of you. I have been broken, and remade. He would not recognise me now."

"You had bad dreams," she said.

He took his hand away from her shoulder, but remained standing behind her. She did not dare to turn around.

"What is in me is never still," Aeglyss said. "I always dream. Of more things than you can imagine. I dreamed K'rina." There was a note of longing in his voice. Wain could hear his breathing. She wanted to look at him now, but was afraid of what she might see. He was too potent, too unbounded, for the eye to bear.

"She loved me, I think. Not as you do, my beloved. Not as you. But in her way." He sighed. "We'll see. I'll have her with me, and we'll see. My hounds are on her trail."

He kissed the nape of Wain's neck. Ice ran through her body, caressed her.

"Wait for me here," he whispered. "I need to talk with the White Owls. They must be made to understand what happened. If not . . . these savages, they live in awe of the Anain. I can't have them running back into Anlane telling tales of . . . I must . . . they must trust me. They must submit."

Wain felt his fingernail slipping down her back, tracing her spine. It was a cold, transfixing sensation.

"I must set my hand firmly upon them. There can be no trust between me and them without that. There cannot be trust . . . except you. You I can trust, Wain, for you are mine. We are one, now. It was the only way I could be certain. Do you understand?"

"Yes," she had breathed, and then, soundlessly, he was gone.

She watched him now, and felt herself to be perched atop a towering cliff, gazing down from some unimaginable height upon that slight figure. Slight, yet wreathed about with terrible glory that none save she could see; radiant with the promise of power, utter and complete.

3

Anain

When the One Race was no more, and the Gods resolved to make five to fill the void its destruction had left, the Gatekeeper first made the Huanin. Next The God Who Laughed made the Kyrinin, and the Light, who sang, made the Saolin. Then the fell Wildling, The Spear, made the Whreinin.

The maker of the last of the five was to be The Goddess. More than any save The God Who Laughed, she loved the green places of the world. More than any save The Raven she saw what lay beneath the world they had made, and saw that not everything that mattered could be touched or held in the hand. Thus she made the Anain, who have no substance save what they borrow from tree and leaf, who dwell in all places and none. And when he saw what she had done The God Who Laughed was pleased and said, "This is a good thing, for you have put life into that which is most beautiful in our creation."

But the Gatekeeper said, "This is a fell thing you have done. These you have made are too potent and too deep. They will not love these others we have made, for all life save their own will seem to them a small and brief thing. They will know too little of death and of failings, and too much of things that are hidden from the others. This is not a gentle thought you have breathed into the mind of the world."

The Goddess was not angry at these words. "These my children will be gentle in their way and in their own manner. But none can be always gentle. Your Huanin, Gatekeeper, will be sometimes fierce. The Kyrinin will be sometimes cold, the Saolin sometimes foolish. The Wildling's wolfenkind will be sometimes most cruel. And my Anain, they will sometimes be more terrible and wondrous than all the others. For every world must have terrors and wonders in it, just as much as gentleness."

from First Tales, *transcribed by* Quenquane the Simple

I

Kolglas was an even more distressing sight than Taim Narran had expected. All through the long march from Kolkyre he had been steeling himself to withstand whatever might await him here, but those preparations made little difference. The town was in turmoil. Hundreds upon hundreds of people were crammed into its streets, its houses and barns. They had come from every corner of the Glas valley; from tiny villages and from lonely cottages in Anlane and the Car Criagar. Some were only passing through, their flight from the Black Road not yet done, and even those who meant to remain here in Kolglas carried fear on their faces. The joy with which many greeted the arrival of Taim and his six hundred men had a strained undercurrent of desperation, of hesitant hope. Ragged, cheering townsfolk clustered along the roadside as Taim led his little army in.

The worst sight was that of Castle Kolglas itself. It stood like a massive, sullen outcast on its tiny island. The causeway running out to it from the harbour was covered by the choppy sea, and Taim was glad of that. From this distance there was little outward sign of the fate that had befallen the castle, but he had no great desire to set foot within those abandoned walls. He knew the keep had been almost gutted and its roof ruined by fire after the

Inkallim had finished their slaughter; he knew that the stables, and the barracks where the castle's meagre garrison had slept, were wrecked. And he knew that if he entered the castle's court-yard he would only be beset by images of the horrors of Winterbirth. He had heard more than enough reports of that savage night to satisfy any curiosity, and to feed his guilt at being so far away when his Blood had needed him.

The market square was crowded with wagons, makeshift shelters and rootless families, making it impossible to find a path through. Taim sent most of his men back to make camp on the south edge of the town, and went in search of someone who could tell him how things stood.

The man he found was Elach Mell, an old warrior who had been quietly seeing out the twilight of his life in the garrison of Kolglas for at least a dozen years. The tone of the few reports he had sent to Taim in the past week or two had been steadfast, resolute. Only now, in the cramped quarters the old man kept next to the square, could Taim see the true extent of Elach's decline. He had never known the man well, and it had been years since they had last met, but his exhaustion was clear. His shoulders were slack, his eyes sluggish. Only the embers of whatever determination had sustained him thus far now remained, insufficient to oppose the persistent weight of all that had happened.

"There's not enough food," Elach said. His voice was flat. "The barns are almost empty. All but a few of the cattle and goats have been slaughtered. We're trying to move people on to Stryne, or to Hommen. Some go willingly, others are reluctant."

Taim nodded slowly. "How many men do you have fit for battle?" he asked.

"Two hundred, if you mean those with any training. A week ago, it would have been three, but . . . well, there're coughs and agues in the town now that winter's taken hold. I've lost fifteen or twenty in skirmishing up the road to Glasbridge. They've thrown some kind of wall across the road, you know, between here and there. Can't get anyone beyond it. And I had to send three dozen to Drinan."

"Drinan? Why?"

"Woodwights. So the folk there claim, anyway. They're convinced there's White Owls on the move." Elach shrugged. "I don't know what to believe these days. There's been some barns burned, some cattle stolen; that much is certain."

Taim stared at the back of his clasped hands in thought. He had hoped for more than two hundred. His Blood had always thought itself strong. Had they been so deluded in that? Where had all that imagined strength gone, to leave them with fewer than a thousand warriors to take the field? He knew where it had gone, of course: it had been whittled away by a few too many years of peace, gnawed at by the Heart Fever, caged and slaughtered at Tanwrye, cut down at Grive, at Anduran and Glasbridge. And in pursuit of Gryvan's victory over Igryn oc Dargannan-Haig.

"We could muster hundreds more from amongst the townsfolk," Elach murmured. He sounded almost reluctant, as if he said such things only because it was expected of him. Taim hid a momentary frown of annoyance behind a hand raised to brush his brow. He had hoped for more in many ways.

"Only those who know which end of a sword to hold," he said. "Fishermen and farmers who've never felt a spear in their hand'll be worse than useless against the Black Road. We'd do well to get whatever hunters and woodsmen there are here organised, though. Get them out into Anlane, to watch our flanks and hunt for woodwights. Send fifty of them to Drinan; get your three dozen men back from there."

Elach shook his head: despondent, rather than disagreeing. "We've lost a lot of them already. The woodfolk, I mean. They've been going out of their own accord, looking for survivors, or for someone to kill. We found the bodies of five yesterday, just inside the forest. I don't know whether or not there're woodwights out there, like folk say, but I do know there's Hunt Inkallim. They've been seen."

"The Hunt?" Taim repeated, unable to keep the surprise from his voice. "I thought . . . we were told it was only Horin-Gyre, and a few of the Battle. You're sure the Hunt's here?"

Elach grimaced. "My scouts have seen their dogs, and heard them. I've stopped sending men up the road. The few that don't die come running back here like frightened hens. But the Hunt's the least of our worries, Taim. Maybe it was only Horin-Gyre when all this started – I don't know about that – but there's a lot more than that come across the Stone Vale now."

The old warrior rose to his feet and stretched his back.

"We're still getting a few stragglers who manage to sneak out through the forest. Some even paddle down the coast holding on to driftwood, but most of those ones drown before they get here, I think. Anyway, they all say there's thousands more Black Roaders coming down from the north. Every Blood, not just Horin; armies at Targlas and Grive, as well as Anduran and Glasbridge. One girl said she'd seen hundreds – hundreds, mind you – of Battle Inkallim marching down past Anduran."

Taim watched in silence as Elach went to the window and stared up at the sky. In the space of a few sentences, the older man had undercut the foundations of all Taim's half-formed plans. Had it only been the exhausted, diminished forces of the Horin-Gyre Blood he faced, he – and Orisian – might have been able to turn them back without any aid from Aewult nan Haig and his host. Now . . . now a multitude of dangers presented themselves to his imagination. Aewult had close to ten thousand men, but he thought he was marching against a far weaker foe. If the Battle itself was indeed fielding hundreds of its ravens, what lay ahead would be far bloodier, far more savage, than any of them had anticipated.

"It's true, is it, that Orisian's our Thane now?" Elach asked, still standing by the window. "You saw him in Kolkyre?"

"It's true. He went by a different road, but he will be here within a few days."

"What times, to have a child as Thane."

"He's no child," Taim growled. "And he's Thane by right, and by duty."

Elach grunted and returned to his chair. "So he is. I pity him as much as the rest of us. His family gone, our lands lost. We'll be lucky if there's more than splinters left of us once the High Thane and the Black Road have hammered away at each other for a while."

Taim slapped the table. "Enough, Elach." He rose and took his scabbarded sword up from where he had leaned it against the wall. "You have a wife, if I remember rightly. Where is she?"

"Stryne. I sent her to Stryne, after Glasbridge fell."

Taim buckled his belt and settled his sword on his hip. "Go and join her. You've done what you can here. Clear whatever you want to take with you out of this place by nightfall. I'll sleep here tonight."

Elach's expression lurched from alarm to relief and back again. He started to protest, without conviction. Taim pulled the door open.

"Don't argue, Elach. The burden you've shouldered here is mine to bear now. Go. Take care of your wife."

Taim Narran slept little that night, and not at all the one that followed. Instead, he laboured. He laboured to put back together what he could of his Blood, and to build for it some defences against whatever lay ahead.

In an inn by the waterfront, he found an Oathman – the only one, it appeared, to have escaped the chaos beyond Kolglas. The man, a little drunk and extremely shocked, was told he was now the Master Oathman of the Lannis Blood. The Naming of infants, the taking of the Bloodoath, the burning and mourning of the dead, all these things must continue. Taim Narran made it clear to the newly elevated Master Oathman that it was his responsibility to ensure they did so.

Men were sent to retrieve everything of value that survived within Castle Kolglas, and Taim had it stored under guard in the town's gaol. He gathered all the merchants to be found in the town together and instructed them in what their Blood required of them in such times. Their consequent generosity swelled the nascent treasury in the gaol a little further. Taim ordered that the size of the town Guard be doubled, and tasked them with ensuring that there was no hoarding of food. He emptied part of the garrison's barracks – sending the warriors to camp outside the town – and had all the sick brought there to be cared for. Fifty volunteers were armed with spears and knives from the garrison's stores and dispatched to Drinan. They carried orders summoning the warriors Elach Mell had sent there back to Kolglas, and commanding them to bring with them all the cattle and grain that Drinan could spare.

Taim himself took thirty of his men along the coast towards Glasbridge. They got less than halfway before they found a pack of Tarbain tribesmen looting and burning an abandoned mill. A few of the northerners escaped; most of them did not. Soon afterwards figures could be seen moving along the forest's edge. Ahead, far up the road, riders were visible. Taim turned his men around and returned to Kolglas. That night he set more than a hundred sentries along the town's northern boundary, and went himself to every one of them in the rain-filled darkness to ensure that none doubted the importance of wakefulness.

He did all this while secretly dreading what would happen if the Black Road came pouring down the coast; knowing that if they did come, his hundreds of men were unlikely to be enough. There would be nothing he could do save stand and die with them, and hope to give the people of Kolglas enough time to escape. He did it all while longing with every fibre of his being to return to his wife and his daughter and to take them in his arms and await with them the birth of his grandchild.

And then, at dusk on the third day, when the Black Road still had not come, a moment Taim had both hoped for and feared arrived. He went with apprehension clenched in his chest and two dozen of his veteran warriors at his side to the southern edge of Kolglas and stood looking down the coast towards the distant sunset. His exertions, and the paucity of sleep, had left his head heavy, his neck stiff, his legs aching. He felt, standing in that gloaming, watching the waves sighing up along the shore, as old as he had ever done. He did not have to wait long. Out of the gathering gloom, coming like a dark, roiling river beneath clouds turned orange and red by the sinking sun, Aewult nan Haig's army arrived.

* * *

Abeh oc Haig brought an unexpected and unwelcome guest with her to the Palace of Red Stone. She was wife to the Thane of Thanes and thus beyond the reach of any disapproval, but Tara Jerain was in any case too well schooled in Vaymouth's manners to betray her irritation. One could not prosper in the ants' nest of aspiration and competition that the city had become without learning to speak only with a smile in Abeh's presence. For Abeh, the world and her life within it were glittering things, filled with glory, fine food and pleasures of every kind. Her husband and sons were flawless, loved by all; their wealth was limitless and resented by no one; every gift that was pressed upon her was born of affection, sired by admiration. Anything contrary to her vision was hurtful, a personal insult. And one did not insult Abeh oc Haig.

Tara Jerain's smile never faltered as she greeted Abeh on the steps outside the palace. The inevitable crowd of maids and attendants bunched behind the High Thane's wife. The line of carriages and horses that had brought them filled the street, amongst them a strange box-like contraption from which the source of Tara's annoyance was being roughly removed: Igryn oc Dargannan-Haig. The former Thane of the Dargannan-Haig Blood was dressed in a fine lace bodice and skirt. His hair and beard, both grown long during his imprisonment, had little silken bows in them. His hands were tied behind his back with a cord of soft velvet, his empty eye sockets – emptied on Gryvan oc Haig's orders when Igryn was captured – were hidden by a band of flowery cloth wrapped around his head.

The sight was as surprising and distasteful as anything Tara Jerain had seen in a long time. Yet her face as she embraced Abeh oc Haig was a study in delight, her voice a smooth melody. Her husband the Shadowhand would have been proud of her.

"You are most welcome, my lady," Tara said. "I am quite delighted, quite delighted."

"Well, it has been too long since I came to one of your gatherings," beamed Abeh.

Her pleasure in her own cleverness was bubbling up, too vigorous to be restrained. She glanced over her shoulder, her chin quivering with anticipation.

"You see I have a new maidservant," she breathed. "Quite ill-suited to her calling, but I was sure you and the other ladies would like to see her."

Two guards were manhandling Igryn oc Dargannan-Haig up the first couple of steps. Abeh's throng of servants laughed behind decorous hands and whispered to one another. Much as Tara would have liked to ignore the humbled Thane's presence entirely, she gave a soft chuckle.

"She seems strangely familiar, my lady. And, if I may be allowed the thought, a trifle old to be embarking on a new role in life."

Abeh glowed with satisfaction. "Well, it is only for today. The Thane of Thanes was kind enough to lend him – her – to me for the occasion." She looped her arm around Tara's and drifted into the Palace of Red Stone. "He was reluctant, really quite reluctant, but I insisted."

Tara smiled. Abeh's determination in pursuit of her own amusement was infamous, but it would have been far better for Gryvan to deny his wife this petty indulgence. Such humiliation of Igryn oc Dargannan-Haig, once it became widely known, would only feed the ire of those opposed to Haig's rule. Igryn might be a prisoner, a traitor condemned by his own deeds and words, but nevertheless he had been a Thane not long ago. Such considerations would not occur to Abeh, of course. She had founded her life, her very understanding of the world and all its processes, on the primacy of her whims.

"Well, do bring him or her in quickly," murmured Tara. "We don't want that lovely hair to be ruffled by the breeze." It would hardly help, but at least they could get Igryn inside the palace and away from curious eyes.

The other guests – most of the wives and older daughters of Vaymouth's great and powerful – had been gathered in the music room for some time. It was the prerogative of the High Thane's wife always to be the last to arrive. There was a stir of interest as Tara and Abeh swept in, which gave way to gasps and laughter when Igryn oc Dargannan-Haig followed them. Tara was gratified to see that at least a few of those present had the sense to be dismayed at the sight of the former Thane.

An attentive flock of admirers descended on Abeh oc Haig at once. Tara took the opportunity to edge up to one of the guards who flanked Igryn.

"Please do not feel you have to stand there like idiots," she muttered in his ear. "There are chairs over there."

"I offend you, do I?" Igryn rasped. The guard laid a hand on the prisoner's arm and squeezed tightly, but Igryn did not appear even to notice it. "It's my sight that's been taken from me, not my hearing. You'll have to whisper quieter than that if you want me ignorant of your contempt."

"It's not contempt," Tara said, gesturing to the guards to remove Igryn to the farthest corner. "But you hardly fit in with the mood of the evening. If you'd rather stand there and have all Vaymouth's fine ladies spitting insults and laughter at you for the rest of the night, you'll just have to forgive me for denying you your wish."

When the musicians began to play, the chatter quietened for a time. They were masterless men from the Free Coast, found by Tara's embroiderer playing at the last night market of the year. Their style was energetic, a novel departure from the light, flowing Tal Dyreen music that had been preferred in Vaymouth for the last couple of years. But their greatest attribute was the singer who soon came to the front. She was an exquisitely beautiful girl, perhaps fifteen or sixteen. And her voice was as sweet and fair as any voice could be. It filled the room like a formless, enchanting quality of the air itself. Even Abeh oc Haig was held and stilled by it for a few moments.

Time passed as it always did at such a gathering: in smiles and murmured pleasantries, in flattery and aimless talk. Tara moved slowly around the room, ensuring that no one ran short of wine or conversation. The singer sang, and everyone praised her voice; some cultivated jealousy of her youth and beauty. A roasted swan, resting on a bed of its own white feathers, was carried in on a huge silver platter.

A serving girl came hesitantly to Tara's elbow.

"Forgive me, my lady, but your other visitor has arrived. He has been taken to the Chancellor's audience chamber, as you instructed."

Tara nodded, and left as discreetly as she could to greet her new guest.

Lammain, Craftmaster of the Goldsmiths, had a sharp, long nose and angular cheeks and chin. It gave him a certain dignity, Tara thought, but it also always made him seem rather gaunt and hungry. And hungry he was, of course, though not for food. In common with much of Vaymouth's population, wealth, power and standing were what he craved.

Tara did not dislike the Craftmaster. He was one of those amongst the city's game-players who had never mistaken her for a mere wife, an empty adornment on the Shadowhand's arm. Lammain had always respected her intelligence, and the particular kinds of influence she could wield. He was, as far as she could tell, one of the few men she had met who was not blinded by her beauty.

"Did they offer you wine, Craftmaster?"

"They did. I declined it. I did not realise you had other visitors this evening. I had no intention of disturbing you."

"Not at all," said Tara as she settled gracefully into a chair. She leaned a little closer to the Goldsmith, with an expression that conveyed both guilt and amusement. "I asked you to call on me today for this very reason. These ladies make for demanding company, you know. A few moments away from them will give me the chance to recover my strength. And it is only polite to give them the chance to discuss me, and my hospitality, without having to whisper."

Lammain gave a brief half-chuckle. "I am sure it is not quite as tiring as you say," he murmured.

"Oh, but it is. The talking is incessant. And the mind must be fast as a deer to keep up with it. One moment it's gossip about some lustful intrigue, the next talk of war. Then it's fretting about the cost of fine cloths. You can never be sure what is coming next. As I left, they were all agog at the news of Gann nan Dargannan-Haig."

"They were?" The surprise in Lammain's voice was far too unguarded to be false. It pleased Tara. So long as she kept the Craftmaster off balance, the conversation was hers to steer.

"You've heard, I assume?" she enquired. "They say he fell off the dock at Hoke, straight into the sea."

"I had heard, yes," Lammain said.

He would have been amongst the first to hear of Gann's demise, Tara knew. The dead man had, after all, been the Goldsmiths' possession, purchased over many years with coin and favours. How her husband had arranged the man's death – and such an appropriately grubby kind of death, at that – Tara had no idea, but that it was a costly one for Lammain was beyond doubt.

"The Dargannan-Haig Blood is having no fortune, is it?" she said. "First Igryn gets himself thrown into a gaol cell, now his cousin manages to die a very common little death. Of course, rumour has it that Gann brought it on himself. I hear he was terribly drunk, and wandering about the harbour at dead of night. It is no great surprise that one with his habits should come to an ugly end."

"Well, I never met the man myself. But yes, he had a certain . . . reputation."

"Still, his death is rather regrettable. It proves the fragility of all our dreams that someone could come within reach of a Thaneship only to be denied by drunkenness and cold water. My husband will be disappointed, when he hears of it. He was most interested in your view, you know, that Gann might be the best choice as Igryn's successor."

"Was he? Well, I am gratified. Though it hardly matters now."

"Perhaps you could consider whether there is anyone else you think well-suited to the task of leading the Dargannan-Haig Blood. I know that the Thane of Thanes took a much closer interest in Gann once he knew of your advocacy. Really much closer. Should you have anyone else to put forward . . ."

She left the suggestion hanging, with a delicate smile.

The Craftmaster's face darkened for a moment before he recovered his self-control. It was only a fleeting slip, and the change had been almost imperceptible, but it was enough to satisfy Tara that she had done what her husband had asked of her.

Mordyn seldom involved her directly in his dealings but on this occasion his enforced absence from Vaymouth had made it necessary.

"Make him doubt," the Shadowhand had whispered to her on that last night – a long night, and gentle, both sweet and sad – before his departure. "That is all that is required. When word comes of Gann's death – and it will come – give the Craftmaster just enough cause to wonder about the circumstances. I need Lammain to consider the possibility that his ambition ran too far ahead of his sense."

"I will give the matter some thought," Lammain now said quietly.

"Do. Well, we neither of us have the time to fritter away on idle chatter, I imagine? Before he left, the Chancellor asked me to make a gift to you in his absence. He had hoped to see you himself before his departure, but there simply wasn't the opportunity. You know how it is, when there are armies marching to and fro."

"Of course. I am not sure what I or my Craft have done to merit a gift from your husband, though."

"Must every gift be merited?" Tara kept any hint of a smile from her face. She spoke softly, precisely. "Just as not every crime is punished, so not every reward is earned."

Lammain nodded. He was watching Tara intently. She wondered if it was hostility that narrowed his eyes, but concluded that it was only concentration.

"Anyway," she continued, her voice now light, glittering, "the gift is not for you, in truth. You know how Mordyn and I have always admired your Craft's dedication to the service of the less fortunate. Your orphanages, in particular. You have two now, don't you?"

"Indeed. Here and in Drandar." The Craftmaster's self-discipline was impressive. His tone shadowed Tara's to perfection, pitched just short of merriment.

"It's a most worthy cause. I will have the donation brought to the Crafthouse in the morning, if that is agreeable? Delivered to the Secretary in person, I imagine?"

"You are most kind, dear lady, most kind. I will ensure that it is expected, and dealt with appropriately."

Tara strolled back towards the music chamber with a light tread. She did not hurry, savouring these few moments of peace and solitude. Her soft footsteps rang faintly along the marble-clad corridor. She wondered how much of the donation Lammain would keep for himself, and for his Secretary. However much was needed to salve the blow of Gann nan Dargannan-Haig's death, no doubt. Which was exactly as Mordyn intended. He would be pleased to hear how smoothly everything had gone upon his return. And that return could not come soon enough for Tara. There was no one else in whose company she could set aside all pretence and be wholly herself.

She could hear the singer's voice, an ethereal shiver through the halls. The girl really was very good, Tara thought. In all likelihood, Abeh would steal her away and have her singing in the Moon Palace within the month. And then, inevitably, her beauty would sooner or later catch the eye of Aewult or Stravan, the High Thane's sons. Whatever happened after she had drawn such attention, it was unlikely to end well for her.

Tara paused outside the music chamber. A single upraised finger was enough to tell the servant there to wait before opening the door. Tara took a moment to run a careful hand over her hair, to settle into place the required bright smile. Then she made her entry.

* * *

The narrow strip of fields that skirted Kolglas – fragments of land gnawed out of the vast forests of Anlane – had disappeared beneath the boots and tents and hoofs and creaking wheels of Aewult nan Haig's host. Hundreds, perhaps thousands, of his men were yet to reach the town, but enough had arrived to transform the landscape. The earth was churned into a great lagoon of mud that curved around the town's landward flanks. It made for a slippery, sodden camping ground; one that would sap the spirits and vigour of the Bloodheir's men. Aewult nan Haig himself, to no one's surprise, found it not to his liking. He claimed finer quarters, in the centre of the town.

That was where Taim went seeking him, but the guards on the gate told him the Bloodheir was not within. Aewult, it transpired, had gone to the sea, to view Castle Kolglas. Taim hastened down through the crowds towards the harbour. The thought of Aewult nan Haig observing the empty shell of the castle in the sea was irrationally distasteful to him. For Taim and everyone else of his Blood, what had happened within those walls on the night of Winterbirth was a bitter memory: painful, but also, in an ill-defined way, shameful. It was all too easy to imagine the Haig Bloodheir having a very different response. It felt rather like having to watch an enemy gloating over the corpse of a fallen friend.

The night before, there had been no opportunity to speak with Aewult at any length. When Taim had greeted him outside the town, their reunion was, if not exactly hostile, certainly cold. The Bloodheir had made it plain that his only interest was in finding himself a warm bed and hot food. Taim had found himself dismissed and all but ignored. Unexpectedly, he slept well that night.

Now, the morning after, he had no difficulty in finding Aewult. The Bloodheir's Palace Shield had cleared a stretch of the quayside and stood like an array of metal-clad statues in a wide half-circle. Protected from the common folk by that barrier, Aewult was gazing out over the choppy water towards the castle. A woman was by his side, wearing a heavy but intricately decorated coat with a thick fur collar. It took Taim a moment or two to recall her name: Ishbel, the companion Aewult had brought with him all the way from Anduran.

Taim slipped between a pair of the silent shieldmen. He was relieved that neither made any move to obstruct him; he was, at least, saved that minor humiliation. He came up to the Bloodheir's side with a small bow. Aewult did not acknowledge his arrival .

"It's a fine castle," Aewult said. He turned to Ishbel, gesturing at the lifeless mass of Castle Kolglas. "Don't you think, my lady? It's a noble setting."

Ishbel gave no sign of any genuine interest. "I suppose it is. If you can call anywhere this cold noble."

Aewult smiled at her.

"It *was* a fine castle," Taim said. "The roof's half gone now. Most that wasn't stone has been burned out."

"You can build it back," Aewult said. The smile vanished from his face as soon as he turned his attention to Taim. "It's nothing that can't be mended, once your young Thane's back on his throne. Where is he, by the way?"

His voice had a powerful edge of threat, of aggression, in it. Where his father Gryvan, in Taim's experience, spoke with subtle daggers concealed behind each word, Aewult flailed around with cudgels.

"I don't know, sire. I have not seen or heard from him since we marched from Kolkyre. We expect his arrival any day, though."

Aewult grunted. The answer clearly did not satisfy him. "You can expect whatever you like. Where did he go? Was it Highfast? That's what Mordyn thought."

Taim had to take a moment to consider his answer. The Blood-heir was unlikely to believe him if he feigned complete ignorance of Orisian's plans. Even so, Taim had no intention of reporting to the Haig Blood on the detail of his own Thane's intentions.

"I think so," he said, endeavouring to sound like a man

accustomed to ignorance of his master's dealings. "He meant to make his way here with some speed, though."

"Did he?"

The simple phrase was bloated with self-satisfaction and affected lack of interest. Evidently, Aewult knew – or thought he knew – something that Taim did not.

Ishbel made a disgruntled sound, faint but pointed. "I'm getting cold here. It's bitter."

"There's snow coming in off the sea," Taim said. He nodded out towards the banks of clouds to the west. They hung like a dismal roof over the grey sea. "Any west wind can bring snow at this time of year. This one's likely to be heavy-laden. Tonight, or tomorrow maybe, there'll be a big fall."

Ishbel grimaced – it was no small achievement to render her exquisite features so unattractive – and pulled that exuberant collar of fox fur tighter about her neck. A pair of women, bent beneath the baskets full of shellfish they carried on their backs, were scrambling up onto the harbour wall. They must have been out along the rocky shore to the south since early morning, Taim knew. The tide had been at its lowest before dawn. Ishbel watched them walking slowly along the quayside.

"I don't how anyone gets anything done in this weather," she muttered. "You should all move south for the winter. Like geese."

"It'll be some time yet before the deepest winter," Taim said.

"Why don't you go back to our chambers?" Aewult said to his lover, and then beckoned one of his shieldmen. "Send an escort back with the lady Ishbel. And have them prepare my horse. I will be needing it soon, and thirty men to ride with me."

"Are you planning to go somewhere?" Taim asked the Bloodheir as Ishbel and a pair of the armoured shieldmen disappeared up the road.

"I am." Aewult turned back towards Castle Kolglas. "I'll be surveying my army this afternoon. I want them to be ready for tomorrow."

Taim hung his head and regarded the cobblestones. Events were already setting off down the very path he had hoped to avoid. Had Orisian been here, there might have been some way out of the trap that Taim could feel closing about him; but Orisian was not here, and Aewult was. Now, Taim knew, a great deal – for him and for his Blood – depended upon what passed between him and the Bloodheir; upon what accommodation, if any, he could find with this turbulent man.

"You mean to offer battle tomorrow," he said, making it a statement rather than a question.

"Not offer. Force. I'll march, and I'll keep marching until the Black Road face me. Either we'll have ourselves a battle or they'll run away back over the Stone Vale. I'd prefer the battle. Not as much glory in chasing sheep as there is in slaughtering wolves."

"You think battle a glorious thing?"

"You do not?" The retort was sharp, angry. A battle with the Black Road was not the only kind of conflict the Bloodheir might be eager to court, Taim thought gloomily.

"I've seen too much of it to think it anything more than a necessity to be endured," he said.

"And you think, therefore, I have not seen enough of it? You think me inexperienced in war, Taim Narran. A child, too callow to lead an army. Is that it?"

"No, Bloodheir. That was not what I meant. I am tired, and I am not as young as I used to be. That is all." It was a lie, but a necessary one. He could hardly tell the Bloodheir that he thought a hothead with a desire to prove himself as quickly as possible made a poor leader for any army.

Aewult kicked a loose pebble into the water. He followed it to the edge of the quay and peered down at the waves.

"Tired and old, indeed," he said without lifting his gaze. "You needn't worry. You can stay here tomorrow, while we carve a path back to Anduran for your Thane. If he ever sees fit to grace us with his presence. Perhaps his duty has called him elsewhere."

The Bloodheir swung about and set off up the road towards the market square. His Shield clattered into loose ranks before and behind him. Taim had to hurry to keep up. He was tempted to ask Aewult what it was he thought he knew about Orisian's whereabouts, but was not inclined to feed the Bloodheir's sense of his own importance.

"The Black Road seems more numerous than we thought," he said as they strode along. "All the reports suggest the Horin-Gyre Blood is no longer the only foe we face. And Inkallim—"

Aewult cut him short with a flourish of his gloved hand. "You and your Thane shouldn't have been in such haste to leave Kolkyre, if you've not the stomach for a fight. I've got enough men here to give me the stomach for anything." He came to an abrupt halt and jabbed a finger at Taim. "You are the rearguard now. Haig'll do the killing that's needed to win this war."

Taim was uncomfortably aware that they were attracting attention. A whole family huddled on the doorstep of a bakery had turned their heads at the sound of Aewult's voice. Half a dozen men carrying firewood down towards the harbour had stopped to watch. Above, an old woman was peering curiously out from a window.

"We should march with you," Taim suggested as evenly as he could. "You've still got hundreds of warriors strung out on the road, not even here yet. My men can kill for you as well as your own."

"I'll tell you what you should do, Captain of Anduran: you should do as I command. I am here, your Thane is not. Unless you can produce him, and have him command you otherwise, you're bound to do as I tell you. Are you not?"

"Yes, sire."

Aewult grunted, a satisfied smirk briefly stretching his mouth, and set off once more. Taim followed with a heavy heart. The Bloodheir was right: in Orisian's absence, he had no choice but to obey whatever instruction Aewult saw fit to give him. Any other course would lead to an open breach with Haig. However appealing that prospect might be in some respects, here and now it would be a disaster.

Up ahead, Aewult's shieldmen were like the prow of a boat, ploughing a path through the thickening mass of people as they drew closer to the square.

"It might be worth delaying your advance a little while, sire," Taim tried again. "Anyone here could tell you there's going to be foul weather the next day or two. Heavy snow'll blunt any advantage you have in numbers, or in horsemen. Wait until your stragglers have caught up. If it's true that the Black Road's stronger than we—"

"If it's true, if it's true. Enough. I will not wait here for your Thane to arrive, if that's what you hope. I have an army, and an enemy within reach of it. If I wait for good weather in this miserable corner of the world, I'll still be here come the spring thaw. Whatever you hoped for when you snuck out of Kolkyre, this is not your battle to fight. Not your victory to win, do you understand?"

"I do," Taim sighed.

"Then bite your tongue. Tomorrow, you'll see what the men of Haig can do. It might be a valuable lesson for you and your boy-Thane."

II

Aewult nan Haig's army was a lethargic thing. It woke out of a cold night slowly, discouraged by the gloomy sky and the sharp-edged wind that was gusting off the sea and carrying tiny, hard flakes of snow. Long after dawn, when they should have been formed into columns or already on the move, men were still clustered around fires, arguing over trifles or silently eating gruel. The whole army stank of resentment and reluctance.

The invisible sun climbed higher. The snow grew heavier and cast a white dusting over the town, the army's camp and the road north. At last, with abundant ill humour, the host began to move. They trudged in their thousands around and through Kolglas, choking every street and farmland path, spilling into the fringes of the forest.

Taim Narran was posted a little way north of the town, five hundred of his men flanking the road. He sat astride his horse and watched Aewult's army pass. He saw some companies he would count as ready for battle: straight-backed spearmen who marched behind a Vaymouth banner; Taral-Haig riders, their mounts clad in stiff hide bards; a loose crowd of skirmishers from the Nar Vay shore, exuding a murderous enthusiasm. Most, though, appeared short on both vigour and spirit. Heads hung low, feet dragged. Few had clothing fit for the wintry conditions. Taim could see canvas wrapped around boots that were too thin now that snow was falling. Many men had removed their helmets and replaced them with warmer, softer caps. The warriors of the Kilkry Blood would have done much to strengthen and fortify this host, Taim reflected, if Aewult had permitted them to gather and march.

Aewult nan Haig and his Palace Shield were like a glittering precious stone set in the tawdry sludge of his army. The shield-men had evidently been polishing their breastplates. Aewult's magnificent horse – a huge beast – had its mane plaited, and its head encased with moulded, hinged silver armour. Some of the shieldmen were beating their drums, though the snow and wind conspired to thin out the sound and rob it of its force.

The Bloodheir peeled away from the column and came cantering up to Taim's position. His Shield followed and drew to a halt in a long, bright line.

"Enough to do what needs to be done," Aewult said with a flourish of his arm. It was not a question.

"I hope so, lord," Taim said.

"You're not to move from this position, whatever happens. I'll send word to you if your company is needed. If my messengers do not find you here, it will count against you when all this is done."

"Of course," Taim said tightly. "I will be here until I am commanded otherwise. Or until night falls."

"Ha!" The Bloodheir turned his horse hard about. "This'll be done long before nightfall. You'll see."

"Dusk comes early at this time of year," Taim murmured, but Aewult was already gone.

As the snow grew heavier, Taim had his men set up tents and move most of the horses into the fringes of the forest for shelter. Fires were lit and pots of broth set over them. A band of Haig warriors detached themselves from the passing army and demanded food and a place by one of the fires. By the time Taim got there and ordered them away, fists were being clenched and insults thrown. They were not the only ones to split away from the great, slow column. A dozen or more sick-looking men sat down by the side of the road and huddled there, despondent and apathetic, while the snow settled all around them.

Taim saw other small groups simply turn around and head back down the road towards Kolglas, like stubborn fish swimming against the current. One such band of reluctant warriors — men from the far west of Ayth-Haig to judge by their accents, and better than half-drunk to judge by their loudness — was intercepted by a harassed-looking captain in the midst of the column, and commanded to resume the march. There were threats, and shouting, and eventually violence. Two men were dead and others wounded before the mutinous company was compelled to obedience. Taim watched all this with a cold sense of trepidation settling over his heart.

The falling snow thinned. The sky lightened a fraction, the wind eased and fluttered back and forth as if unsure of its destination. Taim had dismounted and was sharing a loaf of bread with some of his men. He glanced up, and thought for one moment that he even glimpsed the globe of the sun, smeared through the clouds. It had begun its descent towards the horizon now; half the day was gone. The swirling wind was carrying a faint hint of sound on it. All around, men were waving at their companions to silence them, angling their heads to try to catch whatever message the erratic wind sought to deliver. Taim, like all of them, recognised the sound well enough. It was a formless thing, but he knew of what it was made: feet and hoofs, blades and cries, the clatter of shields and press of bodies. Somewhere far up the road, the head of Aewult's army had found the battle it sought.

The clouds soon thickened and reasserted their grip. The world was returned to a kind of twilight gloom. The wind swung back into the west and drove fresh snow in off the sea. Taim led his horse into the shelter of a clump of bushes and waited there, in silence, with a knot of his most experienced warriors. They watched, without surprise, as the flow of the mighty Haig army along the road faltered and fragmented. Fewer and fewer warriors were trudging up from Kolglas, and ever more of those who did were stopping and flinging themselves down, pulling cloaks over their heads and curling in their protection like soft boulders. Wagons had got stuck in the roadside ditch. The tide of the army slackened. For a short time, there was nothing more than a scattering of men, disorganised and unmoving, strung out along the road. Then the tide was ebbing and, though Taim had heard no command given, men were no longer marching out from Kolglas but back towards it.

Soon after that, the messenger came to Taim: a young man, with blood on his face and a feverish urgency in his eyes. He struggled to control his panting and foaming horse as he shouted his message.

"You're to bring every man you have to the Bloodheir. At once, without delay."

Taim swung up onto his horse and set about unbuckling his shield from where it lay across his back.

"Where is the Bloodheir?" he asked. Already, his men were hurrying to ready themselves.

"Glasbridge! Make for Glasbridge!" The messenger sounded almost angry, though perhaps it was only the backwash of fear. "You'll find the Bloodheir that way."

Taim grimaced up at the waves of snow tumbling down. "I'll be lucky to find him anywhere," he muttered.

"Every man you have!" the messenger cried as he spun away and was carried off by his distressed mount.

"Three hundred," Taim shouted after him, then as much to himself as anyone: "No more. I'll not blindly lead all the strength my Blood has left into this storm."

The wind died as they rode. Fat, heavy snowflakes thronged the air like congealed fragments of cloud. Hundreds upon hundreds of warriors, some exhausted, some wounded, some merely lost, crowded the road. It was as Taim and others had told Aewult nan Haig: this would be snowfall enough to still the world, to confound all the intents and desires of men. Even the rocky shoreline was acquiring a white dusting in the space between each set of waves. The sea receded into obscurity as ever more dense curtains of snow rolled in from the west. The mills and cottages on the landward side of the road faded behind wintry veils. It was, Taim kept thinking as he led his men on along the coast, weather fit for disaster. With every pace his horse took, the road was disappearing beneath its hoofs.

There were corpses – and perhaps the living too, for it was not always easy to tell the difference – here and there along the roadside: black bundles heaped up and now coated with white. Arrows, bolts and broken spears were scattered around, and a few dead horses. Once, without warning, a shower of arrows came skimming out of the snowstorm. There was no way of telling their source. A couple of men cried out, horses screamed. A few riders set off in search of the unseen archers but Taim called them back.

They came to a great swathe of the dead. Bodies were piled up along the line of a ditch and bank – now little more than great white undulations in the earth – that had been thrown across the road. The wounded were crawling around, clambering over their fallen comrades. Some were weeping, some crying out for help. One man, his left arm broken and torn, was stumbling around stabbing feebly, one-handed, with his spear. Perhaps he was killing the enemy wounded; perhaps he was killing the already dead. A score or more of injured Haig men had gathered together, huddling in the ditch, watching one another die.

"Where is the Bloodheir?" Taim shouted down at them.

They looked up at him, and he saw shock, fear, emptiness in their faces.

"Have you a healer?" one of them asked him. "We need a healer."

"Tell me where the Bloodheir is first," he insisted.

They did not know, but Taim left three of his men to give them what aid they could, and get those who would live back to Kolglas. He rode up and over the bank. Beyond, the ground as far as he could see was strewn with bodies. Hundreds had fallen here, warriors of the Black Road and the True Bloods alike, but the battle had moved on. It was somewhere out there, in the grey-white clouds of snow. Taim took his men onwards in search of it.

They were attacked soon after. Seventy or eighty assailants came howling out of a scrawny stand of trees. Not many of them had any armour, or even proper weapons. Fearless, they swept down on Taim's column, brandishing sickles and axes, cudgels and long knives. Many stumbled and fell in the snowdrifts; many others fell as soon as they came within reach of the Lannis men. Enough closed up to turn a short stretch of the road into a brutal little battle. Taim kept his horse on a short rein. He worked methodically, hacking down one attacker after another. It was soon over.

The further up the coast road they went, the more uneasy Taim became. He heard bursts of battle from further inland, never close or clear enough to tempt him towards them. Aewult's great army had been engulfed and dismembered by the snowstorm. A frightened band of Haig warriors came streaming down the road from the direction of Glasbridge. Many of them were wounded, others had cast aside their weapons. As they barged their way past, Taim leaned down and seized one of them by the collar.

"What's happening?" he demanded of the man. "Where's the Bloodheir?"

"Who knows?" the warrior cried, and tore himself free.

More figures were rushing down the buried road in the footsteps of the fleeing Haig company. These were different, though: matted hair, hide jackets adorned with fragments of bone and ivory, long spears with extravagantly barbed points. Tarbains. Taim had fought them once or twice in his youth, when he was scouting into and beyond the Vale of Stones from Tanwrye. He knew how best to meet them. He swung his sword above his head and charged the tribesmen, crying out as he went. His men followed. The Tarbains halted. Some of them launched spears that arced down into the mass of horsemen. Breaks and contortions in the rolling thunder of hoofs told Taim that more than one of the missiles found its mark, but the Tarbains were not inclined to test their skills against mounted men. The whole ragged band of them scattered from the line of the road, streaming inland over a flat, blank white field.

Taim reined in his mount at once, and a single shouted command was enough to call back his warriors. There was no point in wasting time and the horses' strength trying to run down Tarbains in deep snow. They had a more important purpose here. Taim allowed himself to wonder only briefly how he was supposed to fulfil that purpose, if he could not even find Aewult nan

Haig. There was nothing to do put press on down the gullet of this great wintry beast.

The air was now so thick with snow that sight failed beyond two score paces. Taim's world had collapsed to this strange, enclosed white space, beyond which strange sounds – indistinct but terrible – rose and fell. He turned his head this way and that, trying to make some sense of what he heard, but the same blurred cacophony seemed to lie all around beyond the curtain of falling snow. He glimpsed figures and raised his sword; they were gone at once, as if they had been mere momentary darkenings in the air's featureless expanse.

His men were clustered together behind him. Their silence betrayed their apprehension. Taim peered this way and that. Even the course of the road ahead was lost, hidden beneath a white blanket. Anger – a clenched ire born out of anxiety – knotted his stomach. It was impossible to fight like this, half blind and half deaf. He had not led the survivors of Gryvan's war against Igryn oc Dargannan-Haig all the way here just to throw their lives away.

He was on the point of turning his company back when a surge of sound reached him, holding its shape in his ear long enough for him to fix its direction. There was battle somewhere close ahead. He urged his horse forwards, gesturing for the others to keep pace with him. And soon enough there was a trail they could follow: corpses; a broad field where the snow and earth and blood had been churned into a filthy, trampled mess; and voices, screaming and shouting above the ringing of blades and shields. There was a heaving mass of figures. It was a formless thing, a dark, turbulent thundercloud pressed down by the weight of tumbling snow. Amidst it, Taim glimpsed momentary flashes of armour, a torn banner swaying back and forth like the mast of a tempest-shaken ship. It was Aewult's Palace Shield, beset. And where his Shield was, the Bloodheir must be.

"Here you are," Taim cried over his shoulder to his men. He

rattled his sword against the face of his shield. "Here's battle for you! Here's the Black Road, that killed your Thane and burned your homes!"

The charge was reckless and wild, across treacherous ground strewn with the dead, through the blizzard. There was no time to tell friend from foe, only to stab and slash as they crashed into the throng of warriors. Taim's horse reared and stamped, lunged on into the fray. Men and women went down before it. Taim swung and his blade sent someone's helmet spinning away. A spear lanced in across the front of his hips. He hacked down on the shaft and cracked it. His shield shook, and he saw a crossbow bolt fixed there. Another spear punched into his horse's shoulder and stayed there for a moment, dragged from its wielder's hands. It fell away as the horse staggered, sinking, before surging up and on again. Someone – a woman – was running past, fleeing perhaps. Taim cut at the back of her neck.

He could see the Palace Shield, surrounded by a thick press of Black Road warriors. He cut his way towards them, trusting his men to follow. His horse stumbled and its forequarters plunged down. It twisted onto its side, throwing Taim. The snow was deep and it smacked, wet and cold, into his face. It filled his mouth and clung to his face. His body acted without the need for thought. He kept hold of his sword, rolled, and then he was on his feet, spitting snow, in time to turn the first spear thrust aside with his shield. Another came in from his flank, but he was already stepping back and out of its path. A backhanded sword-stroke hit the spearman on the shoulder and knocked him down. In the empty, still part of his mind that took over at such moments, Taim registered his own warriors surging past, saw the mounted figure of Aewult nan Haig up ahead. He heard his horse struggling to rise behind him, spun around and flung a leg across the saddle. It bore him up.

The Lannis-Haig men broke through to what remained of Aewult's Palace Shield. Many of the shieldmen were already dead, crumpled in the snow, their breastplates smeared with dirt and blood. The survivors were fighting desperately to keep the teeming masses of the Black Road from their master.

At first Taim was not certain whether Aewult recognised him. The Bloodheir's eyes were wild.

"Sire, come away," Taim shouted. His horse was tossing its head, shaking. He could not tell how badly it was injured; how much longer he had before it fell again.

"We can't keep you safe here," Taim cried. "There's already fighting far behind us. We must fall back to Kolglas."

Taim saw such loathing, such visceral hatred, in Aewult's face then that he feared the Bloodheir was about to attack him. Instead, Aewult wheeled his massive horse and made for safety. Most of his Palace Shield broke away and followed in his wake, barging through the ranks of Taim's men. A few of the huge armour-clad warriors were too entangled in the fray to escape so easily. Even as Taim watched, one of them went down, a long-handled axe hooking his neck and hauling him backwards out of his saddle.

Aewult was instantly out of sight, vanished into the white void that surrounded them. Taim swept snowflakes from his brow with the back of his sword hand. There was nothing to be gained by fighting on here. The Black Road warriors were too numerous, and dozens of them were already spilling out over the snowfield in pursuit of the Bloodheir.

"With me, Lannis!" Taim cried, and drove his horse after Aewult.

One of his own men crashed to the ground in a spray of snow and earth. Taim turned to help him, but was too late. Half a dozen Black Roaders fell upon the Lannis man like hounds on a stricken boar. Taim battered them aside and killed one with a single blow to his head. The dead rider's horse struggled to its feet and hobbled a few paces before slumping down again.

"Inkallim!" Taim heard someone shouting.

He looked. The last of the Bloodheir's Palace Shield to have remained behind was unmounted, standing with his feet widely spaced and both hands on the hilt of his upraised sword. It was a stupid pose, Taim though. Either the man was ill-trained, or his mind had been clouded by shock or fear. Blinking through the falling snow, Taim saw the mass of the enemy back away. Inexplicably, a space opened, a moment of silence stretched itself out. Then a figure was coming, out of the crowd, out of the snow: a tall, rangy woman with hair as black as ink tied tightly back. She came with long strides. Snowflakes spun about her, tumbling in her wake. She wore a rigid dark cuirass of hard leather. Two swords were sheathed on her back. As she came up to the shield-man she reached back over her shoulders and swept the blades free.

Taim was held, gripped by this most awful of sights: a fell raven of the Battle, come like the very animating spirit of this gelid killing ground to mark his flight. Aewult's abandoned shieldman steadied himself, prepared to meet this new opponent. He was huge, at least a head taller than her, and as broad-shouldered as she was lean. His sword snapped down, beginning its killing arc. And then there was only an instant's blurred movement and the Inkallim was beyond him. She was lowering her twin blades, and she was staring at Taim. Behind her, the shield-man toppled.

Light blades, one a fraction shorter than the other, the old, appraising part of Taim's mind noted. Single-edged, they had to be wickedly sharp to fell a man in such a way. And she must be a rare talent to wield them with such precision: one of those blades had opened the shieldman's throat as it passed. Taim felt a cold challenge in the gaze that the woman fixed on him. Once, when he had been younger, it might have lit an answering anger in him; he might have sprung forwards to meet that challenge, whether it was imagined or real. Not now, though. He hauled his horse around and kicked it into a gallop.

The Lannis-Haig riders pounded through the ever-deepening snow. It was chaotic, dangerous. They could not see what lay before them, nor what came after them. They rode down several of the Black Roaders who were pursuing Aewult, but of the Bloodheir and his surviving Palace Shield there was no sign. As he charged along, forcing his way to the head of his straggling company, Taim locked his mind onto a single, sharp idea. He had done what he could for Aewult, discharged his duty; now all he cared about was bringing as many of his men as possible back to Kolglas. Whatever battles were still being fought out in the snowstorm, there would be no resolution. Friend and foe alike were blind, lost. The most anyone could hope for on this bloody, white day was to live, and see tomorrow.

He slowed his men to a walk, reordered them into a column. Their losses were not desperate, but enough to pain him; enough to hollow him out a little with premonitions of guilt, of sleeplessness. Then, allowing, just briefly, his head to hang down and his eyes to close, he grasped for the first time the full extent of his heart-sick weariness. He was, in a way that did not befit the highest warrior of his Blood, tired to his very bones of leading men to their deaths. He had thought it would be easier now that he faced the Black Road, a true and lasting enemy of his Blood, but it seemed even that salve for his uneasy heart was inadequate.

Taim lifted his head once more. A fresh wind was picking up, coming in off the estuary and swirling the snowflakes in a fiercer dance. The cold was numbing his face. He could hear the sea on the rocky shore off to his right, and that was enough for him to cling to. So long as they kept moving, and kept that sound close upon their flank, Kolglas was within reach. He laid a hand on his horse's neck, and could feel the unsteadiness of its stride, the faltering of its muscles. It did not have long left, he thought.

They had to fight more than once. The blizzard had taken the battle and twisted it, crumbled it into the chaos of a hundred grim, brutal little struggles. Small bands of warriors stumbled back and forth through the blinding storm, flailing about in knee-deep snowdrifts, crashing up against one another, killing, dying. When Taim led his dwindling company back to the ditch and dyke that they had found covered with the dead and wounded on their journey out, fresh slaughter was being done there. New layers of corpses were being laid down over those – already snow-covered – that had fallen earlier.

Taim and his men cut their way through. He lashed out all around him, in a kind of surfeited stupor. Again and again he felt his sword jarring in his hand as it met flesh, armour or shield, but he hardly knew whether he struck friend or enemy. He constantly expected his horse to die beneath him, to pitch him down into the dark red slush. Somehow, it did not, and it bore him through the battle, up over the bund and across the ditch beyond. And then there was no one left to oppose them. There was only the snowstorm, and the long march back to Kolglas, and the hundreds or thousands of others, stunned and exhausted, lost and empty-eyed, who were trudging back in that same direction through the last dwindling light of the day.

At last there came a time when Taim was in a stable in Kolglas, and the blizzard was outside, beyond wooden walls, and he was hauling his saddle from his horse's back with aching arms. The great animal shook. He went to fetch water and feed for it, but when he returned it had collapsed. So as night fell and the snow kept spinning down out of the darkness, he sent the stablehands away and stood in the light of a guttering oil lamp and watched his horse die there on the straw.

III

Beyond Highfast, the road that Orisian and the others followed soon sank into decrepitude. It snaked across a saddle between two rocky peaks, then down a steep valley. As it went, it crumbled. Its

surface grew ever more pitted and broken. Water and frosts and
rock falls had eaten its fabric away over the years, reducing what
must once have been a great highway to an uneven, unreliable
track. Once, in the time of the Kingship, there would have been
many traders and travellers following this route through the
Karkyre Peaks and on towards Drandar. Now the hamlets and
inns that lined the way were ruins; the road stumbled pointlessly
in its decay towards a wilderness of hills, forests and Kyrinin
lands.

Orisian rode at the head of the column with Rothe and
Torcaill. The band of warriors that followed was somewhat
reduced. Orisian had ordered four of them sent north by way of
Hent to find Taim Narran at Kolglas and tell him what was happening; Torcaill had picked out another half-dozen and sent them
ahead as outriders. Though an undisputed part of Lheanor oc
Kilkry-Haig's domain, these were wild lands. Orisian did not ask
whether it was Kyrinin or human bandits that Torcaill feared, but
it hardly mattered. They saw no living thing save birds and occasional wild goats silhouetted on the ridges high above the road.

They made good time on the first day. Only once were they
delayed: a cascade of water plunging down from the heights had
cut away a swathe of the road, turning it for some little distance
into the bed of a churning mountain stream. The horses crossed
easily, if hesitantly, enough. Yvane, still obstinately refusing to
ride, grumbled and moaned about her wet feet.

By the time dusk was coming on, they had almost escaped the
Peaks. The valley that carried the roadway down had opened out.
Trees and shrubs now lined the gentled river. Grass and rushes
sprouted amongst the rocks, even in the midst of the road.
Ahead, dark in the faltering light, woodlands could be seen scat-
tered across lower ground.

They camped on the valley floor, far enough from the river's
course that no sudden flood would catch them unawares but close
enough that spindly alders could give them some shelter from the

wind that had followed them from the Peaks. While Torcaill's men set up their few simple tents — not enough to shelter everyone — and lit fires, Orisian went to find Ess'yr and Varryn. They were filling waterskins from the river. As Orisian drew near, Ess'yr threw back her head and poured a stream of water into her mouth. It splashed across her chin and ran down the smooth sweep of her neck. She wiped her lips and held the skin out to Orisian. He shook his head.

"No, thank you."

The two Kyrinin had their spears with them, and Varryn his bow.

"You don't plan to rest tonight," Orisian said, disappointed. He had hoped to speak with Ess'yr, share food with her perhaps as he had done before, when they crossed the Car Criagar. Catch fish, he thought, as they had once done at a tiny stream in those distant forests.

"We need less rest than Huanin," Varryn said, standing up. He tied the fat waterskin to his belt. "And the enemy may be near."

"I don't think so," murmured Orisian, still watching Ess'yr. There was a life, an energy, in her now that he had not seen for some time. That part of her that had been so oppressed by confinement in Kolkyre and Highfast was stirring again, remembering itself. She moved quickly, precisely, as she sank the mouth of her waterskin below the surface, then raised and stoppered it.

"But you cannot know," Varryn said. "We will know, because we will see with our own eyes."

Orisian smiled, despite himself. "Of course. I'd sooner trust your eyes than those of Torcaill's scouts, in any case."

Ess'yr stood up, pushing the hair back from her face with both hands.

"You'll be back before morning?" Orisian asked. "We plan to move on as soon as there's any light."

Ess'yr nodded. "Long before."

"Good." Orisian gestured at the river. "I'll see if I can trick some fish out of there, the way you showed me."

Ess'yr glanced at the water slipping by. She gave Orisian a smile — a momentary, faint thing — and bent to pick up her spear. "It is good to break a fast on fish," she said.

After the two Kyrinin had drifted off into the deepening darkness, Orisian did make a brief attempt to feel out some fish lurking under the soft bank of the river. The icy-cold water was discouraging, and he very soon began to feel foolish. Here he was, a supposed Thane, scrambling about on a river-bank trying, and failing, to catch fish to please a woman who probably thought of him as nothing more than a chance companion. He sat on a hummock of wiry grass and silently berated himself.

"Feeling a bit solitary?" Yvane said behind him, making him jump.

"I'm fine." He stood up and brushed dirt and fragments of grass from his legs. "How are your feet?"

"Warm. I toasted them by one of the fires. You might want to come and join us. Eshenna and your man Torcaill are liable to be calling each other names soon. Not good for the harmony of the camp."

"Harmony doesn't seem to be anyone's first concern these days," Orisian muttered as he followed her back to the tents.

In the midst of the encampment, around the largest of the fires, twenty or more men were sitting cross-legged. They were quietly consuming their meagre rations while Torcaill and Eshenna argued across the flames. Rothe, standing at the very edge of the pool of yellow firelight, looked almost amused.

"Enough," Orisian said without waiting to hear what the subject of the disagreement was.

Torcaill clamped his mouth shut. Eshenna looked more inclined to continue the dispute but satisfied herself with taking a mouthful of hard biscuit.

"What are you arguing about?" Orisian asked Torcaill.

"She says we are moving too slowly," the warrior replied. "I say it's not safe to move faster. Not during the day and certainly not at night."

Orisian glanced at Eshenna. The *na'kyrim* returned his gaze but said nothing.

"Will you walk with me?" he asked her, and led her away from the fire. Yvane followed, as did Rothe a little way back.

"It's not easy for some of these men, you know," Orisian said once they were out at the furthest limit of the fire's light. "They have never known a *na'kyrim*, never had to trust anyone not of their own kind. Most of them would rather be heading north, to fight for their homes and families."

"You are their lord, are you not?" Eshenna asked. "It should not matter to them what is easy and what is not."

Orisian shook his head. "They know me little better than they do you, and they've not much more reason to trust me. No one ever thought I would be Thane, Eshenna. Not them, not me."

The *na'kyrim* shrugged and folded her arms across her chest. "I only wanted them to understand," she said. It was no apology, but her tone was subdued.

"Understand what?"

"That there is urgency here. K'rina is not far. I can hear the sound of her mind, close. But if there are White Owls hunting her too, they will not stop in the night. They will not rest. If they reach her first, and take her back to Aeglyss, all this effort will have been wasted."

"I know." Orisian sighed. "For these men, these are difficult things to understand. They know nothing of the Shared, had never heard of Aeglyss until they left Highfast. It's not the world they live in."

"It is now," muttered Yvane behind him. "They just don't know it yet."

Orisian glanced at her over his shoulder. "That might be true but, if so, they'll have to learn it for themselves. I can't make them believe it just by telling them it's so."

"The Shared is in chaos," Eshenna whispered. "It shudders at the movement of the Anain. And Aeglyss himself is there, not just the stain of his corruption, but his mind itself: reaching out. K'rina is at the centre of this. I know it."

"Is that true?" Orisian asked Yvane.

She shrugged. "Couldn't say for certain. I've no great talent for sifting out the patterns. If you're asking me whether my head aches worse every day, whether I feel a shadow spreading, then the answer's yes. If you're asking me whether I think I should have stayed behind in Highfast, the answer's maybe. That should tell you something."

"Whatever the truth is," Rothe said from out of the darkness, "you'll not persuade Torcaill to move any further now. Not at night. If there are White Owls out there, we'd all be feathered with arrows by dawn. The blacker the night, the more numerous the arrows."

Orisian regarded his shieldman for a moment: a dark mass with the flames of the fires leaping behind him. He was right. Even Orisian knew that only the direst, most overwhelming need would persuade warriors of his Blood to confront Kyrinin at night, when human eyes and ears were at such a disadvantage. They had been skirmishing with the White Owls in Anlane, and even with the Fox, for generations, and had learned the lessons such experience taught.

"I'll speak to Torcaill at dawn," he said to Eshenna. "We'll make as much speed as we can tomorrow. That's the best we can do."

In such poor light, he could not see her face clearly, but he did not doubt there was frustration there.

Orisian was awake when Ess'yr and Varryn returned. He had hardly slept at all, disturbed by the hard ground beneath him, the intermittent patter of rain on the tent and Rothe's snoring. When at last he drifted off into shallow sleep he was soon awoken, startled by the piping calls of some birds flying over. Unable to recover the threads of slumber, he struggled out stiffly from beneath the coarse blanket and left the tent on his hands and knees. Rothe stirred behind him, but did not fully wake.

Outside, the slight lightening of the eastern sky said dawn was near but not yet breaking. Others – a few weary warriors – were also awake, shuffling through the near-darkness, trying to restart fires, or just standing in the fine misty drizzle with blankets and cloaks wrapped about them. There was no sound save an occasional cough, the crackle and hiss of wet wood resisting feeble flames, the soft voice of the invisible river.

Orisian drank from a waterskin hanging outside his tent. He was standing there, wondering whether to get back beneath the shelter of canvas, when the Kyrinin came out of the gloom. They appeared amongst the tall, thin alder trees as sudden and silent as deer emerging on the edge of a forest. Both of them were soaking wet, their hair matted down and heavy, their clothes darkened by the rain and covered in muddy stains.

Varryn went straight to the large fire at the heart of the camp and squatted down beside it. The warrior who was feeding twigs and kindling into the faltering flames regarded this Kyrinin newcomer uneasily, perhaps suspiciously, but said nothing. Ess'yr paused at Orisian's side.

"Did you find anything?" he asked her softly.

"We saw sign of the enemy. Half a day towards dawn from here, by human pace."

"Coming this way?"

She shook her head. "They do not seek us. Not yet."

"But you did not pursue them." Orisian glanced across at her brother, silent and thoughtful by the fire. "I feared you might not return, if you found sign of White Owls you could hunt."

"There will be hunting soon. And killing."

It was an incomplete answer, Orisian knew at once. He could not tell whether it was some subtle sign in her tone or expression that betrayed her, or whether he had come to know just enough of how her – and her brother's – mind worked to anticipate her evasions.

"Do you think I am still in need of your protection?" he murmured, unwilling to allow anyone else to hear these words. "You think your promise to see to my safety not yet done with?"

Ess'yr returned his intent gaze, and for a moment he was captivated once again by those flinty eyes and the depths of grace they seemed to hold. The pale blue lines tattooed across her face were faint in this pre-dawn light; they almost danced with a life of their own at the corners of his vision. He could think of nothing else to say.

"Did you catch fish?" she asked him.

Orisian blinked. "What?"

"In the river."

"Oh. No."

She dipped her head, drawing his eyes down to her waist. A single silvery fish hung there, tied to her belt with strands of woven grass.

"I knew you would not," Ess'yr said.

The derelict road bore them on down the valley, in amongst clumps of trees and long stretches of wet, boggy ground. Behind them, the Karkyre Peaks were hidden by thick grey clouds of mist and rain. The horses were subdued, discouraged by the foul weather. Those who rode them were little more enthusiastic, but at Orisian's urging Torcaill did keep them to a steady, remorseless pace. Ess'yr and Varryn trotted along parallel to the column of warriors, drifting in and out of sight as the drizzle thickened and then slackened off again. They kept up easily with the horses.

Yvane did not fare so well. Orisian had known she would not.

He and Rothe dropped back along the line of men and rode beside the *na'kyrim* for a time. She said nothing, made no complaint, but was obviously struggling. The road surface was scored across with little gullies, strewn with loose stones and scarred with pits where the cobbles had disappeared altogether. More than once Yvane stumbled. Had she been human, it would have been impossible for her to continue on foot; because she was not, Orisian felt, it was merely a bad idea.

"You'll turn an ankle," he called down to her eventually.

She ignored him, though he did hear what might have been a grunt – of either exertion or dismissal.

"Get up behind Rothe." Orisian saw the expression of alarm that contorted his shieldman's face.

"I managed to climb the Car Criagar, up and down, many times on these two feet," Yvane said. "I walked the length of the Vale of Tears more than once. I can manage this road."

"She doesn't like horses," Rothe said. "That's fair enough. It's her choice."

Orisian frowned at his shieldman, but Rothe was now staring fixedly ahead, fascinated by the back of the nearest warrior.

"Ride with me, then," Orisian said.

Yvane kept striding on. If anything, she picked up her pace a little, presumably hoping to either dissuade him or leave him behind. Irritated, Orisian gave his horse a sharp nudge and brought it to a halt across Yvane's path. She almost walked into its shoulder. The lines of warriors parted around the two of them and flowed on.

"Listen," said Orisian, "you will slow us down, sooner or later. You encouraged me in this undertaking, and I won't have you now hindering me out of stubbornness, or whatever it is. I also won't leave you behind on your own. Therefore, we are going to stand here and argue about it until you ride."

Yvane glared up at him, drops of water beading her hair. She blinked misty rain out of her eyes. Orisian did not flinch as he once might have done. Instead, he raised his eyebrows expectantly and waited. It was Yvane who yielded.

"I never mastered the trick of riding. Tried a couple of times, at Koldihrve. Neither attempt ended well. Not for me, at least; the horses seemed to quite enjoy it."

"All you have to do is hang on."

"That is much what I was told on previous occasions."

"But this time you just have to hang on to me, not the reins or the horse."

Yvane displayed neither grace nor good humour, but she did, eventually, allow herself to be hoisted up behind Orisian. She clutched him so tightly about the midriff that he had to ask her to loosen her grip more than once.

The sky cleared, the air grew cold. Forest closed in along either side of the road. Everyone became tense, now that they could not see more than a few dozen paces in any direction. The tallest trees – elegant ash and soaring oak – almost touched their outermost branches together across the road. Orisian and the others advanced beneath a skeletal roof of leafless boughs.

Eshenna rode beside Orisian and Yvane for a time. Her pony was looking bedraggled and sorry for itself, but walked doggedly on amongst the warhorses.

"I'm feeling dizzy," Eshenna said. She spoke to Orisian, but he had the feeling that her words were addressed to Yvane more than anyone. "If I close my eyes, I lose balance; my head whirls. I can't hold on to a thought for more than a few moments."

"I know," grunted Yvane into Orisian's shoulder.

"Can you still lead us to this woman?" Orisian asked.

Eshenna nodded. She was gloomy, her face drawn and lifeless as if she was sick.

"It feels as if she's close. It's getting hard to tell. Such storms are running through the Shared that it's . . . difficult. The Anain, Aeglyss. It's all too much."

"Are the Anain here?" Orisian murmured. "Watching us?" He

remembered, clearly, what Ess'yr had told him of the Anain, when they were in the Car Criagar. She had spoken of those then as though they were always present, as though the land was always inhabited by their incorporeal minds.

"We are beneath their notice," Eshenna said, and grimaced. "They are no more likely to watch us than they are to watch a mouse, digging about in the moss. Still, they are here. They move, like ships, and we are just twigs caught up in their wake."

"We might have been beneath their notice once," Yvane muttered, "but now, who knows? The *Hymyr Ot'tryn* is near."

"What's that?" Orisian asked over his shoulder.

"It's the Snake name for what you would call the Veiled Woods."

"I've not heard of it," Orisian said, but then hesitated at a flickering of memory. "Perhaps I have. In stories, maybe."

"A stretch of forest, not far from here. One of the places, some say, where the Anain come a little nearer to the surface of the world." Yvane glanced across at Eshenna. The younger woman was tight-lipped, staring at her pony's neck.

"Even the Kyrinin get shivers down their backs thinking about that place, for all that they imagine the Anain are more or less benevolent," Yvane went on. "They're not stupid enough to think you could ever call them friendly. Even in the best of times."

In places, the surface of the old road was slick with wet, rotted leaves. Too few wheels and feet had passed this way, in recent decades, to clear the detritus of each autumn. In the cracks and crevices and ruts, soil was accumulating. Grass had taken hold between and across cobblestones. The deeper they went into the wooded landscape, the more and more the road they travelled came to resemble little more than an overgrown grassy track. Where the turf was thickest, there were sometimes bulbous anthills dotting the sward, and swathes of mushrooms bubbling up. Saplings, some more than twice the height of a man, grew in the middle of the highway, straggly things straining thinly upwards in search of light. Their hidden roots had lifted the road's surface, tilting the stones up on their shoulders.

Orisian grew ever more uneasy and doubtful of his choices. The further Highfast fell away behind them, the more remote seemed his reasons for coming this way. As the wilderness swallowed up the road before his eyes, so he felt as if it was drawing him into itself, distancing him ever more completely from the world of strife and conflict that lay beyond these narrow, tree-crowded horizons. A part of him – he wondered if it might be the honest part – accused the rest of cowardice. Did he secretly prefer to be Thane of just this small company, lost in this wild place where none could require great martial deeds or weighty decisions of him? Did he fear marching at the head of an army, facing the challenge of Aewult nan Haig and the Shadowhand, more than he feared whatever threat the forest, the White Owls, rumours of the Anain, could offer? Every step along this crumbling road was beginning to feel like flight. The trust he had placed in Eshenna, Yvane and the other *na'kyrim* seemed less certain with each passing moment.

As night began to fall, a rough wind shook its way through the treetops. Torcaill turned the column off the road and chose a small clearing for a campsite. His warriors were silent and subdued. They disliked the forest, its suffocating density. Orisian wondered how much longer these men would follow his lead without question. The wind was rising, rocking the trees and rustling through the undergrowth. Those who had tents struggled to stake them into the ground. The men who must sleep without shelter were casting about for places where they might find some small protection from the elements.

Rothe tried to light a fire. The wind kept swirling down into the clearing and scattering the flakes of bark that he had cut for kindling. The shieldman muttered under his breath as he set down his flint and scooped the bark back into a little pile. Orisian squatted beside him.

"There's a lot of unhappy men here, aren't there?" he said softly.

Rothe glanced at him, then concentrated on striking sparks.

"It's not of much consequence, whether a warrior's happy or not. He does as he's commanded. You needn't worry about that. However much any of them grumble, they'll follow you."

Orisian wished he could share Rothe's confidence. He glanced round, to find Ess'yr standing behind him. She was watching Rothe's hands as he methodically chipped spark after spark out of the flint.

"We heard the enemy," she said. "Before. They call like birds."

Rothe looked up at that. Orisian stood, feeling the stiffness in his legs and back as he did so. His body had still not reconciled itself to so much time spent on horseback.

"White Owls?" he asked her. "Are they near?"

She gave the slightest, most delicate of shrugs. "Cannot say. Perhaps not. They moved . . ." she stretched a graceful arm out, a little south of east. "But others might be near. The weather favours the hunter."

As if to emphasise her words a violent gust of wind rushed through the clearing, tumbling twigs and dead leaves along. Orisian ushered Ess'yr to one side, putting a little distance between her and the closest of Torcaill's warriors. He might have touched her elbow, or her back – applied a gentle pressure to indicate his desire to move – but there was something in the simple thought of such contact that made him nervous.

"Yvane and Eshenna were talking about the Anain before," he said, once he was confident that none could overhear them. "They say they're awake. Moving. And that we're close to places . . . to their places."

Ess'yr gazed back at him, waiting for a question. In the half-light of dusk, her face seemed to him like a soft mask; the gentle curves of her tattoos like some pattern impressed upon pale silk. It was too dark for him to see her eyes clearly. They were shadows.

"Is it true?" he asked. "Do you think they're here, around us?"

"Always," she replied, and he heard her voice quite clearly even though the trees all about were roaring and creaking in the wind. "We walk on their backs. When we touch a tree, we touch their arm. The roots are their bones."

"They're waking, though. That's what all the *na'kyrim* say: they're moving closer to the surface. Why? Do you know?"

"Such a thing is not to be known. They are not like us, not like Huanin or Kyrinin. You do not ask why the river flows, or why the fire moves as it does. If the Anain rise, they rise. If they act, they act. That is all."

"Yet your people seek their favour. Your *anhyne*, the catchers of the dead. They guard you, don't they?"

Ess'yr regarded Orisian inexpressively. She blinked, sheathing and then unsheathing the deep, dark pools that her eyes had become.

"My thought is that the Anain favour none and nothing. Some of my people say they ended the war between Huanin and Kyrinin to end our suffering. I think not. It think they ended it because it disturbed the balance in their world. If we are beneath their gaze, if they wake, we will not choose the ending. The seal pup does not choose if the storm takes it out to sea. The storm does that."

Later, as Orisian lay in his tent, his mind sank down into a half-sleeping fog. The rushing of the wind through the trees was transformed into the breaking of waves. He saw himself standing on the shore looking out towards Castle Kolglas. The sea was high, far higher than he had ever known it. Huge foaming breakers roared in and pounded at the isolated castle. It was breaking apart beneath the onslaught. He felt an awful dread churning in his chest.

He woke once. The gale had fallen away. Cold prickled across his cheeks. He could hear Rothe breathing. He closed his eyes and slept.

IV

Four men died in the night. A hard frost had come, brittling the grass and casting its white sheen over everything. The ground crackled beneath Orisian's feet. He left a trail of dark prints behind him, pressed into the cold dusting. He shivered and sniffed as he walked.

Rothe showed him the bodies. One – a guard – lay at the foot of a shallow slope, stretched out against the thick base of a tree. The other three lay where they had settled down for the night. In the evening they, like everyone else, had wandered about beneath the trees, pursing their lips and weighing up the options. They had chosen a place where the ground seemed even, the grass dry, and they had unrolled their sleeping mats, made a pillow of their jacket or shield or a rock. They had lain down and pulled their blankets tight about them. And they had died there, silently, in the darkness. Their throats had been cut. Their blood had made puddles on the forest floor.

Orisian looked into the face of the corpse nearest him. He looked away again quickly, repelled by that too-familiar vision of death, but he had time to see the bruises on the man's face where someone had roughly clamped a hand over his mouth.

"They killed the sentry first," muttered Rothe. "Then these three, just because they were within reach, on the edge of the camp."

"Kyrinin?" Orisian asked dully.

"Beyond doubt. I've seen this kind of thing before, in Anlane."

"They could have killed us all."

"There may only be a handful of them. Perhaps someone stirred while they were about their work; perhaps they thought they were about to be discovered. They'd always rather be cutting throats in the darkness than facing up to a real fight."

"It's a pity Varryn and Ess'yr were sleeping on the other side of the camp. They might have heard something."

"Perhaps."

Torcaill was going from corpse to corpse, collecting swords. He paused beside Orisian.

"We should turn back, Thane," he said. "There'll be more dead if we don't. I can't put outriders ahead of us now. They'd not survive half the day."

Orisian took one of the sheathed blades from the warrior and turned it in his hands. There were notches and crude patterns scratched into the scabbard; the metal cap on its end had a simple design of dots punched into it. An incongruous little strand of red-dyed string was tied about the hilt.

"What's this?" Orisian asked, running a fingertip over the string. "Do you know why he had this on his sword?"

Torcaill frowned at it. "No, sire. A token from some girl, perhaps. Or a reminder of some enemy he had killed. I don't know."

"What was his name?"

"Dorvadain. Dorvadain Emmen."

Orisian glanced over his shoulder. Varryn and Ess'yr were there. They had come silently across the frosted grass and now stared at the dead men. Orisian looked back to the sword in his hands for a moment, then returned it to Torcaill.

"Will you do something for me?" he asked Varryn quietly.

The Kyrinin waited.

"I want to know how many White Owls there are. Where they are, where they are going. I don't want to be surprised by them again. You can move faster than we can; see things we cannot. And you know them better than we do."

Varryn regarded him with the usual still, unreadable eyes. Yvane walked up behind the two Kyrinin, peering over their shoulders and wincing a little when she saw the bodies.

"Of course he'll go," the *na'kyrim* said. "Never known a Fox that'd pass up the chance to stick a spear into a White Owl."

That brought no more response from Varryn than Orisian's question had, but the Kyrinin warrior did turn to Ess'yr and murmur a few fluid words in the Fox tongue. Yvane brushed past him and pointed at the frost-blighted ground around the corpse of the guard.

"They left enough of a trail for even a human to follow, I should think," she said to Orisian.

Orisian noticed Torcaill's scowl at that, but ignored it.

"If we all go running off into the forest after them, we'll end up dead," he said to Yvane. "You know that as well as I do. They might not even know Varryn is on their trail."

She shrugged, and blew out a breath that steamed into the chill air. "Probably true. I'm not so sure we won't end up dead anyway, mind you."

"Did you sleep badly?" Rothe muttered. "You're in a foul mood this morning."

Yvane glared at the shieldman, who smiled as innocently as Orisian had ever seen him manage. The *na'kyrim* stalked away. Orisian gave Rothe a prod on the shoulder as they watched her receding back.

"You wouldn't be trying to pick a fight, would you?" he asked. "Quality of sleep's not the best subject to discuss, these days."

Rothe muttered a half-hearted apology, and went to help Torcaill move the bodies.

Orisian found Eshenna rolling up her thin sleeping mat. The skin beneath her eyes had a dark, almost bruised tinge to it. Little sleep, and less rest, he assumed. He squatted down beside her. She did not look up, concentrating on tying up the mat with a loop of cord. There was the very slightest tremor in her hands as she worked, he thought. It might have always been there, but if so he had never noticed it before.

"I cannot go on much further," he said quietly to her. "I have to turn back, head for Kolglas soon. Perhaps I've already come too far. Everyone else seems to think so."

"I don't. Nor does Yvane."

"No. But you are only two. Men are dying now, Eshenna."

"We are the only two who understand even a little of what is happening." She looked him in the eyes then, and her gaze was strong and firm. "You know that. It makes a difference."

"It makes some difference," he murmured. "But you have to tell me she's close, Eshenna. I can't just keep marching deeper into the forest."

The *na'kyrim* returned her attention to her rolled mat, slinging it across her shoulder.

"She is close. Today, we'll have her. Tomorrow, perhaps."

Varryn and Ess'yr trotted past, spears in hand. They wove their way between the trees and disappeared, vanishing in an instant into the forest as if they had stepped across some intangible, impenetrable barrier. Orisian stared after them briefly, then rose and went to tell Torcaill to prepare his men for the march.

They went quickly now. Anxiety gnawed at Orisian, fraying the edges of his temper and patience. An emptiness, almost a hunger, had settled into the pit of his stomach that he somehow knew could only be relieved by finishing this; by finding K'rina, or finding White Owls, or death, even. What form the culmination took mattered less to him than that it came soon. He disliked that feeling, and mistrusted its origins. There was something in its texture that felt not wholly his own.

The ancient road that had brought them this far had lost its struggle against the suffocating forest. It was gone, buried beneath layers of leaf, moss, root and soil. Nothing was left to mark its course save the occasional worked stone poking up through the green and brown sward, and once a cluster of low ruins of to one side, draped in ivy, crowded with saplings.

Yvane was persuaded to share Rothe's horse for a time. The *na'kyrim* glowered, and every now and again shot dark looks in Orisian's direction, as if accusing him of some kind of betrayal, but she made less protest than he had expected. Eshenna rode near the front. Her head hung low, and bobbed in time with her mount's tread. She did not sleep, though; merely suffered. Whenever Orisian glimpsed her face, it was crunched up in a shifting mix of pain and concentration. Now and again she would grunt, sometimes wince. Late in the morning, she grew still. Her horse drifted to one side of the column and dropped its head to tug at a clump of long grasses.

"That way," she murmured, when Orisian and Torcaill flanked her in consternation. She waved an arm imprecisely. What remained of the road they had been following curved away; Eshenna was pointing into deep forest.

Torcaill looked doubtful, at best.

"You're sure?" Orisian asked quietly. It was too late to refuse this woman's guidance now, after they had come so far.

"She's that way," Eshenna insisted dully.

So they drove into the wild wood. Branches scratched at their faces, fallen timber blocked their way. Tangled, leafless bushes caught in their stirrups and snagged their horses' tails. Birds scattered from their path, chattering alarm calls into the stillness of the forest. Their pace slowed, even as the oppressive sense of fear and foreboding grew.

They found another trail, and followed it. It was wide enough for two or three to ride abreast, but no more. They ate in the saddle, passing biscuits and waterskins from one to another. It left Orisian still hungry. His eyelids grew heavy as the day turned past its midpoint. His thoughts wandered, shapeless.

He recognised the sudden sound as soon as he heard it, but could not name it: that snapping, hissing flutter like a score of breaths abruptly expelled. He turned in time to see a flock of arrows darting out from the forest along the track. They rattled in on the column of men and horses. Someone cried out. A horse reared. He looked for their attackers, but there was nothing save the dark thicket of tree trunks. And now another scattered flight of arrows flashing through the crowd of his men. One rider slumped out of his saddle.

"Go!" Torcaill was shouting close by. "Ride on, ride on!"

Orisian's horse sprang into a gallop. He was not certain whether he had kicked it into motion or whether it was just carried along by the sudden rush of all the other riders. They surged down the track. Orisian felt and heard an arrow smacking into the shield slung across his back. The horse ahead of him veered to one side, stumbling and faltering on suddenly flimsy legs. Orisian glimpsed the fletching of an arrow protruding from its neck. Thundering on by, he turned his head to see the animal crashing through a bush and falling, spilling its rider. He lost sight of both the man and his mount.

The forest seemed to press ever more closely along the path. Orisian expected the lithe figures of Kyrinin to emerge at any moment. The horses stretched their legs, though, and hammered on and on, until the forest thinned a little and the trail opened out.

Rothe reined in his mount next to Orisian and reached across to pull at the arrow embedded in his shield. Yvane, clinging to the burly warrior like a limpet, looked queasy.

"Are you wounded?" Rothe demanded. "Were you hit?"

Orisian shook his head. "You?"

"No." Rothe grunted as he finally freed the arrow. He snapped its shaft and threw the two pieces to the ground.

Orisian looked around for Torcaill. It was hard to tell, amidst the throng of riders milling about, how many might have fallen. He glimpsed the young man at the rear of the company, sword in hand, expression grim and angry.

"Torcaill," Orisian shouted. "Are they coming after us?"

"I can't tell. We should put more ground between us and them, anyway."

Orisian hauled his horse's head around. The animal resisted, almost as if it too dreaded what lay behind them, and he had to dig his heels into its flanks to move it. He worked his way to Torcaill's side. The two of them stared back down the path. It looked like any other woodland trail: a muddy stretch of wiry grass, bare overhanging branches and twigs bobbing in the faintest of breezes. There was no sign of life.

"How many men did we lose?" Orisian asked.

"I'm not sure. Two, I think. We've others injured, though, and some of the horses. Still, we were lucky."

"They're only playing with us," rumbled Rothe, coming up behind them. "Chipping away. Come, Orisian. You shouldn't linger in the open like this. There must be bodies between you and any arrow's flight."

"He's right, sire," Torcaill said, sheathing his sword. "You should stay in the midst of us. We won't see them coming next time, either, unless we're luckier than we've any right to expect."

Orisian allowed himself to be shepherded into the centre of the column, like some prized lamb kept in the heart of the herd.

"We could use your Fox friends now," Torcaill muttered as they moved on down the trail. "Will we be seeing them again, do you think?"

"Yes," said Orisian tightly. "Yes. We'll see them again."

* * *

Kanin oc Horin-Gyre had discovered depths of exhaustion such as he had never before imagined. He bore half a dozen small wounds – cuts and many-hued bruises – but it was lack of sleep that had sapped his strength, and the emptiness that came in the aftermath of battle. He was limping heavily: he had torn, or strained, something in his knee during the battle, leaping from the back of his dying horse. It hardly hurt, but the joint was enfeebled.

His Shield followed behind him through the streets of Glasbridge. Igris still carried, like a fool, the stick that he had tried to persuade Kanin to lean upon. A Thane, the victor in savage battle, should not be seen humbled by such a minor

injury. The streets were soft with slush and treacherous under-
foot, but Kanin would rather fall than hobble along like an old
man.

After the battles he had won at Grive and Anduran, he had felt
a dazed exultation, a lifting up of his heart and a sublime affirm-
ation of the rightness of his deeds. No such exalted feelings
attended upon the brutal victory won in the snowstorm on the
road to Kolglas. The struggle had been unlike anything Kanin
had previously experienced: desperate, seemingly never-ending.
Wreathed by snow and cloud, there had been no time, no location
to the slaughter. It had simply existed, a world unto itself, and all
purpose had been lost save the imperative to slay one man, and
then the next, and the next.

Driven back from the earthen wall that the Inkallim had raised
across the road, almost overrun by the hordes of the Haig Bloods,
he and his dwindling and scattering companies had fallen back
towards Glasbridge, turning again and again to face another
charge, to die. Eventually, lost, adrift in the blizzard, they had
turned for the last time and stood in the calf-deep snow to await
fate's resolution. And there had been enough blood shed there to
leave them wading in it. Kanin had known he was going to die
then, and had felt no great sorrow at the thought. But he had not
died, and the enemy had instead faltered and then fled. The
battle was won, by the snowstorm and by the army Fiallic the
Inkallim and Temegrin the Eagle had brought down upon the
flank and the rear of their enemy.

There had been ravens of the Battle Inkall fighting and dying
at Kanin's side all through the long day, with Shraeve at the
forefront; there had been scores of commonfolk from the north,
come across the Vale of Stones to stand with Horin-Gyre. All
these had been there in the fields of snow, but not Wain. His
sister had insisted on remaining in Glasbridge with the vile
halfbreed who, impossibly, she had brought back with her from
Anduran.

Wain was, in manner and character, unrecognisable. Kanin's heart ached to think of it. Her face and voice were as they had always been, but what lay behind them had changed. Since her return, she spoke only of things that Kanin did not wish to understand: Aeglyss, the Kall, storms, all-consuming fires and terrible, wondrous fates. Half of what she said was incoherent, little better than the ravings of some mind-addled crone; all of it was spoken with a strange intensity.

As far as he could tell, nothing Kanin said reached her any more. She would not be parted from Aeglyss; she would not participate in any calm, reasoned conversation that Kanin attempted. That part of her that had always burned fiercely, with faith and hard certainty, now seemed to have overwhelmed all her sense, all her restraint. The sister Kanin loved, and respected above all others, had been taken away from him by these strange changes. And he was all but certain, in his deepest instincts, that Aeglyss was in some way responsible.

At the very thought of the man, Kanin let out a wordless snarl of anger and contempt. For want of any other way to release his frustration, he slapped his thigh with an open palm as he strode along. Nothing, it seemed, would keep that half-human wretch from interfering. Now, when Kanin had almost started to believe that he was lying dead in some distant ditch or copse, here he was again, poisoning everything with his presence. And when Kanin had argued that the halfbreed should be killed, Wain had stared at him as if he was a petulant child, and turned away from him. She had set her back to him; dismissed him. Nothing could have caused him greater pain than that.

Even Kanin could tell, though, that Aeglyss was not quite the same man he had been when last they met. Now the *na'kyrim* stank of confidence and capability. He had not only some kind of woodwight honour guard, but also Wain, her Shield and another few dozen warriors who seemed inexplicably intrigued by him. Even Shraeve and her company of ravens had been seen coming and going from the huge house where Aeglyss had settled himself.

And then there were the dreams. Kanin had not slept well for several nights. His slumber was disturbed by dreams that he could not clearly remember, but which he always felt had involved Aeglyss. And if he ever did secure a long spell of sleep he would invariably awake filled with inexplicable anger, or with his heart racing, or fear twisting in his stomach.

A twinge of pain shot through Kanin's knee as he limped up a gently sloping street. He winced and, reluctantly, reached out to Igris for the walking stick. The shieldman handed it over without comment.

A woodwight came darting around the corner. Kanin was so astonished that he did not react. Igris was more alert, and more governed by deeply ingrained instincts. The shieldman swept his sword from its scabbard and lashed out at the speeding figure. The Kyrinin leaped and spun, evading the blow with barely a break in his stride. He sprang away down the street. Bemused, Kanin glanced around to find two more White Owls appearing, arrows already at their bowstrings. They took aim, and in no more time than it took Kanin to turn his head, the fleeing figure was reeling, two feathered shafts standing in his back. He fell into a puddle of melt-water.

The two who had killed him retreated back around the corner, slipping fresh arrows free from their quivers as they went.

"The whole world is going mad," Kanin muttered.

He limped forwards and beheld a startling scene. White Owl Kyrinin were killing one another. A brutal, dazzlingly fast struggle played itself out. There were already several bodies lying in the mud and slush. As Kanin watched, two more wights broke away and tried to flee. They were shot down just as the first had been. Whatever the argument had been about, it was clear that one side had won. The last of the defeated was pinned down to the road, stabbed with many spears. She writhed there for a moment or two. A muscular warrior with the most dramatic facial tattoos Kanin had ever seen on a woodwight leaned down and stabbed her in the chest. As the woman's convulsions stilled, her killer straightened and looked towards Kanin.

The Thane of the Horin Blood had no intention of showing any interest in the doings of these Kyrinin intruders. Had Wain not insisted upon it, he would never have allowed them – or Aeglyss – to enter the town. He led his Shield past the White Owls, through a gate and into the wide cobbled courtyard beyond. This was the extensive house that Wain and Aeglyss and all their companions now occupied. Previously the possession of some senior official in the Woollers' Craft, it was an elaborate conglomeration of courtyards, workshops and apartments. The place still had the smell of wool and hides and oils lingering about it.

"Wain!" he shouted, standing in the centre of the courtyard. He turned around, pivoting on the stick, shouting her name again.

He saw her at a window. She peered out from under the eaves. Drops of water were falling from the lip of the tiles.

"With me," Kanin snapped at Igris. "The rest of you remain here. Keep clear of the woodwights. I don't want any trouble."

He was disgusted, but not surprised, to find Wain in a bed-chamber, watching over the slumbering form of Aeglyss. Kanin had thrown the door back with a clatter, but the *na'kyrim* did not stir. A single glance was enough to convince Kanin that the half-breed was sick. His skin had a sheen of sweat, though its pallor was cold. He had thinned in the time since he had disappeared from Anduran, as if gripped by some wasting affliction. Kanin could see the shape of his bones across his brow, in his cheeks and jaw.

"There are woodwights slaughtering each other in the streets," the Thane said to his sister. "What's happening?"

"A dispute to be settled," she said flatly. "There was an incident at Sirian's Dyke, involving the Anain. Some of the White Owls wavered in their loyalty. It seems it became necessary to come to a final decision on the matter. It is best not to let doubts linger."

Kanin stood in silence for a heartbeat or two. He was frightened. The sister he had loved and relied upon all his life was as unfamiliar to him now as the most distant stranger. Once they barely needed to speak to understand one another's intent; now when they talked it was as if they did so in different languages. He had lost his only true friend here, and was bereft.

"Wain, listen to me. This is all wrong. What are you doing here, amongst woodwights and . . ." he stabbed a finger towards Aeglyss ". . . and halfbreeds? This is no place for you, sister. We've won. The way to Kolglas is open to us now. We don't need all this."

She set herself between him and the bed, a resolute wall. Kanin stared at her in anguished confusion.

"You don't understand," she said. "We need him."

"What are you doing? Wain, what are you doing? You'll put yourself between me and this creature?"

His passion washed over her, finding no purchase.

"He is important to us. To everything," she said placidly.

"This is madness." In his desperation, Kanin cast about in vain for words that might rouse her from whatever torpor had taken hold of her mind. He wanted to seize her and shake her, but was terribly afraid that she would fight him if he did so.

"Not madness," Wain insisted. "This is fate, revealing itself to us. You will see, I promise you. We are only at the beginning of things, Kanin. Great, wonderful things." There was at last some emotion in her voice, but it was only a pained need for him to understand. "We draw near to the unmaking of the world, don't you see? He is the herald of all that. The key to it."

"Him?" Kanin shouted, surrendering to fury. He pointed again at the pallid, emaciated *na'kyrim* lying on the bed. "Look at him, Wain! He's barely even alive."

"You see only the least part of him there. There is one he wants at his side. He has gone in search of her, to guide her to him. He swims in oceans we cannot imagine, brother. He becomes them. I will watch over him until he wakes."

Kanin cried out in disbelief. He could feel his face reddening, could feel anger shaking his hand.

"Come with me," he implored her. "You need rest. We'll go back to Anduran. We've done all that could be asked of us here."

"I cannot leave him now," Wain said, quite calm and soft but obdurate. "Do you not feel it? Sleeping or waking, he is spreading his shadow across us all. His will colours every thought, every mood now. It forces . . . change. Movement. Why do you suppose the Kyrinin have come to such strife amongst themselves? Why do you suppose our army fights with such vigour; is so hungry for death's embrace? Because Aeglyss has changed, and changes all of us now."

Kanin stepped to one side, thinking to pass around his sister. He did not know quite what he would do if he could reach Aeglyss: kill him, or merely wake him? He did not care.

Wain shifted to block his way again.

"I am to watch over him until he wakes."

Kanin hung his head. He was unused to the kind of impotent uncertainty that filled him. Whatever doubts or hesitations might occasionally have beset him in the past, he had always been able to draw upon the reserves of his faith, or upon the support of Wain herself, to find a path. Now he felt bereaved, and the one he would otherwise have turned to for aid was the one he had lost.

"There is to be a council, Wain," he murmured. "Fiallic, and the Eagle, and Goedellin and all the captains are gathering on the southern edge of the town. We should be there. There are decisions to be made. Fiallic wants to drive on to Kolglas and beyond as fast as the weather will allow. Temegrin resists."

"Fiallic will have his way," Wain said placidly. "You go. I will remain here. Our victory in this war – and we will have victory, brother – will not be shaped in the council tents of the Inkallim or the Gyre Blood. You will see, in time."

Kanin left, desolate. Going down the stairs, his knee almost betrayed him. He slumped against the wall. Igris tried to help him down the last few steps, but Kanin pushed him off.

In the courtyard, he found his Shield clustered around a water barrel. They passed around overflowing cups as they watched the Kyrinin dragging the bodies of their fallen comrades in from the street. The dead were piled against a wall, beneath the overhanging eaves. Kanin angrily gathered his warriors and led them out.

Shraeve was arriving just as he left, at the head of a dozen or more mounted ravens of the Battle. Several bore fresh wounds. The Inkallim had fought savagely. Shraeve nodded down at Kanin as he hobbled past her horse.

"You're going to the Eagle's council, Thane?"

He nodded without looking at her, angry now – at himself and at Igris – for the presence of the walking stick upon which he leaned. The Inkallim had proved themselves valuable allies at last, but in Kanin's mind their past betrayals of his Blood were not undone. And Shraeve was still an arrogant, abrasive presence.

"I thought you might be there too," he muttered.

"I am not needed there. Fiallic is Banner-captain. He is the will of the Battle here. And I am interested in whatever your sister has got herself involved in. That halfbreed of yours really has proved to be remarkably surprising, don't you think?"

At that, Kanin could not help but glare up at the woman.

"He's mad," he snapped. "And dying. You waste your interest, raven, by spending it on him."

"Oh, I don't think so. My instincts tell me otherwise. You might find, Thane, that a great and terrible fate is unfolding itself here. We will see, no doubt. We will see."

V

The Elect's every instinct, of body and mind alike, howled with alarm, cried out for flight. It took a determined effort to hold her gaze upon the abomination before her.

She had come here, climbing up through the keep of Highfast, in answer to a call only one closely attuned to the Shared could have sensed. It was the call of sudden change, of the sudden bursting in of brilliant light as a shutter is pulled back. She had been alone in the midst of the keep, returning from a brief, uncomfortable meeting with Herraic. They had been discussing the care of the Chancellor of the Haig Bloods, who lay unconscious, near death, in Herraic's own quarters. The Captain was nervous, unsettled by such unforeseen disturbance of Highfast's normal routines, and the meeting had been a little bad-tempered.

Cerys was still turning it over, wondering whether she should have been quite so curt with the man, when her mind was struck numb. Alone in a narrow corridor, she had staggered, would have fallen had she not reached out and pressed a hand to the dank wall. And then, shivering, she had tipped her head back and gazed up at the ceiling. But it was not blank stone that she saw, and not with eyes that she looked. Down, down, through the walls and the gutters and the passageways of Highfast, power was pouring. A dark, malignant torrent of delirious potency cascaded through the Shared, and she knew, without question, from whence it came.

So she had climbed, heavy-legged and fearful, hoping that someone else might join her before she reached her destination, someone to share the burden of witnessing whatever awaited her. And hoping, at the same time, that no one else would come, for she was the Elect and the *na'kyrim* of Highfast were her charge, and she must guard them against this. At the door of the Dreamer's chamber she had hesitated. It had taken every fragment of will she could muster to force herself to open that door and to step inside.

It was not Tyn, not the man she had viewed with affectionate concern for all these years. It had his form, it was made of his stuff, but it was not him. The fact that this cadaverous figure moved and spoke gave it the semblance of life and familiarity, but they signified little more than the writhing of maggots beneath the hide of a dead cow. The maggots did not give the cow life. This was not the Dreamer awoken. Aeglyss wore Tyn's body like a cloak.

"I don't like this skin," the abomination slurred, holding up a gaunt hand and staring at it.

"Set it aside, then," said Cerys. "Remove yourself. Return to your own skin. Your proper place."

Tyn grimaced. His gums were white, those teeth that remained jaundiced.

"What do you think that would achieve? He is gone, the one who inhabited this shell. Gone, utterly. His mind was a frail thing, almost wasted away. I cut it free. I watched it . . . melt into the Shared. You should not mourn it. There was almost nothing left of him even before I came."

Cerys closed her eyes. She gripped the iron chain around her neck with one hand. She had no way to tell whether Aeglyss spoke the truth. If she could have reached out into the Shared with her mind, perhaps she might have caught some hint of Tyn's presence and thus discovered whether or not he persisted, unhomed. But she no longer dared to let her awareness extend into even the shallowest fringes of the Shared. Such was the turbulence, the turmoil, surrounding Aeglyss that she knew she would be unable to hold on to any sense of herself. Already her head spun and she had to fight back waves of nausea.

"Don't close those lovely eyes, lady. You should look upon me – look upon this – in wonder. I thought you were all scholars here. Aren't you? Here is something you've never seen before."

When she looked upon him, it was with all the contempt she could muster.

"You think yourself clever, do you?" she spat.

"I don't think clever is quite the word for it. No, not clever. I don't have the words that would fit this. But come, let's not be cruel."

The blanched head rocked on its flimsy neck. The mouth sagged open, giving out a faint groan. Cerys felt the tumult in her mind recede a fraction. Her thoughts were no longer buffeted quite so viciously this way and that. It was as if Aeglyss had sucked back into himself some small portion of whatever poison it was that leaked out from him into the Shared. The effort it took was evident from the tremors that shook Tyn's shoulders. He barely controls this, the Elect thought. It is too much for him.

"You are uninvited," she said. "I did not invite you into this place any more than Tyn invited you into his body."

"You should thank me for the mercy I've shown him. Have you heard of the Healer's Blade? Every healer who travels with the Black Road army carries one, to end the suffering of those whose wounds cannot be healed. This old man was no different. I cut him loose from this rotting shell. It was only an anchor, holding him back; he'd long ago surrendered himself to the Shared."

"I will hold no debates with one who steals the bodies of others," Cerys said and turned on her heel. The door was only a few paces away. She felt an urgent need to put its solid oak between her and this obscenity.

"You will not turn your back on me!" cried Aeglyss from Tyn's throat. "You will not!" The words were ragged, but the fury that informed them was real. And it burned not only in that voice; in the Shared, it was a howling storm of ire.

The world lurched sideways beneath the Elect's feet. Or was it she who veered and swayed? A wind blew through her mind, so loud and hard that it snatched away her thoughts and sent them swirling off into nothingness. The door for which she reached, the wooden peg that would lift its latch, receded, rushing away into the distance. The floor snapped up and crashed against her knees.

Then it twisted itself, slammed against her head. The world had
turned itself on its side. The bottom of the door stood vertically
before her eyes. In the narrow gap between door and flagstone
flooring, she saw the warm glow shed by some torch out in the
passageway beyond. It looked safe, comforting and immensely
distant. Someone was whispering in her ear.

"Don't turn your back on me. This is a sanctuary, isn't it? For
my kind? For all our kind? That's what I'd heard. You can't cast
me out. Never again."

Billowing white cloth – the hem of Tyn's gown – brushed over
her face. Naked, near-skeletal feet were walking away from her.
She heard the creak of the door on its ancient hinges and then it
was closing, and the hunched, frail figure had passed out into the
passages of Highfast.

"Cerys. Cerys."

Someone was speaking her name. Why? Could they not see
that she was asleep? She was so tired.

"Elect." The voice was more insistent now. Someone was lifting her, sitting her upright. She wondered why her bed was so
hard, so cold.

She opened her eyes. She was on the floor of the Dreamer's bedchamber. Amonyn knelt in front of her, holding her arms, gazing
at her with an expression of such pained concern that she wanted
to cry and cup his face in her hands. She did not, because others
stood behind him and, whatever there was between Amonyn and
her, it was a private thing.

"Are you injured?" he asked her. She had always loved his
voice.

"I don't think so," she murmured. "Only bruised. Help me
up."

He did so, and her dizziness was such that she might not have
managed it without his help. She leaned against him. She felt
sick.

"What happened?" she asked.

Amonyn shook his head. "We don't know. Tyn came out, you did not, so we came looking for you."

"Tyn. No, not Tyn. Where is he?"

"In the keep's kitchens. Mon Dyvain and Alian are watching him, but he will not speak to them. We know it's not Tyn, though. Is it . . . Mon Dyvain claims it is Aeglyss."

Cerys could only nod.

"How?" Amonyn asked.

"I have no idea," she sighed.

"Everyone is frightened. He trails fear behind him. Bannain has gone to fetch Herraic and his warriors."

Cerys forced herself to stand up straight. She breathed deeply, building walls against the pain and terror that were echoing through the Shared.

"I doubt whether swords can help us with this," she said. "It would be Tyn they struck, not Aeglyss. I don't know if the Dreamer is truly lost to us, but I'll not see his body harmed until I am certain his mind is gone. Come, help me to the kitchens."

"He has refused to speak to anyone."

"He will speak to me. I am the Elect."

They went down the stairway in silence. Fear and anxiety went with them, as present and immediate to their minds as heat or cold would be to their skin.

The *na'kyrim* had their own kitchens, deep down in the rock of Highfast's foundations. Those at the base of the keep served the castle's human inhabitants only. Normally, Cerys imagined, there would have been some maids or cooks milling about. Now she found them deserted, save for Mon Dyvain, Alian and the unnatural intruder over whom they watched. The servants must have fled at the sight of this grim, corpse-like figure.

Tyn – she could not help but think of it as being the Dreamer still – was hunched over one of the kitchen tables, gorging himself on scraps left over from whatever meal the garrison had recently taken. He gave no sign of noticing the arrival of Cerys and the others who followed in her wake. Mon Dyvain glanced at her. He said nothing, but his confusion and distress were obvious.

Cerys drew closer to Tyn. Instinctively, she put the table between her and the gaunt figure. It was not, after all, Tyn.

Aeglyss looked up, fragments of meat protruding from between his lips.

"This body starves, yet no food seems to assuage the hunger," he said indistinctly.

"He . . . it . . . has not left the chamber you stole it from for thirty years. You tax it beyond its limits."

Aeglyss chewed and swallowed, all the time staring at Cerys. He held a stub of bread in one hand, but made no move to tear at it.

"What do you want here?" Cerys asked, as calmly as she could. Now, being so close to him, being the focus of his attention and thought, the nausea was returning. She rested a hand on the table top, partly to steady herself and partly to ensure some connection with the real, tangible world.

Aeglyss made a strangulated, choking sound. It took her a moment or two to recognise it for laughter.

"Isn't it sanctuary that any of our kind coming here always want?"

"It is intended to be a place of safety, yes. The one whose body you have stolen thought it so."

Aeglyss threw down the hunk of bread angrily. "I stole nothing! Are your ears all blocked up with dust? I told you, he had abandoned this shell. Gone. He was almost gone."

"And what is he now? Does he still live?"

Aeglyss leered at her. "Do you want him back? Is that what you want?"

Cerys gasped as sudden pressure encircled her head, like bands of steel or hard hands seizing her skull. Diffuse spots of light danced across her vision. Behind her she heard a thump. She

looked round to find that Alian had collapsed, and lay unconscious on the floor. She was capable of no more than that quick
glance, for the pain redoubled itself. Her knees trembled and she
had to lean on the table to prevent herself from falling. Then, just
as abruptly, it was gone. Light-headed, she blinked and breathed
deeply.

"Yes," Aeglyss murmured. "It's what you want. Of course it is.
You should be glad for him, to have sloughed off this carcass. But
no. You'd have him back here. Very well, Elect. Should I call you
Cerys? I have your name, you see. I pluck it out of the air, out of
the Shared."

When she made no reply, he shrugged Tyn's bony shoulders.
He took a step – slightly unsteady, frail – away from the table.

"I did not mean to come here, anyway. I was seeking someone
else entirely. She . . . well, no matter. There's time. But it wasn't
sanctuary I sought, not here or anywhere. Not any more. There's
to be no sanctuary for me. And I need none. You know that, don't
you?"

"Yes." She saw no point in trying to conceal the obvious from
this creature. His presence filled the kitchen, echoed from the
blank stone walls, gazed out from behind her own eyes just as she
did herself.

"Yes. I'll make this bargain with you, Elect. Cerys. You can
have this sickly thing back. I'll take myself away and leave it
empty for him to reclaim, if he has the strength or the desire to
do so. But first, but first . . . you'll show me what you have here
behind these famous walls, and you'll tell me what it is you think
I am. You're supposed to be wise here, the wisest in all the world,
when it comes to the Shared. If you can prove that to me, you can
have your precious Dreamer back."

A sudden commotion made them all turn towards the doorway. Bannain rushed in, and behind him came Herraic, the
Captain of Highfast, and half a dozen of his warriors. Herraic
already looked alarmed. Cerys wondered what Bannain had told

him; whatever it was, she feared how the Captain would react. She held up her hands to the warriors as they arrayed themselves on either side of Herraic.

"I think there's no need for this," she said.

Every human eye was on Aeglyss. They stared at this ghastly apparition in horrified fascination. None of them would have seen Tyn before. Only *na'kyrim* ever entered the Dreamer's chamber. The figure now before them must appear to be a corpse, dead and on the verge of decay yet still, impossibly, moving.

"I am sorry for the disturbance, Captain," Cerys said, with an apologetic nod of the head. "We need not trouble you or your men, I think. This is a problem we can deal with ourselves."

Herraic looked both suspicious and relieved. He was as transfixed by the sight of Aeglyss as any of his warriors, but managed to tear his gaze away to concentrate on Cerys for at least a moment or two.

"Bannain said—"

"Yes," Cerys interrupted him. "We thought we might need your assistance, but it seems . . . perhaps we were mistaken. It would be best if we took ourselves back to our own chambers. I will speak to you later, if I may."

Herraic did not seem convinced, but he and his men withdrew.

"Feeble little allies you have here to protect you," Aeglyss scoffed as the sound of footsteps receded down the corridor. "Should you ever meet them, you'd find mine rather more impressive."

"No doubt," Cerys muttered. Alian, still prostrate, was waking. Amonyn crouched over her, hands cradling her head. Faint though it was, Cerys could feel the shifting pattern in the Shared as he wove what comfort he could for Alian out of it. To her consternation, Aeglyss clearly caught the same scent, for he stared at Amonyn.

"I'll make no bargains with you," she said hurriedly, eager to distract his attention. "But I'll speak with you further, if that's what you wish. Our rooms, our libraries, are not in this part of Highfast. Will you come with us?"

"Very well."

Bannain and Mon Dyvain escorted him out, keeping him at more than an arm's length of distance. Cerys followed, but paused to kneel at Amonyn's side and whisper to him:

"How is Alian?"

"She will recover soon enough. His strength — his weight — took us all by surprise."

"I will talk to him; do what I can to persuade him to leave."

"Whatever happens, we cannot offer him any aid," Amonyn murmured. "His presence is as dark, as deranged, as anything I've ever felt."

"I know. He could . . . this might end badly. Once Alian is on her feet, go to Herraic. Tell him as much, or as little, as you see fit, but make sure he understands that there is something very dangerous inside Highfast now. And that, despite anything I might have said, we might need his swords."

Cerys had descended into the rock of Highfast many times, over many years. It was the only place that had ever felt like a home to her, the only place to which she had ever belonged. Its sounds, the cool stability of its stone, the deep, old quality of its air: all these things had, for as long as she could remember, been comforting companions. Now, following Aeglyss and the others down, everything seemed to be imbued with foreboding. The distant hum of the mountain breezes sounded threatening; the air stirred with uneasy eddies. Her home had been rendered inhospitable to her by this uninvited guest.

She felt strangely empty, though. Powerless, as if she was standing in the path of a great rockfall and could do nothing but remain, staring up at the boulders rushing towards her. It seemed very cruel to her, that she should have the misfortune to be the Elect of Highfast in such times.

They put Aeglyss into a small antechamber adjoining one of the disused dormitories. It was dank and cobwebbed, but he did not seem to notice. He sat at the old, split table there and waited. Cerys sent the others away. She was afraid of what might happen, even though she had no clear idea of it.

"Do you know this man whose body you have stolen?" she asked Aeglyss once they were alone. "His name is Tyn. He was born near the Kyresource Lakes. His mother took him to Kilvale when he was only a few weeks old. She protected him for a time, but she died when he was young, and he . . ."

"Enough!" The anger – and pain, perhaps – in that word shook Cerys.

"Enough," Aeglyss said again, quietly this time. He rested his elbows on the table, lowered his head to his hands. "Talk, talk. You think you can solve everything, trick anyone, with talk. Is that all you do here? I was told you had books here, and learning; that you were great *na'kyrim*, with great understanding of the Shared. Inurian came from here, did he not?"

"He did," breathed Cerys. She felt as if she stood upon fragile ice that cracked under her feet, a torrent roaring beneath it. She wanted to retreat, but did not know which way to turn. Aeglyss lifted his head once more. There was a vicious, contemptuous smirk on his haggard face.

"You want to ask me about Inurian," he growled.

She shook her head, just once, in denial. She did not trust herself to speak.

"Oh, but you do. I can see it in you. You loved him. Why? What was so deserving about him? He was not remarkable. Just another poor halfbreed like you. Like me. Tell me what he did to earn such affection."

Again Cerys shook her head and bit her lip. But she could feel his will upon her now, prising open her mouth, breaking down whatever wall she might try to raise in her mind.

"Tell me!" he insisted.

"He had a good heart," she gasped. "His instinct was always to listen, to understand, to be patient. He knew more than most of us ever can about other people, and yet still he liked them. Loved them. That is what he did to earn affection."

Tyn's face twisted, distorted by whatever powerful emotions tormented Aeglyss. Cerys could hear his confusion, his hurt, ringing in her ears. There's a child in there somewhere, she thought.

"A good heart," Aeglyss mimicked her. "A good heart. I didn't find it so. Not at all. I didn't find it so. He'd have nothing to do with me, fool that he was. And yes, I killed him. That's what you want to know, isn't it? I killed him. I put a spear through him."

To her numb astonishment, Cerys saw that he was weeping. Tiny tears tracked down Tyn's pale, sunken cheeks. His lips trembled. His hands were clenched into fists.

"I killed him." His grief was such a potent thing, so limitless and invasive, that Cerys found her own eyes moistening, her own throat tightening. The borders of her sense of self were overrun.

"I still hear his voice, though, sometimes," Aeglyss groaned. "I feel him, at my shoulder, watching. How can that be? Tell me that."

"The Shared remembers many things. All things. It is not Inurian you sense, but the memory of him. The memories of him that all those who still live carry with them; the echo of the pattern he himself made in the Shared before he . . . before you killed him."

Cerys could not tell how much of what she felt was her own grief, her own anger, and how much belonged to Aeglyss. She – all of them here in Highfast – had concluded some time ago that this man had played a part in Inurian's death. For that, she despised him. Yet she pitied him too. Or perhaps she was participating in his own corrosive self-pity.

"There's so much I don't know," he said. "He could have helped me, guided me. I think . . . sometimes I feel like I am losing myself. Do you understand?" He flicked a needful glance at her. "Even now, I am here, in this shell, and I do not fully understand how I came to be here. My body lies somewhere back in Glasbridge, and I can see it, sometimes, through her eyes. Through Wain. I . . . Oh, I have done a terrible thing to her. Terrible, but beautiful.

"I can't hold on to myself. It's all too much. And the Anain. I hear them, feel them, circling about: great beasts in the darkness. I know they're there, but I can't see them, can't drive them off. They tried to kill me, you know. To silence my thoughts, tear me apart. But I turned them back. I am stronger than they knew. But, please . . . please help me. You must."

"They tried to kill you?" Cerys murmured. She struggled to focus her thoughts. The effort needed to concentrate was painful, draining. But if the Anain had risen against this man it confirmed many of her worst fears. That they should have done so and failed in their intent . . . terrified her. For a single *na'kyrim* to have such innate, raw strength in the Shared that he could withstand the Anain was, to the best of her knowledge, unprecedented. And if the contest of wills between two such immense forces continued, any and all caught between them or around them faced ruin. Disaster.

Aeglyss laughed again. All his sorrow and fear and regret were snuffed out, like a covered candle flame.

"Now you see a little of what I am. What I am capable of. Don't you, Elect? You glimpse the faintest outline of what I am becoming. What I have been made. And now you're afraid of me."

"What . . . what happened? Something happened to you, some change was worked upon you."

His face – Tyn's face – stilled. He stared at her, and looked in that moment empty of any life or thought or feeling.

"I was beaten, and broken, and left on a stone to die. By my own people. Betrayed. It will not happen again. I shall put my will upon them, upon all of them. I am beset by enemies, Elect.

Always. Always. Therefore, I must gather true friends about me, and I will make them fear me and love me and there will be nowhere that closes its doors against me. The world has ever been a cold and heartless place. I will teach it to be more forgiving."

"You must release Tyn," Cerys said faintly. She had never felt such despair, and that feeling was, she was certain, entirely her own.

"I will. When you have shown me your libraries, when you have told me all you know of the Anain, and armed me against them. When you have helped me control the fires that burn in me, or convinced me that there is no one here capable of helping me in that. I will release him, and leave this place, when you have proved yourselves my friends, Elect. Only then."

VI

"If we do not feed her she will die," Cynyn observed.

The three Heron Kyrinin were crouched atop a steep earth bank, staring down at the *na'kyrim* who lay on the path below. K'rina was awake, but her eyes had lost their focus and her breathing was shallow, flighty. She lay on her back, her arms spread out. She had not moved, other than to make one failed attempt to rise, since before midday; evening was close now.

"It cannot be just hunger," said Mar'athoin, not bothering to conceal his puzzlement. "It has only been three days since she ate. Long for a Huanin, perhaps, but one of the *na'kyrim* should not succumb so quickly." He glanced at Sithvyr in search of confirmation.

She looked away. She had lost interest in this adventure, and took every opportunity to make clear her desire to turn for home. They had been gone from the secure, familiar marshes of the Heron homelands for fifteen days now, had passed even beyond the borders of Snake lands: enough to fatten their reputation amongst the clan's warriors a little. Enough, Mar'athoin hoped, to show Sithvyr that he might be worthy of her affections.

"No," he mused. "Not just hunger. It is her mind, her spirit, that is coming loose."

The *na'kyrim* gave out a faint groan. She rattled out a few words in the Heron tongue: "My boy. Beloved boy." Then more – incomprehensible to Mar'athoin and the others – in the Huanin language that some in Dyrkyrnon spoke.

"She is done," Sithvyr said.

"No," said Cynyn in surprise. "See, she rises."

And rise K'rina did, coming feebly to her feet and staggering onwards.

"I say she is done," Sithvyr insisted.

Mar'athoin watched as the *na'kyrim* stumbled off down the path, remorselessly following whatever mad call drew her. There must be a terrible need in her, he thought, to drive her weakened frame on thus.

"She must fail soon," he said. "It would be fitting that we bear witness to it if she does. Then we can carry word back to Lacklaugh and he will know we did not turn aside at the end. He ran well with my father when they were young. They shed blood together. Let us see in the morning."

The *na'kyrim* did not falter all through the night. Against all sense, she struggled on through the darkness. She strayed from the trail she had been following, though it was impossible to say if the straying was by choice or by blindness. She led them across high ground of rough grass and rushes, scattered trees twisted and stunted by the wind. They followed in silence.

And dawn showed them a thing none had ever thought to see in their lifetimes. Spread out below them was a vast bowl of land, two days wide: a sprawling forest cupped in a gigantic hill-circled hollow. Over and amongst its serried ranks of trees hung a tattered shroud of fog. Like clouds strewn over an inverted sky, strands of obscuring mist stretched far and wide across the hidden wilderness.

The three Kyrinin stood atop a crest of high ground, gazing at the immense landscape. Below them, K'rina was toiling down the rough slope, drawing ever nearer to the wisp-thin borders of the mist sea.

"Have we come so far?" Cynyn murmured.

"It seems so," said Mar'athoin. "I did not know this was where her course would bring us."

"She means to enter," Sithvyr observed, staring at the fading back of the *na'kyrim*. "There is a decision we must make."

Mar'athoin nodded. "I did not know . . ." he murmured.

"But we cannot turn away now," said Cynyn. His excitement was close to the surface. "No matter what becomes of the mad woman, she has brought us to a place of wonders. We must walk a little way at least beneath the mists. We must."

"It is not only wonders that the tales of this place recount," Sithvyr said.

"I know, I know. But to say we have breathed those airs . . . who else of our clan could claim that?" The youngest of them was smiling as he let his gaze roam across the half-obscured forest.

"I think Emmyr came here once," Mar'athoin said. "He does not speak of what he saw."

"And we need not. But I do not wish to say that I stood upon its very threshold and turned aside," Cynyn insisted.

Mar'athoin glanced at Sithvyr. She answered his questioning look with a tiny shrug.

"I am curious," she conceded.

"Very well," said Mar'athoin. "We follow. But only a short distance. I will not let this woman draw us deep. Our promise to Lacklaugh is fulfilled; he could ask no more of us than this."

They entered the *Hymyr Ot'tryn*. The mists that dwelled there, the lingering exhalation of The Goddess, closed about them. This had been her land since the beginning of the world. The Wildling never hunted here, the Walking God never trod its paths; but The Goddess had come here often and, though she was gone with all the others, her breath remained on the still air.

The three Kyrinin went with light feet and heavy hearts. Every mist-muffled sound gave them pause, every flitting shadow drew their eye. They did not speak, but flashed curt messages to one another with the hunting language of fingers. This was a place thick with otherness, wrapped not only in fogs but in ancient tales. It was known that in the *Hymyr Ot'tryn* the forest slept lightly. The smallest disturbance might rouse it.

They passed in and out of bands of mist, feeling its damp fingertips on their faces. Nothing was dry here. The ancient, wrinkled trees were dark with dew, the ground fat with moss and mud and grassy hummocks. Streams ran between weed-clothed boulders. Little ponds and marshes would appear out of the vapours and then disappear once more as they skirted round them. Autumn lingered here, long after the new winter had banished it elsewhere. The grass was still bright, the willows and alders and ash trees still held many leaves that were only now browning and curling. The soil was soft. The *na'kyrim* left a clumsy trail of deep footprints sunk down into the yielding ground.

At length, Mar'athoin halted and the three of them gathered on the huge rotting trunk of a wind-thrown tree. He pointed ahead and then at his ear. Cynyn and Sithvyr frowned in concentration, cocked their heads at an angle. After a few heartbeats they both nodded. They could hear the *na'kyrim*'s laboured breathing, a few dozen paces away. She was no longer moving.

A part of Mar'athoin – the larger part – hoped that this might be the *na'kyrim*'s end. He was glad to have walked in the *Hymyr Ot'tryn*, and glad for the story he would be able to tell when they returned to their homes, but each step further into the forest's dank heart felt like trespass. He felt unwelcome here. It was not a giving land such as the marshes where the Heron dwelled; it was unknowable, belonging only to itself.

Sithvyr was signing to him. She thought they had come far enough, seen enough. She thought, as Mar'athoin did himself, that they were unwanted here. Cynyn would be disappointed, but the time had come to turn back.

A faint crack turned all their heads. It was a soft-edged sound, as if some rotten bough had been gently snapped. In its wake there came a vanishingly quiet rustling: the sound of leaf-heavy twigs in a breeze. Yet there was no breeze.

Mar'athoin rose. He began to move towards the source of the sounds. He could no longer hear the *na'kyrim*'s breathing. Cynyn and Sithvyr looked unsure but they followed him, hanging back. In this land of clouds he could see no more than a few paces ahead. The mist hung thick amongst the trees.

He smelled broken earth; a sharp, green hint of new leaves; a hard edge of water sprung from underground. It all spoke to him of a rising, a breaking of buds, a stirring of insects among the loam. None of it belonged here in the winter.

With each step his heart beat faster and a new prickling wave of unease ran through his skin. He risked a glance back over his shoulder. Cynyn and Sithvyr had stopped. He saw in their faces what he felt in himself: hesitation, uncertainty, the germ of fear. One more step, he told himself, and then again, and another. But his throat was tightening, his chest aching as if the very mist was squeezing him. The scents assailing his nose grew stronger and more potent until he could almost see their colours. And was there a sound? A wet shifting, a slithering of mud?

One more step and there was something at the limit of his sight: a slow roll in the undergrowth as if some great slumbering beast had turned over in its sleep. Mar'athoin paused, feeling the cold sweat across his forehead. His mind was reeling, spinning. At the base of a great tree there was a thickening of creepers and twisted bushes, a swelling in the moss-covered earth. He narrowed his eyes. The mists thinned. He saw a fore-arm, wrapped in a thorny bramble stem that tightened its twisting grip as he watched. He saw a face held between two sodden pillows of moss that pressed slowly, slowly together. He saw the grey eyes of the *na'kyrim* drift towards him, and the minute movements of her lips.

"Help me," Mar'athoin heard K'rina whisper. And even as he heard the words, he saw a coil of dead, brittle creeper unfurl itself and flex bright leaves.

He fled. He ran without care or caution, back the way they had come. Only one thought was clear and hard in his mind: their journey was done, for here in the *Hymyr Ot'tryn* they had come to the very extremity of the world a Kyrinin could know. Nothing remained now but to fly back to the safety of the *vo'an*.

Cynyn and Sithvyr sped after him, silent. They must taste the horrors on the air as well as he could, but they had not seen what he had.

"Anain," Mar'athoin shouted to them as he ran. "The Anain have taken her."

* * *

"I've lost her," Eshenna murmured.

"What do you mean?" Orisian asked, frowning at the *na'kyrim*.

"She's . . . gone. I can't feel her mind any more."

Orisian shot a questioning glance at Yvane, who shrugged.

"I can't tell. The Shared's become too loud for me to think straight. I barely know where I am, let alone anyone else."

"You can't lose her now," Orisian snapped at Eshenna in exasperation. "We've come too far. You said we were close; within reach."

They were sitting in the open, on the northern slope of a ridge of high, grassy ground that hunched up above the surrounding forests. Chains of low hills stretched off into the distance. The

Karkyre Peaks, distant and cloudy, thronged the western horizon. Torcaill and his warriors were tending to their horses, and to their own wounds. Twice in this long afternoon they had been beset by the arrows of invisible enemies. Three men lay dead somewhere back along the trail they had followed through the forest and out onto this bare ridge. All of it in answer to Eshenna's insistence that K'rina was so close that they need press on only a little further.

The *na'kyrim* had an anguished expression on her face now. Her eyelids were fluttering, her head rocking back. Orisian was suddenly afraid that she was going to faint away. He seized her arm, holding her upright.

"Eshenna! What's happening?"

"The Anain," she breathed. "There's terrible power, all around. I can't see anything else. Gods, we're too small to be in the midst of all this."

Orisian shook her, overcome by a surge of fear and frustration.

"It's too late! We're here! Tell me where the woman is, Eshenna."

She recovered herself for a moment, met his gaze steadily, then grimaced and closed her eyes. She gestured towards the summit of the ridge behind them.

"Over there. She was close, beyond the rise, but then . . . I don't know. She disappeared."

There was a chorus of shouts. Orisian glanced round. Men were hauling themselves onto their horses. Others were pointing back down the slope towards the treeline.

"It's a false alarm," Yvane muttered.

For a moment Orisian did not know what she meant, then he saw the two lean figures jogging out from amongst the trees. He recognised them at once: Ess'yr and Varryn.

"It's all right," he shouted at Torcaill.

The warrior had already reached the same conclusion himself. He calmed his men, stood expectantly watching the two Kyrinin coming up the slope towards them. Ess'yr and Varryn passed him by, ignoring every curious gaze as they made straight for Orisian.

He stood up to meet them. Ess'yr had a bow again, he saw at once. Someone – some White Owl – must have died to give her that.

"The enemy fill the forest like deer," Varryn said curtly. "We could not kill so many in five days of hunting."

"Where?" Orisian asked. He could not take his eyes off Ess'yr. She was breathing deeply, a faint flush of exertion colouring her cheeks. She looked alive, full of renewed energy. There was dried blood on the arm of her jacket, but it looked to be someone else's, not hers.

"Behind you," Varryn said, "and beside you. All around. They are searching."

"For K'rina. As we do."

"Perhaps for her. For us, now. And for you."

Torcaill and Rothe came striding up, urgent questions evident in their expressions.

"They will be on you here very soon," Varryn continued.

"How many?" Torcaill demanded.

Varryn did not look round at the warrior, but down at the spear he held lightly in his hand.

"As many bows as you have swords," he said. "Perhaps more."

"At least in the open we can see them coming," Rothe muttered.

Orisian knelt again at Eshenna's side. The *na'kyrim* was more composed now, though she still seemed distressed.

"How close is she?" he asked her gently. "Can we reach her? We have no more time."

"I don't know. Perhaps. She was very near, before I lost my sense of her. If we could find her trail, or some sign of her . . . perhaps. Your Fox are good trackers, aren't they?"

Orisian looked up at Rothe, and then at Torcaill.

"We have to try. There's still a chance to do what we came here to do."

He could see the doubt in Torcaill's face. It went unvoiced, but it was there. There was no instinct of obedience, Orisian thought. No immediate recognition of the authority of a Thane. It would have been better to have gone to Kolglas, to face what had to be faced there. But that was an old choice, taken and fixed. There could be no turning aside from this road now, only a race to its ending.

"Get the men mounted," he said dully. "We have to move on quickly."

They crested the ridge, and beheld a strange sight. Beneath them, stretching away into a haze of mist, stood a sea of dark treetops. Here, surrounded by hills, was a forest where no wind stirred. Strands of fog hung over and amongst the branches, like impaled fragments of soft, translucent cloth.

"The Veiled Woods," Yvane murmured in Orisian's ear. She rode with him once more now, to free Rothe for any fighting that might come. "That's not what I would have hoped for."

"If that's where she is . . ." Orisian let the sentence trail away. Nothing he could say would make the forest below appear any less threatening, or decrease the apprehension that filled him at the sight of it.

"Best to tread lightly, when the Anain are stirring," Yvane said. "If we can."

Rothe drew his horse to a halt beside them.

"Not seen anywhere less inviting in a long time," the shield-man observed gruffly.

"That, we can agree on," muttered Yvane.

Torcaill's warriors were strung out along the ridge top, almost as if they were drawing up in formation to charge down upon the army of mist-armoured trees. Torcaill himself was twisted in his saddle, looking not at the Veiled Woods but back down the slope they had climbed. Ess'yr and Varryn, standing close by, were facing that way too. They were speaking softly but urgently in their own language.

With Yvane pressed up behind him, Orisian could not easily turn or see over his shoulder. He had to wrestle his horse around in a tight half-circle. He saw at once what the others had. Shapes were moving at the edge of the forest: indistinct flickers of movement in that boundary between the light of open ground and the gloom of the woods. Insubstantial things, at this distance, but there could be no doubt what they were.

Torcaill came riding down the line of horsemen.

"Do you mean to press on, sire? Into those woods?"

Orisian nodded.

"Very well," Torcaill said without hesitation. "Get your Kyrinin to lead the way. They're our best hope of finding the woman. I'll leave a dozen men here, to delay pursuit. They'll have the slope to favour their charge, if the woodwights come out from amongst those trees."

They went steadily down towards the Veiled Woods. Ess'yr and Varryn ran on ahead. No one spoke. The mists settled about them, and the trees closed over their heads.

VII

The Veiled Woods quickly defeated the horses. Before they had gone more than a few dozen paces in from the edge, a thick mass of looping bramble stems and contorted undergrowth blocked their path. There was no track to follow here, not even a suggestion of one. Ess'yr and her brother darted easily through the thicket and disappeared. The horses baulked. The ground was uneven, rippled by rocks, roots and dead wood half-hidden by wet grass. The trees, which had seemed tall and stately from the distance of the ridge crest, were in fact crowded, twisted and misshapen, thrusting their branches out at odd, low angles to obstruct any man on horseback.

"Get down," Orisian told Yvane. Once she had done so, he dismounted too, and stood by his horse's head, patting the bridge of its nose.

"We have to go on foot," he said to Rothe. "It'll take far too long if we try to ride."

"We can lead the horses."

Orisian shook his head. "Too slow."

Torcaill rode over to them, his horse picking its way carefully, setting down each hoof as if it did not trust the ground.

"No way through for horses," Rothe told him.

"No."

"We'll lose touch with Ess'yr if we don't keep up," Orisian said, feeling the first intimation of desperation.

There was a sudden sound: a muffled, rising rumble like far-off thunder. All of them looked back the way they had come, but the trees and low fogs blocked any view.

"They're charging," Torcaill said, tense. "So soon. I thought it'd take longer. Or that the wights would turn aside and look for a way round."

"The White Owls are in a hurry," Orisian said. "Just like us. This isn't just some raid they're on. It's more important to them – to Aeglyss – than that. They won't turn aside, or hide away."

Somewhere at the rear of the weary bunch of riders, someone shouted out, "I see them! Wights coming!"

"Go, if you must," Torcaill snapped down at Orisian, already turning his horse. "I'll send some men with you on foot, and come after, if we can curb the pursuit here. I'll not just abandon our horses to the wights. We'll need them yet."

Orisian saw no point in arguing.

"Stay with Torcaill," he said to Yvane, and then, "You too, Eshenna. Rothe?"

With that, he started to run, fearful of being unable to find any sign of Ess'yr or Varryn beyond the thicket. He barged through the tangled undergrowth, feeling it rip at his clothes and snag his hair, but not caring. Rothe came blundering after him.

"Slow down, Orisian," the shieldman shouted at him. "Wait for the others."

Orisian waded on, fighting the resistant vegetation like the current of some fierce river that he was trying to cross. He burst free of its tenacious grip at last, and stumbled on over the scattered debris of a giant tree that had long ago fallen and been eaten into fragments. He could hear Rothe's heavy tread close behind him. Further back, someone – one of Torcaill's warriors – was cursing the brambles.

Orisian ran around a stagnant pond of murky water, sprang over a rotted, split stump. Still he could not see Ess'yr or Varryn, or any sign of their passing.

"Ess'yr," he shouted, and regretted it instantly. The cry sounded far louder, in the limp, damp air that lay beneath the trees, than he had expected. He imagined it ringing out through the forest, turning the head of every living thing. He told himself that any White Owls would not need his voice to find him, but it was small comfort.

Then he saw Ess'yr up ahead, standing beside a moss-wrapped tree, and relief washed through him.

"Come," she said as he reached her. "Quickly. There is scent. Perhaps it is her."

And with that she was already spinning on her heel and running on, deeper into the Veiled Woods. Rothe drew level with Orisian and laid a hand on his shoulder.

"I think I heard fighting, perhaps. Back behind us. Not sure."

"They've got her trail," Orisian said – hoping, believing, that it was true.

He set off after Ess'yr.

There was a dark scar across the forest floor, running up to the base of an ancient tree, where the turf and moss and leaf litter had split – or been torn – apart and peeled back to expose the earth. Orisian crouched down next to it and dug his fingers into the loose soil. It had a warm, wet smell.

"It seems fresh," he said. There were still insects crawling across the loam, still worms writhing in it.

Varryn went on a few paces and bent to examine the grass.

"Not long," Ess'yr said. "We are very close behind her."

"She was here? Is this to do with her?" Orisian asked, wiping his hand on some moss.

Ess'yr was watching her brother. "With her. There is the smell of *na'kyrim* here. Or with the Anain. We walk in their sight. They are awake, in this place. Can you not feel it?"

Orisian frowned. He felt the age, the eeriness of the Veiled Woods, but surely that was just to do with the old, twisted trees, the moist air. He looked again, with more careful eyes, and saw the moss – rich and luminously green – that clothed rocks and fallen timber, saw the leaves, some brown, some yellow, some even a blotched green, that still clung to twigs. He breathed in deeply, and felt the softness of the air in his chest. It all felt like a place out of its season.

Rothe was at his side, breathing heavily.

"You must stay closer to me," the shieldman grumbled. "The White Owls'll be fast enough to flank us, get ahead of us even, however hard Torcaill tries. This is not the kind of place I'd choose to go up against Kyrinin. Where are those men who're supposed to be with us?"

He glared around, as if to blame or accuse the forest itself as the origin of all their woes. There was, behind them, perhaps the sound of someone crashing through the forest. It might be one or more of Torcaill's warriors. Orisian was not sure how long they had been running for, how far behind his supposed escort might have fallen. It seemed improbable that any White Owl would make so much noise, but he was nevertheless disinclined to shout out to whoever it was.

"I don't think Kyrinin are the only things we've got to worry about here," he murmured.

Rothe looked at him, troubled. "What does that mean?"

Orisian shook his head. "It doesn't matter." And it didn't. There was nothing that Rothe, or Torcaill, or any of them, could do about Anain. He straightened himself and turned round. "Come on – we have to keep up with Ess'yr and Varryn."

The two Fox were trotting away, heads down like hunting dogs following a scent. Rothe stared after them.

"We need those men," he said. "If we get too strung out in here, we'll never find each other again. None of us can match those two's pace." He nodded after the disappearing Kyrinin.

Orisian sighed, looking first after Ess'yr and then back the way they had come, searching for any sign that Torcaill and the others were approaching. Somewhere, distantly in that direction, he thought he heard shouting. A few small birds were hopping, chattering, through the canopy above.

"What we came for is close," he said. "Ess'yr and Varryn are certain of it. If the White Owls reach the woman before we do, everything has been for nothing. Come on."

He went without waiting to see Rothe's reaction. He did not need to; he knew that his shieldman would follow. The two of them, struggling to match the pace of their Kyrinin guides through the tangled forest, stumbled over hidden rocks, stamped down on brittle, rotten branches, crashed through nets of briars. Ess'yr and Varryn, as far as Orisian could tell, made not a sound.

The woods were suffused with a strange, pale light. The flat white vapours that draped the treetops were quite motionless. Everything felt vaguely unreal to Orisian. Then he heard a bird call, from somewhere off to his left. It was an unfamiliar sound. He risked a glance that way as he ran. There was nothing to see but the silent throng of contorted tree trunks. A sudden dip in the ground almost sent him sprawling down, and he had to return his attention to his feet.

There was another call, perhaps closer, though it was hard to judge on the still, heavy air. He looked again. And this time he saw a flutter of movement. He slowed despite himself, looked again. Something moved, far out amongst the mist-blurred green and brown of the forest.

"Keep going," Rothe snapped, running up behind him. "It's too late to stop. We have to stay with them now."

Orisian ran faster, vaulting over a fallen tree; glimpsing the profusion of tiny mushrooms that had burst up out of its crumbling wood. To his surprise, he found Varryn kneeling amongst willow saplings, an arrow set to the string of his bow.

"Go," hissed the Kyrinin. "Follow Ess'yr."

Orisian ran on wordlessly, glancing back only once; seeing Varryn drifting through the undergrowth, as intent as any hunter. Ahead, Ess'yr had increased her pace. She ran in bursts: a few long, lithe strides, then a moment of casting about, then another surge forward. Trees flashed past. They were going much too fast for any hope of quiet now. Orisian could hear Rothe crashing along behind him like a boulder tumbling downhill.

Above the noise of their own haste he heard a faint, far-off cry. It was too light, too thin to be born of a human throat. Then another sound: a clattering, rattling cadence that rushed up close and then stopped. It came again and he glanced sideways in time to see an arrow tumbling through scrub, its flight unbalanced and broken by the undergrowth. It glanced off a tree trunk and dipped into the ground, sinking to its flights in yielding moss.

"Faster," shouted Rothe.

Orisian's thighs and calfs burned, but he stretched his legs and drove on after Ess'yr. His shield thumped rhythmically against his back. He leaped across a tiny stream, so overgrown with ferns and choked with mossy stones that the water only betrayed its presence by its gurgling voice. He wanted to draw his sword, but was unsure whether he could do so without falling, or at least slowing down. He was on the verge of making the attempt when he rounded the great fat trunk of a wizened oak to find Ess'yr crouched in a tiny glade. She was at the side of a woman who was lying face down in the grass beside a massive fallen tree.

Orisian bent down, panting for breath. Ess'yr glanced at him. "This is the one," she said. "She still lives."

Orisian turned the prone woman over onto her back. She was light in his hands, almost as if her clothes were empty. Her *na'kyrim* face was neither old nor young, neither beautiful nor plain. It was painfully thin, though. Her deathly-pale cheeks, smeared with streaks of dirt, bore dozens of tiny scratches. As though, Orisian thought, she had been assailed by a flock of birds. Or thorns, perhaps; thorns, and roots and twigs. Her breathing was shallow. She smelled – he leaned closer – of the wet earth and decaying leaves. Her simple deer-hide dress was caked with soil and was full of little rips.

"Move her," Ess'yr said. She hooked a hand under the *na'kyrim*'s armpit. Orisian got to his feet and took hold of the collar of the woman's dress. Together, they dragged her up against the great wet bulk of the fallen trunk. The woman's eyes were open. The pupils moved this way and that, but they had no grip upon the world.

Then Rothe was thumping over the grass towards them, shouting as he came, "Get under cover. Leave her, Orisian! Get under cover. They're coming."

Orisian hesitated. He looked at Rothe, scanned the forest behind him and saw nothing. Rothe had his sword in one hand, his shield still slung across his back. With his free hand he seized Orisian's upper arm and thrust him away from the *na'kyrim*.

"Get behind the tree," the shieldman shouted.

Orisian obeyed, soft rotten wood crumbling beneath his hands and feet. "Get her!" he cried.

Ess'yr vaulted over the huge fallen tree trunk, reached back and hauled at the *na'kyrim*. One-handed, Rothe lifted the insensate woman and pushed her bodily over the dead tree. She slid onto the sodden grass beside Orisian. Rothe followed her. There was a dull thud as he did so and he went unsteadily down onto his knees, with a disgusted grunt. Orisian reached out to steady the big man. Ess'yr was quickly stringing her bow, bending low to stay out of sight.

An arrow was embedded in the back of Rothe's leg, driven deep into the meat of his thigh. Without thinking, Orisian reached for it and snapped the shaft off. Rothe gasped in pain, but was already unbuckling the straps of his shield and settling it onto his left arm.

"Keep low," he rasped. "Come on, get your shield ready."

Orisian tried to do as he was told. His fingers were clumsy, unable to move as fast and nimbly as his mind desired of them.

Ess'yr had an arrow at her bowstring. She scurried a few paces away from them and peered over the tree trunk. There were a couple of hollow cracks as arrows smacked into the dead wood, the whispering flight of two or three more that flashed overhead and disappeared into the forest. Ess'yr rose to a crouch and loosed off an arrow in reply.

"How many?" Rothe demanded of her as she sank back down, reaching for another shaft.

"Enough," she said calmly.

"Enough for what?" the shieldman muttered in exasperation.

Orisian had sword and shield ready now. He stayed in a low crouch, trying to ignore the fluttering heartbeat he felt in his throat, the cold sweat on his brow and his palms.

"Where's Varryn?" he asked.

"They are coming," Ess'yr said. She spun, still sunk down on her haunches, and sighted along the length of the great tree trunk. A figure rounded its far end, where its root plate stood tall: a Kyrinin, a man with a tattooed face. Then Ess'yr's arrow was lodged in his chest and he was pitching backwards.

"Behind you," Ess'yr hissed, casting aside the bow and taking up her spear.

Rothe and Orisian both looked over their shoulders. Another White Owl warrior was leaping over the tree trunk, little more than a spear's length away. Rothe surged up before Orisian could

move. Shieldman and Kyrinin crashed together. Orisian heard
gasps of violently expelled breath as the two of them fell in a
tangle. The White Owl was faster, more agile, than Rothe; he
rolled and swept up onto his feet, already in a low fighting stance.
Rothe was still scrambling to get upright.

Orisian rushed at the back of the White Owl. He knew at once
that he was too slow. He could see the Kyrinin turning, the tip of
his spear snapping round at stomach height. Something else
hammered into Orisian from the side, knocking him flying. He
hit the ground clumsily, his sword pinned beneath him. He was
distantly aware that his shin had smacked against a sharp-edged
rock, but the pain was carried away, for now, on the flood of the
moment.

He sat up, managed to get his sword out from under him. A
blur of closing movement gave him enough warning to lift his
shield. It took the spear thrust close to its centre and trapped the
point there, holding it fast. Orisian tried to roll onto his feet, but
the White Owl still had hold of the spear. A single hard tug was
enough both to twist Orisian onto his knees and to pull it free of
the shield. Orisian watched the butt of the spear sweeping
towards him. He could see it coming, it seemed slow, it seemed
that he had plenty of time to block it with his sword; yet his arm
was only now beginning to move, far too late. The moment
passed. The butt of the spear leaped into his face. He felt the skin
under his cheekbone split. He felt a rush of hot, wet blood in his
mouth. One eye was awash with blinding light. He slumped
sideways, flailing with his shield. A blow landed on it. He
blinked and saw the White Owl standing over him, readying
another stabbing lunge. He slashed at the Kyrinin's legs with his
sword. The Kyrinin sprang out of reach.

Ess'yr came from behind and drove her own spear into the small
of the White Owl's back. He arched, his mouth silently stretched
open. Ess'yr tripped him and pinned him to the ground. Orisian
swayed onto his feet. He still could not see properly. He spat teeth

onto the muddy grass. Blood and saliva trailed from his mouth. Through the showers of blurry lights that cascaded across his vision, he saw White Owls spilling over the huge fallen tree. Rothe was still fighting, bodies at his feet. Ess'yr tried to wrench her spear free, but it resisted. She released it and turned to meet the wave of assailants with a knife.

Orisian stumbled forwards. The White Owl that Ess'yr had impaled was stirring, clawing at the ground. The spear protruding from his back jerked and swung about. Orisian hacked at the back of his head, felt the blade meet bone, and stepped over him. There was a terrible anger howling inside his skull, a vast roaring filling his ears.

Ess'yr dodged the thrust of a spear, stabbed its wielder in the groin. A second White Owl reached her before she could untangle herself, knocked her down. Orisian cried out, bloody spittle filming his lips, and sprang forwards. There was no room in his mind for thought, but his body took over, leaped up, brought the sword down on the Kyrinin's shoulder. Orisian heard the clear crack of bone breaking. The White Owl fell, within reach of Ess'yr and her knife. Orisian rushed on beyond.

He ducked behind his shield and charged, meaning to drive his way to Rothe so that he could stand back to back with his shieldman. One Kyrinin darted out of his path; the next, he crashed up against and pressed to the thick bole of the dead tree. The White Owl writhed and strained, gripping the rim of Orisian's shield with one hand and pulling it this way and that. Another was coming from the side. Orisian managed to turn aside the incoming spear with a wild sweep of his sword, but the movement left him open with his blade down and wide. The Kyrinin recovered more quickly, brought the spear back up, then jerked. An arrow was in his side. Another darted in beside it. He fell. Orisian had no time to think. The White Owl he had pinned against the great log was too strong for him to hold. He hacked at the exposed legs below his shield until the Kyrinin went down.

He saw the *na'kyrim* woman they had come for curled up against the tree trunk like a child, a dead White Owl laid out beside her almost as if they were a sleeping couple. He saw Varryn coming sprinting from amongst the trees, and behind him human figures: Torcaill's men. He saw Ess'yr, a spear in her hand once more, trading blocks and blows with an opponent. And he saw Rothe, down on one knee, shield up to block one attack, sword parrying another, nothing left to block the third that punched a spear deep into his shoulder.

Orisian lunged forwards. He was in amongst them. Blows landed on his shield, on his hip. Someone went down on his left. He looked, terrified, but it was not Rothe. The shieldman had got back to his feet. His shield arm was hanging limp, defeated by injuries old and new. He cut down one of the White Owls in front of Orisian, stretched out sword and arm, pushing Orisian back.

"Stay clear," Rothe said. Then something hit him at the base of his neck. There was blood there. The shieldman's eyes flared for a moment. Varryn brushed past them, spear and elbows jabbing and stabbing. One of Torcaill's warriors crashed by. Rothe took an uncertain step backwards, and toppled.

Orisian heard the clatter of spears, the gasps of pain and exertion, felt the impact of bodies falling or feet stamping. He saw only Rothe. He dropped his sword and fell to his knees at his shieldman's side. Rothe was watching him. Only his eyes moved. He coughed and blood bubbled out across his lips and beard. Orisian shook his shield free, cast it away. He cupped Rothe's face in his hands. Strands of blood were falling from his own mouth. The wound in Rothe's throat was gurgling. Rothe blinked, again and again. His gaze never faltered, never left Orisian's eyes. Orisian pressed a hand to Rothe's neck. The blood flooded slickly out between his fingers and across the back of his hand. Dark. Remorseless.

"Wait, wait," Orisian heard himself saying.

Rothe blinked once more. And then never again.

VIII

"What would you have me do?" Cerys asked wearily. "Kill him?"

She looked from face to face. There was no challenge in her gaze. The question was an honest one. She had no answers of her own.

Of Highfast's Council, Eshenna was gone, and Alian remained too sick, too crippled by the presence of Aeglyss, to rise from her bed. The others sat here, enmeshed in worry, seeking solutions to a problem that all of them, Cerys suspected, knew was beyond them.

"No," Mon Dyvain murmured. "We cannot cut down the Dreamer, or allow Herraic's men to do so. Can we? We cannot give up on him so easily."

"Hardly easily," Amonyn said. "But I agree. There is still some hope, however faint its light might be. His body lives, even if another dwells in it. His mind might yet return. Aeglyss must exhaust his patience soon."

Cerys sighed. So often, over the years, she had found Amonyn to be of the same mind as her in all things. So often, his calm confidence had been an aid to her as she bore the heavy duties of the Elect. Now, though . . . now she was not so sure. Aeglyss showed little sign of running out of patience so far, though he had been shut away in a long-disused bedchamber for a full day and night now. They took him food and water, and Cerys had given him false promises of further discussion, even aid. Through it all, he had barely spoken. He simply stared at anyone who entered the room. They all left disturbed and distressed.

Amonyn smiled at her. It was a weary smile, but heartfelt. He clings to the possibility of escape from this net we're caught in, she thought. Through all his weariness, he finds cause for hope. Amonyn had gone without sleep now for a longer spell than was wise. Until he was summoned to this gathering, he had been constantly at the bedside of Mordyn Jerain, tending to the

Chancellor's grave injuries as only he could. It had drained him, left him more emptied out than Cerys had ever seen him. Such use of the Shared was always punishing, but now, with everything twisted out of recognition by Aeglyss, it was doubly so.

"No."

The word was spoken with such precision and firmness that it caught all of them unawares. Olyn, the blind old keeper of crows, sat with his arms folded across his chest, his brow furrowed in grave concentration.

"No?" Cerys asked quietly.

Olyn shook his head, blinked his milky eyes.

"Tyn is gone. The one who lives now in his body is a plague. Nothing will remain unruined if he persists. He is a blight upon this world, and all that's in it. You all know it, but won't face it. You all see it. Even these blind old eyes of mine can see it. Who'll deny it?"

The old man's lips were trembling. His long silver hair shivered as he turned his head this way and that. It cut Cerys to the quick to see this gentle man so distressed.

"None of us could deny that Aeglyss fouls the Shared with his—"

"No," Olyn snapped. He laid his hands on the table. They were shaking, trembling against the wood. "Not fouls. Corrupts, wrecks. Never, never . . . there has never been the like of this. I've lived too long that I should be here to learn of it." He was almost weeping. Cerys looked away. "Am I the only one who dreams of nothing but death and suffering and rage? Who is afraid, at every waking moment, lost to fear? Who can hardly walk in a straight line sometimes, so violent are the storms that buffet my thoughts? Am I?"

No one said anything. Cerys had her hands on her iron chain of office, but the cold metal offered none of the reassurance it sometimes did. What use an Elect, or a Council even, rendered so impotent?

"I am not the only one," Olyn said. "We can feel death, in the Shared, spreading its raven wings. Its shadow will fall across all things and all peoples. They do not know it yet, but we do. And its cause, its seed, is here, in Highfast. In Tyn. We should kill the body he is in, and hope against hope that in doing so we may harm him. Nothing else makes sense."

The premonition of something awful came to them all in the same moment. A stillness, a profound hesitation as if every living thing had paused, then the blinding, dizzying surge of raw power through the Shared. Olyn cried out. Cerys staggered to her feet.

The door to the meeting chamber crashed open. A *na'kyrim* was there, but Cerys could not be certain who: her vision was fragmenting.

"Elect," the newcomer was gasping. "Come – please come. He is . . . he has gone mad."

Cerys reeled out into the corridor. She could feel Aeglyss inside her skull. Or, at least, she could feel the Shared, but it was no longer easy to tell the difference between the two. She walked into a storm of the mind, and it was as ferocious as any gale that had ever lashed at Highfast.

"Find Herraic," she gasped, unsure whether anyone could or would hear her. "Bring his men."

This was terror beyond anything Cerys had ever known: all-embracing, crippling. It howled inside her. She lurched from one side of the passage to the other, fending off the walls as they swung towards her. Every bone, every muscle in her body burned with the desire to run, but run where? Everything around her was warped and twisted. The Shared overwhelmed her, bleeding through and hauling her into madness. The room in which Aeglyss was locked was close, but it might as well have been half the world away.

Her hands scraped along the hard walls of Highfast, but her feet stumbled across a sward of green grass; grass that writhed and flailed, animated by the vast will of the Anain. She smelled the deep, hot, ancient soils of endless forests, chokingly oppressive. The passageway down which she stumbled contorted itself into a chaos of shadows and light, of vague figures that ran alongside her, calling like birds, or screaming in fury. She could hear blades clashing, she could smell the sea, she could feel the blasting heat of a great fire on her face. None of it was real, and all of it was real, for it was flooding out of the Shared and into her. A thousand truths, unfiltered, harvested from all across the world, out of memory and experience, all pouring into her mind and tearing it asunder. And all overlaid by the savage, embittered anger of one man.

Then someone took hold of her hand. Someone was murmuring her name, laying down soft walls of protection around the bruised periphery of her mind. It was Amonyn, of course; there, at her side amidst the madness, easing her back towards a clear sense of herself. She held on to him tightly, and pressed her face into his shoulder for a few moments. When she felt strong enough to look up and into his eyes, she saw there such an enervated, haunted spirit that it almost broke her. But she said nothing. There was nothing to say. They went onwards together.

One of Herraic's men was hunched down outside the door, his spear lying forgotten at his side. He had wrapped his arms about his knees, pulling his legs in to his chest. He was shaking. Amonyn knelt beside him while Cerys opened the door. She half expected to die in the next few moments.

There was an overturned table. The mattress of the bed had been shredded, its horsehair stuffing disgorged in great black drifts across the floor. The shards of a clay jug were scattered across the room, a great swathe of wet stone on the wall showing where it had struck. And there was blood: on the sheet, on Tyn's crooked fingers, and on his face, where Aeglyss had clawed furrows out of the flesh of his cheeks.

The eyes that turned upon Cerys were bestial. The snarl was something that could only come from an animal's throat. Yet he wept, and the grief and pain that swirled about him and buffeted her senses belonged to something more than a beast. He gave no sign of recognising her; she barely recognised herself, for she was adrift now, in the limitless Shared.

"She is gone," he howled, and the sound staggered her, sent her to her knees, hands clasped uselessly over her ears.

"Lost in the green." He tore at the gown he wore, ripping open its front, revealing the white skin and the cage of the ribs beneath. "Taken from me. Again, and again, and again. Always to be taken from me."

He was hobbling towards her, like some tottering corpse. Cerys tried to get to her feet, but he had hold of her and there was a strength in him far greater than anything Tyn's wasted muscles could have allowed. His fingers dug into her shoulder, crushing down onto bone. She cried out. He lifted her onto her feet, as if she was a child's straw doll. He pressed her against the wall.

"How?" he shouted into her face. "Tell me! Why have they taken her from me? Dragging her down into the . . ."

His voice faltered. He gagged and spluttered as if choked by his own rage.

Cerys took a feeble hold on his wrists, but could do nothing to loosen his grip upon her. There was blood on his arms. She could feel it flowing beneath her fingers, from wounds in Tyn's wrists. How much blood could there be, in this emaciated body?

"Aeglyss," she murmured. It was not her that he raged against, she knew. The violence that set the Shared afire was not directed at her. It was uncontrolled, unfocused.

"Let me help you," she managed to say. But he did not seem to hear her.

"They'll not have me. Not!" He spat the words. His spittle was on her lips, across her eyes.

Then Amonyn was there, hauling at Tyn's arms. Aeglyss turned and looked upon Amonyn, and Cerys felt the contemptuous hatred surge like a boiling thundercloud. She opened her mouth to cry out in warning, but there was no time. Aeglyss released her, she slumped; he struck Amonyn, just once, across the head.

Amonyn fell, and in that fall somehow the greatest extremities of blind fury were spent. Tyn's bony shoulders went slack as he stared down at the prostrate figure. Cerys could breathe again, could give her thoughts some kind of form. She steadied herself on her feet, still leaning against the wall. She thought she could hear footsteps, somewhere off in the maze of passageways, drawing closer.

"The healer," Aeglyss murmured, still staring at Amonyn. He knelt.

"No," Cerys whispered, unsure of what it was she denied, or feared.

"Be silent. Liar. You think I don't know your lies? Your deceit?"

She felt cold.

"You're less than nothing. All of you here, little rats hiding in your tunnels. There's nothing for me here, nothing that you'll give me. Ha! Nothing's given. Only taken."

He caressed Amonyn's slack face.

"You think I don't know you have secrets? You think I don't know you mean to betray me? I know betrayal, as I know water and meat and the turning of the seasons. It is . . . it never changes."

"No," whispered Cerys. She pushed herself away from the wall, reaching for him.

"Be silent." And she was, for her throat clenched itself shut and she could draw no breath, and her legs and her arms were twigs, grass. She fell.

"Each day, I grow stronger," Aeglyss said softly. "Each day, I sink deeper. I learn. Things are revealed to me." He leaned down close to Amonyn, sniffing at him. "You *na'kyrim*. You . . . half-breeds. There is nothing you can keep from me. You, least of all."

He rose, and loomed over Cerys. She was stretching out an arm, trying to take hold of Amonyn's hand. She did not want to die, but she wanted him to die even less.

"You were my own kind," Aeglyss was saying. She paid him no heed. All that mattered was that she touch Amonyn, that neither he nor she should be alone. "But you want nothing to do with me. I know that. So be it. I am not of your kind any more. I am something else, and I am to have nothing: no companions, no sanctuary, no . . . It does not matter. The Anain may hunt me, take everything that I love, if they want. You can plot against me. No matter. I take what I need, Elect. There is to be no more trust, no more talking. Not in all the world."

He came down onto his hands and knees, crouched over her like a dog. She felt his lips brushing her ear.

"You should not have tried to keep secrets from me. I know you have the Shadowhand here, Elect," he said. And then he collapsed. Tyn lay curled on the floor, his shallow, rattling breath the only sound save the heavy footsteps of Herraic's warriors coming running.

* * *

They buried Rothe in the clearing where he had fallen. Torcaill was disapproving, Orisian knew, eager to be away from that threatening place with its smothering mists and enclosing trees, but he said nothing. Eshenna and Yvane were uneasy, fearful no doubt of any intrusion upon this domain of the Anain, but they raised no complaint. Orisian dug the grave himself, first with a short blade one of the warriors lent him, to break open the soft, wet earth, then with his hands, clawing out great fistfuls of the black soil. Others helped, but he barely registered their presence or their exertions.

The few horses that had not been lost in the sprawling, frantic pursuit and skirmishing through the forest grazed on the glade's wet grass. Ess'yr and Varryn sat on a log, watching. Sentries looked nervously out on all sides, knowing they had little chance of anticipating any attack. Torcaill himself knelt, cleaning Rothe's sword. All of this Orisian knew, vaguely, was around him. It seemed like nothing to do with him. He just dug.

They lowered Rothe into the ground. Torcaill laid the sword on his chest, folded his arms across it. Then Orisian laid Rothe's shield over his hands. As he straightened, the warriors – not many more than twenty of them alive now – stepped forwards, ringing the shallow grave. As one, they bent and began covering Rothe with earth. Orisian watched that face he knew so well gradually, incrementally disappear.

"He deserved a pyre," he murmured. His jaw throbbed. His mouth was swollen and tasted foul, of blood and ruin. He could not speak well, or clearly.

"He did," Torcaill agreed. "But this is the best we can do for him. It's better than others have had, today."

"They all deserved better. But him especially."

After it was done, they covered the grave with dead wood and stones.

Orisian sat, numb and cold, while one of the warriors – he did not even know his name – cleaned the dried blood from his face. Probing with his tongue, he could feel the empty sockets of the teeth he had lost. It was not until the needle and sinew began to close up the great gash across his cheek that he felt the pain. It was sharp and insistent enough to cut through the fog that enshrouded his mind. He closed his eyes and endured it as the stitches went in.

Afterwards, Ess'yr beckoned him over. She said nothing, but made him sit at her side. She had collected a few clumps of some pale green moss-like plant. Now she chewed on a little of it. After a few moments, she touched a thumb to his chin and pressed his mouth open. She removed the moist, pulped mass from her own mouth and gently pressed it into the space between his cheek and gum. The juices that oozed from it made his wounds sting.

Wreaths of mist drifted amongst the treetops all around. Orisian stared blankly at them. His gaze slipped down and rested on K'rina. She was sitting cross-legged, rocking back and forth. She turned her hands over, and back and over again, examining them as if she had never seen such strange objects before. The tiny scratches all over her skin were like a fine net. No word, no sense, had passed her lips since they had found her; no sign that she was anything more than a madwoman, lost in the forest. That was the treasure Rothe and the others had died to deliver into Orisian's hands.

Someone shouted out. Men were running. Ess'yr was on her feet, raising her bow.

"They're coming again," Orisian heard. It might have been Torcaill's voice. He looked at Rothe's grave. Someone leaped across it, rushing with sword drawn to meet whatever danger now came.

Dull and distant, without thought, Orisian reached for his own blade and rose to his feet.

* * *

For two days they waited. Guards stood outside the door behind which the monster lurked. Or possibly lurked. Cerys and others went back and forth from that gloomy chamber, spending hours at Tyn's bedside, and learned nothing. They found nothing save silence, and a dead, empty space in the Shared. The Dreamer breathed, his eyes moved beneath their lids, but there was no life in him. His body was truly a shell now, an empty, abandoned shell. There was no Tyn, no Aeglyss. The wounds in his face and his wrists dried, but did not heal. Cerys sat and stared into that gaunt face, as if by merely looking she might find some answer. But none came. The Shared was still, unresponsive. The Dreamer did not stir. The iron chain around her neck grew heavier.

Amonyn lay in his own quarters, alive but bruised both without and within. Herraic came to see Tyn himself, and fretted and frowned impotently until Cerys asked him to leave. Mordyn Jerain hesitated between life and death, his wounds half-healed. Olyn stayed in the crows' roost, and would not emerge. Highfast was paralysed, prostrated by trepidation and gloom and uncertainty. Snow fell, and laid white blankets across the roofs and battlements and courtyards.

During the short hours of daylight, the Elect could busy herself with her duties. She could find enough activity to fend off the darkest of her thoughts. It was an illusory, temporary calm but necessary. At night, she had no such defences, and could not even take comfort in Amonyn's company. Guilt and doubts circled her, snapping at her.

She wondered if she had failed Tyn, through some lack of wisdom or lack of knowledge in the ways of the Shared. Not for the first time, she thought of Inurian. He might have been Elect instead of her, had he stayed in Highfast. Had that been what he wanted from life. Would his failures have been less?

Now and again, in the sleepless night, Cerys would shake and scold herself for giving in to such futile self-doubt. It served no purpose to play these games. What was done, was done. Still, dawn would find her at the Dreamer's bedside. She rested her elbows on his sheets, held her chain of office clasped in her hands. She closed her eyes and wondered if Tyn was still there, somewhere, and if he would hear her when she asked for his forgiveness.

Then, on the morning of the third day: "Elect."

She opened her eyes. Tyn was gazing at her. He was smiling. And it was not Tyn.

"They are here."

He was rising from the bed, casting aside the sheet. She could only watch.

"Did you think I had gone? No, Elect. Just waiting. I do not mean to leave this place empty-handed. And I do have friends, after all. Would you like to meet them?"

He came around the bed to her side, took her hand in his. There was no warmth in his skin, only the cold of dead flesh.

"Walk with me, Elect. Show me your mighty library, your precious store of wisdom that fills you with such pride."

She saw – or thought she saw – him enshrouded by a vast cape of shadow that swelled up behind him like a living thing. It drowned out the world, leaving her alone with him, the two of them alone in a dark domain where the very air was made of his thoughts, the ground upon which she walked was made of his hatred for her and for all things.

They moved, though she could not say which of them led the other. A door opened, and there were men there. Warriors. Guards, she vaguely remembered. She saw them faintly, as through a veil. They were saying something, but their words were only sounds that fluttered up against her and fell away, spent and meaningless.

"No," she heard Aeglyss saying, and his voice was all about her, in her blood and her bones. "The Elect and I are going to the library. You, you are going to the gates. Open them. Open Highfast."

He drew her onwards, through corridors. They passed by torches burning on the walls. Aeglyss took one and lit their way with it, though the shadows stayed all around them, and the light seemed sickly to Cerys. She recognised the passageways they walked along, knew that they were familiar, but they belonged to someone else, to another life.

They entered into a great chamber, where daylight spilled in through high windows, and there were ranks of writing desks. Cerys smelled parchment and ink and dust. She knew this place. There were people here: just one or two. They were afraid. They cowered. Aeglyss could taste their fear, and she could too. It was a sharp, acrid touch on her tongue, in her nose.

Aeglyss turned around and around, arms outstretched, the flame of his torch crackling.

"Look, Elect. What a wonder."

She looked, and saw books, and rolls of parchment and shelves. The Scribing Hall, she thought. The library.

"Tyn? Elect, what is happening?" someone called.

She frowned in the direction of the voice. A man was there, half-hidden behind one the desks. He stared out, fearful. Bannain, she thought to herself. I remember his name.

"Nothing," Aeglyss shouted. Then he had hold of the front of Cerys's dress. He dragged her close to him. She did not resist, for he was already all around her.

"Wake, Elect. Wake up. You should see this."

She plummeted back into her body as if falling from a great height into a pool of cold water. She gasped for breath. Her head spun.

"What a task," Aeglyss cried. "What a burden, to watch over all this for so many years."

"Leave us!" Cerys shouted, her mind tumbling away into panic.

"No! Whose gratitude have you earned by all these years of devotions? What have you achieved by storing up the past here, making it so precious?"

"Please. Please."

She cast a desperate glance sideways. Bannain and two scribes were rising hesitantly.

"Forget them," Aeglyss hissed. "I am here to relieve you of your burdens, Elect. All of you. Memory is no longer needed, for what is to come will be unlike what has been before. There are to be no more secrets. I declare the past dead. Your task is done with. Are you not pleased?"

"Release me." She struggled against him, but his grip was firm.

"Oh, I intend to. I will take the weight of your responsibilities from your shoulders."

He threw her down, and she sprawled to the floor, sending a

chair skittering away across the flagstones. He was laughing. Savage glee poured forth from Tyn's stale throat, coarse and wild. Cerys got to her feet.

Aeglyss strode down a rank of shelves, drawing the flame of the torch he carried across the books and the scrolls and the manuscripts.

"No," Cerys shouted, but he ignored her.

Gouts of black smoke burst up. She could see flames taking hold. Everything that mattered about Highfast was here, in this hall. And Aeglyss laughed as he swept the torch back and forth. Cerys moved towards him, but Bannain was faster. He darted forwards, and as he did so he faded. He folded the Shared about himself for a heartbeat, spilled the Elect's gaze off his back. He was gone. Gone to her, but not to Aeglyss. Tyn's arm snapped around. Sparks erupted in a frenzied cloud as the torch struck Bannain on the side of the head.

He crashed against one of the desks. Aeglyss followed him, kicking aside a chair that came between them.

"You think tricks like that will work on me? That is my ocean you're swimming in, child."

Bannain groaned and rolled onto his side. Cerys glimpsed a red welt across his temple. She cast about for something, anything, to use against Aeglyss. Smoke was thickening the air now, rasping down into her chest with every breath. The sound of the hungry, consuming flames filled her ears, and their hateful, triumphant light danced across the walls. She took up a chair and rushed towards Aeglyss.

He crouched and struck Bannain's head again and again with the torch. Embers spun away across the floor. There was a stench of burned hair and flesh. Bannain was not struggling. Aeglyss laughed.

Cerys smashed the chair across his back. It burst into fragments. He staggered up, dropping the flaming brand. He spun and seemed to Cerys to fill her vision. Sheets of flame were roaring up the shelves and walls behind him. He bore down on her. There was blood in Tyn's long hair: ruby strands in that silver waterfall. Smoke billowed across his shoulders.

He took hold of her chain of office and twisted it in his hands, tightening it around her neck.

"Did you want to kill me, Elect? Is that what you wanted?"

There were others beating him, trying to drag him off. He roared defiance and pulled the chain tighter and tighter. Cerys clawed at Tyn's face. She opened fresh cuts over those that already disfigured it.

"My spears are at the gates, Elect. It is done. I will make war on all the world, if it makes war on me."

His restraint was crumbling. His wild, blind rage roared through the Shared. He was a terrible thing, she saw now. Worse even than they had feared; more consumed by hate and anger, more potent. He was a tempest that would not cease until it had brought all the world, and all the Shared, to ruin.

Cerys clutched at the chain. So many times she had felt those iron links beneath her fingertips. She smelled his blood, and the smoke. She began to thin. The Shared pulled her gently apart, like a soft breeze working upon the morning's mist. Tyn's face was twisted into a furious mask of hatred. She felt something cracking and collapsing in her throat. She saw flames, all around her. Her hands, pale, beautiful, lifted for a moment before her eyes, then dropped. Though she thought her eyes were still open, there was only darkness after that. She surrendered, and let herself end, and fall backwards, dissolving, away and down into the limitless depths.

* * *

Herraic Crenn dar Kilkry-Haig could smell smoke. Its acrid taint suffused the air of Highfast. He set down a half-eaten apple, and sniffed.

Herraic was a man aware of his own shortcomings. He sometimes regretted them, in a detached and melancholic way, but
had long since stopped imagining he could change himself. As
distant cousin to the Thane, he might have expected swift elevation to some lucrative or responsible post; instead, he had filled
a succession of undemanding and at times almost trivial pos-
itions. For several years he had been harbourmaster, not of Kolkyre
or Donnish but of Skeil Anchor, a drab and quiet port frequented
only by fishermen and sealers. He had briefly been Captain of the
Guard in Stone, a remote town of just a hundred families on the
upper reaches of the Kyre. Now he commanded the tiny garrison
of Highfast. None was the kind of role that delivered wealth or
fame.

Even so, as Captain of Highfast he had found a degree of con-
tentment. Nothing of any great consequence ever happened here
amidst the Peaks. His responsibilities were simple and therefore
within his capabilities: ensuring the safety of the *na'kyrim* who
dwelled in the castle's roots, keeping the road out to the west
clear of thieves, and maintaining order amongst the few inhabitants of the nearby mountains and forests. Those inhabitants
were self-reliant, solitary folk who made almost no demands upon
his attention. The sense of having at last found a task to which he
was suited had engendered a certain peace in Herraic's heart.

That peace had been shattered by recent events. He seldom had
cause to spend much time with Cerys and the other *na'kyrim*, but
their agitated and despondent state had communicated itself to
him over the last two or three weeks. Then the Lannis-Haig Thane
had arrived, causing Herraic to fret over everything from the
dilapidated appearance of the fortifications to the dismal near-
dereliction of the stables in which the Thane's horse had to be
quartered. And shortly after, Herraic found himself playing host
to the Shadowhand himself, and in a gravely, perhaps mortally
wounded condition at that. The infamous Chancellor would have
died by now, but for the care of the *na'kyrim* healer. He still might.

Finally – the torch to the pyre of Herraic's dwindling ease – there had been the mysterious business with the *na'kyrim* risen from his bed after years of dreaming. Herraic had not fully understood the explanation of that, though it had all sounded to him unpleasantly like the kind of thing that went on in olden days, when halfbreeds wielded terrible power.

Now, when he had rashly started to think that things could not get any worse, might even be showing some signs of improvement, he smelled smoke. It was not the familiar oily stink of lamps, nor the homely scent of charcoal from kitchens or brazier. This was a drier, stronger smell. It reminded him of a long ago day when wildfires had torn through the grasslands around Skeil Anchor one parched summer. He knew at once that whatever was burning should not be. He left his quiet chambers and went out into the deep courtyard before the main keep, to discover a world abandoned by reason, plunged into derangement.

Distraught voices and smoke coiled up out of Highfast's guts. People were running. The crows had burst in black profusion from the roost in the cliff face above the gorge and plumed and tumbled upwards like a thousand leaves caught on a hot wind. They spun screaming about the man-made pinnacles of Highfast. Herraic saw *na'kyrim* darting from passageways, across doorways; he saw men of his own meagre garrison running to and fro, and those who had come here with the Shadowhand, gathering and shouting, and glaring about in anger and alarm.

The smoke carried with it fear beyond anything it should naturally have induced: fear that seeped in through the nose and eyes and ears and twisted itself around Herraic's mind, dizzying and nauseating him. His heart raced, as if meaning to tear itself apart. He found images of blood and violence rushing through his head, invading him. When he tried to shout out commands, an inarticulate, barely human wail escaped his throat instead.

He heard the deep, rumbling, grating sound of Highfast's

main gate opening, and turned in confusion. The inner gate already stood open, as it always did during daylight. Herraic could see down the long tunnel that ran out to the bridge and the road and the mountains. There were figures struggling with one another, down there at the end of the passage. They seemed impossibly distant. Herraic had to narrow his eyes to hold back the blurring waves of distortion that threatened to sweep across his vision. They were his men, fighting with each other there at the outer gate: one trying to push it closed once more, the other trying to prevent him. Herraic was dumbfounded.

Someone brushed past him, almost knocking him over.

"It's the library," they were shouting. "The halfbreeds have gone mad. They're killing each other."

Herraic's hands were shaking now. Savage emotions – terror, fury – that were not his own had him in their grip. He was watching, in disbelieving shock, his own mind, his life and everything he had ever thought to be true, all coming apart.

More figures running now, up from the gate, through the passageway, like rats rushing up out of the earth towards the light, towards him. Woodwights. Herraic heard himself laughing at the sheer insanity of all this. There were arrows in the air, ringing off Highfast's ancient stone. Men were dying. He saw it, but no longer understood it. The Captain of Highfast fled, weeping as he ran.

Herraic hid in a long-abandoned storeroom until the cacophony, both outside and within his skull, subsided. He could not tell how long it took, for he was alone and lost and besieged. As the noises – terrible noises, death cries, screams – fell away, so the relentless, disorientating waves of fear receded. His breath came more easily. His mind fell back into a shape he could recognise. And as it did so, he understood that whatever had happened, it had not been a natural thing, of the natural world. It had been some strange intrusion of the inhuman, incorporeal domain of the *na'kyrim* into his own. He went, still trembling, to discover what kind of disaster had befallen the castle he had been meant to hold. He held his sword out in front of him, knowing that it was far too late for such a gesture, but clinging to that small token of defiance, and the illusory capability it suggested.

There were still fires burning somewhere. He could smell them, and the sky above Highfast was stained with their black-brown breath. He found bodies. In the courtyard, in passageways, in the stables and the kitchens; human and Kyrinin, and *na'kyrim* too. Some of his men had made a stand in the stables, it seemed, for their corpses were piled there, with horses dead alongside them. There were dead woodwights, stretched out on the cobbles of the yard, and in doorways leading off it. Amongst them, the corpse of the *na'kyrim* whom Herraic had seen in Highfast's kitchens. He had looked dead even then. Now, he had assuredly passed into the Sleeping Dark. Cerys had always called him the Dreamer, but he would be dreaming no more dreams. To judge by the contortions of his limbs, the dried blood on his face and his arms, and his fixed expression of horror, his death had been cruel.

Herraic wandered amongst all this in a daze. He thought at first that he might be the only one left alive, but one by one other survivors came out from their hiding places. Herraic saw in the eyes of every one of them the same stunned vacancy he felt himself. They all looked as though they were only just waking, after a punishing dream.

An old *na'kyrim*, a little man, was amongst them. He came blinking into the watery light of the courtyard. Herraic, collecting weapons from the bodies of his men, saw the halfbreed shuffle to the centre of the courtyard and stand staring down at the body of the Dreamer. The old man had a piece of wood in his hands, which he kept turning and grasping. It took Herraic a moment or two to recognise him. He could not remember his name, but this was one of those who had come to Highfast with the Lannis Thane, only to remain here when Orisian moved on.

"He's dead," Herraic murmured to the halfbreed. That piece of wood in his hands was a half-finished carving, he could see now. The outlines of tiny figures had been cut, but they remained vague and ill-defined, as if they had been frozen in the act of emerging from the wood.

The *na'kyrim* was shaking his head, and worrying away at the carving with his trembling hands.

"No. Not him. Not dead. Sad to say. Oh, sad to say. He was only visiting. Only passing through."

Herraic frowned, not understanding. He was distracted by someone shouting his name from one of the windows of the keep. He looked up, squinting against a brief flash of the sun through a crack in the clouds.

"Captain!" he heard. "The Shadowhand's gone. They took him."

4

Shadowhand

Power loves not the light of day, nor the attention of curious eyes. In darkness it thrives most. Examined too closely, it withers. A lord may send his army hither and thither, but the true testing of his power is in those places where his army is not. Has he sunk the roots of his power deep enough into the earth of his lands? Has he sent its long fingers far enough through the backstreets and alleys, into the drinking dens and the lending-houses, so that he may gather them unto himself and hold them firm without a single swordsman?

When a man may whisper in a close ear, and that whisper be repeated far away and many moons later, then he has power. When a man may speak against another, and that other be brought to ruin and rue by nothing more than those words, then he has power. And if a man can act without the appearance of action, and bring about great change without the appearance of desiring it, then he has power.

Ask me not who the most powerful has been, for I know not his name, and nor do you. The greatest power will have been cultivated in the shadows, and the further into darkness and secrecy it was sunk, the mightier will have been its exercising.

from The Huanin Lords
by an unknown hand, writing amidst chaos at the
beginning of the Third Age,
translated from the western form of Old Aygll

I

A kind of fever had taken hold of Kolkyre. The ancient city was convulsed by anger, riddled with fearful rumour. The ferment was such that Anyara began to think that normal conversation was no longer possible. Every exchange she heard seemed to be conducted either in whispers or in the anguished, strident tones of outrage or grief. The death of Lheanor oc Kilkry-Haig had shaken his city out of balance.

The dead Thane was burned in the gardens that ringed the Tower of Throncs. The fire raged, turning pyre and corpse into a great column of flame, noise, smoke and heat, killing the grass around and beneath. The gardens would be scarred, at least until this winter was done with. As would the people of Kolkyre, Anyara thought, as she watched the faces of those come to witness the conflagration: distraught, stunned, vacant.

Roaric was there, arm about Ilessa, his now-widowed mother. Ilessa was weeping silently. The new Thane of the Kilkry Blood looked like a man barely in control of his emotions. His eyes were locked on the heart of the flames, as if there was nothing in his world save that fire, and whatever burned within him.

Cailla the kitchen maid had been put into an unmarked grave outside the city walls. On the very night of her burial, so Anyara had heard, someone had dug up and dismembered the old woman's body. Roaric had spoken of Cailla only once within Anyara's earshot.

"I would have her alive if it was possible," he had said, "so that I could kill her again."

Now the Thane was silent, like everyone else gathered about the crackling pyre. Lagair Haldyn was there, his expression unreadable, a knot of Haig warriors around him and his wife. Aewult had left a hundred or more men in the city, under the Steward's command; just enough to keep resentment simmering amongst Kolkyre's inhabitants.

A rising, gusting wind whipped the flames back and forth. Waves of heat came and went across Anyara's face. She grieved for Lheanor. She had liked him. But the thoughts that smudged her vision with unshed tears were of her own dead father, Kennet, and of Croesan her uncle, and all the others of her family who had died. No one was left now save Orisian, and he had gone from her, out into an unsafe world.

Coinach her shieldman moved a little at her side, breaking her mournful reverie. He turned his face away from a blast of hot wind, and in doing so caught her eye for a moment. He gave her a faint, sympathetic smile.

The flames were dwindling, past the peak of their intensity. The centre of the pyre fell in, belching out a swarm of sparks. The wind took them and tumbled them away. They flared and died amongst the apple trees. Horns were blown. Their mournful voices drowned out the roar of the fire for a time, echoing off the smooth stone of the Tower. It was that sound, filling the whole world, that made Anyara weep at last. It carried every loss, every grief, within it, and it was, briefly, too much to bear.

She saw, as she brushed a tear from her cheek, Lagair the Steward moving away. He and his wife and their accompanying warriors turned and shuffled through the crowd. Roaric was watching them go. The Thane's gaze was so sharp with loathing that Anyara feared, then, for the future.

On the day after Lheanor's burning, Anyara went to visit Jaen Narran in her chambers in the town barracks. Coinach accompanied her, as always. She would be surprised now if one day she turned around and did not find him there, silent, attentive and observant.

If Anyara did not know better, she might have thought Taim's wife flustered by her arrival. The woman rushed around, clearing unnecessary space on the table, searching for her own cloak. They were to go together to visit the few dozen Lannis folk who still lived in squalor in Kolkyre's northern parts. The plan had been agreed the day before, so Anyara knew it was not surprise that made Jaen fuss so. Rather, she imagined, it was the anxiety that affected everyone in the city, like an affliction leaping from one warm body to the next through touch or breath or glance. And for Jaen, as for Anyara, its edge could only be sharpened by the knowledge that someone precious to her was still facing immeasurable danger.

"I brought as much as I could from the Tower kitchens," Anyara said. Coinach, who had carried the sack of ham and bread and apples for her, set it down on the table with a thump.

"Good, good," Jaen replied without looking up. She was burrowing now in a chest, digging amongst blankets in search of something.

"How is your daughter?" Anyara asked.

Jaen straightened, clutching a thin shawl in her hands. She settled it about her shoulders.

"Well, thank you, lady. Her husband takes good care of her. He will make a good father to the child, luck allowing."

"Luck allowing," Anyara said, nodding.

"I have some stew I made," Jaen said, pointing to a lidded iron pot that sat by the fire. "I thought some warmth would be welcomed, now that the weather's set in its cold path. Nothing worse than not having hot food in winter."

"No," agreed Anyara.

"You've no word, I suppose, from the north. From home?" Jaen asked the question almost nervously, almost as if she doubted her right to venture it. Or perhaps it was the possibility of an answer that she shied away from.

"Nothing," Anyara said, with a shake of her head. "The Bloodheir must be in Kolglas by now, but there's been no word of what's happening come back to the Tower of Thrones yet. Not that I've heard, anyway. You'll be one of the first to hear, Jaen, when there is anything."

The woman nodded, and smiled sadly.

"Should we go, then?" she suggested.

They went out into the streets, wrapped against the wind-driven flecks of snow, and headed north. A couple of Taim's warriors – some of the handful he had left behind when he marched for Kolglas – went with them, carrying the food. They walked a little ahead, to clear the way, but in truth there were no crowds to part. The streets of Kolkyre, emptied by cold air and cold hearts, were seldom busy these days. The faces of those others they did encounter were grim. The death of a Thane would always dispirit his people, but the manner of Lheanor's demise had done more than that: it had made them bitter and suspicious as well as grief-stricken. None – so Anyara hoped and believed, at least – looked upon her with hostility. Perhaps it was only that she reminded all those who recognised her of the cruelty of the times they lived in.

They heard the mob before they saw it: a maelstrom of angry voices. At once, Coinach slowed and put a restraining hand on Anyara's arm. The noise was fat with violence. Jaen pulled her shawl tighter about her. A crowd of figures poured around a corner and onto the street ahead of them. It came surging up like a debris-laden flood wave. Two men ran at its head, fleeing it, but unable to outpace it. They were Haig warriors.

Coinach pushed Anyara unceremoniously towards a doorway. She did not resist, but managed to grab hold of Jaen's shoulder and pull her along with them. The mob came rushing on. The objects of its fury crashed past the two Lannis men before they could get out of the way. The sack of food from the Tower's kitchens fell and emptied its contents across the roadway. The pot of Jaen's stew clattered down. The crowd poured around the Lannis warriors without pause, blind to them.

"What's happening?" gasped Jaen.

Anyara, pressed into the doorway by Coinach, said nothing, but she had no doubt of what would happen if the crowd caught their quarry.

Peering over Coinach's shoulder, she saw one of the Haig men go down, the other turn, trying to draw his sword. The mass of their pursuers broke over them and boiled around them like wild dogs biting at sheep. Bodies crashed against Coinach – Anyara felt the impacts through his chest – but no one had eyes for anything except the two fallen men. Anyara saw a heavy lumber axe rising and falling, a long staff beating down again and again. Fists. Boots. Jaen was hiding her eyes. Anyara longed to, but did not.

The storm blew itself out. The crowd scattered. Some of its members fled, running as if pursued by the horror of what had happened. Other lingered. Some spat on the two battered, crumpled corpses; some simply stared down at them, as if surprised by their own handiwork. Coinach carefully stepped away from Anyara. He had his sword in his hand.

"We should get back to the Tower," he said.

Anyara, still standing in the doorway, her arm around Jaen, nodded.

Late that evening, Anyara was alone in her room in the Tower of Thrones, repairing the stitching in the sleeve of a dress. It was not even her dress – just one of those that Ilessa had found for her – and she could have summoned a seamstress to undertake the task, but she found the repetitive, precise movement went some way towards calming her thoughts. It required just enough concentration to keep at bay the worst of the memories and worries that might otherwise intrude.

Coinach admitted one of the Tower's maids. The young girl bobbed her head respectfully.

"The Thane has asked for you, my lady, in the hall."

Anyara hesitated. She was not dressed for an appearance before Roaric oc Kilkry-Haig and any others of Kolkyre's elite who might be present.

"I should change," she said.

"N-no need, my lady. The Thane . . . he said to bring you as I find you. As quickly as I could."

Anyara set aside the dress on which she had been working and stood up. She did not want to leave this quiet room and submit herself once again to the grim atmosphere that prevailed beyond its door, but at the best of times it would be unwise to refuse a summons from a Thane. And these were not the best of times, and Roaric was not the most even-tempered of Thanes.

She and Coinach followed the maid down the long spiral stair and were ushered into the hall through a small side door. Many others were there before them: officials of the Tower, Ilessa and the Thane himself, sitting straight-backed and hard-faced on his great wooden seat. Roaric noticed Anyara as soon as she entered and beckoned her over. She went, with no little trepidation, and bent her head to listen to his murmur.

"I am glad you could join us. I wanted you to see what is about to happen. To see that the Kilkry Blood is unbroken, and still mindful of its enemies as well as its friends. Stand close." He gestured towards a nearby gap in the ranks of the assembled audience. Anyara went to stand there and await events. She glanced questioningly at Coinach, but the shieldman just gave a shrug. He looked no more happy to be there than Anyara felt.

The main doors swung open and Lagair Haldyn marched purposefully in, flanked by Haig warriors dressed in ceremonial finery. Anyara's heart sank.

"Steward," Roaric said equably before Lagair could utter a word, "I heard you wished to speak with us. I am at your disposal."

"With you, sire. Not with your entire household."

"Well, on this occasion I think you had best take what you find," Roaric said, much less warmly now. "I will be retiring to my chambers shortly, and interring my father's ashes tomorrow. My time is limited."

"Very well." Lagair was, as far as Anyara could tell, untroubled by the hostility of his reception. "What I have to say is no secret.

My demand is a just one, and I will gladly let any hear it who wish to listen."

"Demand? This is not the place for demands, Steward. This is the Tower of Thrones, and I am Thane in it. Not Bloodheir, mark. Thane."

"You may call it what you wish, Thane, once you have heard it," Lagair said tightly. "Whatever name you give to it, though, I will have it answered. Two men of the Haig Blood were slain today. Men who marched from their homes to come to the defence of your Blood, and who would have died in that defence if called upon to do so. Instead they died like animals in a back-street of this city, set upon by your people. Beaten to death like—"

"I heard that they brought trouble upon themselves," Roaric interrupted him.

Anyara realised she had clenched her hands into fists. She forced her fingers to uncurl, willed herself to conceal the tension she felt. She had the sense that everyone around her was holding their breath.

"Did you?" cried Lagair, outraged. "Brought it upon themselves? Invited a mob of savages to murder them in the street?"

Roaric leaned forwards a fraction. "I heard that they were drunk, and were abusing the memory of my own dead father. I heard that they said none but an old fool would die by the hand of a kitchen maid. I heard that they said the Kilkry Blood could not keep its own Thane safe, let alone its borders. That we would be nothing without the Haig Blood to fight our battles for us."

"You mean to excuse this deed by reporting gossip and rumour, then?" the Steward snapped.

Anyara did not know if either of these two men possessed enough restraint to back down. Roaric, she imagined in alarm, might even be capable of assaulting the High Thane's Steward.

"I make no excuses," the Thane said.

"Because you think none are required," Lagair said accusingly.

Looking beyond Roaric, Anyara could see Ilessa, his mother, sitting at his side. She was staring down at the hands cupped in her lap, but Anyara could see the sorrow and alarm on her face. She knows, Anyara thought, what dangerous territory her son ventures into.

"Aewult nan Haig himself left those men under my command," Lagair shouted. "I will have an answer to their deaths! I want the men who killed them brought to judgement."

"Not possible. We have no names. The Guard found nothing but the two bodies, no sign that anyone else had been there."

"I want them brought to judgement," Lagair repeated, low and firm. "And I want rightful payment for their families, their widows."

"Rightful payment?"

"A silver bar for each child they left behind them when they marched. Five, I believe."

"For two drunkards?"

"Warriors! Men who served your master, Thane, and marched upon his command to defend your lands from the Black Road."

"While he lived, and while I was Bloodheir, my father was my only master," Roaric said. "I may be Bloodheir in name no longer, but still I am gladly subject to him. To his memory, to the honour he is due. The men who died soiled that honour."

Anyara saw the slightest movement of Ilessa's hand. The Thane's mother reached discreetly out and touched him on the arm. At first Anyara was not sure whether Roaric had even noticed, but he moistened his lips and his gaze went for a moment to the arched stone roof of the hall.

"I have heard your petition, Steward," the Thane said. "Let me think on it."

"Not for long, sire," Lagair muttered. "Not for long."

"I will not yield!" Roaric cried, red-faced with anger.

Anyara could hardly bear to watch. The Thane and his mother

confronted each other across a narrow table in one of the side rooms off the hall. All Roaric's fury, so barely controlled during his exchanges with the Steward, had burst out now, in the privacy of this tiny chamber. Anyara alone had been brought – by Ilessa, not by Roaric – to stand witness. Why, she could not imagine. It was a scene that should have been played out between the two of them alone.

"I will not," the Thane repeated. "They died the death they deserved, and Gryvan oc Haig will get nothing from this Blood in answer to their deaths. You think he'll shed a tear when word reaches him of my father's death? Do you think so? Or do you think he'll laugh, and fill his cup with wine, and drink to the health of the bitch who killed him?"

"I do not care what the High Thane does or thinks," Ilessa said wearily. "Your father – my husband – is dead and will remain so whether Gryvan laughs or weeps at the news. He will remain so no matter how loudly you argue with the Steward. It is not something that can be undone, any more than can your brother's death."

Roaric thumped the table with his fist and spun away.

"I am not a child, needing lessons in my own grief."

"You are no child," Ilessa agreed quietly, "but you are my son. And you are not so old that there are no lessons left for you to learn. None of us are."

Roaric slumped into a chair against the wall. He glared at his mother, but could not maintain his indignation.

"What would you have me do?" he asked her.

"You could take counsel with our friends, if nothing else," Ilessa said, glancing meaningfully at Anyara. "This is thin ice, Roaric. Every time you deal with the High Thane, or his heir, or his Shadowhand or Steward, it is thin ice. And if you stamp so hard that it cracks beneath your feet, it will never be just you who'll fall through it. Never."

Roaric glared at Anyara. She longed to be elsewhere. It was not her presence that so infuriated Roaric – she hoped not, at least – but his anger, or grief, was so all-encompassing that she did not trust him to see clearly.

"Your brother is not here," Ilessa said to her gently, "but in times such as these Lannis and Kilkry have always walked in step. We both stand to lose – have already lost – a great deal. There should be no secrets between us."

"No," Anyara agreed, "but I don't think I can speak for Orisian, if that's what you want. He didn't . . ." She shrugged. "I'm not sure what he would want me to say."

"I don't ask you to speak for him, though I do not doubt he would be happy to have you do so. I only ask you to tell my son whether you are content to see him risk an open breach with the Haig Blood, now that their armies are your best chance of recovering your home."

Anyara thought she caught a glimpse in Ilessa's face, just for a moment, of the great ocean of weariness and sorrow that lay behind her words. After all the loss the older woman had suffered, she was still trying to hold on to what remained of her family, to protect her people. She knew her son too well, Anyara suspected. She was afraid of what Roaric might do. That was why she had brought Anyara into this little room: she had feared she was not strong enough to influence her own son alone.

"There's no need to say anything," Roaric said. "I know the answers to my mother's questions already."

"You could arrange for the men who did the killing to disappear from Kolkyre," Anyara suggested. "Let them escape to Il Anaron, or into the Vare Wastes. They might not be found for months, once they're out of the city. Or never."

Roaric acknowledged the idea with a half-nod, though he did not look very enamoured of it.

"And we can spare some silver, if the Steward wants to insist on it," said Ilessa. "The Haig Blood has always been easily distracted by glittering things, and Lagair is more bluster than anything. He doesn't care about the men who died, he's just fearful that Aewult will blame him for their deaths. He has to show that he did something about it."

She was leaning heavily on the table now, tired. She lacked the strength for all of this, Anyara thought. Too much had happened too quickly for an ageing body and heart to bear.

"We'll have nothing left with which to buy food for our own table soon," Roaric muttered. "But yes. Perhaps. We can throw some more silver at them, if we must. What is all this obeisance, this submission, meant to achieve, though? For us, I mean? Our Blood? There's no purpose to it, if it doesn't even buy us peace, or safety within our own borders. Cannoch let Haig raise itself up as highest amongst the Bloods to spare our people unending strife. My father suffered Gryvan's arrogance for the same reason. But if all we've gained is the right to have Haig armies marching back and forth across our lands at will . . . the honour of paying so that they can plot and scheme in their palaces . . ."

He thrust himself up out of the chair, full of renewed exasperation and anger. He pointed at Anyara.

"What has the Lannis Blood gained by making obeisance to Gryvan oc Haig? All its lands are gone. That's how much Haig cares about us, about the unity of the Bloods. That's Orisian's inheritance. We've got the Black Road bearing down on our borders, and we're forbidden – forbidden! – to gather our own armies. All the men I brought back from the south, the ones who haven't already died for Gryvan oc Haig, have scattered: gone back to their postings, or their homes, by Aewult's command."

The Thane paced back and forth, his arms swinging. Ilessa was hanging her head. Anyara wondered whether Roaric truly could not see how drained, how much in need of gentleness, his mother was. Perhaps not. She understood a little of how he felt. Blind rage was not a wholly unreasonable response to much of what had happened.

"All right," Roaric said. He gave every appearance of talking to himself now, of voicing the struggle between his warring instincts. "All right. We'll find an accommodation with them in this. We'll show enough obedience to keep the Steward happy. I'll not have one man punished for those deaths, though. Not one. And I will have my army back. I don't care what Aewult nan Haig thinks, he can't tell me, in my own lands, what to do with my own warriors. I'll send messengers tonight. The Steward won't be so sure of himself if we've five thousand swords gathered within the city walls."

The Thane stalked out with only the most cursory of glances at his mother.

"You will have to forgive him," Ilessa said. "This is hard for him."

She went slowly, hunchbacked, fragile, to the chair that her son had vacated. As she sank down into it, she closed her eyes. Anyara watched her exhaustion and grief take hold of her.

"It is hard for all of us," Anyara said. "You need rest, I should think."

"Oh, yes. I do need rest. I need to sleep. But when I do, I dream of grief. I miss my husband very much."

"Yes," Anyara murmured. She had no idea what she could, or should, say. Ilessa deserved comfort, she deserved kind words and more. Nobody, Anyara was beginning to think, received what they truly deserved. "I didn't know him well, but . . . he was a kind man, I thought. Good."

"He was good," Ilessa said. She nodded, her eyes still closed, a weary frown still across her brow. "He often said that there were too few good men left in the world. One less, now. And the world much darker to my eyes."

Anyara began to back away, edging towards the door. She felt guilty at her inability to offer this woman any succour, though such profound, private sorrow was, in her experience, not often salved by the sympathy of others anyway. Ilessa summoned up a rueful smile from somewhere.

"We're all to suffer loss this winter, it seems. All to take on our own burdens. You carry yours well, Anyara. Your father, your uncle, would be proud of you, and of your brother. I am sorry to draw you into the sorrows of my family as well. You deserve better, but . . . I do need help. My son does."

"I'll give you whatever help I can," Anyara said sincerely. "I don't know what it is you think I can do, though."

Ilessa rose to her feet. She had recovered some of her poise.

"Roaric is young. He has been Bloodheir for only a few weeks; Thane for just days. It will take time for him to . . . he makes everything a personal matter. Always has done. Any blows against our Blood, against our honour or pride, he feels landing on his own back. Every failure or shortcoming that he perceives in himself, he makes into a crisis fit to convulse nations. Your presence alone will help. Anything will, that reminds him there are others – your Blood, not least – with much to lose if he mis-steps.

"His father . . . Lheanor spent half his life restraining himself, submitting himself and our Blood to slights and petty humiliations. He did it to preserve the peace. It cost him a great deal of his pride, and of his strength. He missed the young, fearless man he had once been. Oh, you should have seen him when he was young. He thought himself reduced by time, but I loved him just the same, and never thought the less of him. He served his people better than they know."

Ilessa sighed. She regarded the worn surface of the table thoughtfully, brushing it with her fingertips as if it was spread with some fine, soft material.

"Is it true that you saw the Haig men killed?" she asked Anyara quietly.

Anyara nodded. "It was not . . . pleasant."

"I am sure. Times like these bring savagery closer to the surface. I think perhaps men like Aewult, like my son, do not fear it, or hate it, quite enough. Perhaps, if they are given the time to do so, people will remember the value of the peace that our forefathers built. Perhaps they will understand the sacrifices that are needed to sustain it."

II

The pervasive tension of Kolkyre wore Anyara down. Like a ramifying spider's web, it seemed to have infiltrated every alleyway and courtyard. She tired of it, and when she woke to find a rare morning of vast, cloudless skies and still, clean air, she took Coinach and half a dozen other Lannis men and rode out into the low hills east of the city. She wanted some open ground beneath her, some movement.

The land here was rich and fertile. The gentle dips and slopes of the rolling hills were swathed in grass that even at this time of year had a lushness to it. Her horse stretched its legs, as if it too had tired of the narrow horizons of stables and city streets. She let it run, and the rush of cold air across her face filled her with a fierce exuberance. The speed was almost enough to make her think that she could outpace all the woes of the world, that peace lay only just beyond the next rise.

Her horse pounded across a slope. The thudding of its hoofs in the soft earth was a drumbeat to match her exhilarated heart. A flock of little birds burst up from the grass ahead, and horse and rider chased them, almost as if one more bound might bear them up into the great sky. Anyara heard herself laughing, the sound tumbling away in her wake, spilling back over her shoulders. Freedom and forgetfulness were just there, just ahead: a few more strides, one more surge of effort from the great animal beneath her, and she would be free.

The shouts of her escort drew her back. That sense of weightlessness was gone and she was pressed into her saddle, hauling at the reins to slow her mount. Coinach drew level with her. He was flushed, his cheeks red.

"You must be careful, lady," he said a little more loudly than Anyara thought was necessary. "There could be holes for the horse to trip in, a hidden ditch."

She grinned at him. "You are an old woman, Coinach. I suspected as much. Doesn't this lift your spirits? Don't you feel better for some clean air? It's put a fine blush on your cheeks."

The shieldman half-raised a gloved hand to his face in surprise, but snatched it back down again. Anyara laughed again and nudged her horse on, turning up the slope.

"Look," she said, "we'll go to that barn up there, see what's over the rise. We can rest then, if you like."

The building was empty, though in good order. The lands around Kolkyre had been feeding fine horses and sheep and cattle for centuries, making their owners wealthy, their Thanes powerful.

Anyara dismounted in the lee of the barn and tousled her horse's mane.

"Thank you for that," she whispered in its ear.

Coinach had a couple of the other warriors quickly search the barn, and did not descend from his own mount's back until he was assured that they were alone on this lofty ridge. He brought some bread and cheese and a flask of wine to Anyara.

She sat on the edge of a stone watering trough and ate. The view was not as dramatic as some she had seen – in the high Car Criagar or even from the rocking deck of the Tal Dyreen ship – but it felt amply vast enough for her today. The waters of Anaron's Bay were a soft grey mass beyond Kolkyre. They looked calm and peaceful. The grassy humps and hollows that rolled down towards the coast were gentle, tamed. Even the farmhouses and barns and stables scattered across the landscape had, in her eyes, a solid, safe look to them.

"I never really knew that Kilkry had such rich grazing lands," she reflected.

Coinach, loitering nearby, took a step closer.

"They've always bred the best horses here, lady. So they claim, anyway. You know what they say: the Storm Years were ended from the back of Kolkyre's horses."

"I know. I'd just never really thought about it. Are you not eating?"

The shieldman shook his head.

"Sit, then," said Anyara.

He hesitated, but did settle himself onto the rim of the trough, keeping a respectful distance from his charge.

"When we visited Kolkyre before . . . when my father was alive . . . we never went outside the city walls," Anyara mused. "It's a pity. He would have liked a ride like this."

"It will be better to ride out from Anduran, along the banks of the Glas."

"I suppose so. You're so sure we'll be back there, then?"

"Of course," Coinach said. "The fishing boats will be sailing from Glasbridge again. The drovers and shepherds will be grumbling in Targlas. The Thane and his family will ride to the hunt in Anlane. Everything will be as it was before, one day. You'll see."

"I hope you're right." But she knew better. Whatever happened, nothing would be quite as it was before. Her father would not be there, nor Inurian. She and Orisian would never be children again. And she would never be able to look upon Castle Kolglas without seeing death, or Anduran without feeling fear, or the distant peaks of the Car Criagar without feeling cold.

"I hope you're right," she said again. "It's the waiting that's so hard. I feel trapped. I did not want to stay here. I should have gone with Orisian, or with Taim Narran. I should have made them take me."

"We cannot always do as we want. Sometimes we must do what is required of us."

Anyara frowned at him, and the shieldman looked abashed.

"I am sorry, my lady. I speak out of turn." He averted his eyes.

"Don't worry," Anyara said. "I expect you're right. But didn't we agree you were to call me by my name?"

He nodded.

"I don't suppose you wanted to be shieldman to a woman, did you?" Anyara asked. "You're better at doing what is required of you than I am, clearly."

"I serve the Blood. I think guarding your back is good service. You and your brother are all we have left."

Anyara stared off over the undulating lowlands. Where moments ago she had seen escape in these huge spaces, now she felt small and exposed. It was absurd, unfair, that such burdens should have fallen upon Orisian's shoulders. Armies moved, Thanes jostled for power, cities burned, and somehow amidst all of that her brother, and she, had become important. The boy and girl who stole bread from the kitchens of Kolglas, chased one another up and down its stairwells, played tricks on Ilain and the other maids: those people were no more, in the eyes of the world.

Far off to the north, where distance blurred and muted everything, a stain was spreading across the land. Like a trickle of dark water, a mass of figures was slowly flowing down the road. Anyara narrowed her eyes. She could make out no detail.

"Look," she said.

Coinach followed her pointing finger.

"The Bloodheir. It must be."

"That or the Black Road," Anyara muttered.

The shieldman shook his head once, emphatically. "No. We would have heard long before now if it was them. It must be Aewult."

"Either way, it's not likely to be good tidings. We'd have heard before now if Aewult had won a great victory, too. Wouldn't we?"

Coinach did not reply. Anyara was not even sure he had heard her question. He stared out, from that quiet rise of grassy ground, towards the distant, indistinct army moving down the road towards Kolkyre.

"We should get back to the city," he said. "Whatever's happened, now's not the time to be out here."

For an instant Anyara was in the grip of a child's frustration at being deprived of some treasured possession. She did not want to return to Kolkyre. She wanted to stay here, with the grass and sky and the horses, and recover that brief feeling of freedom. She wanted to know nothing of armies and Bloodheirs and battles won or lost. The feeling subsided as soon as she told herself how foolish it was, but it left traces: a soft sorrow, a fragment of apprehension.

She turned, heavy-hearted, back towards her horse.

"Come, then. But we'll go slowly. I want a little more of this air yet."

The mutual loathing that seethed between Aewult nan Haig and Roaric oc Kilkry-Haig was so potent as to be almost visible, like a sickly miasma staining the air. It made Anyara want to turn away or shrink back amongst the small crowd of officials and warriors that had gathered to witness the confrontation. Had the two men been lowly townsfolk, confronting one another on the street, their acid tones and blatant contempt would have presaged certain violence.

Aewult was seated on a wooden bench outside his huge white tent in the midst of his army's encampment. The Bloodheir's refusal to enter Kolkyre had unsettled both the city and the Tower of Thrones. For the last day and night Anyara had heard many servants and officials muttering in consternation, asking one another whether Aewult's rejection of Kilkry hospitality was studied insult, veiled threat or careless oversight. Or, perhaps, admission of shame; for everyone knew, by know, that the Bloodheir had been humbled by the Black Road. The story of the disastrous battle in the snowstorm was on everyone's lips.

It was not the state of Aewult's mind that occupied Anyara's thoughts, though, but the consequences of his failure; his betrayal, she was inclined to think, whether caused by incompetence or malice. Kolglas was gone, she heard. Drinan overrun by White Owls. Hundreds of Lannis folk dead or captive or unhomed. The battles still to be fought would not even be fought on Lannis ground now. It was too late for that. The Black Road had swallowed up her Blood, in its entirety. And of Orisian there was no word.

Pennants flew from the poles at each corner of Aewult's sprawling tent. They cracked in the wind. The heavy canvas walls shook and strained against the pegs and ropes that held them down. Anyara wished she had tied her hair back. It kept straying across her face.

"I left a thousand men to stand at Hommen," Aewult nan Haig was saying, "and twice that many stand astride the road between there and here. They will hold our enemy until I have the fresh companies I need. Nothing has been abandoned, Thane, and you'll not speak such an accusation again in my presence."

"What makes you think a thousand men can hold back the Black Road at Hommen when you failed with ten thousand at Glasbridge?" demanded Roaric.

The Kilkry Thane was a splendid sight. Anyara had never seen such a luxuriant cloak – black velvet and fur, trimmed with gold thread – nor gloves of such fine leather, nor a scabbard so encrusted with silver and gems. For once, Aewult was overshadowed.

"Taim Narran is there too, with what's left of Lannis strength," the Bloodheir snapped. "They need hold only for a few days. Long enough for more companies to come up from the south. Once I've made good my losses, we'll drown the Black Road in its own blood."

"I've close to five thousand men gathered in the city. I mean to send some of them to Hommen. It's my town. My border. You cannot forbid that."

"I ordered your army disbanded, Thane. I forbade its assembly. Little good that did me! It was not needed, and still it is not needed. *This* is the army that will break our enemy." Aewult flung out an arm, clenching his fist as if to take hold of all the men and horses and tents and wagons arrayed around him. "This is the host of the True Bloods, and I am its master."

"This is a beaten army. That's all." Roaric's voice was rising perilously, punching out against the wind. There should be no audience for this meeting, Anyara thought, but Aewult had insisted on receiving Roaric and his entourage in the open. He meant, perhaps, to ensure that everyone saw and heard his resilience, his steadfast determination. Having lost one battle, he was intent on proving that he could still triumph in a contest of wills, even when his opponent was a Thane. It did not bode well for Roaric oc Kilkry-Haig. Anyara wondered if he understood that. She wondered, too, at Aewult's insistence that she should accompany the Kilkry Thane. That did not bode well, either, but exactly what it foretold, she was not sure.

"It was not our enemy that defeated this army, but foul weather and foul friends," rasped Aewult.

Anyara blinked at that, wondering for a moment whether she had misheard the Bloodheir in the blustering wind. She glanced at Coinach, but her shieldman was glaring at Aewult nan Haig. Looking around, Anyara saw much the same rapt expression on almost every face. In some, it was tinged with hostility or contempt; in others, a harsh approval. Anyara found herself afraid of what might happen. There were many armed men here, of both the Haig and Kilkry Bloods, and the pervasive tone of anger and accusation was taking them in its grip. The only people present who seemed to be truly relishing the course of events were Lagair Haldyn and Ishbel. The Steward bore the look a man who thought himself vindicated. Aewult's graceful lover, standing as close to him as anyone, had an expression of glee, as if the malign energies imbuing the scene filled her with a kind of intoxicated joy.

"But for the snowstorm, I would have had the victory," Aewult continued. "And but for Taim Narran's tardiness, and disobedience, I'd have had it still, no matter what obstacles the sky put in my way."

The anger that filled Coinach at her side was all too obvious to Anyara. She shared it, but knew that now was not the moment to let it show. Aewult was goading, goading. Like a man provoking fighting dogs to violence, he would not rest until this contest had been won and lost. His pride required it; nothing less would ease the humiliation he must feel at having failed on the field of battle. We're all to pay the price for the Bloodheir's shame, Anyara thought.

"Your army's not marching anywhere, Thane," Aewult muttered. "Not yet. There are matters we must discuss, matters the Steward tells me have not been satisfactorily resolved in my absence."

Roaric cast a baleful glare in Lagair Haldyn's direction.

"It is being dealt with," the Kilkry Thane growled. "There is nothing to discuss."

"I disagree," Aewult snapped. "I disagree. I am told there has not yet been justice. Punishment. I am told the murderers of Haig men remain free. Therefore there are matters to discuss. Don't test me, Thane. I will not be tested, and if you insist upon the attempt, you will lose." Those last words were precise, pointed; each one a finger jabbed at Roaric oc Kilkry-Haig.

The Thane looked enraged, but somehow he restrained himself. Anyara did not see how he could win this argument. Sooner or later, he must give way to the demands of the Haig Blood. But there was something in Roaric's nature that rebelled at the thought of bending with the wind. Perhaps he imagined that he could make the world other than it was, rebalance its various powers, by sheer force of will. If so, he was mistaken. Anyara could have told him all he needed to know of the inadequacy of will in the face of obdurate fact. But he would not have listened. She could almost see, in front of her now, any gains won by Ilessa's calming influence being swept away on the rising tide of Roaric's anger.

"Come away," she whispered to Coinach.

He hesitated, but she was insistent. "I'll not listen to this nonsense any more. We're serving no purpose here except to give Aewult an audience for his play-acting. He won't even notice I'm gone."

They slipped back through the few ranks of onlookers, and retrieved their horses from the care of Aewult's grooms. They began to pick their way out through the maze of the vast camp that lay like a stain across the ruined fields.

This was a world unfamiliar to Anyara, and one far more unsettling to her than she had expected. A world of haggard, stubbled men who watched her pass with hungry eyes, of stinks and raucous noise, mangy dogs and dull-eyed horses. She heard soft curses, in distant accents, and ribald laughter. She saw men arguing over a dead goat, and playing dice, and eating mud-like stew from wooden bowls. The smoke of a hundred campfires, whipped along by the gusting wind, needled her eyes.

A flock of children, filthy and excited, spilled across the path in front of her. They were in their own world of adventure, blind and deaf to the harsh scene all about them. Two of them, wrestling, spilled a pot that had been warming by a fire. They were chased off with a torrent of abuse boiling about their heads.

"What a place for children," Anyara murmured to Coinach.

"They might not have known any other life," he said. "There are worse ways to grow up."

They could see the long line of Kolkyre's wall, the lean spike of the Tower of Thrones jutting up beyond it like a watchtower of giants. Just this once, the city looked appealing, the wall a comforting promise of seclusion and safety. It was to be denied them, though.

Aewult's shieldmen came running down the track, mud spattering their greaves and breastplates. Half a dozen of them blocked Anyara's way. They stood, she thought, with comical rigidity, like an honour guard arrayed for some grand occasion. Somewhere amongst the tents crowded along the side of the track, someone laughed and mockingly applauded. One of the armoured manikins stepped forwards and grasped the bridle of Anyara's horse.

"The Bloodheir requires your—" the man began, peering up from beneath the rim of his polished helm.

"Release the lady's horse," Coinach said levelly, nudging his own mount forwards to loom over the shieldman.

The man's mouth gave an irritated twitch, though he continued to watch Anyara rather than Coinach.

"Your presence is required by the Bloodheir. Turn about, and we will lead you to—"

Coinach's horse eased forwards, its chest brushing the warrior away from Anyara.

"Coinach . . ." she began.

"You should not address a Thane's sister with so little regard for her station," he was saying, loudly but still quite calm. "Nor take hold of her horse without invitation, I think."

"Coinach!" she snapped, fearful for him. He looked around at once, attentive.

"Don't," she said.

He looked a fraction disappointed.

The two of them turned their horses and headed back into the heart of the great army, escorted by Aewult's Palace Shield.

"Perhaps you misunderstood," Aewult said, smiling. "Were you not told I wished to speak with you, lady?"

Anyara tried to smile as well, but her lips were stubbornly set in a half-frown. At least Aewult had brought them inside his huge tent, and spared her the misery of a crowd of onlookers. But Roaric was gone, and all his attendants and officials. She and Coinach were alone here now, and she felt as if they had been abandoned amidst enemies. It was foolish, she told herself. However hateful he might be, Aewult would not dare to harm her. The two warriors of his Palace Shield who flanked him looked more like ornament than threat. The one other person present did, however, exude vicious intent: Ishbel, dazzling in a finer dress than any Anyara had ever worn, wore a look of such poisonous hostility that Anyara found it almost laughable.

"You were bored, were you?" Aewult asked. "By my discussions with the Thane?"

Anyara shrugged a little, nodded a little. Suitably ambiguous and inoffensive, she hoped.

"Not the sort of thing likely to entertain ladies, I know," Aewult said, smirking.

An oaf, Anyara concluded. She finally managed a smile. Let him think me empty-headed if it pleases him, she thought. He appeared to like his women thus.

"Well, you're here now. Were you offered wine? Or some dainties, perhaps? I have cooks who can make pastries even out of mud, you know."

"I don't need anything," she said as gracefully as she could manage.

"Very well. I am concerned, Anyara. The Thane has not been able to allay my concerns, but I expected nothing else. You, though . . . I am sure you are of more reasonable character. I am certain of it. However, you must be frank with me. Will you be so?"

"Is there something you wished to ask me, then?"

"Your tongue seems to have softened a little since we last

spoke. That is encouraging. Perhaps it was the wine that spoke then, was it?"

Had the Bloodheir known what barbs of invective seethed behind Anyara's clamped lips, clamouring for release, he would not have been so encouraged. But she was determined to maintain a placid demeanour. The days when she could afford to speak without thinking, and without care for the thin skin of others, were gone.

"Anyway, here is the matter that concerns me." Aewult leaned forwards in his great chair, resting his elbows on its carved arms. "Your brother seems to have disappeared. And I have heard – this is not something to be repeated in other ears, lady – I have heard that my father's Chancellor, who followed in your brother's wake, has suffered a most unfortunate accident."

"I am sorry to hear that," Anyara lied.

"Indeed. I am sure. As, no doubt, Roaric in his little tower will be when he hears of it. Neither of you as sorry as I am, I suspect. Not, I can assure you, as sorry as my father is going to be when word reaches Vaymouth. And my father's anger can be a terrible, terrible thing. You understand my difficulty?"

"I am not sure I do."

"Ah. I am told Mordyn Jerain was taken to Highfast, but whether he will live or die I do not know. He was gravely injured, my lady. Gravely injured. Nobody seems to know how or why this has come about. Perhaps your brother might be able to shed some light in the shadow. I would ask him if I could. But I am told he is no longer at Highfast. We do not know where he is, and cannot ask him the question. Can we?"

"I do not know where he is, if that is what you want to ask me," Anyara murmured. To have this loathsome man scratching at wounds so raw and painful was sickening.

Aewult's dissatisfaction was obvious in his face. He sat back in his chair, tapped his heel a few times at the hard earth beneath him. He stared at Anyara, his brow clenched into a frown.

"She's lying," said Ishbel.

"Don't you dare . . ." Anyara snapped, all restraint lost and forgotten in that one moment.

"Quiet! Quiet!" Aewult cried. To Anyara's relief and bitter pleasure, he turned his ire on Ishbel. "Keep quiet. Don't interfere in this. It's not your place."

The woman's face burned, and Anyara saw in that angry glow a promise of lifelong enmity. She did not care; relished the thought, almost.

"I was not served as well as I thought to be by your esteemed captain Taim Narran, in the battle," Aewult said. "And our cause was not served at all by your absent brother. The High Thane's Chancellor himself, riding after your brother, has been struck down by some unknown hand. I find myself suspicious; my trust thinning. There are questions here that require answers. Sureties that must be given, I think."

"Sureties?"

"Indeed. You, in fact. If your brother cannot be found, I must invite you to attend upon your High Thane in Vaymouth. To give reassurances and to offer some explanation. There must *be* some explanation, you understand, for recent events. Good faith must be demonstrated. Loyalty proven."

Anyara's mind was racing. For all that Aewult appeared calm and collected, there was panic in this. He feared the blame, and judgement, and shame, that would come from defeat, and from the loss of the infamous Shadowhand. He was lashing out in all directions, fumbling for others to shield him from it all: condemning Taim Narran, pushing Roaric to utter rebellion or disloyalty, casting the Lannis Blood in the role of traitors or cowards. It was clumsy, blundering, but dangerous too.

"You cannot refuse," Aewult said quietly. "You know that, of course. I speak for my father in all things. And I wish you kept close to my Blood, lady, henceforth. Until matters become clearer, at least. I have already sent to the Tower of Thrones to have everything you might need brought out. I am sure Roaric will understand that you choose to be the guest of the Haig Blood for a little while."

And I, thought Anyara, am not at all sure that he will.

III

Like an immense shoal of fish seething in the shallows of some cold ocean, the great army of the Black Road swirled over the snow-blanketed lower reaches of the Glas valley. It was hungry, and eager, and incapable of remaining still. More companies kept coming south across the Vale of Stones, many of them now the trained warriors of the other Bloods, whose Thanes scented triumph and did not wish to see it solely claimed by Horin and by the Inkallim. As every new band arrived it was swept up into the army, and caught up in the frenzy of anticipation.

Kanin had taken part in every discussion amongst the supposed masters of this ever-growing force, but he had said little. There were too many people, and too much hunger both physical and spiritual, assembled here for any conclusion to have been reached other than the obvious: to rush on down the coast, give battle at every opportunity, pursue their collective fate to its utmost limits. An unspoken consensus had been reached, that no culmination was any longer possible save one that was vast and violent. Temegrin the Eagle had whined and obstructed, raised objections and reservations, all to no avail. He alone imagined that events could any longer be the subject of reasoned debate. The Black Road had hold of them, and would carry them helplessly into whatever future lay ahead.

Many tributaries were feeding the rising flood of enthusiasm. Kolglas had been overrun and sacked. Drinan had been burned, its inhabitants slaughtered, by White Owl Kyrinin. The vanguard of the Black Road army was already on the borders of

Kilkry-Haig territory, poised to sweep on past the little town of Hommen. And nowhere in all this frenzied, impulsive advance had they encountered more than token, delaying resistance. The great army of the Haig Bloods they had faced, and beaten, in the snow outside Glasbridge had crumbled away.

All these victories served to stoke the fire that burned in every heart, but none had greater impact than the news from further south: Lheanor oc Kilkry-Haig was dead, cut down in his own feasting hall by the Hunt Inkall. The Battle was fighting side by side with the commonfolk; the Hunt was killing the greatest foes of the Black Road; the Lore marched amongst the warriors, lending their authority to the struggle. Temegrin, the timorous Eagle, could vacillate all he wished, Kanin reflected as he marshalled the meagre remnants of his own Blood's army on the fields outside Glasbridge. His solitary counsel of restraint would be drowned out. Futile.

There were only a few hundred swords left for Kanin to command. Such was the price his Blood had paid to open the way. He had heard that Vana his mother had dispatched another two or three hundred warriors – the very last that could be spared – but they were not here yet, and there was no time to wait. The Glas valley was emptying, disgorging its conquerors on down the coast towards greater prizes.

Kanin rode along the front rank of his spearmen, drawn up with admirable precision across the grass. They were hungry, like everyone else, and tired. He could see that in their faces. But they made no complaint, showed no reluctance. Many hundreds of their comrades had died since they had marched out from Hakkan all those weeks ago. Perhaps more than any other company in this great patchwork army, they desired an ending – clear, dramatic – to all of this that made sense of what had gone before. There were even a few dozen Tarbains: dishevelled and subdued, clustered behind their glowering chieftain. Their desires, no doubt, revolved around loot more than glory or fate's vindication. Still, they would serve. Every spear that marched behind Kanin made his Blood's place in this war a fraction less tenuous and inconsequential.

He looked around for Igris. The shieldman was hanging back, muttering something to another of Kanin's escort.

"Igris! We're still short, are we not? I thought another hundred at least."

"Some . . ." The shieldman looked uneasy, fumbling for words.

"Come on," Kanin snapped. "Where are they?"

"With your sister, sire. Eighty of them, I was told."

"Eighty?"

"Yes, sire. The . . . the halfbreed is awake again. Your sister and him have come out of the city. They're by the river." The shieldman gestured in a vague northerly direction.

Kanin was incredulous.

"Why wasn't I told?"

"We only got word . . ." Igris began, but Kanin was already wheeling his horse away and digging his heels into its flanks.

His path through the chaotic army was constantly obstructed. Here it was a wagon of charcoal, bogged down in a slick of deep mud; there a mule driver furiously beating one of his animals that had fallen, exhausted or injured; next a column of Lannis captives — mostly women — being marched for no obvious reason from one place to another. In places there were thick forests of tents sprouting from the fields, and hundreds upon hundreds of people swarming about them. Kanin rode past a gigantic, roaring fire, around which Tarbains were shouting and gesticulating while a small group of Inkallim looked on.

As he drew closer to the Glas River, and to Glasbridge itself, Kanin found his path becoming clearer. There were still little encampments scattered about the fields, and small companies moving back and forth, but here, so far to the rear, he was amongst the dregs and detritus of the army. Many of these people would be going no further. They were the injured, the enfeebled, the mad or the predatory. He saw one man sprawled half in and half out of a ditch, insensible through drink or sickness. Dark water reached to his thighs. He might be dead come nightfall, unless someone dragged him out. No one was likely to, Kanin guessed.

There were plangent cries from the sky above. Kanin looked up, and saw vast, straggling arrowheads of seagulls passing overhead. They were coming down the line of the river, making for the open sea.

He brought his gaze back down and saw what he had come searching for. Out of place amongst the disorder all around, an organised column was moving northwards along a faint track that ran parallel to the river. Kanin kicked his horse on and as he drew nearer he could see that the company was a strange mixture. There were dozens of ragged figures – commonfolk of the Gyre Bloods who had come across the Stone Vale on their own initiative – and plenty of warriors too. Some, Kanin saw in disgust, were indeed drawn from his own Blood. And leading the way were twenty or thirty Kyrinin, with two figures riding at their head: Wain and Aeglyss.

The mere sight of his sister riding alongside the halfbreed was enough to reawaken Kanin's anger, never far beneath the surface these days. Every morning he woke to find his mind already teeming with bitter thoughts of Aeglyss. At any moment during the day when there was nothing to distract him, he could be seized by a surge of despair at the thought of losing Wain. For he had lost her, in all meaningful senses. Ever since her return to Glasbridge, she had chosen to incarcerate herself, never leaving the *na'kyrim*'s side while he lay insensible. Again and again Kanin had sought her out; always, when he did so, she was distant and uninterested. It was as if everything they had shared since they were children, all the connections and understanding they had accumulated between them, had never been. Nothing had ever caused him quite such pain.

He walked his horse into the ranks of marching White Owls without a moment's hesitation, using its strength to barge them aside and plough through to his sister. He heard what he imagined were hissed curses directed at him, and felt his horse start at a blow across its haunches, but he ignored them. He had eyes only for Wain.

She looked round as he fell in beside her. Her expression was blank. She was neither pleased nor perturbed by his arrival.

"What is happening?" he asked her.

Aeglyss, a little way ahead, spoke without looking round.

"Please don't delay us, Thane. We have important matters to attend to."

Kanin bit back his fury and contempt, keeping himself focused upon Wain.

"Where are you going?" he asked her.

"To Kan Avor," she said flatly.

"Why?"

"Because it is the heart of things," Aeglyss called back over his shoulder. "Because it is empty, and should be filled. Because others are coming to meet me there, with a precious cargo."

"Kan Avor is empty because it waits for Ragnor oc Gyre to take his rightful place there," Kanin snapped, "not so that some deranged half-wight can foul it with his presence."

"Come with us, brother," Wain urged. There was almost some life in her voice with those words. They carried need in them, but not affection.

"No. You come with me." He reached out for the reins of her horse. She did not resist as he steered her out from amongst the files of Kyrinin. Aeglyss, though, turned his own mount – a thin, miserable-looking animal – towards them. Kanin saw the half-breed's face for the first time then, and it was an unpleasant sight. He might have risen from his sickbed, but he still looked like a man upon the very threshold of death. His eyes had sunk back into his skull, pouched in dark pits.

"Do not try to impose your will here, Thane," Aeglyss said. In the same moment, Kanin felt a shaft of piercing pain flash through his head and lodge there like a hot blade driven into his temple. He winced and involuntarily closed his eyes for a moment.

"Let her go," he heard Aeglyss saying, and found that both his hands were back on his own reins. He blinked, still beset by throbbing pain, and saw Wain turning back to rejoin the column. They were all marching on, as if nothing had happened. Even, Kanin saw, the dozens of warriors of his own Blood.

"Stand aside," he shouted at them. Some looked up at him, and he saw doubt, fear perhaps, on many faces. Several faltered and even halted, sending disruptive ripples through the column.

"Come away from there, all of you," Kanin cried. First one or two, then ten and twenty, fell out of their marching order and came across the muddy grass towards their Thane. Aeglyss was still there, watching with a cruel smile on his face.

"Pay him no heed," the *na'kyrim* said to the warriors. "You know where we are going, and why. You know where fate's course will be decided." He almost whispered it, yet Kanin heard the words clearly above the tramp of feet. He felt the immense weight of command they carried, the overwhelming will that informed them. He understood for the first time that Aeglyss truly had changed into something more than he had once been.

"Stand still," Kanin shouted, aware of the edge of alarm that distorted his voice. "You will not defy your Thane in this!"

Some of the warriors were already turning away from him. Others hesitated, looking in confusion at him or at Aeglyss or their comrades. Growling, enraged, Kanin side-stepped his horse towards Aeglyss.

"If you think you can usurp my authority . . ." he began, but the *na'kyrim* was already returning to the head of the column.

"The authority here is your sister's, Thane, not mine. Wain! Let him see."

The dullness he saw in Wain's eyes as she halted her horse and stared back was enough to break Kanin's determination. Never had she seemed so lifeless to him, so empty.

"Get back in line," she shouted. "We march to Kan Avor."

The warriors did as she commanded them, and Kanin lacked the will to challenge Wain's command in their presence. He watched the motley band snaking past him for only a few moments, then spun his horse about. The pain his head was subsiding, but not that in his heart.

Igris and others of his Shield had caught up with him, but he ignored them as he rode back towards the army. He saw Shraeve and two dozen of her ravens watching, like a flock of their namesake birds attending a carcass. And he did feel as though something was dying, though he did not know what it was.

As he drew near to them, the Inkallim moved off, following after Aeglyss, Wain and their motley company. Shraeve gave Kanin a wry smile and nod of her head as she rode by, but he barely registered it. One figure remained behind, standing in Kanin's path: Cannek, the Hunt Inkallim, with two massive hounds sitting motionless on either side of him.

"A moment of your time, sire?" Cannek said.

"Not now." Kanin twitched his reins, keeping his uneasy mount beyond reach of those dogs. There was nothing, at this moment, that he had to say to one of the Inkallim.

"Ah, a pity," Cannek called. "Just this, then: if you ever want to discuss the halfbreed, you might find me an attentive audience. Remember that."

Kanin glanced, reluctantly, down at the man. "What does that mean?"

"Only that he might prove an interesting subject for discussion. Shraeve, our fierce raven, certainly seems to think him of interest." Cannek gazed after her disappearing form. "I do too, though perhaps in different ways."

"Now is not the moment to play games, and talk in fogs."

"Oh, this is no game, Thane. Not at all. I find some things strange, that is all. And I am not alone in that. It seems to me the mood has changed since that *na'kyrim* appeared. Do you not think so? There's a certain bloody hunger, a certain shortness of temper, in the air; more than we might expect even from such an army as this. A certain disturbance of dreams, by all account. We – Fiallic, wise Goedellin himself – understood that the halfbreed's place in things was to keep the woodwights in step with our purposes. That your sister had him harnessed. Yet now . . . well, it's less clear who wears the harness. And I hear his unnatural talents are not quite so meagre as we once thought they were. He humiliated Temegrin quite thoroughly, by all accounts."

Kanin stared at the Inkallim. Cannek had folded his arms, his hands embracing the knives that lay sheathed along his wrists. The man looked self-satisfied, smug almost; yet his gaze was serious.

"I am of the Hunt, Thane. It is in my nature, my upbringing, to see things that might not be there, to fear betrayals, conspiracies. Dissent. Tell me, am I seeing things that are not there?"

"Where is Shraeve going?" Kanin asked quietly.

Cannek flicked a brief glance after the receding Battle Inkallim.

"She is tasked with keeping a watch on the halfbreed. And – forgive me – on your sister. You are not alone in wishing to see Wain safe, you know. Our masters are curious; less certain than they were, just a few short days ago, of whether Aeglyss . . . matters or not. Perhaps Shraeve has her own interests, too. She has always, I think, been plagued by an enthusiasm for the most extreme twists and turns in fate's path."

Kanin eased his horse onwards. Cannek's two hounds turned their heads to watch him move away, all feral, predatory attention.

"I am not in the mood for discussion," Kanin muttered.

"As you wish," he heard Cannek say behind him, lightly, as if it was a matter of little consequence. "Should you find the mood upon you, no doubt you will be able to find me."

Kanin moved through the day in dreamlike detachment. Around him, the army roused itself into fragmentary motion. It moved, company by company, away from Glasbridge, tearing up the fields and tracks with its feet and wheels and hoofs as it went. Kanin allowed it to carry him with it. He rode amongst his warriors like flotsam on the current of war. He noted only in the most distant of ways the hamlets, cottages and mills they passed as they made their way down the coast, as shapes signifying nothing. He barely heard the pulsing sighs of waves on the rocky shore or the cries of gulls overhead.

He was moving away from Wain, and though it felt like disaster he did not know what else he could do. It was fate that bore his sister off down whatever path she was following: ineluctable, remorseless. It was fate bearing her away, just as it had cheated him of the chance to put an end to the Lannis line for ever. He knew it was fruitless to rage against the insensate force of the Black Road, but he could know that without feeling it, instinctively, in his heart. He found it impossible to accept that fate would enact itself through a halfbreed, through one who was himself surely faithless, empty of any urge save his own inhuman survival. Aeglyss. That was the rock around which the tides of Kanin's thoughts surged. He could not free himself of the image of the *na'kyrim*, the memory of his vile voice.

They reached Kolglas in darkness. There were still bodies in the streets, still ruins smouldering. The town was in chaos. Houses were being emptied of goods, and cattle slaughtered in the main square. Kanin hated it, as on this day he hated everything. There was battle to be had, somewhere further on and further south, and what he wanted now was battle: the clarity of slaughter. He ignored the muted protests of his warriors, and marched them on into the night.

* * *

The boy was screaming, each lash eliciting a howl more piercing than the last. And each howl, Theor noticed, caused a faint twitch at the corner of Ragnor oc Gyre's mouth. The two men – First of the Lore Inkall and High Thane of the Gyre Bloods – sat opposite each other across the dining table and did not speak. The sound of the punishment going on outside made conversation difficult. Ragnor sought to conceal his evident discomfort by concentrating upon the food, but it was a thin pretence.

The Lore Inkall did not indulge in excess, whether of food or drink or anything else, no matter how elevated the guest. Only salted fish, nut bread and apples had been served, on simple wooden platters, with a watery ale to wash it down. It was, no doubt, not much more to the High Thane's taste than the beating outside was, but he would have known what to expect. He had chosen to invite himself to the Lore's Sanctuary, after all. Had he wanted luxury, he could have asked Theor to attend upon him in his own halls in the city down below.

The sounds of distress subsided to a more muted sobbing, and then fell away altogether. Theor pushed his half-emptied plate to one side and leaned back in his chair.

"The boy was a thief and a hoarder of food. And worse, perhaps."

"Worse?" the High Thane asked through a mouthful of ale-soaked bread.

"A would-be stealer of secrets, we think. He had coins hidden in his chambers that came, most likely, from Wyn-Gyre coffers."

Ragnor smiled. He had recovered much of his composure, now that his ears were not being so harshly assaulted. "You accuse Orinn oc Wyn-Gyre of seeking to spy upon the Lore Inkall, First?"

Theor gave a consciously nonchalant shrug. "The Thane might have known nothing of it. The boy may be innocent of anything more than thievery. It does not matter. He has been punished. He will either learn from it, or not."

"I imagine it matters to him," Ragnor muttered.

"If he has the mettle required of a Lore Inkallim, he will come to understand that fate is blind to his innocence or otherwise, as it is to his suffering. He was whipped. It is in the past now, and of no consequence. He will resume his candidacy, and we will see in due course what fate has in store for him. Should he fail the creed again, he will die."

The High Thane belched. Theor grimaced in distaste and looked away. Ragnor had never pretended to graces he had not been born with. Just as he did not, in recent years at least, pretend affection for the Inkallim that he did not feel.

Ragnor drained his tankard of ale, and peered into the empty vessel as if it contained some noisome dregs.

"Your ale matches your food in quality," the High Thane observed.

"Perhaps you should have visited Nyve," Theor suggested. "He would have served you *narqan* there. It might have been more to your taste."

Ragnor set his tankard down and shrugged. "*Narqan's* drinkable. I don't find it as . . . repellent as some. But I don't think it's the Battle I need to be talking to, is it, First?"

"I do not know."

"Of course you do." Ragnor let a little of his irritation show: a momentary tightening of his brow, a curl of his lip. He is angry, then, Theor thought. He had suspected as much, but until now the High Thane had concealed it well, by his standards.

"I want to show you something," Ragnor said. He pushed his chair back and stood, brushing crumbs from his chest. "Come with me, would you?"

Theor frowned. "Where? I thought we were to talk here."

"Just to your gates."

"I am an old man, High Thane. I am not given to taking strolls in the snow."

"Don't be difficult, First," sighed Ragnor. "The High Thane of the Gyre Bloods invites you to walk with him a little way, so that he might show you something of interest. You can humour him, can't you? Or is even that beyond the Lore Inkall these days?"

Theor complied. He followed Ragnor out. Snow was falling on the Lore's Sanctuary, as it had been now for more than two days. Big, buoyant flakes drifted down in thick flocks. The pine trees amongst which the buildings clustered were heavily burdened with snow; now and again, some branch would spill its white cargo in a soft, tumbling collapse. The paths along which First and High Thane walked had been cleared by candidates, otherwise they would have been almost impassable. This, for Theor, was one of two times of year when the Sanctuary was at its most restful and peaceful. The snow made it a silent, still place. As did, in other ways, the hot, windless days of midsummer, when warm air pooled beneath the pines and all was languid and lethargic.

The two men tramped along the stone path, between dirty banks of snow piled up on either side. The High Thane's Shield, and Theor's attendants, came behind them, but not so close as to hear what passed between them. The wooden gates in the encircling wall of the Sanctuary stood open. Ragnor planted himself in the centre of the gateway, facing out. The land fell away beyond him, sweeping down in a long, pine-clad slope to the valley floor and the great sprawl of Kan Dredar. The High Thane's city was all but obscured by the teeming snowflakes.

"You cannot see as well as I hoped," Ragnor grunted.

"I can hardly see a thing." Theor made no effort to disguise his ill humour at being brought out here.

"You can see the one thing that matters, I think. Look. No, there: the road south."

"A somewhat darker area of the blizzard, perhaps."

"Close to four thousand of my warriors marching south. That's what you see, as well you know."

"I knew they were gathered. I was not aware they had started their march. It hardly seems the weather for it."

"It's not." The High Thane's patience was thinning out. "It's not even close to the weather for it. Half a thousand of them might be dead of cold or exhaustion or hunger, or lost, by the time they reach Anduran. But I have little choice in the matter, do I?"

Theor looked sideways at the High Thane and shrugged. He turned and walked back into the Sanctuary. A candidate – a young girl he vaguely recognised but could not have named – had appeared from somewhere with a birch broom. She shuffled along backwards in front of him, sweeping the freshly fallen snow from the path.

"Look where you're going, child. You'll only fall over if you do it like that."

He could hear Ragnor stamping after him.

"I could hardly keep my warriors sitting around Kan Dredar idly sharpening their swords," the Thane of Thanes growled. "Not while half my people march off into the south of their own accord. Did you know one of my iron workings has closed, because there's not enough workers left?"

"I did not know that, no," Theor said.

The First led the High Thane back into the little courtyard around which the offices of the Lore were arrayed. Cord shackles still hung from the whipping post in its centre. The snow around it was flecked with red, like dye spilled on linen.

"Nyve has left me little choice but to send my army south. No choice at all, I'd say. Not once the Battle marched."

"I do not interfere in the doings of the Battle, High Thane. I am not in a position to question his actions. No one is, unless you can find one of his own captains willing to challenge him for his rank. The Lore's territory is . . ."

"Oh, don't be ridiculous. Don't insult me."

Theor ignored the High Thane's anger. Over to one side of the courtyard, beneath a wooden awning, steam was drifting out from a serving hatch in the wall. A couple of young Lore Inkallim were standing there, their hands wrapped around hot cups.

"Look." Theor pointed. "They've got some milk heating there. It's years since I had hot honeyed milk. Shall we?"

Ragnor made an indeterminate sound – half-groan, half-growl, not remotely enthusiastic – but followed Theor, crunching across the snow. The two Inkallim shuffled away at a flick of Theor's hand. A serving woman ladled the thick white liquid into cups and handed them to the First and the High Thane, then sank back into the musty darkness within and disappeared.

Theor watched the fat snowflakes bobbing down as he drank. He really did like honeyed milk. The reality did not quite match the remembered delight of it, but it was good enough. A slab of snow slipped from the roof and rushed down into the courtyard, making a soft thump as it landed. Ragnor oc Gyre was not drinking.

"The Haig Bloods can field twice as many warriors as we can," he said quietly. "More."

"Warriors, yes." Theor nodded. "I'm sure that's true. But will their commonfolk take the field? Can they match our thousands, with their hot hearts, their faith burning in them, that rush to serve the creed in battle?"

Ragnor sniffed at his steaming cup, and took a hesitant sip of its contents. He grimaced and emptied it out onto the snow at their feet.

"They're soft. We all know that. But they're too strong, Theor. You underestimate Gryvan oc Haig. He may be soft and slow, but only like a bear, fresh out of its winter sleep. If you prod him hard enough, he'll have your arm off. What was the Hunt thinking, to kill a Thane? Gryvan may have been no admirer of Lheanor's, but he'll not sit by while we merrily cut down his liegemen like that.

If you – if Nyve, and Avenn, and all these thousands of common-folk you're so pleased with – force us into unrestrained war with the Haig Bloods, we will end up with his foot on our throats, sooner or later."

"You do not know that."

"No, of course I don't *know* it. But I *think* it. I apply a little sense, a little thought, to the world as I see it, and I find it to be a reasonable expectation."

"The future is not a matter of reason." Theor smiled, wearily. He, and his fellow Firsts, had known that Ragnor's commitment to the rigours of the creed was not all it might be. They had known, ever since Vana oc Horin-Gyre intercepted his messenger, that the High Thane had long ago lapsed into the mistaken view that some kind of accommodation was possible with the Haig Bloods. Now he heard Ragnor condemning himself out of his own mouth.

"What seems reasonable is of no consequence," the First continued. "You know that. Fate can overturn, disregard, discard reason as it sees fit. The course of the Black Road is not set by reason, or by the judgement of men, or by what we in our narrow way call sense or thought. It is set by the tales inscribed in the Last God's book. It is set by what he reads there."

The High Thane, his lips pursed, regarded his fine leather boots. He was, Theor knew, not stupid enough to attempt to debate the elements of the faith. Ragnor had never been stupid. And when he had been young he had been full of energy, hunger. That he had become something else as he grew older was a source of regret rather than resentment or anger. It was as it must be. Fate had decreed that for this little time, the Gyre Blood and the Inkallim would follow paths that diverged a fraction. It did not matter. One day – this year, next, a thousand years from now – everyone, everywhere would be walking in one path, that of the Black Road.

"Call off your ravens, First," Ragnor said. "That is all I ask. For the good of us all. Temegrin complains that the Battle and the Lore are making themselves masters of the army in his place. Anything that draws Gyre and the Inkallim apart serves the creed ill, does it not?"

"Temegrin's counsel has been found wanting, I hear. He has tried, at every turn, to curb the ambition of your people, whose hearts cry out not for such timidity but for fate's cleansing judgement. Perhaps you should have sent another of your captains, one more . . . eager. Unless you approve of his caution, of course."

"I would put every sword I have in the field to prevent Gryvan coming north across the Vale of Stones, but if you try to force me – to shame me – into fighting a war in the Glas valley, and outside Kolkyre, and beneath the walls of Vaymouth, you will fail. You can have these few thousand to feed into whatever slaughterhouse it is Nyve means to build for our people down there, but I will not see our Bloods throw away every last life in pursuit of the impossible."

"The impossible?" Theor murmured. "We do not know what is or is not possible, High Thane. We can never know that. It is in the nature of fate to surprise us."

IV

Every few days, Magrayn bathed Torquentine. Bowls of water, infused with herbs and scents, were carried down into the cellar where he dwelled, then jars of unguents and oils. All those who brought them were sent back up into the complex of ramshackle houses above; only Magrayn remained to kneel beside the great man on his bed of pillows.

She peeled Torquentine's clothes back to reveal his vast bulk. She was gentle and precise as she washed his blotchy skin. The cloths she used were the softest to be had in Vaymouth. The soothing ointments she worked into the fleshy folds of his torso were the most expensive, the oils she spread over him the rarest. It took a long time, and through it all she and Torquentine exchanged not a word. There was silence there in the cellars beneath Ash Pit in Vaymouth.

Only after it was all done, and he was dressed once more and the cloths and bowls and jars had been cleared away, did Torquentine turn his affectionate, one-eyed gaze on his door-keeper. His visage was far from perfect – bloated, scarred – but hers was still more imperfect. Her nose was a misshapen stump, her face a mass of purplish blemishes.

"Thank you," Torquentine said.

Magrayn only smiled: a lopsided gesture, since the King's Rot had reached the muscles of her cheek and lip before it receded.

"I've got a craving for lemon tarts, Magrayn. You know the ones I mean?"

She nodded. "I'll send someone out for some." The words were indistinct, as if her tongue had been bloated by a bee sting.

"Sweet Magrayn. I'd be lost without you. Well, not lost pre-cisely." Torquentine gave a short laugh as he gestured towards the low ceiling with fat fingers. "I am fortunate in always knowing, without fail, where I am, since I am never anywhere else. Let me kiss those gentle hands."

He laid his lips softly on the back of each of Magrayn's hands in turn. She slipped out of the chamber. In her absence, Torquentine's one good eye soon closed. He clasped his hands, resting them on the huge swell of his belly, and hummed a few phrases of a melody. The tune grew softer and softer until it faded away. His jowly head slumped forward, only to jerk upright once more at Magrayn's return. She carried a bowl, covered with a cloth.

"Jemmin has gone for the lemon tarts," she reported as she knelt down on a cushion at her master's side. "But there's this in the meantime."

She drew the cloth away and held the bowl up so that Torquentine could see its contents. He smiled.

"Preserved pears," he said as he plucked one from the bowl.

"The Calasheen sent them up from Hoke."

"There's a man who knows how to please," Torquentine said. Sticky juice glistened on his lips as he sucked down a sliver of pear. "Did he send any news of note along with them?"

"Gann's killers are dead, and their killer too. There's no word of any witness. People talk, of course, and gossip; but there's none left could track the death back to the Calasheen, or through him to us. None save the Shadowhand himself, of course."

"Ah, I know you too well, dear Magrayn." Torquentine wagged a finger at her. "I hear the worry you do not speak. You think me rash, to have accepted this commission?"

Magrayn shrugged. "It's dangerous, that's all. People care when someone like Gann nan Dargannan-Haig dies. They become curious."

"You're right, of course. Perhaps I should have turned the Shadowhand away this time, but he's a potent friend to have. And the more he asks of me, the more I can ask of him. He gave me Ochan, didn't he? Ochan the Cook! What kind of man gives himself childish names like that?" He selected another morsel of pear. "And before you say it, dear lady, I know Ochan's hardly a fair trade for Gann, but not every exchange need be equal in the scales from the first day. We'll reap a rich harvest in the years to come, I promise you that. We're hand in hand with the noble Chancellor now."

Magrayn looked sceptical but said nothing. She set the bowl of pears down on Torquentine's broad stomach and went slowly around the chamber, setting out new candles to replace those that had guttered in the last few hours. She lit the wick of an aromatic oil burner. A sweet scent seeped into the air.

Torquentine sucked juice from his finger.

"Have you any other news to fend off boredom with?" he asked.

Magrayn returned to his side.

"Melmon Thyr is complaining. Says all the fighting in the north has ruined his trade. Too risky for his mule men to get in and out of the Vare Wastes, with all the armies marching up and down the road. One of them was already caught by a passing Haig patrol, apparently: got himself flogged and gaoled in Kilvale for smuggling."

Torquentine grunted. He held a slice of pear up before his eye and subjected it to minute examination. "Melmon means to soften my sympathies, to ease the blow of a meagre trickle of coin back into my vault, I suppose."

Magrayn shrugged.

"You are more voluble than ever today, my dear," Torquentine remarked, smiling. "No matter. I think this is a puzzle that I can solve unaided. We have that lumber merchant in Kilvale. The one whose cousin's in the Guard."

"Thune."

"Have him buy Melmon's man out of gaol. Tell him he'll be reimbursed in due course. And send word to Melmon that I expect him to apply more imagination to his efforts. If his dealings with those bandits in the Vare are going poorly, he must find other outlets for his energies. I will be expecting no less from him by way of share this year than I received last."

He handed the bowl back to Magrayn. A single lonely piece of preserved pear remained, disconsolate in a pool of sugary liquid.

"Here, take this away before I gorge myself. He's right, of course. Nothing worse for business than all this strife. Creates too much uncertainty; puts people too much on edge. Makes everyone suspicious, watchful." He shook his head dolefully. "Erodes trust."

"Nobody seems to think it'll last much longer," Magrayn said as she ran a cloth around the rim of the bowl.

"Maybe, maybe not. Nobody thought the Black Road had it in them to bring down Anduran, but look what happened. Never occurred to anyone they could reach inside the Tower of Thrones and put an end to old Lheanor. Dangerous to make too many assumptions, I think. People have grown soft and lazy, if they think the Black Road'll be easily undone. Did you ever find out what became of Kennet oc Lannis-Haig's children, by the way?"

"They turned up in Kolkyre. Rumour has it that they brought half a dozen Kyrinin and *na'kyrim* with them. The boy – Thane, now – has disappeared again, last I heard. The girl's still in Kolkyre, as far as anyone seems to know."

"I see. Nothing of much interest there, then. Really, is there nothing happening for me to ponder on?"

"Cold Crossing's tomorrow," Magrayn said.

"Ah, yes." Torquentine's expression brightened a little. "Always gain to be had from the day of the Crossing. Do we know who's going to win?"

"There are three or four who have a chance, I believe. No certainty, this year."

"Pity. The more certainty there is, the more profit's to be made from overturning it. Well, no matter. Always good sport to be had with the crowds, if nothing else. How many of our little rascals will be plying their trade tomorrow?"

Magrayn glanced up at the ceiling. Her disfigured lips moved as she silently counted off names.

"Thirteen," she said after a moment or two.

"Good, good. That should ensure a multitude of cut purses and lightened pockets. Do go and see if those lemon tarts have arrived yet, if you'd be so kind. I find my desire for them so distracting."

Magrayn left. Torquentine's gaze rested upon the door long after it had closed behind her. He swallowed a mouthful of air and belched it out again.

"Not good," he murmured to himself, alone with his pillows and candlelight and the still, sweet-scented air. "Soft and lazy. No good will come of it . . ."

* * *

The Cold Crossing was a tradition with more than two hundred years behind it. There were many contradictory tales of how it began, back then when the Bloods were young, but all agreed on the name proudly borne by the victor of that first race: Hedrig the Fish. Every year a platter of solid silver was made and offered as prize, and every year it was decorated with leaping, darting fish. Three of the Crafts, and the Haig Thane himself, took turns to pay for the trophy's making. Whoever's coin had bought it, though, it was always known simply as Hedrig's Plate.

This year, it had been Gryvan oc Haig's duty to provide the Plate. The Thane of Thanes had, inevitably, left the practicalities to his Chancellor. And Mordyn Jerain had, in turn, delegated the responsibility to his wife, passing on Gryvan's sole instruction in the matter: the platter was to be the most dazzling, the most expensive, ever offered. Tara had taken him at his word. Tremannor, famously the best silversmith in Vaymouth, had spent months upon the task.

Now, on the bleak day of the Crossing itself, Tara Jerain rode her finest bay mare in the wake of the wagon that bore the Plate, its guards, and Tremannor himself, towards the great wooden platform on the bank of the Vay. A dozen or more of her household were around her, and behind them several ranks of Vaymouth's Guard. The Thane of Thanes himself was up ahead, leading the way. He wore his great crimson cloak on this day of spectacle, its radiant expanse spread over the haunches of the huge white horse that bore him. Cries of adulation, of formless excitement, accompanied his progress through the crowd.

In the last half-century, the Crossing had become one of the events that gave Vaymouth's year its shape and structure. It was a last, defiant expression of the city's insatiable hunger for activity before the shorter days and colder nights of winter took a firm hold. During the week preceding it, a temporary town sprang up outside the city walls, on the northern bank of the Vay. Tents crowded along the fat brown river like a forest of mushrooms bulging up out of the earth. Horses and cattle were traded there, and furs of every kind and quality. Fishermen netted the river and sold their catch from stalls, even from their moored boats. Hot sweet wine was ladled out of great cauldrons. Despite the vagaries of the weather at this time of year, the event drew in folk from as far away as Drandar and the furthest reaches of the Nar Vay shores. In past years, many would even have come up from Dargannan-Haig lands to the south, but the ruin of that still leaderless Blood had rendered the roads to and from Hoke dangerous for travellers. They would, most likely, have been unwelcome guests this year, in any case.

Tara had never liked the Cold Crossing. The crowds were too tumultuous, the mood too coarse and raucous, for her liking. Tonight, if recent Crossings were anything to go by, once the great and the powerful had returned to their palaces in the city there would be drunken fighting, grubby little deaths, amongst the stalls and tents of the huge encampment. The excitement of the day's events, combined with the loss of hard-earned coin in foolish wagers and an inexhaustible supply of powerful drink, always seemed to culminate in such excess. For now, though, there was only merriment and feverish anticipation of what was to come.

A flurry of children swirled by, shrieking in excitement and caught up in their own games. Tara watched them pass. She felt a momentary stirring of the normally dormant regret at her own childlessness. Twice, she had lost a child of Mordyn's before its proper time. The losing of the second had almost killed her. After that, he had extracted a promise from her that there would be no further attempts. Such pain and fear and grief had possessed him then that she had given the promise almost willingly. On those rare occasions when she thought of taking it back, she closed her mind against the thought.

The long wooden dais from which Vaymouth's elite would watch the day's events was already crowded. Gryvan oc Haig and

Abeh, his wife, mounted its steps and were swallowed up by the admiring host. Tremannor and his apprentices carried the plate onto the platform to a chorus of admiring gasps and even scattered applause. Tara, happy on this occasion to remain largely unnoticed, followed with her attendants.

The competitors — muscular young men one and all — were lined up on the short, muddy grass at the river's edge. All were naked, save for coloured caps, and liberally smeared with goose fat that gave their pale skin a sticky white glaze. Some were shivering already, beset by the sharp wind that came up from the sea. The great expanse of the river before them was dark and choppy, speckled with little foamy wave crests. It seemed likely that the Vay would claim at least one or two victims this year, and that only fed the eagerness of the surging crowds. A line of Guards from the city, wielding clubs with impartial and indiscriminate enthusiasm, held back the mass of spectators.

From amongst the crowd on the dais, the Craftmaster of the Vintners stepped forward. He opened a scroll and began to shout out the full list of competitors. Each name was greeted with a burst of noise, mingling exhortations to vigorous effort in the challenge to come and predictions of dismal failure. Once the Craftmaster had furled his scroll and retired, it was the turn of Gryvan oc Haig himself to come to the front of the platform. Kale, the High Thane's chief shieldman, was at his shoulder, stony-faced. Tara could not remember ever seeing the man smile. He surveyed the crowd now, as he seemed to survey everything and everyone, with suspicious disdain.

In one hand Gryvan carried a bright bronze gong, in the other a little iron hammer. There were cries for silence. The swimmers shuffled forward to the very edge of the river bank. Gryvan turned this way and that. He held the gong up, letting the vast assemblage of his people see it. The wind caught his cloak, setting it billowing. In such moments, Tara mused, the High Thane did have the look of a king. Gryvan beat the gong with the hammer, the crowd roared and the swimmers flung themselves into the turbid rushing waters of the Vay. The Cold Crossing had begun.

As a long communal bellow of encouragement rose from the mass of spectators, serving girls brought beakers of wine and tiny pastries for the elite gathered on the High Thane's dais. Tara Jerain tasted both carefully, with diligent attention, to arm herself with some harmless pleasantries about them for the small talk that was bound to ensue. Both were good, but neither were exceptional. She recognised the wine as a Nar Vay imitation of a finer original from the vineyards around Drandar.

"Oh, look, one of them's floundering already," said one of the court ladies nearby, a ripple of mirth in her voice.

One of the swimmers did indeed appear to be in difficulty. He had turned back before making even a quarter of the river's breadth. Clearly labouring, outmatched by the chill of the water and the powerful current, he was the target of hundreds of abusive catcalls from the bank.

"He'll not be winning the favour of any girls tonight, with a performance like that," Tara observed. Everyone laughed in agreement.

As the luckless man hauled himself out onto the mud, several people threw food and pebbles at him.

"Most mysterious to me, some of your traditions," someone said at Tara's elbow.

She glanced around to find Alem T'anarch, the ambassador of the Dornach Kingship. He was a handsome man, but prone, like many Dornachmen, to an occasional haughtiness that made him difficult to warm to.

"Not only to you," Tara replied with a fleeting smile. She had no wish to appear rude or dismissive, but it would not be advantageous to be seen spending too long in conversation with this man, given the current mood of Gryvan's court. Relations with the Kingship, never warm, had reached new lows once Gryvan found Dornach mercenaries fighting against him during Igryn's rebellion. Tara knew the High Thane had only decided at the last moment .that T'anarch should even be allowed to attend the Crossing.

"Not good for swimming, I would have thought," the man murmured. "These cold waters, I mean."

"Yes. I imagine you never have to put up with such chilly amusements in the Kingship."

"Oh, it can be cold, my lady. In Evaness, in midwinter, I have seen snow."

Tara nodded, content to let matters rest there. She had said enough to appear cordial, not enough to attract the attention of any observers. The ambassador was, however, gently persistent.

"A pity that he cannot be here, your husband. Must be even colder in the north."

"It probably is," Tara agreed. She was careful not to let her irritation show. Alem T'anarch was an intelligent, capable man. He must know perfectly well that no one of any consequence would want to be seen enjoying his company while he stood in such ill favour with the High Thane. "Perhaps you should ask one of the servants to find you some warmed wine, Ambassador, if our weather is displeasing you."

"No need. Have you heard when the Chancellor will be returning, tell me? I have asked, but cannot find an answer."

A flurry of shouts drew Tara's attention back to the river. Halfway across the leaden mass of the Vay, amidst the crowd of flailing arms and backs, it appeared that another of the swimmers was being overcome by the current and the cold. A single pale shape was parted from the rest, carried off downstream. The man's yellow-capped head bobbed in and out of sight; at this distance there was no way of telling whether he was being pulled under or whether it was only the waves obscuring him. Further down the bank a little boat had been launched, two burly men hauling at their oars in an effort to reach the swimmer. On the basis of past experience there was a good chance they would not succeed. Sometimes the bodies were never found.

"I ask only because his voice would be valuable now, I think," Alem said. "He is missed. Wise heads are, in times of difficulty."

Tara had always been steadfast in distancing herself from the kind of matters that absorbed Mordyn's attention. She worked in a different arena, collecting – sometimes shaping – gossip, making gifts to good causes, cultivating the company of merchants, musicians and craftsmen. Except on those rare occasions when her husband felt it useful, such as her recent audience with the Craftmaster of the Goldsmiths, she stayed out of the dealings of Thanes. This Dornachman knew that. Why, then, seek to interest her in his only too well-known troubles?

"I am sure my husband will return soon," she said, smiling. "I do not follow such things closely, of course, but by all accounts it will not take long to settle matters with the Black Road."

Alem T'anarch gave a little nod of his elegant head.

"Time is ever the heart of things. And war, or threat of it. A shame, that such violence should be required in the north. It is never the desire of the wise, violence. I hope, at least. Not when there are ways of avoiding it."

"Indeed," Tara said. She took a small, decisive step away. "Excuse me, Ambassador. I must have a few words with Abeh oc Haig. I promised to provide some musicians for her gathering at the White Palace tonight."

"Of course. Mention my interest to your husband, if it please you. Should you send him a message. Tell him I hope the Thane of Thanes will benefit from his counsel once more, soon."

Tara frowned a little as she worked her way through the throng towards Gryvan's wife. She was annoyed with Alem T'anarch, but concerned too at the implication of his words. The Dornach ambassador was evidently a troubled man. That he should try to involve her in solving his troubles had more than a whiff of desperation about it. Perhaps he feared an irreparable breach between his masters in Evaness and the Haig Bloods. It would be no surprise: Mordyn had told Tara more than once that there would be war between Dornach and Haig in their lifetimes. As far as she was aware, though, that confrontation was supposed to be some time off yet. Perhaps in her husband's absence Gryvan oc Haig was allowing his contempt for the Kingship to run away with him.

Abeh oc Haig was an avid spectator of the Crossing. Her maids had cleared a space in front of her to ensure an unobstructed view. The High Thane's wife did not even glance round as Tara came up at her side.

"Can you see who is winning?" Tara asked, managing to feign at least a little interest.

"Not really. Three or four of them seem to have left the others behind, though."

"Perhaps there will be a contest to the end this year, at least," Tara murmured. Last year, one young man had so easily outpaced all the others – including the youth who had been confidently expected, and heavily backed, to win – that there had been a general sense of disappointment, not to mention suspicion.

"We may hope so," Abeh agreed. "Did Alem T'anarch tell you who he favoured for the race?"

"No, my lady. He didn't. I imagine the Ambassador's favour would sink any swimmer it was attached to, in any case."

Abeh gave a girlish laugh. "Well said. He spreads gloom wherever he goes, these days. Oh, look. There goes another one."

One of the swimmers was drifting. He was fortunate: a rowboat hovered only a short way downstream, and the current looked set to carry him onto its prow.

"The Plate's impressive," Abeh observed. "You chose well, in picking Tremannor for the task."

"I am glad you approve."

"I was discussing it with the High Thane last night. We thought perhaps you could speak to Tremannor – tonight, or tomorrow, as you see fit – and convey our gratitude to him once again. And express to him our hope, our expectation, that now that he has reached this pinnacle of his art, he will not find it appropriate to accept any commission to make the Plate for future Crossings."

"Of course." Tara dipped her head a fraction to signify acceptance of the task. "Though it will be the High Thane's task to provide Hedrig's Plate once again, in four years' time. Perhaps I should suggest that Tremannor refuse any such commission for . . . three years?"

Abeh grunted in dry amusement. "If you wish. We are thinking of using him to make a gift for the new Kilkry Thane, in any case. A chain, we thought, to wear about his midriff."

"By all accounts, Roaric oc Kilkry-Haig would not fully appreciate the artistry of one such as Tremannor," Tara said.

"Of course not. The man probably wouldn't know the difference between a pebble and a ruby if they were both set down before him. But that's not the point."

"No." Tara hesitated, then decided to venture onto trickier ground. "Extraordinary, don't you think, the way they managed to reach old Lheanor? Right there, at a feast in his own Tower, by all accounts. I heard the woman even poisoned half the kitchen staff, to get herself next to the Thane."

Abeh wrinkled her nose in distaste, and gave a little sniff. Talk of death, talk of anything of any consequence, would only spoil her immersion in this lively, light day. But Tara knew that Abeh, Gryvan, all of them, had been shaken by Lheanor's death. No one had thought the Black Road could hide so deeply, and for so long, so close to the heart of a Blood. As soon as the grim story reached Vaymouth, purges amongst the staff of every palace in the city had begun. Maids and cooks and grooms who had given good service for years had been turned out onto the street, or worse, for want of a convincing answer to some question, or a suitably loyal, submissive expression on their face.

What Tara feared was not betrayal within the walls of her own palace, though. No, what left her feeling as if she lived now beneath a constant shadow was the knowledge that her husband was there, in the north where Thanes were dying, and traitors were lurking. To lose Mordyn would be more than she could bear. It would be to lose the best reason she had – had ever had – to wake in the morning. And there was nothing she could do to ensure his safe return; only wait, and hope, and dream of the day when this fear would be lifted and he would be with her again.

"They're almost there," cried Abeh in a burst of excitement.

Way out across the river, the pale shapes of the swimmers were just visible, labouring through waves. It made Tara think of debris, on the sea. They were almost at the far bank. It was impossible to say who was in the lead, but to judge by the cheers rising from the small crowd gathered over there it was a close race this year. The wind had strengthened and was peeling spray off the crests of the waves, blasting it downriver. The bobbing, multi-coloured heads of the swimmers came and went, obscured and revealed. Even the rowers in the longboat that waited to bring the winner back and present him to the High Thane, so that he could kneel and have the Plate pressed into his hands, and hear the adulation of the masses, even those rowers and steersmen were on their feet, shouting encouragement. And all Tara Jerain could think was, Oh, what does it matter? Don't you know that more important things than this are happening? Darker things. Things that could yet put cracks into this bright, glittering, empty delight.

V

He breathed, and the air was rough and jagged in his throat. He blinked, and the light sent splinters of pain back into the hollow cavity of his skull. He lifted a hand, and his arm felt distant, as if it belonged to someone else. Mordyn Jerain, the Shadowhand, came slowly back to himself.

There was a pillow under his head, a coarse linen sheet beneath his fingertips. He could hear someone moving, soft shoes on stone. His eyes no longer wanted to open. His head ached.

"I am thirsty," he managed to say.

"Wain, pour some water from that jug," someone – a man – said, in a voice so smooth, so richly contoured that it made Mordyn think of flowing honey.

He tried, and failed, to part his eyelids.

"Let me help you," came that voice again. "You must sit up if you're to drink."

Then there were hands on his arm and shoulder, lifting him. Someone moved the pillow so that he could rest against it. The pain in his skull was unremitting.

"Where am I?" he asked. "Highfast?"

And there was laughter at that. The voice previously so unctuous and rich became strained, agitated.

"Highfast? No, it's not Highfast. Not at all." A finger pushed at Mordyn's eyelid, lifting it. In the flare of harsh light, he glimpsed pale skin, a long and bony hand. "You'd know that soon enough if you'd open your eyes and look around."

From the other side of the bed someone else was putting a beaker into his hand. He raised it and forced down a mouthful or two of water.

"You'll damage him if you're rough," a woman said. The words might have implied compassion or rebuke; the voice that carried that was so emotionless, though, that they did neither. It was a cold statement of fact.

The man snorted. "He's well enough. They mended his skull."

Mordyn blinked again. He had to force his eyes to open against the intrusive, painful light. Tears formed as he winced and looked around him. The first thing he saw, the thing that snagged and held his attention, was the *na'kyrim* staring back at him. The man looked sick. The skin of his face was blotched and bruised, the shape and line of the underlying bones starkly visible. He watched Mordyn with an eager hunger that would have made the Shadowhand recoil had he possessed the strength to move.

"Welcome back," the *na'kyrim* said, and he smiled in a way that put Mordyn in mind of the half-mad diseased beggars of the Ash Pit in Vaymouth.

The woman took the beaker from Mordyn's hand and refilled it. He turned his head to follow her. She was impressive: sleek hair, an erect and powerful posture. There were rings on her fingers, and hundreds of others – of a more functional kind – in the vest of metal she wore over a padded shirt. The Shadowhand's mind was sluggish, as if numbed by the pain in his head. He had to concentrate to string thoughts together. The woman was strong, and armoured. Her voice – what little he had heard of it – wore an accent he could not attach to any of the lands of the True Bloods. Improbable as it seemed, then, could she be of the Black Road?

"Anduran?" he murmured, turning back to the *na'kyrim*. "Is this Anduran?"

"No." That pale, gaunt head shook. The *na'kyrim* straightened. He flicked one of his thin fingers at the wall. "This is older stone. Nothing of Sirian's making."

The woman returned the over-full beaker to Mordyn. His hand was unsteady. He spilled water on his chest as he drank.

"You are in Kan Avor," she said. "I am Wain nan Horin-Gyre."

Sister to Kanin, Mordyn thought at once. The Horin Blood sent its best, then, to fight this war. There could be no worse company for the Chancellor of the Haig Bloods to find himself in. He had no idea how he could have come into such an absurd situation. He remembered . . . a stone road, amidst stone mountains, and nothing thereafter. Could this all be just a feverish dream, tormenting his mind while his body lay in some distant, safe bed?

The *na'kyrim* was leaning over him again, smiling, regarding Mordyn with carnivorous glee. His face was so close that Mordyn shrank away from it, repulsed by the marbling of blood vessels and bruises.

"She is Wain, Chancellor, and I am Aeglyss." He laid the tips of his white fingernails on Mordyn's cheek, and the Shadowhand found the muscles in his jaw taut, his teeth grinding together. Tremors ran across his brow and scalp, like maggots swarming under his skin. "Remember my name, Chancellor. You will come to know it well, for we've a great deal to talk about, you and I."

Mordyn felt sweat on his brow as Aeglyss backed away. A rootless fear was roaring in his mind, a wind bursting open shutters and bullying its way around the room of his skull. The beaker of water fell from his fingers, soaking the sheet over his stomach and hip. He had to clench his hands into knots to prevent them from shaking. Something in this halfbreed undermined all the precious self-control and clarity that Mordyn so valued. Desperate for something to hold on to, he looked back to Wain nan Horin-Gyre.

"I can speak for Gryvan oc Haig," he said, almost ashamed at the strain in his voice. "I will gladly talk with you and your brother; not this other, this *na'kyrim*. I don't know how he comes to be serving you, but he has no place amongst the councils of the great."

Aeglyss was laughing, a sound both sickly and invasive, clambering in through Mordyn's ears. Wain was silent, her face a passive mask.

"You are labouring under a misapprehension, Chancellor," the *na'kyrim* said. There was harsh amusement in his tone. "It's disappointing. Given what little I know of you, I'd have expected you to grasp the situation more quickly."

Reluctantly, Mordyn turned to Aeglyss. He had never been this close to a *na'kyrim* before. Were their grey eyes always so like chips of cold stone? Was their skin always so corpse-pale? Did the object of their attention always feel so assailed, so over-whelmed?

"You think me Wain's servant, perhaps?" Aeglyss asked with a lopsided smile. He stretched one arm out towards Mordyn, turn-ing it to expose the underside of his wrist. The cuff of his jacket slid back a little way, revealing a swollen, scabbed wound. "I ceased to be anyone's servant the day they put stakes through my arms. I learned then that a servant buys nothing but cruelty with his service. That loyalty is unknown to all of you with pure, unpolluted blood running in your veins."

He interlaced his fingers to make a double fist of his hands. Mordyn could not look away, though he longed to. That fear was still there, tearing at his thoughts.

"Let me show you," whispered Aeglyss, then more loudly: "Wain. Thane's sister. Kneel for me, my beloved. Show this noble man how much of a servant I am to you."

Out of the corner of his eye, Mordyn could see Wain doing as she was bid. Aeglyss did not even glance at her.

"Do you see, Chancellor? Do you understand? It is not the Horin-Gyre Blood you will be taking counsel with. It is not Wain who holds your life in her hands. It is not the Black Road that rules here. Come, I will show you."

Kan Avor was all mud, ruin and rot. What had once been streets were now little more than soggy culverts ankle-deep in silt and decaying vegetation. Some of the buildings must once have been grand but the ones that still stood were now crumbling and gutted. Those walls that retained more than a few courses of stone bore dark, mouldy bands on them: the high-water marks left each winter when the Glas Water had been at its fullest flood. But the dam that had created that great lake was gone now, of course. The waters it had restrained had poured away and ravaged Glasbridge on their way to the sea. Freed from its watery imprisonment, Kan

Avor was revealed as nothing more than the sodden, rotting skeleton of a long-dead city.

Mordyn Jerain hobbled along behind Aeglyss. Wain supported him, without which aid he would not have been able to walk. Every movement of his head triggered a pulse of pain. His body was feeble. He felt like an old man.

"Keep moving," Aeglyss muttered. "If you stand still for too long, you're likely to get stuck in the mud." He laughed to himself.

In a small square, bordered by half-tumbled, roofless houses, people were labouring to clear away the silt that the Glas Water had left behind. They dug down to the ancient cobblestones, unearthing all manner of debris as they did so: roofing tiles, shattered pots, even bones. The mud was piled up at the edges of the square. Water oozed out from these mounds, spreading in a filthy slick across the newly exposed cobbles.

In the centre of the square, a broken statue lay in two pieces. It looked like the image of some tall and noble man, though it was so chipped and pitted and stained that it was impossible to be certain. Whoever's glory it had been meant to extol, it no longer served that purpose: the figure had shattered across the waist, leaving legs and barrel-chest divided and forlorn.

Aeglyss lingered beside the head of the fallen statue. He looked almost wistful as he touched the cracked stone brow.

"I don't know," the *na'kyrim* murmured, as if in answer to some silent question.

Mordyn had to lean his weight against Wain. He hated such vulnerability, but his muscles and bones had nothing to offer him. He felt sick.

"Who are these people?" the Shadowhand asked.

Aeglyss lifted his head and looked around the square. For a moment, he seemed puzzled, like a man suddenly waking and not knowing quite where he was. A woman stumbled past, carrying a wicker basket of mud on her back. Aeglyss watched her empty it out, turn around and come back for another load.

"I don't know. Oh, does it matter? They're . . . followers, if you like." Again, he laughed, in that disconnected, abrupt way. He was, as far as Mordyn could tell, quite mad.

"Come," the *na'kyrim* said. "This isn't what I wanted you to see. Not all, at least. I'll show you. Can you climb some steps, great Chancellor?"

Mordyn started to shake his head, but lancing pain arrested the movement.

"No," he groaned.

"Well, try. For me. You need to see for yourself. Everyone does."

Wain helped the Chancellor to follow after Aeglyss. They moved away from the square, picking their way amongst ruins. Mordyn glimpsed indistinct figures here and there. There were men and women, human and Kyrinin, digging, gathering, watching, or just standing staring up at the sky or at leaning walls and broken-topped towers. Mordyn could not find purpose or pattern in anything he saw, and could not tell whether the lack was in him or in the world.

There was a stretch of wall, thirty or forty paces long, standing alone. Whatever buildings it had connected or guarded were gone, slumped into rubble. It was crenellated, with a flight of worn steps running up to the battlements. Aeglyss climbed up, beckoning for Mordyn to do likewise.

"I can't," he muttered.

"Of course you can," the *na'kyrim* snapped irritably. He stopped halfway up the flight of stairs and turned. "You will. You're stronger than you imagine. Lift your foot. One step at a time. You're not so tired; not so weak. Climb up, Chancellor."

And Mordyn's weariness abated. The ache in his head receded, still there but set behind some softening barrier that left someone else to suffer it, not him, not now. Wain's hand was at his elbow, easing him towards the steps. He drifted up them without feeling them beneath his feet. Then he was standing atop the orphaned wall, and the pale light was hurting his eyes. He winced against it.

"Look," Aeglyss said at his side. "What do you see?"

The Chancellor looked and saw before him the edges of ruined Kan Avor, bleeding without clear boundary into the surrounding marshes and fields. The grey of fallen stone gave way bit by bit to the brown and green of mud and grass, and the black of still pools. There were distant copses, far-off barns and farmhouses like smudges on his eyes; a dark line, tracing the weaving course of a river. And beyond, high ground: ranks of hills and mountains rising up to merge into the featureless sky.

"What do you see?" Aeglyss asked again.

Mordyn narrowed his eyes. He saw figures moving across this great indistinct landscape. Small groups of people, out in the fields, following invisible tracks. Some were on horses, some on foot. Some came in wagons, some walked alone. He could see a dozen, two dozen, three.

"They don't even know why they're coming," Aeglyss murmured. "They just come. It is like . . . do you suppose the geese know why they turn south when winter is come? Or do they just wake one morning and find that they must fly? Perhaps their hearts just long for the sun that has abandoned them, and that longing carries them aloft, and southwards, without them ever knowing its intent. Do you think that might be so, wise Chancellor?"

"I don't know. I never troubled myself over the motives of geese."

"Ha. No. Why should you? You are one of the great, and the powerful, of course. You have no need to concern yourself with such things. Well, I'll tell you what I think, shall I? Would that interest you more?"

Mordyn closed his eyes for a moment, and turned his head away from the *na'kyrim*. He was afraid of this man.

"They don't know why they come, these pilgrims," Aeglyss

continued. "I do. I know. They come because they have desires, and questions, and instincts, and longings; and because, to each and to all of these things, I am an answer. They come because the light of the sun will always draw life to it, without reason and without understanding. And I am that light. In the Shared, I now burn brightly, Chancellor. They cannot see it, cannot comprehend it, but they feel it. They feel the promise of glory, or of change, or of death, or of peace. They know, in their hearts, that something great and strange is happening here. So they come."

Mordyn made to descend the short flight of steps. He felt dizzy and unstable, exposed.

"Stay," Aeglyss whispered, and Mordyn's body obeyed before his mind had even made sense of the word. "I am beset by enemies on every side, Shadowhand. My own kind, your kind. The Anain. I must armour myself. I must have friends, who will stand by me. I must have shield and sword, to protect myself and to strike out at those who would drag me down. I've learned well; slowly, but well. There are only friends and enemies. Nothing in between. So you must be a friend to me, Chancellor, or you are nothing."

The *na'kyrim* turned and gazed out across the vast valley floor. A cough hunched his shoulders for a moment, then he straightened. He wiped spittle from his lips with the back of his bony hand. There was something in his eyes, as he stared out, of wonder, or awe.

"This is what I wanted you to see. To understand," he said softly. "It is not the Black Road that rules here. It is me. Or what burns in me."

Mordyn was left, for a time, seated on wet stone, his back resting against the stub of a fallen pillar. His memory, his sense of himself, came and went. He was not certain how he had come to this place. It was some kind of empty hall, only half-roofed. There was wet moss beneath his fingers, growing in the cracks of the flagstone floor.

He could hear voices, sometimes loud and near, sometimes faint like weather far beyond a distant horizon. There were people standing close to him. One was the Horin Thane's sister. She watched him, but did not speak to him. Warriors were gathered about her. Her Shield, perhaps. He was almost certain that the women of the Gyre Bloods sometimes had Shields, in mimicry of their menfolk. It was not only his hunger, or the pain in his head, that made it so difficult to dredge up such fragments of knowledge. To his profound distress, his mind, always his most prized possession, was unruly, sluggish. His every thought writhed and slipped away from him almost as soon as it was begun. There was something in the air of this place, in its foetid, decaying presence, that was inimical to sense and to order.

No, he told himself. That was a half-truth. It was the strange, mad *na'kyrim*. He was the source of the imbalance that afflicted everything here. Somehow, he was staining everything with his own delirium. Mordyn felt as if he had fallen into some fool's story, of the mad times when halfbreeds wielded awful power, and bent the shape of the world to fit their own desires.

He realised he was slumping slowly to one side, his head lolling down towards his shoulder. He struggled to right himself, sighing at the discomfort such movement caused him. There were Kyrinin in the chamber now. His erratic vision turned them into tall, sweeping blurs. A vast terror shook the Chancellor of the Haig Bloods then, feeding off his helplessness and his pain. It receded, but left him feeling like a child, lost and confused, surrounded by things he could not understand.

The *na'kyrim* was there, face to face with Wain nan Horin-Gyre. Mordyn longed to close his eyes and shut out these vile visions, but he was transfixed. The sickly, half-human Aeglyss was smiling, whispering in tones of silver and velvet, cupping the woman's chin, tipping her head back, tracing the line of her lips with a single fingertip. It looked obscene. Then the *na'kyrim* was turning his head, looking towards Mordyn. The smile remained in place. Splitting, bleeding lips stretched back to expose yellowing teeth. Mordyn felt that terror stirring again, reaching its tendrils up towards him.

"You look hungry, Chancellor. Shall I have someone fetch you food?" Even as he stared at Mordyn, and spoke to him, the *na'kyrim*'s finger was stroking the skin of Wain's throat, a vile caress. "Mutton, perhaps. It's spitted outside."

Mordyn blinked. He could not tell whether he was hungry or not, whether the emptiness he felt was of the stomach or the heart.

"Go and cut our honoured guest some meat, Wain," Aeglyss murmured. He came and squatted down in front of the Chancellor.

"You're fragile, Shadowhand. It hurts, I know. But you are not going to die. You will heal."

"How . . . how did I come here?"

"Ha! A shame you slept through the whole adventure! I stole you away, from the greatest castle in all the Bloods. I did, and my White Owls. Oh, Chancellor, what wonders you poor, common Huanin are deprived of. What marvels you are blind to. I can feel the grass beneath their feet when they run, I can hear the wind in the trees above them. I can whisper in their heads and in their hearts, and they will do as I bid them, even if they never hear me."

Someone else was moving behind the *na'kyrim*. Mordyn squinted, but his eyes were rebellious and faltering. He could see only that there was someone standing there, a woman perhaps. Hair as black as ink; something – sticks? The hilts of swords? – protruding from her shoulders.

"Is this truly the famed Shadowhand?" he heard her ask. A cold voice. He heard nothing in it save the wintry north, and hardness.

"Ah," Aeglyss whispered without looking round. "They are interested in you, Chancellor. Of course they are. You're a prize indeed. The ravens come to circle you. Perhaps they think your corpse is ready to be picked clean."

"He could be of great value to us." the woman said.

"Us?" Mordyn could see that Aeglyss was smiling. "I haven't decided yet, Shraeve. I haven't decided what his value is. But remember, in the days to come, that it was I who found him, I who brought him here."

Wain returned and knelt at Mordyn's side. She pressed a fragment of greasy mutton into his mouth. Its juices filled him with an urgent hunger. He chewed it and swallowed it down. It rasped a hot, painful track down his gullet.

"I don't know what hold this madman has over you, lady," he whispered, "but you must take me away from him. You must talk to me. I can make agreements . . ."

"Be quiet." Aeglyss had risen to his feet. He kicked Mordyn's foot. "She won't bargain with you. Leave us, Wain. Wait for me. I will come to you soon."

Mordyn watched in despair as the sister of the Horin-Gyre Thane meekly dropped a few more slivers of meat into his lap and retreated. He was not the only one to observe her departure with interest.

"Does Kanin know you've got her so well-trained?" the woman Aeglyss had called Shraeve asked. "Whatever you've done to her, he'll not forgive you for this. Tell me, for I would know: is this the work of Orlane? Do you think yourself him, reborn?"

"Don't speak of her," Aeglyss snapped. "Or of things you don't understand." Mordyn felt the command like a blow upon his breastbone, a lance punched through his chest, even though it was not directed at him. The tall woman withstood it. But she could not meet the halfbreed's gaze. She bent her head away. Inkallim, Mordyn thought, belatedly understanding Aeglyss's reference to ravens. Even Inkallim will not face him down.

They locked Mordyn in a chamber that stank of rotting weed and noisome mud. A grey-brown sludge covered its floor. Black and green mould patterned its walls, following each seam and crack.

Carved pillars flanked the door. A stone bench was cut into the bay of the window. There was a wide grate in which fierce fires must once have burned. Now there was nothing, save the cracked wooden pallet on which Mordyn lay, and the thin moth-holed blankets they gave him to cover himself.

He lay there and willed his fear into submission. He denied the pulsing ache in his head until it slipped into the background. He begged himself to rise above the harrying doubts and distractions that dogged his every thought. Slowly, in the night's darkness, he gained some small mastery over it all, and was, for a time, himself again. There was always an answer to every question; a chink in the defences of every obstacle that lay athwart his path. He struggled to make himself believe that, alone amidst the city's foul decay, and tried not to think of what lay outside the locked door. He tried not to imagine what might lie beyond that one cold night's horizon.

VI

"I'm told that Avann oc Gyre held audiences here, in this very chamber, before he fell foul of the High Thanes of Kilkry."

Aeglyss walked slowly, a little unsteadily, around the periphery of the columned hall.

"Do you like it, Chancellor?" he asked.

They were high here, by the broken-topped standards of Kan Avor: two storeys above the mud that passed for ground; two flights of coiled, slippery steps above the highest water marks the flood had imprinted on the buildings. The planking of the hall's wooden floor was intact, but overlaid, in places, by moss and slime. Great thick beams still supported the roof above, but there were holes that had admitted the rain and the wind and light. The columns on which the beams rested were pitted and eroded. The stone bench that stood at the far end of the hall was spotted with patches of lichen. There was a smell of soft, saturated timber.

Mordyn Jerain hardly noticed the damp and the decay and the stenches any more. Three days and three nights he had been here, trapped in this mad, corrupt nest of snakes. He thought it was that long, at least. His senses, his awareness of what was around him, came and went. Sometimes, momentarily, he forgot who he was. The only thing he never forgot was Aeglyss. The malignant presence of the halfbreed was everywhere, in the walls, in the air he breathed, in the interstices of his thoughts. When he slept, the Shadowhand dreamed dreams that he did not believe were even his own. He dreamed of forests, and of fires, and murder and rage, and all of it, he was almost certain, was born of this creature who was twisting the world into an imitation of his own diseased mind.

Mordyn's body was recovering slowly. But his heart, his spirit and his hope were being picked, bit by bit, apart. He had given up trying to speak to Wain nan Horin-Gyre. She was nothing more than an obedient hound at the halfbreed's heel, of no more consequence or significance than the Kyrinin who came and went at his command, or the scores of men and women who milled about Kan Avor's rubble-strewn streets. There was, Mordyn now knew, nothing here that mattered save Aeglyss. But he had no idea what to do with that knowledge, or even where it had come from, how it had infested his mind. He had never imagined that the world held such things as this halfbreed. He had no weapons in his armoury of manipulation and influence that could serve against such an opponent. And though despair was no part of his nature, it was taking hold of him.

"Come here," Aeglyss said, beckoning Mordyn to join him at one of the windows.

The halfbreed laid a spindly arm across Mordyn's shoulders. Its touch filled the Chancellor with revulsion, though there was no weight to it.

He was alone here with the *na'kyrim*. Wain and some of her warriors waited outside, on the stairway. He could kill Aeglyss before they could possibly intervene; throttle the vile life out of him perhaps, or beat his head to a pulp on the stone window ledge. He could do it. His body was strong enough. Not his heart, though. Not his will. This man cannot be killed, some awed part of his mind whispered to him, any more than the wind could be dragged out of the sky and crushed in your hands; any more than winter could be slain, with axe or fire or storm of arrows.

"Look at that." Aeglyss extended a crooked, wiry finger.

Below, in a wide street, a crowd was gathered. It surged back and forth, like a mountain stream plunging and swirling in a rocky bowl. In its midst were three figures: mud-streaked men clad in simple clothes, flailing about with clubs and staves.

"Thieves," Aeglyss whispered in Mordyn's ear, holding him close. "Farmers who lost their land, I suppose. They stole food from us in the night, killed one of Wain's guards. They thought themselves safe, hiding down by the river. But no. My White Owls can find anyone, if there's a trail to follow."

The crowd – a jumbled mixture of warriors, and Inkallim, and men and women as ragged as the farmers were – howled and roared and drove the captives up and down the street. One of the men slipped and went down. The throng flowed over him, trampling.

"Can you feel it?" Aeglyss asked. "The need they have, for blood."

Mordyn shivered, though he was not cold.

"I don't know, you see," Aeglyss hissed, "whether it is mine or theirs. Whether I . . . make it, or whether it came here in their minds, already nestled there. There's too much I don't know. Don't understand."

A rock struck one of the farmers on the side of the head. Blood at once ran down his face, and he staggered, lifting his hands in a vain effort at protection. Someone stabbed a spear into his stomach. A sword slashed in and lifted a part of his scalp away from his skull. The man fell, silently.

A small band of Kyrinin appeared at the end of the street.

"Ah, look now," Aeglyss breathed. "Now they'll have what they want. Now the beast that's in them will be fed."

He leaned forwards out of the window, his arm slipping away from Mordyn's shoulder as he did so. The Chancellor sagged a little at the sudden removal of that terrible, weightless burden.

"Let the White Owls have that last one," Aeglyss shouted down. Every face, every gaze, was drawn by his cry. The sound was not loud, but penetrating, as if it was the voice of the city itself, emerging from the stone and the earth. "Let his punishment be at their hands."

He looked back to Mordyn and smiled. The crowd parted and the few Kyrinin came softly through it. The last surviving prisoner was weeping and shaking. He made no attempt to flee; simply stood there, and beat his chest in despair. The Kyrinin took him and bound his hands and his feet and laid him down in the middle of the street. A perfect circle of silent, attentive observers formed. There was an awful stillness about the scene: an expectant, anticipatory thrill. Mordyn could feel it himself, the yearning for this moment to culminate in cathartic violence.

The Kyrinin tore the man's shirt from his body. Two of them produced knives. They began to carve long strips of skin away from his chest.

Aeglyss closed his eyes and lifted his head back and breathed in deeply, as if inhaling the screams.

"Sit, Chancellor. You must be tired." He took Mordyn to the ancient bench and settled him onto it. "Thanes sat there once. And now you."

Mordyn had to press his hands down against the rough stone to hold himself steady and erect. Aeglyss lowered himself onto the floor and sat there, cross-legged. The robe he wore was filthy, its hem frayed. He was looking at his fingernails. Delicately, he lifted one away from its bed. It fell like the petal of dead flower. Aeglyss grunted. He lifted the exposed fingertip to his mouth and licked it, watching Mordyn now.

"Too much for this poor body," Aeglyss said. He sounded sad and tired. "My exertions in securing your presence here . . . I reached a little too far, I think. I am learning, but too slowly. Too slowly."

He coughed, and bloody saliva crept over his chin. He dragged the back of his hand across it.

"I don't know what to do with you, Shadowhand. You're too precious a thing to be given up to the rest of them. They'd squander you. Waste you. Yet . . . oh, to put her aside would be too much for me. Too cruel."

He hugged himself, wrapping his chest in his arms. Rocking. There was a sudden redoubling of the screams outside. Mordyn started at it. Aeglyss did not seem to hear it.

"I can't. I can't. How has it come to this? What did I do that such miseries should be visited upon me? I had no choice. That's the truth in this. They'll none of them love us, Shadowhand. Never. No matter what service we do them. They'll always try to cast us out, curse our names, sooner or later. Or try to kill us. They'll stake us up on stones."

He sprang to his feet and strode forwards. Mordyn felt as though his skull would split asunder, such was the pressure building there. He closed his eyes, but still saw shadows and light moving on the inside of his eyelids. All reason was leaking out of his world. The *na'kyrim*'s voice was within him, just as much as it was without. Nothing would still it. A fingertip prodded at his eyelid. He jerked his head to one side. A hand brushed his cheek.

"You think they love me now?" Aeglyss asked softly. "The White Owls, the Black Road? All these cold hearts yearning for slaughter? They don't love me. None save Wain. Perhaps you think I love them? The White Owls are the people of my mother, but I don't love them. Horin-Gyre is the Blood of my father, but I'll not love them."

Those taut lips were at Mordyn's ear now. The words spilled from them, a mad, angry tumble. Mordyn heard them, but barely grasped their meaning. It was the sound of inchoate madness that held him, that made his heart flutter.

"I'll climb up on their backs, I'll raise myself up on the mounds of their corpses. But I'll not love them. There's no love, for the likes of you and I. We're the outsiders, the hounds they want to run at their heels. They work us hard, and feast on the fruits of our labour, but it's scraps from the table we get. We were born in the wrong place, or of the wrong father, or at the wrong time. You think Gryvan oc Haig loves you for what you've done for him? No!"

Mordyn groaned. He would fall away into unconsciousness in a moment, and he longed for that release. But even as he thought of it, the battering waves of darkness receded.

"Forgive me," he heard Aeglyss say. "I must learn restraint. There is so much I still have to learn. I know what I must do with you, Chancellor. It's just . . . it's just that I fear to . . ."

The halfbreed's voice was moving away. Mordyn cautiously opened his eyes. Aeglyss was stumbling across the floor, his feet scraping over the wooden boards. He drifted around one of the soaring stone columns.

"I've known from the first moment I found you. I made terrible sacrifices to bring you here. Terrible. Someone . . . important slipped through my fingers. The only one I could have trusted. The only one. Stolen from me, because I indulged myself; lingered in that awful place, and called my warriors to fetch you out of there. I lost her. And gained you, Shadowhand.

"Now that I have you, there will be none to gainsay me; none to deny me. They will not turn me away from their tables when they see that I hold the famed Shadowhand. They will not shut me out from their councils. No, they will beg me, they will entreat me, they will seek my favour. Mine! You can aid me, but I know . . . I've learned that aid is not given. Not when I ask for it. I must take it. Take what I need to put myself beyond their reach, beyond everyone's reach."

He stopped, poised in mid-stride, teetering like a frail, half-felled tree. He cocked his head to one side.

"Here they come. Now we shall see. Now there will be a decision."

He looked towards the door, and it swung back on its rusted hinges. Wain stood there, seeing and dismissing the hunched figure of the Chancellor with a single sharp gaze.

"Temegrin is coming," she said. "He has fifty riders at his back."

Aeglyss nodded heavily. "He means to kill me, I think. Well. It's good. Let him, if he can."

More than two hundred marched out to meet the Eagle of Ragnor oc Gyre's army, and even then Kan Avor was not emptied. Kyrinin warriors, Battle Inkallim, Wain and her Shield and fifty of her Blood's spears, a hundred folk from the valleys and mountains of the distant north. They walked out through the city's tumbled wall and onto the icy, wet fields beyond. Aeglyss and Wain led them, with Shraeve a few paces behind, and Mordyn Jerain at their side. They had put a cord around the Chancellor's neck, and led him liked a leashed dog.

Aeglyss stumbled often as he walked. It was not only that the ground here was treacherous, sucking mud beneath a thin skin of ice, more marsh than solid earth; his legs seemed unequal to the task of bearing him. Wain helped him with one hand, dragging Mordyn along with the other. The great muted company drew itself up in loose array and stood watching Temegrin and his band of warriors come cantering up with the sinking orange sun at their backs, flags and pennants flying, mud and water and shards of shattered ice churning beneath the hoofs of their horses. Mordyn could feel their approach in his legs, rumbling up from the ground, shaking his bones. They looked magnificent, these warriors from beyond the Vale of Stones.

Temegrin sprang down from his horse, his feet crunching through ice as he landed. His coarse-skinned face was flushed with anger, Mordyn could see. He tried to remember what he knew of this man. He had certainly had reports of him, but so sluggish and disjointed had his memory become that he could not dredge them up. There were eagle feathers fluttering at the top of his boots as he stamped up towards Wain and Aeglyss. Silly, Mordyn thought. This is no place for birds. Not even eagles.

"So it's true," Temegrin snarled at Wain. "This is Gryvan's Chancellor?" He looked at Mordyn with avaricious loathing.

"It is," Wain said.

The Eagle grinned. "I thought it impossible, when I was told. I had the man who first reported it beaten for spreading lies and rumour. But behold! The Shadowhand himself."

A dozen of his warriors had dismounted and lined up behind him now. Mordyn stared at the ground. This was humiliation more than he could bear, to be gloated over like a prized exhibit at some Tal Dyreen slave market of old.

"But when did you mean to send word to us, Wain?" he heard Temegrin asking, his voice seething with threat. "I had to come all the way from Kolglas to see with my own eyes, for we've had no word from you of this great boon that fate has granted our cause."

She made no answer, and that angered the Eagle still more.

"How did he come here?" he shouted.

"Ask your questions of me," Aeglyss said softly.

Mordyn risked a glance sideways. The halfbreed was standing limply, shrunken and fragile amongst these great warriors in their mail shirts. Mordyn could hardly bear to look at him, for dread burst in through his eyes at the very sight of that stooped frame. Temegrin perhaps could not yet see it, or sense it, for he ignored the *na'kyrim*. He reached out a huge gloved hand, stretching to take from Wain the cord that bound the Chancellor. She twitched it out of his grasp.

"Don't try my patience, lady," the Eagle snarled. "I command the High Thane's army here. You'll surrender this man to me."

"He is not for you," Aeglyss said.

"Silence! Silence! Don't dare speak to me, halfbreed."

Temegrin shook with rage. He swept his head back and forth, contemptuously surveying the strange throng assembled before him.

"Shraeve," he shouted. "Is this what the ravens have come to, consorting with halfbreeds and wights and traitors? Where does the Battle stand in this?"

"I am here to watch, and to learn, and to witness fate's unfolding of its intent."

Temegrin threw his hands up in exasperation. "Madness! Wain, out of respect for your father and your brother, I give you this chance to come back to the straight and level path. Come away from this place. Bring the Shadowhand with me to Kolglas, and you will be honoured amongst—"

"She will not go with you, Eagle," Aeglyss interrupted.

At that, Temegrin finally turned his full, ferocious attention upon the *na'kyrim*. He took two long, fast strides to stand in front of him.

"I told you to hold your tongue. You are not fit to speak, or to breathe, in the company of the faithful. Of warriors. Of humans."

Then, to Mordyn's horror, Aeglyss turned his head and looked directly at him. And smiled. A sad smile, fit to break a man's heart. The Chancellor was filled up with fear at the touch of that smile, taken by a sudden urge to cry out a warning to Temegrin, to fall to his knees and hide his face in his hands.

"You see," whispered Aeglyss, and Mordyn did not know if the words were spoken out loud or only in him, for him. "You see. This is how it will always be. Hatred. Always."

And it seemed to Mordyn that Aeglyss was growing, and spilling a shadow from his shoulders and from his long hair, and that the air was thickening, the light of the setting sun an orange mist that turned everything to its own sickly shade. And the great crowd of his followers was stirring, rising up and murmuring.

Temegrin lunged at Aeglyss, who made no attempt to avoid his grasp. Mordyn groaned, unable to breathe now, seeing everything with a terrible clarity. His ears were ringing.

The Eagle had Aeglyss by the throat, both hands like claws, and was bellowing into his face.

"What will you do, mongrel? What do you think you can do? You're nothing! I could crush your neck, break it, with one hand. What are you going to do?"

And Aeglyss, inexplicably, was grinning at him: a mad, wet grin.

"We're none of us more than sticks in skin, Eagle," he hissed between taut lips. He raised his frail hands, set one on each of Temegrin's forearms.

The Gyre warrior was a powerful man. Aeglyss was almost nothing, like the survivor of a famine. His form was all bone and angles. Yet, impossibly, it was the Eagle who released his grip, who found his arms forced back and held fast by those lean inhuman hands. Temegrin's face was twisted by some sort of horror or pain. Aeglyss had hold of his wrists, and was laughing.

Temegrin's warriors started forwards, swords leaping from their scabbards.

"Hold!" cried Aeglyss, like a storm. Mordyn cowered, swords fell from stunned hands. Mail-clad warriors fell to their knees and dug their hands into the mud.

"Did you see?" Aeglyss shouted. "You saw him lay his hands on me? He meant to kill me. Did you see?"

The crowd at his back was roaring, a deep howl of incoherent fury. But within that cacophony the *na'kyrim*'s voice was an iron thread.

"He asks fate to choose between us. So be it."

Mordyn heard the crack of bones breaking, like wet sticks. Not just once, but twice, then again and again: a ripple of tiny, sharp, savage sounds like the fracturing of an ice sheet. But it was not ice that was breaking. It was Temegrin's arms. They crackled. The Eagle screamed and fell to his knees. Aeglyss stepped forwards and stretched those shattered arms up, the hands at their extremities fluttering limply.

"I am chosen! I am chosen! I am chosen!" Aeglyss cried it out again and again. The sound fell upon the Eagle's warriors like blows, clubbing them back and down. Mordyn fell to his hands and knees, retching dryly. Only Wain did not stir at the torrent of power rushing out from the *na'kyrim*. She watched, quite still, as he stared madly down at Temegrin's tear-streaked face.

"You chose the wrong mongrel to make an enemy of this time, Eagle," Aeglyss said.

The *na'kyrim* reached down and pulled a short knife from Temegrin's belt. The warrior's arms fell back to his sides, and though he wailed at the agony of it, he did not – could not – move. He knelt there, raging and sobbing, and Aeglyss pushed the knife deep into the side of his neck, twisting it.

Temegrin fell onto his side, dead weight. Aeglyss dropped the knife, raised his hand, with the Eagle's blood thick upon it. He stumbled forwards, amongst the Gyre warriors. The frozen marsh splintered beneath his feet.

"It is done. It is done. There's to be nothing now, not for any of us, but fire and blood and a rising-up until all the world lies beneath us. Come with me. I am its herald, and its bearer, and its sword. I will give you shelter."

Mordyn watched them scramble out of the *na'kyrim*'s path, saw the horror in their faces. And felt what they felt, bursting in his

own breast: the awe and the wonder and the dazzling light that
fell from Aeglyss, the certainty that here was the centre of the
world, the seed of everything that was to come. It was an invasion, a foreign intrusion that overwhelmed his own deeper
repulsion and disgust; but it was irresistible.

Aeglyss fell, slapping down into the sodden soil.

Wain dropped Mordyn's leash and ran to the *na'kyrim*'s side.
She knelt there and cradled his head in her hands.

"It is done," Mordyn heard him murmur. "Carry me back. My
legs are gone. I am empty."

VII

Mordyn did not see Aeglyss again until the afternoon of the day
after Temegrin's death. He was left, all that time, alone in the
decrepit chamber that had become his gaol cell. No one brought
him any food or drink. Such thirst afflicted him that he licked
moisture from the walls, until ice began to creep across the
stonework.

He was frightened now. Not just for himself, but for everything he had left behind when he rode out of Vaymouth. It felt
tremendously distant, that vast and bustling city, as if it belonged
in a world wholly unconnected with the one that he now inhabited. His Palace of Red Stone would be shining in the
sharp winter sun. Tara would be soaking in the hot baths she
loved at this time of year. The streets would be aswarm with
visitors to the winter markets. Gryvan oc Haig would be in his
high Moon Palace, dreaming of glories yet to come.

All of it seemed unutterably warm, and safe, and unreachable,
to the Chancellor in his cold imprisonment. And fragile, too.
Everything he and Gryvan had built over the last few years, all the
wealth and power and future conquests they had worked to secure,
now struck Mordyn as flimsy, illusory. Sitting here in Kan Avor,

overshadowed by the baleful, ubiquitous presence of Aeglyss, the Chancellor could no longer believe in the permanence of any earthly, mortal power, or the solidity of any wall. There was now, he feared, nothing left for the world save a dark descent into madness and destruction. Nothing of his labours would survive, nothing of his loves. What he had seen and felt here in the Glas valley admitted of no other possibility, in his besieged mind.

Mordyn struggled ineffectually against the encroaching despair. It leached out of Kan Avor's ruined fabric into his heart. When Wain nan Horin-Gyre came for him, with her Shield grim and silent about her, he made no complaint or resistance. He allowed them to take him out into the bitter air. There was a fine crystalline dust of snow across the city, glinting like innumerable minute fragments of glass. There were icicles hanging from the ruins. His breath steamed in front of him.

On the street, in between heaps of mud that had been cleared from the roadway, columns of men and women were forming up. Scores of cruel faces watched the Chancellor shambling past. There were Kyrinin, lean and pale, and horses, great dark beasts, with the warriors who had escorted Temegrin to his death astride them.

The Chancellor was taken up the spiral staircase and dragged into the columned hall from which he had watched the slaughter of the Lannis farmers in the street below. Aeglyss was there, slumped on the stone bench at the far end, and Shraeve the Inkallim, with her raven-black hair and dead eyes, and a single tall Kyrinin whose face was an intricate dance of blue curls and curves. The *na'kyrim* did not look up as Mordyn was brought in.

"Bring him here. To me," he said, and his voice was feeble.

Two of Wain's Shield took hold of Mordyn's arms, swept him down the centre of the hall and cast him onto the wooden floor in front of Aeglyss. The halfbreed's naked foot, Mordyn saw, was trembling, twitching in tiny spasms.

"Come here, Shadowhand," Aeglyss hissed at him.

Mordyn wanted nothing more than to haul himself away, put as much space as he could between himself and this monstrosity. But a compulsion was upon him, and he slid himself forwards and rested his back against the stone bench, almost touching the *na'kyrim's* legs.

"Send your warriors away, Wain," Aeglyss said, at last lifting his head a little, staring out from under his creased and gaunt brow. "You do not need your Shield here."

The warriors did not hesitate, Mordyn saw. They did not wait for Wain's command, or even look to her for assent. They turned and went silently from the hall. Wain herself stood still and limp, watching Aeglyss. Shraeve, leaning against one of the stone columns, snorted in amusement, or perhaps contempt.

"Be quiet," Aeglyss muttered, sounding more weary than angry. He rose to his feet and tottered away from Mordyn, stooped and unsteady. It put the Chancellor in mind of the aged cripples that haunted Vaymouth's streets, or the dying, wasted victims of the King's Rot. It was absurd to be afraid of such an enfeebled figure, yet Mordyn knew, with an absolute certainty that was beyond the argument of his eyes, that fear was justified.

"It is not what I intended," Aeglyss said as he shuffled down the hall's length. His bare feet made soft scraping sounds. "You understand that, Wain?"

Mordyn saw her nod.

"None of it is as I intended. The Anain . . ." He shook his head convulsively, shivered. "I did nothing to harm them, yet they come for me. I went seeking her – K'rina – but they stole her, and I found this one instead."

He turned, halfway down the hall, and glanced back at Mordyn. It was a casual, cursory glance.

"And now that fool . . . that idiot of an Eagle . . . has forced me . . . Left me no choice, Wain. You see? The storm is breaking, and I must armour myself against it, or it will consume me. All of us."

He laid a hand on Wain's cheek. Her eyes half-closed at the touch, and Mordyn thought he glimpsed both ecstasy and horror in her face, just for a moment, before it settled back into blank repose. The lone Kyrinin had turned away, moving soundlessly to gaze out from the open window.

"I have the Chancellor of Gryvan oc Haig," Aeglyss said, letting his hand fall away from Wain's skin. "I cannot turn away from that. Cannot set aside what is being offered me. Everything, everything is possible."

His voice was rising, taking on a shrill, unstable edge.

"Shraeve, do you understand?" He was staring at the Inkallim. She remained silent, unmoving. "I can only hold one mind. Securely, unbreakably. Only one. Oh, I must crack my own heart today. Do you understand?"

Aeglyss was wringing his hands, kneading them together like a man consumed by uncontrollable grief.

"I cannot . . . I am too weak. Even Orlane could not do more. If I lay myself across two of them I will be too thin, too feeble." He turned back to Wain, who was watching him without any hint of emotion, and smiled at her through tears. "Forgive me for my weakness, beloved. Forgive my failings. If I had known . . . I did not know I would have to take away what I have given you."

He spun away again, as if he could not bear to set eyes upon her. "Raven, do you not understand? We must have this . . ." Aeglyss extended a bony finger towards Mordyn. The Shadowhand shrank away from the gesture. "I must. And to have him, I must give up what I hold most dear. But it would be too cruel to leave her without that light, now that she has known it, to withdraw the shelter of my wing. She would not understand it . . . me. She would not forgive."

He hung his head.

"Shraeve?" he said. Plaintive. Imploring. Insistent. "Have you not yet seen enough? Do you not yet believe in what I make possible?"

The Inkallim stared at him for a moment or two, then slowly, slowly, she turned her head towards Wain nan Horin-Gyre. Mordyn felt himself, and all the world, poised between two forms, caught in a shapeless moment beyond which it might become one thing, or another, wholly different.

"Shraeve," Aeglyss whispered.

And she was moving: one long stride, and two, and one of her blades was coming out over her shoulder. Mordyn wanted to close his eyes, but could not.

Wain stood quite still. She was watching Aeglyss, though his back was turned to her. Her face was calm. It remained so even as Shraeve reached her, and even as the blade descended. Mordyn saw metal flash down, heard a dull sound, a soft breath. Aeglyss howled, and the pain in that cry struck the Chancellor blind and deaf and stilled his mind and froze his heart. He drifted in a small death of darkness and silence.

"Do you see? Do you see?"

Mordyn Jerain blinked and came back to himself. He did not know how long he had been lost. He was still slumped where he had been before, against the bench where the long-gone Gyre Thanes once sat. He could still hear the dripping of water, still feel the grain of the floorboards beneath his fingers.

But now Aeglyss had hold of his head, one hand pressed to each of Mordyn's temples, and the *na'kyrim* was leaning in to fill his field of vision.

"Do you see?" Aeglyss demanded again. His voice filled Mordyn with grief, and with anger and with fear. It crowded out his own thoughts and left no room for his own feelings. He could not breathe. Nor could he turn his head, but out of the corner of his eye he could see a body on the ground, and Shraeve standing over it. She still held her sword. It hung straight down at her side. Something – blood – was dripping from its tip. The Kyrinin warrior was at her side, staring down at the corpse.

"Do you see what I have given up for you, Shadowhand?"

Aeglyss demanded of him. His eyes were bloodshot, tear-filled, anguished. "Do you understand the price I have paid? What I . . . I have killed a Thane's sister for you. One who loved me. Would have loved me for ever, without fail. Are you worthy? Are you . . ."

The *na'kyrim* broke off, turned away, shaking and choking. Freed of the pressure of those mad eyes, Mordyn could suck in a great breath of air. He lifted his arm. Never had he felt so devoid of strength. Aeglyss recovered himself and fixed him once more with an unrelenting gaze. Mordyn felt a mounting pulse in his head; not his own heartbeat, it was faster, harder than that, hammer blows pounding against the inner curve of his skull.

"Now," rasped Aeglyss, "now you will see what wonders I can bring, Shraeve. Now you will see that you are right in thinking me the answer to the world's need."

Mordyn tried to struggle, he commanded his arms and legs to lash out. Yet they barely stirred. The strings that bound his body to his will were loosened. He made to cry out – he did not know whether in fear or abuse – but no sound louder than a croak escaped his constricting throat.

"There is no more time," Aeglyss whispered. "Not for any of us. No more time for hiding or hanging back. We must race now, Shadowhand; race for the sun and the light and the glory. And death will take the hindmost."

Mordyn felt tears on his face. The hands that clasped his head were throbbing, beating against his temples with their insistent heat and force. His sight was blurring and darkening from the edges. He felt himself to be falling away inside his own head, descending into darkness. He could see nothing but those in-human eyes before him. They were dwindling, but it was him who was receding, not them. And in the space he left behind him, another was rushing in, and he could feel the grief, the exult-ation, the delirious potency of that other as if they were his own.

The Shadowhand briefly imagined himself embracing Tara, his

precious wife; smelling her hair, feeling her cheek against his. He managed, just for a few transitory instants, to hold her, and feel again the wonderful lightness of love. Then he was pulling away even from her. He reached out as he fell, but she was gone. He was gone.

* * *

The shutters were closed in the Palace of Red Stone. The fires and the braziers were stoked up, curtains drawn across every door. But still Tara Jerain felt cold. Ever since the Crossing, Vaymouth had been in the grip of chill winds coming down all the way from the Karkyre Peaks, perhaps from the Tan Dihrin itself. They laid frosts across the gardens and the rooftops, had even once, briefly, locked every drinking trough and washerwoman's tub in ice.

The Shadowhand's wife walked alone through the echoing corridors of the Palace at dusk. She carried a candle, cupping its flame with her hand, following its shimmering light down the marble ways. She had nowhere to go, and nothing to do, this night. Her maids were drawing her a bath, and spreading fresh silks across her bed, but she was restless and not yet ready to sink back into the warm waters or into sleep.

Each of the last half-dozen evenings had been the same. With the onset of dusk, Tara found her mood darkening in turn. An imprecise, indefinable anxiety began to seep into her thoughts. She could settle to no task, and find no distraction. This fretful stirring of her mind forced her body into motion. It brought no great easing of her worries, but the act of pacing through the halls and passages kept them in the background.

And what was it that so undermined her ease? She could not say, though of course her persistent fear for her husband's safety was a part of it. Word had come to Vaymouth of Aewult's defeat – humiliation, some murmured when they thought themselves safe from prying ears – outside Glasbridge, but her unease had already taken root before that grim news. Perhaps it was only weariness, for her sleep had been a poor and wretched thing for some time now. She woke in the morning with heavy eyes, and a heavy heart, and fading memories of distressing dreams. She was not alone in suffering thus, she had gathered. There was something in the season, or in the air coming down out of the north, inimical to restful sleep, it seemed.

A movement of the chilly air shook the flame of the candle, and she paused for a moment to ensure it did not falter. A chink, somewhere, in the palace's defences. She would have one of the maids go in search of a shutter left open, or a door ajar. Tara wanted the palace sealed, impenetrable to the winter.

She walked on. There was no sound save the soft tread of her slippers. The silence was not peaceful, though. It was, she now thought, oppressive as never before. She would like it to be broken, and with one sound above all others: Mordyn's voice, ringing from the stone and marble walls, echoing through the chambers. Nobody seemed to be able to tell her where her husband was, or why she had received no word from him. He had marched with Aewult, someone told her, and returned with him to Kolkyre; he was in the Tower of Thrones, locking horns with Roaric oc Kilkry-Haig, another said. Or, inexplicably, had he gone to Highfast, as one rumour had it? She did not know. But she did know that she wanted him back, warming her bed and her heart and armouring her against the chills of winter. Perhaps only then would she sleep deeply again, and only then would the mist of unease be lifted.

Tara's maids had put scented oils in the bath. She smelled them before she entered the room and felt the hot steam. Braziers were burning here, and oil lamps. She pinched the candle out and handed it to one of the girls. Another took her velvet robe from her shoulders as she shrugged it off, and gathered her clothes as she shed them. She stepped into the bath. They left her alone then, and she closed her eyes, and felt the tingle of her immersed skin, breathed in the perfumes and the heat. She closed her eyes, and tried not to think of Mordyn, and of his absence.

VIII

Anyara refused to think of herself as a prisoner. She stubbornly behaved as if she were an honoured guest, and Aewult nan Haig and his followers conspired in that pretence sufficiently to give it a semblance of credibility. The tent she was housed in was enormous, with heavy canvas walls that were hung, inside, with fine rugs. Wooden planks had been laid for flooring, and a partition raised to give her an almost private bedchamber. She could come and go as she pleased, though the world of a huge and, she could not help but feel, hostile army camp was not appealing. The limits were unspoken, and she chose not to test them. She knew well enough that if she tried to enter Kolkyre, or to stray far beyond the bounds of the encampment in any direction, she would find her way obstructed. The obstruction might be polite, even deferential, but she did not doubt it would be firm.

Coinach took this gentle imprisonment far worse than she did. She remembered a gaol cell in Anduran, when her captors, the Horin-Gyre Blood, had been much less soft-spoken; he saw only insult and humiliation and his own failure to discharge his duty as her shieldman.

"Don't be so miserable," she said to him one day. "I don't care what you think, I say it's no part of your task to go picking fights with the High Thane's entire army."

Coinach sat on the edge of the cot where he snatched brief spells of sleep – though only during the day, when Anyara was awake; he insisted on keeping solitary, wakeful watch all through the night – and glowered at her in a way that she was not sure was entirely fitting for a shieldman.

"You can't cut me a path out of this with your sword," Anyara insisted, "so stop daydreaming about it. It's no help to me to have you moping around."

"It is unforgivable that they should make a hostage of a Thane's sister."

"Maybe it is. But listen to me. What matters here is that we try to make sure Orisian still has a Blood to be Thane of, when he gets back from wherever it is he's gone. If staying here, or going to Vaymouth even, is what's needed to keep Aewult from losing his mind completely, I'll do it."

It was easy to summon up such words when talking to Coinach, but Anyara was a less compliant audience for herself. At every mention of her brother's name, she had to crush the doubts and fears that swirled up within her. Only by denying them her attention could she keep the tears from her eyes, and keep putting one foot in front of the other. Wherever he was, whatever had happened to him, there was nothing she could do about it now. There was little she could do about her own situation, either, and though she secretly dreaded the prospect of being carried off to Vaymouth, that sentiment too she chose to ignore.

One morning, the sides of the tent were stiff and creaking with a hard frost. The water in the bowl by Anyara's bed was frozen. Lying there, bleary-eyed and with a neck aching from the overly soft pillow, she could hear Coinach moving about in the outer part of the tent. Perhaps he thought he was being quiet, trying not to disturb her, but she could hear him pulling back the flap of the tent, gasping softly at the cruelly cold air that must be greeting him. She smiled a little to herself at that. She heard muffled voices, and a rattle of pots. One of Aewult's cooks was bringing food – usually a thick oat porridge with bread and honey – and handing it over to Coinach. The shieldman insisted on tasting everything that was provided for Anyara to eat before it got anywhere near her. She had told him she thought it more than a little unlikely that Aewult meant to poison her, but in this at least he was immovable.

His expression was grim when she finally emerged to break her fast.

"What is it?" she asked as she sank into one of the cushioned chairs that they had been given.

"The word is that the Bloodheir's blockading Kolkyre."

"What?"

Coinach shrugged. "I don't know if it's true or not. That's what the cook says. A test of wills between Aewult and Roaric. The Bloodheir wants the men who killed his warriors while he was away, and Roaric won't hand them over. And now, apparently, he's saying he won't make any payment to the families of the dead men until Aewult's paid for all the horses and cattle the army's taken."

Anyara groaned.

"Aewult wants the Kilkry army that Roaric's gathered in there disbanded all over again, too, I think," Coinach added glumly. "The Thane refuses, of course. And . . . well, it sounds as though Roaric's demanding that you be returned to the Tower of Thrones."

"Oh, so now I'm to be some little token for these . . . idiots to fight over?"

"He's only trying to stand by you, to get you out of Aewult's grasp."

"No, he's not," Anyara snapped. "He's trying to undo every insult he thinks his Blood has suffered at the hands of Haig. He's trying to prove he's strong enough and big enough to be Thane, and to face up to Aewult." Her shoulders sagged, and she stared down into the grey porridge in her bowl. "Oh, I don't know. I'm sure he thinks he's helping. Aewult's the wrong man to try to prove himself against, though, and this is the wrong time. Can't he see that? Has everyone lost their mind?"

"He's got a dead brother and a dead father burdening him," Coinach murmured.

"We've all got the dead to deal with. All of us."

"Yes. Of course."

On Anyara's third day in Aewult's camp, Ishbel came to see her. Anyara was surprised at her own indifference to the intrusion. The woman, standing smug and sneering in the great tent's entrance, clearly had no purpose there except to gloat, yet Anyara found herself unmoved.

"Not as comfortable for you as the Tower of Thrones, I imagine," Ishbel said. She had a little flock of maids fluttering about behind her. They laughed.

Anyara and Coinach were sitting cross-legged on the planked floor. He was showing her how to sharpen the knife he had given her. She glanced up, then turned her attention back to the blade.

"I've seen much worse," she said.

Ishbel said nothing for a moment or two, but Anyara could feel her presence, and her self-satisfied smile. She concentrated on the weight of the whetstone in her hand, and the movement of the knife across it.

"Should I lend you some of my maids?" Ishbel asked. "Or some clothes, perhaps? I know how the subject of rain capes interests you. I have some I could spare you, to keep the cold and the wet off."

"I'm sure," Anyara muttered. "Your master has provided what servants I need, though, and I've cloaks enough."

"He's not my master."

"No?" Anyara looked up and smiled thinly. "My mistake."

Ishbel left with a frown on her face, stamping her feet as she went.

"Needs to learn some manners," Coinach observed.

"I don't suppose she needs them, so long as she's got the Bloodheir's favour to wrap herself up in."

Boredom, and the excess of thinking time that came with it, was Anyara's greatest discomfort. She asked more than once to meet with Aewult, hoping against hope that she might be able to soften him, but the message always came back that he was too busy. She practised knifework with Coinach. He was a patient teacher, hiding well whatever reservations he felt about the exercise. The nights were the worst. The camp was never quiet, and all through the hours of darkness she could hear voices and the creaking of wagon wheels and the movement of canvas on the breeze. She dreamed – when she slept at all – in indistinct patterns of shadow and fear.

No one could, or would, tell her what was to happen. Every morning she woke half-expecting that there would be a battle, or that she would be sent off to Vaymouth. Each day those expectations went unfulfilled, until Anyara began to feel as if there was nothing to the world save this great encampment with the city silent and sealed beyond it, and that it could continue like this indefinitely.

Then they brought Taim Narran to see her. The Captain of Anduran was grimy and battered. There were rents in his tunic, bruises on his face. He was clearly exhausted. Two of Aewult's Palace Shield escorted him and stood there, all armour and pride, as he greeted Anyara.

"Leave us," she said to them. Both of them looked at her, but neither moved. For the first time in days her anger surged. "Get out. I am sister to a Thane, and I will talk to this man in private. Get out!"

The two huge shieldmen glanced at one another, and after a moment's silent consideration they retired from the tent.

"What's happening?" asked Taim as soon as they were out of earshot. "Has Aewult gone mad?"

"Who can say? I'm safe enough, I think. But where's Orisian, Taim? That's what matters."

"I don't know," he said, anguished. "I don't know. I'm sorry. He never reached Kolglas. I hoped . . . I hoped he might be here. Or still at Highfast, perhaps?"

Anyara shook her head. The thought came to her, as it often

did now, that the last time she had seen her brother she had been angry with him, frustrated at being left behind in Kolkyre. She dreaded the possibility of that being their last parting, and of anger being its tone. Somehow, it left her feeling that she owed him all the courage and discipline she could muster to face Aewult, and his father, and the whole Haig Blood if needed.

"Gods, everything's coming apart," Taim muttered. "What does Roaric think he's doing, picking fights with the Bloodheir? The Black Road's stopped, for some reason, between here and Hommen, but when they come south, every man – every sword – will be needed if there's to be any chance of turning them back."

"Perhaps they've come as far as they can," Anyara said, her mind still tangled up in thoughts of Orisian.

"No," Taim said firmly. "They've overrun every obstacle put in their path. We stood for a day or two at Hommen, but we had to retire as soon as they brought up their full numbers. If Aewult hadn't fallen all the way back here, his whole army'd have been destroyed by now. No, they've some reason of their own for pausing. But it's only a pause. They'll be here before long, and Aewult will be lucky if he's not outnumbered when they do reach him. There's more of them than we ever imagined was possible."

Anyara nodded, hardly listening. Her eyes drifted down. Where was Orisian? If the Black Road reached Kolkyre before . . . something pierced the veil of her preoccupation. She blinked.

"Where's you sword, Taim?" she asked.

He looked down at the empty scabbard on his hip. When he lifted his head again, Anyara was not sure what she was seeing in his expression. It might almost have been shame.

"I am a prisoner, my lady. It has been taken from me."

At that Coinach, who had been a silent observer thus far, stepped forwards.

"Aewult would not dare—" he began, but Taim Narran cut him short with a sharp look.

"The Bloodheir dares to issue commands to our Thane's sister. Why should he hesitate to make a mere warrior his prisoner?"

"On what grounds?" Anyara asked.

"That I failed him at Glasbridge; brought too few men, and too late, to his aid in battle." Taim spoke the words without inflection, as if reporting the dry details of some dull conversation. "After we retreated from Hommen, I meant to stand again, but Aewult summoned me. And took my sword from me when I arrived."

One of the shieldmen outside pushed aside the flap at the tent's entrance. He bent and stared in.

"Enough," he said. "Come away. The Bloodheir said a brief visit only."

Taim Narran did not hesitate. He gave Anyara a shallow bow, and turned to submit himself to the custody of the Palace Shield. Coinach growled in pure anger.

"This cannot be," he said.

"Look to your charge, shieldman," Taim snapped at him. "That is where your duty lies. Do not fail in it."

Aewult's huge shieldman put a rough hand on Taim's shoulder and hurried him out of the tent. Anyara followed and faced the armoured giant.

"Listen to me," she said as calmly and clearly as her ire would allow. "This man is an honoured warrior of my Blood, and valued by his Thane. You will treat him with respect and leave him his dignity. If not, I'll make such trouble and noise that you will have to bind me, and put me in shackles at his side. Tell your Bloodheir that."

* * *

Hommen was a strange place: two distinct settlements, living uncomfortably side by side. Down on the sea's edge, a fishing village, with a harbour wall of boulders and a short wooden quay that stood on pole-legs crusted with barnacles and weed. Up on the hillock to the south, an abandoned stone watchtower with a slate roof, and a flock of two dozen cottages clustered around it in memory of the protection it must once have offered. Linking the two, a short, straight track flanked by drystone walls. Where that track crossed the main coast road, there were gates and a toll-house for tithe-collectors, a little barracks and a hall, hay barns and a wayfarers' inn.

A few days ago, Kanin oc Horin-Gyre guessed, there were probably a good three hundred people who called Hommen home. Now, none. Most had already fled by the time the Black Road arrived. Those who had remained, out of sickness, or despair, or determination to defend their homes, were dead. No one had been spared this time, no prisoners taken. The army that had descended upon Hommen was a more furious beast than that which had taken Anduran or Glasbridge.

Kanin had been at the forefront of the slaughter, cutting his way up to the base of the leaning watchtower, with his Shield about him and a hundred or more Tarbains howling up behind. It had been unwise, perhaps, with his knee still unreliable and sore, but he had needed that violence and danger. Several of the enemy had taken refuge in the little tower, and barricaded it against him. He burned them out, and those that did not emerge to die on the waiting blades and spears were choked by the smoke or consumed by the flames. The charred tower now had a drunken angle that suggested its life was almost done.

Much of the army had pressed on, and was further along the coast pursuing, or destroying, the scattered warriors of the True Bloods who made repeated, if half-hearted, attempts to block the road. Kanin, spent and tired, had let it rush on without him. He and his weary company remained in Hommen, stripping it of every supply it could offer. The forces under his command were larger now than they had been before the battle. Many common-folk of his Blood had emerged from the ranks of the greater host, especially after his reckless display during the fighting. He had armed them as best he could; given them captains and at least a semblance of discipline.

Kanin could not fully explain, even to himself, his reluctance to follow the main body of the army in its rush onwards. When asked, he pointed at his knee and said it needed time to heal, which was at least partly true. It would have been more wholly true to admit that there was something he found untrustworthy in the mad fervour that had taken hold of almost everyone. It was not just a result of the domination that the Inkallim had achieved over the multitude; there was a kind of frenzy that seemed to him to have taken root of its own accord, and was now feeding on itself. He could catch hints of it in his own black moods and his hunger — sated, for now at least — for bloodshed.

There was another strand to Kanin's reluctance that he shied away from examining too closely. Each stride he made down this long road — so long that he knew if he followed it far enough it could carry him to the gates of Vaymouth, and beyond — each stride took him further from Wain, and that felt, at some basic, instinctive level, wrong. Whatever delusion she had slipped into, whatever strange hold she had granted the *na'kyrim* over her, she remained the most important thing in Kanin's life. They had begun this war together, and no matter what triumphs might lie ahead down the coast road, he became more certain with every passing day that they could only be hollow and meaningless for him without Wain at his side.

So Kanin lingered, and slept in a fisherman's house on the quayside, where he could breathe the cold sea air. Snows fell. Hoar frosts cloaked the quay. Ice lay in sheets on the paths. In the north, he realised, up on the furthest coasts, in the inlets and bays, the sea would be frozen now: great flat plains of ice over which snow like dust would spin and twirl in the biting wind. The thought made him long, for the first time since he had left Castle Hakkan, to be marching home. There were others who could fight this war that his father had sired, through him and Wain. He was Thane now. He had a Blood to lead, lands to secure. A widowed mother to greet.

They were thoughts ill-suited to one supposedly faithful, above all things, to the creed. The Black Road was on the brink of its greatest victories in centuries. It was a time when the faithful should be exultant, eager for further glories, determined to test fate's sympathies to their utmost limits. But Kanin did not feel these things. Not any more. It was failure – cowardice, perhaps – but all he truly wanted was to turn back, gather his sister into his company once more, and march away over the Vale of Stones and back to Castle Hakkan. He hung there, in Hommen, suspended; unable to bring himself to march on, unable to commit himself to retreat.

Bands of warriors and stragglers, and beggars and the wounded, moved back and forth up the road like shoals of fish caught in powerful tides. Much of the movement seemed aimless. There were occasional bursts of violence: small slaughters, petty murders. One day, Temegrin the Eagle came pounding up the coast at the head of a column, thundering through the snowbound village in a cloud of steaming breath. Kanin watched him pass with little interest.

Kanin gathered about himself a makeshift household of cooks and servants, grooms and messengers. He had thirty or more women and old men brought down from Glasbridge – slaves – and set them to work gathering food, filling Hommen's barns with stores against the deepening winter. He was standing on the wooden quay, watching some of those sullen Lannis labourers casting weighted nets out along the shore when Igris brought a filthy, sickly-looking woman before him.

The shieldman had a firm grip on the collar of the woman's worn hide jacket, holding her up so that she had to walk on the balls of her feet. She appeared to be terrified. As Kanin regarded her, her eyes widened and she struggled half-heartedly.

"Tell him," Igris hissed. "Repeat what you said to me."

Kanin raised his eyebrows expectantly.

The woman groaned and tried to look away. Igris shook her, like a huge doll. She was limp and defeated.

"Tell him!" the shieldman shouted.

"What is it?" Kanin asked quietly.

"I heard — I heard," the woman stammered. She was Wyn-Gyre, Kanin thought, by her accent. She hesitated, and he saw that she was weeping. Then it came out in a torrent: "Dead, sire. Dead in Kan Avor. Temegrin the Eagle and . . . and your sister. Both dead. It's become a mad place. But they're dead . . ."

Kanin had hold of her shoulders then, and she wailed at his crushing hands. He took her from Igris, lifted her bodily from the quay and held her there in front of him. He could see, in inexplicable detail, every stain and smear of grime on her face, every lash aound her eyes, every crease in her trembling lips.

"Wain?" he asked.

"Dead," cried the woman, flinging the word out as if to rid herself of it.

Kanin could not move. His limbs were stone. He stared into those frantic eyes and did not understand what he saw there, or what he heard.

"Sire . . ." someone — Igris? — said.

The sound freed Kanin. He turned and took one pace, carrying the woman by her shoulders. She hung slack. A slab of meat in his iron grip. But she was light, lighter than flesh; just skin. He threw her. She tumbled, screaming, out and away, down to crash into the thick, dark water. The sea parted and vomited up a plume of spray and closed, rocking, over her.

"Find out if it's true," Kanin said to Igris as he watched the pale form struggling to regain the surface. He could see her mouth opening and closing, her frail hands clawing at the water.

"It may be," the shieldman murmured. "Others came with her. They told the same tale."

"Find out," Kanin repeated, the words dead on the air as they fell from his lips.

Igris turned and went, crunching up the snowy track. The woman's head broke the surface. She gasped and flailed about. Her face was white now, corpse-pale. Kanin looked along the shore. The fisherfolk were standing still, watching, their nets in their hands. When his gaze touched them, they shook themselves and turned away and cast their nets once more. Down below the quay, the woman was crying for help. He could hear her fingernails on one of the stanchions.

"Aeglyss," Kanin whispered.

5

Thane

What, then, is a Thane? Some will tell you that a Thane is a proud or greedy man who makes himself a lord over others the better to satisfy his basest hungers. I tell you, my beloved son, that this is not so. Rather, a Thane is a servant. He serves his people, and all people, by standing between them and the darkness.

There is an impulse in this world, and in we its peoples, towards destruction and decay. Ungoverned, we will always, sooner or later, tear down whatever we have built, unlearn whatever we have learned. If there are to be no Gods to give us order, we must impose order upon ourselves lest we sink for ever into a chaos of cruelty and suffering. Such was the darkness we fell into at the departure of the Gods. The Three Kingships lit our way out of that shadow, but only for a time. The War of the Tainted, the Storm Years that came after it: the ruin of that thin pretence that we were anything more than the corrupt inhabitants of a failed world.

Now we have made the Bloods, and we have made Thanes, and we do not yet know whether this will be more than another thin pretence. You will be Thane after me, dear son. You will be heir to whatever I build. For good or ill, you must take what I pass on and shape it and hand it on yourself to those who come after. Such is the burden of Thanes: to take what is bequeathed to them by the past and make of it the present; to hold the present in their hands and shape from it a future for their heirs.

Some may love you, but others will curse you and defame you and be jealous of you. Pay no heed to those who berate you. Pity them, rather, for the failure of their memories, their wilful ignorance of the fallibilities, the vast imperfections, at the root of our kind. Take comfort that you fulfil a noble duty. There must be laws, and Thanes, and order. They are our only armour against our own malignant instincts.

from To My Son and His Sons Thereafter
by Kulkain oc Kilkry

I

Orisian left a trail of dead men behind him on the journey out of the Veiled Woods. One of those corpses weighed more heavily upon him than all the others combined, but each added its small burden. The White Owls harried them, like wolves at the heels of a dying stag, coming close enough to snap and wound, but never committing to a final, fatal struggle. Men died with arrows in their back, or with their throats cut while they stood watch in darkness.

Torcaill did his best to keep the battered company moving, resting only briefly, never straying out of one another's sight. Orisian's respect for the man grew. He was tireless, resolute. But for all his efforts, everyone knew that it was upon Ess'yr and Varryn that their best hopes of survival rested. The two Kyrinin ranged through the Veiled Woods without pause, ahead and behind, day and night. They moved soundlessly through the misty forest, quartering the ground in search of scents and sign. No one – Orisian least of all – tried to give them any commands. They were fighting their own war, generations old, against their clan's enemy, and they knew its methods and necessities better than anyone. This was, in a way, what they had been seeking ever since Koldihrve, and now that it had come they went about their work with silent, bloody intensity.

The horses, that Torcaill had so wanted to keep, were long gone, abandoned to the wilderness. They could only have slowed, rather than aided, their flight through the tangled forest. The Veiled Woods seemed almost to be folded in upon themselves, trees and brambles and rocks and moss all bent inwards and intertwined in vast confusion. And all dripping wet, suffused with cloud, green and loamy. Not a place for humankind. Perhaps not even a place for Kyrinin, for whenever Orisian caught a glimpse of Ess'yr and Varryn their manner suggested a caution and unease that he did not think even their struggles with the White Owls could fully explain.

The oppressive otherness of the place ate away at his own spirit. Constantly, out of the corner of his eye, he thought he caught some fleeting movement. Whenever he followed such a hint with his gaze, he found nothing; just the mute vegetation, the still, convoluted trees. But there was something here, something more than human or Kyrinin, of that he became certain. The grass on which they walked was that of autumn, not winter. The leaves on the bushy undergrowth were still a patchwork of reds and browns and mottled greens. The tiny streams that gurgled their rocky way across the forest floor seemed to be giving a voice to a saturating presence that hung, untouchable, in the air and the soil. Sometimes, Orisian was almost certain the treetops stirred when there was no breeze to move them, and at night there would be sudden creakings and crackings as if the oaks and willows were twisting themselves into new shapes. He thought constantly, and fearfully, of the Anain.

Much of the time, they had to carry K'rina. The thin *na'kyrim* was often too feeble to walk, though whether it was feebleness of mind or body none could be certain. The raw scratches that had covered her when Orisian first saw her quickly faded into a dull net of scars, flat across her skin. Her distress came and went, with tears and with kneaded hands and trembling brow. Her eyes darted this way and that, or lay dead and sightless in their sockets; her lips shivered and worked in silent flurries, or locked themselves into taut closure. But never did she utter a word. Never did she give any sign of knowing where, or who, she was.

Neither Eshenna nor Yvane could tell Orisian what had happened – or was still happening – to K'rina.

"Will she recover?" Orisian asked Eshenna when they paused, sitting for a time on boulders cloaked in lichens. "Can you not even tell me that?"

"There's nothing there," Eshenna said. "She's gone. Empty."

Yvane shook her head slowly. "Not empty, I think. A dead space in the Shared, but it's concealment, not emptiness. There's something there."

"So that's what all this has been for?" Orisian asked. "You cannot even tell me what prize it is we've won with all these deaths." He spoke carefully, wary of his battered mouth. It hurt less now, though there was sometimes still a dull throbbing in his jaw. The stitched wound in his cheek itched, and stung when he stretched it. His tongue was tender, and constantly stumbling over the unexpected gaps amongst his teeth.

Yvane scowled at him. "Her name's K'rina, if you remember. And whatever has happened to her, I doubt she chose it. Look at her. Do you suppose she's happy with the way things have turned out?"

Orisian sighed, and tugged at the grass. He was angry; at himself, the White Owls, Eshenna, the world. Even through that obscuring anger, though, he knew that however desperate was his desire to assign blame, K'rina deserved none of it.

"No," he muttered. "How did she come to this state, though?"

"The Anain," Yvane said. Eshenna winced at even the word, and the older woman shot her an irritated glance. "We're amongst them here. I can feel them, hear their movement. And K'rina is a part of it, somehow."

"And Aeglyss?"

"He has receded, a little. Sunk back into whatever hole his skull has become, since . . ." Yvane faltered. She did that more often now, running aground on her own feelings, or fears.

"Since Highfast," Orisian finished for her, and she nodded.

It had come late one morning, perhaps the first after Rothe's death, though Orisian could not be sure, for the passage of time had become an indistinct thing to him for a while. Eshenna had been suddenly on her knees, fists balled and pressing down into the mossy grass. She wailed, and the sound was so piercing and anguished that it turned every head, arrested every stride. Yvane had gone to help her, but she too was shaken by something, sent staggering. Orisian held her up, trying at the same time to reach out a hand to touch Eshenna's back.

"What is it?" he had asked them.

"They're dying," cried Eshenna. "Disappearing."

"Who?" He looked from Eshenna to Yvane, frightened by the extremity of whatever had taken hold of them.

"Highfast," Yvane stammered. Her arm was shaking in his grasp. "Cerys is gone. Oh, he's too bright, too dark . . . he's burning them away. He's a beast, a great beast gone mad."

"Save us," Eshenna had said then, and Orisian heard a terrible, hopeless pleading in her voice.

"There's nothing but death," Yvane said, more controlled but still unsteady and bleak-faced. "*Na'kyrim* are dying, in Highfast. Aeglyss is there. For a moment . . . for a moment, there was no difference. He was the Shared, and it was him."

Ever since that morning, Eshenna had been withdrawn. Haunted. She had been, when Orisian first met her in Highfast, urgent and eager; hungry, almost, to leave it behind and step out into the world. What had happened since then, Orisian thought, had been too much for her. Just a few days. That was all it took. That part of him still capable of sympathy regretted the savagery of the lessons the world had seen fit to teach her. But such sympathy as he could summon up was tinged by a cold recognition that such was the nature of the times in which they lived. If Eshenna was paying a price for her curiosity, it was less than others had paid for the recent twists and turns in the path of the world. He disliked the ease with which such thoughts occurred to him now, but he could not deny them.

They exerted little control over the route they followed. They went where ground and thicket and pursuit permitted, and that meant south and west, towards the towering Karkyre Peaks that they could sometimes glimpse through gaps in the branch-woven roof of the forest. However much Orisian wanted to retrace their steps to Highfast, Ess'yr told him with casual certainty that to attempt it would mean death on White Owl arrows or spear points.

"We'll be out of here soon," Yvane said to Orisian, as they sat sharing some of the last hard oaten biscuits.

Orisian looked around, aware that his sight and his thoughts alike were blurred and clumsy. They had been on the move since long before dawn, blundering their way through wooded gullies and rocky thickets. It was miserable, and punishing, but preferable to the alternative of waiting, motionless in the darkness, for Kyrinin to creep out of the moonshadows with murderous intent.

"Out of where?" he asked. "The Veiled Woods, you mean?"

Yvane nodded, trying to break a piece off a biscuit with her teeth, failing, and staring doubtfully at it. "The ground's been rising under us since daybreak. Haven't you noticed that the mountains are near?"

Orisian peered up through the latticework of branches over their heads. His eyes had, this morning, been fixed on the ground beneath his feet. He saw now that Yvane was right. The Karkyre Peaks were close. He could see the texture of their sunlit eastern slopes, and of the clouds around their summits. The snow, white strands laid down in the crannies and crevices of the high rock faces.

"No choice but to press on, unless you mean to stand and fight," Yvane muttered.

Orisian said nothing. He gazed up at those lofty slopes. He could almost imagine what it would be like to be up there – high and fresh, washed by the cold winds, with wide-open views – instead of here, trapped in the suffocating woodland.

"I doubt if the White Owls will keep chasing us all the way across the Peaks," Yvane said. "Not really their sort of hunt, out in the open like that. Mind you, I'd never have believed they'd come all the way through the *Hymyr Ot'tryn*. Kyrinin'd usually rather lose a finger off their bowstring hand than risk disturbing the Anain. Whatever – whoever – is driving them, it must be strong. Hard." She paused. "Where do you mean to go, then?"

Orisian lowered his eyes. "Once we've shaken off the White Owls, then we'll see. Kolkyre, at first, I should think."

He glanced across at K'rina. The mute *na'kyrim* was sitting with her back against a grassy bank, turning her head this way and that in an effort to avoid the waterskin that Eshenna insisted upon holding to her lips.

"I'll have to find Taim," he said. "I've let him down."

"You think so?"

"I should have gone to Kolglas. We gained nothing at Highfast, and nothing out here." Again, that quick, surreptitious flick of the eyes towards K'rina. "Rothe's died, and the others, for nothing."

Yvane sniffed. She gave up gnawing at the biscuit and put it back into the folded square of burlap from which it had come. "I don't think so. Not at all. Whatever's happening here, it matters. The Anain have put their mark on this woman. I can't tell you what it means, but I can tell you it matters."

"Enough for Rothe to pay for it with his life?"

"He chose how he died. That's the best any of us can ever hope for, that choice."

"You think he chose that?"

"Maybe he chose it the day he took whatever oath it is you make them take. Your shieldmen. He took that oath willingly, I imagine? You didn't have to force him?"

"Of course not."

"Then he chose the possibility, at least. Accepted it."

Orisian almost hated Yvane in that moment; hated the ease with which she talked of such things. But he lacked the will to take issue with her.

"Don't let it harden your heart too much," Yvane murmured. "Don't let it cloud your vision. Hatred, anger: those are the commonest offspring of loss. Doesn't mean they're the best. You Huanin are always making the past master of the present. You make yourselves willing heirs to every grievance of your forefathers; let the burden of every loss or sorrow bend your back. It's the choices you make for yourself in the future that matter, not those you inherit from the past. That's all I'm saying."

"My vision's not clouded," Orisian muttered, wincing and sighing in pain as his tongue faltered over the ruin of his jaw. He put a hand to his cheek, feeling the stitches there and the angry, swollen crust of the wound.

"You think not. But you should be careful of your feelings. We all should be. The Shared is untrustworthy now. It's thick with rage, bitterness. Give it space, and it'll take root in your head, feed off your own feelings. Twist them. None of us is beyond its reach."

Orisian let his hand fall back into his lap. He was so tired, in heart as well as body. He could not see how any of this could come to any good, how there could be healing at the end of this. Too many people had died, now, and too many wounds had been inflicted for there to be any dawn at the end of this night. He had never understood, while his father lived, quite what afflicted Kennet after Lairis and Fariel died. Now, he thought he could glimpse a little of it. It had been absences. The absence of hope, the absence of meaning and sense from the world around him.

"Rothe was a good man," Yvane said. Her voice was heavy. For the first time since he had met her, Orisian thought he heard true, deep grief there. He looked at her.

"I don't think he would regret having died in your defence," she said.

K'rina coughed, spluttering out the water Eshenna had trickled into her mouth. Orisian looked across towards the two *na'kyrim*. Eshenna was distressed. She edged away from K'rina, defeated.

"No," Orisian murmured. "He wouldn't have regretted it."

They came to the edge of the Veiled Woods amidst a misty rain that hid the mountains ahead of them. Everyone climbed up out of the forest onto open hillside with a collective sense of relief. For the first time in days Orisian heard something close to laughter in the voices of Torcaill's men. Torcaill himself had an air of renewed determination.

"Where now?" the warrior asked Orisian.

Orisian looked back at the thicket from which they had emerged. Ess'yr and Varryn were still in there somewhere. There had been no sign of White Owls since dawn, and none of the Fox either.

"Eshenna," Orisian called out. "Do you know where we are?"

She shook her head.

"Closest food and shelter is likely to be Stone," Yvane muttered. "Never been there, but it's on the Kyre, high on the western side of the Peaks."

"We'll try for there, then," Orisian said to Torcaill. "And then Kolkyre, as fast as we can. Give the men a little rest, and food."

"Might be best to put some more ground between us and the woods," Torcaill suggested. "We could climb higher before resting."

"No. Once we're moving I don't want us stopping until we have to. We'll rest here for a little while."

They settled on the damp grass just beyond an arrow's reach from the trees. Torcaill shared out food and water amongst his men. Both were running low. No one had eaten as much as their hunger demanded since the day they had entered the Veiled Woods. Orisian sat facing down towards the forest, watching its edge through the drizzle. He waited as long as he thought he dared, then a fraction longer. He could hear the warriors behind him, further up the slope, growing restive. Just as he rose reluctantly to his feet, he saw what he had been hoping for: Ess'yr and Varryn coming out from amongst the trees. They loped up, heads angled away from the rain.

Varryn was injured, Orisian saw. A strip of hide was tied about his shoulder, holding a wad of moss or herbs over a wound. It did not seem to hamper him.

"The enemy falter," Ess'yr said. "They have not enough heart for the chase. If they come further, it will only be few."

"Good," Orisian said, and smiled. "Good. We mean to go on, across the Peaks."

Ess'yr nodded. "We will follow your trail. Guard your heels. Fox know high ground better than White Owl."

Varryn spoke quickly and sharply to his sister in their own tongue. Orisian caught the tone, even if he could understand none of the words: argumentative, contradictory. Ess'yr murmured a soft reply. Varryn turned his gaze upon Orisian. There were flecks of blood laid over the warrior's tattoos, tiny dark, dry spots across his cheek. There was no way to tell whether it was his own or someone else's.

"I ask something of you," Varryn said.

"What?" Orisian asked. Ess'yr was turning away, moving off across the fall of the slope. Orisian watched her go.

"Tell my sister you need us no more," said Varryn. "Tell her it is done. There is no promise to hold her. No need."

"You want to leave?" Orisian asked him, still unable to tear his eyes away from Ess'yr's retreating back.

"You go where we are not welcome. Our fight is with the White Owl."

Ess'yr squatted down, laying her bow and spear out on the grass. Orisian looked at Varryn. The Kyrinin's gaze was intense and demanding.

"And Ess'yr does not want to go?" Orisian asked. "Is it the *ra'tyn*? The promise she made to Inurian?"

"Tell her there is no need," Varryn said.

"I don't think your fight is only with the White Owl, any more than mine is only with Horin-Gyre," Orisian said. "Things have changed. We're not just fighting the old battles any more."

"Nevertheless. I ask you to release my sister. She does not see clearly in this. She sees in you the . . . child, the memory, of the *na'kyrim* she loved."

"Inurian," Orisian snapped. "His name was Inurian." He knew Varryn had never been fond of Inurian, had undoubtedly disapproved of his sister's involvement with him. His temper was too easily stirred to let such things go unchallenged now.

"Will you speak to her?" Varryn asked, unmoved.

Orisian looked at Ess'yr once more. Could she hear what they were saying? He was not sure. She gave no sign of it, but he had grown used to a paucity of signs where the Kyrinin were concerned. She was balanced on her haunches, unstringing her bow, or replacing the string. She did it, as she did everything, with delicate, careful hands.

Nothing good had come out of all that had happened since Winterbirth, save perhaps this, Orisian thought. Save Ess'yr. He did not know whether she only saw in him a reminder of Inurian and, he found, he did not care. A multitude of thoughts jostled for his attention, each momentary and passing. If Varryn and Ess'yr went alone back into the Veiled Woods, or tried to make their way north, they would surely die. The distances were too great, the dangers too numerous. And he did not want this parting. He was selfishly afraid of it, of the loss it would entail.

"No," he said. "We're all fighting the same battle, even if you don't believe it. I won't send her away. I'll not tell her — or you — either to stay or to go. She can make her own choices in this. We all do."

Varryn stalked away from him without another word. Orisian hung his head for a moment, and then turned to tell Torcaill to ready the company for the mountains. He found Yvane staring at him. The na'*kyrim* was sitting cross-legged, absently scratching the back of her hand and watching him with rare intensity.

"What?" he asked her.

She shook her head, and dropped her gaze to her hands. "Nothing."

II

As they struggled through the Karkyre Peaks, Orisian was constantly beset by images and memories of the Car Criagar. Now, as then, there was snow and biting winds, though the cold was not quite as deep and his clothes offered more protection. Now, as then, he fought as much against grief and fear as he did against the elements and the brutal terrain. This time, though, he was possessed of an anger that had not been in him before. It was a hard and uncomfortable sensation, lodged like a splinter in his mind. He distrusted it, and doubted it, but could not — or did not want to — rid himself of it. He thought he had learned that vengeance could not heal his wounds, yet now he found himself craving it. The desire crept up on his weary thoughts every now and then, twisted them into the certainty that what was required was death, and yet more death. Every time he lapsed into such bitter reverie, he had to shake himself free of it. And every time he felt a little more distanced from himself, as if he was becoming a stranger inside his own skull.

They followed goat trails through the stone wilderness of the

Peaks, and saw no one. They moved slowly. The paths were narrow and often little more than scratches on the sheer flanks of the mountains. Two of Torcaill's warriors were carrying wounds that hampered them, and K'rina had to be helped and herded like a weak child. Eshenna too was tiring. They had to stop often, and rest as best they could on the exposed slopes.

There was little talk. It was not just weariness, Orisian suspected, but apprehension at the thought of what might await them once they left the Peaks behind. He felt like a sailor returning from a long voyage, without word of what to expect on his return, but filled with presentiments of ill tidings. He told himself that he would most likely find Aewult nan Haig triumphant, the Black Road driven back from Glasbridge and Anduran. He tried to believe it. And in any case, he wondered, if that was indeed what they found, what then would Rothe and the others have died for? Nothing more than the faulty instincts of their Thane?

Every night, there was the threat of a renewed assault by White Owls. Each night it did not come, and slowly the fear of it dwindled. Ess'yr and Varryn still hung back, disappearing from sight for as much as half a day at times. They – or Ess'yr, at least, for Varryn had not spoken to him since the day they left the Veiled Woods – brought no word of pursuit when they returned from their wanderings. The relief Orisian felt at that was muted and sour. It was too late for Rothe. He asked himself again and again whether he would have followed Eshenna out from Highfast, had he known what would come of it, and never found an answer.

Stone lived up to its name. It was a broad sprawl of rock-built cottages above the gorge of the Kyre river. There was a quarry full of massive stone blocks and boulders beside it, as if some giant of the One Race had taken a huge bite out of the mountainside and spat out the shattered remnants. They came to the village from the north, crossing a saddle between two jagged peaks in the teeth of a bitter wind. The roaring river lay between them and Stone, and swaying over the foamy waters was a fragile-looking bridge of rope and planking.

Even reaching the bridge was an unnerving task, for the trail cut its way back and forth down an almost sheer cliff. It was littered with loose pebbles and riven with cracks. Every moment of their descent seemed laden with the possibility of disaster. His first few tentative paces onto the bridge convinced Orisian that it was at least as full of unfortunate potential. It swung and shifted beneath him like a living thing, responding to every surge of the wind. He grasped the rough rope tightly and kept his eyes fixed on the cluster of houses ahead.

People were gathering there: a small, curious crowd of onlookers. Orisian could guess how cautious and uncertain he and all the others must appear as they crept across the flimsy span. He did not care. Stone looked bleak, and rough, and impoverished, but it was a welcome sight. Only now, seeing those low, solid huts and the lights burning in the windows and the woodsmoke being whipped away by the gale, did the Veiled Woods and the White Owls and even the Anain feel as though they were at last falling away behind him. As he stepped off the last wet wooden plank and set his foot down on rock, it was like crossing a boundary, returning to a world more familiar.

He turned to watch Torcaill and Yvane and the rest struggling across the bridge. Eshenna had to coax and edge K'rina across, the two women almost embracing. Orisian was assailed by the image of the two of them toppling and plunging into the torrent, carrying with them the last vestige of sense to all that had happened. Only Ess'yr and Varryn, bringing up the rear, were casual, striding nonchalantly without so much as a glance down.

Torcaill stood at his side, clearly relieved at having survived the crossing.

"Here comes the welcoming party," the warrior grunted.

Four men were tramping down towards them, led by one who looked like he had been hewn from the fabric of mountains himself: burly, grey-bearded, rough-skinned and carrying a long spear. He rested its butt on the ground and stood tall before Orisian.

"Don't get many strangers coming that way," he observed gruffly.

"I'm not surprised." Orisian grimaced. "That bridge isn't the most easy of approaches."

"I am Captain of the Guard here," the old warrior said. He was looking beyond Orisian, and his surprise at what he saw – fighting men, *na'kyrim*, Kyrinin – was obvious. He shifted his weight uneasily, tightened his grip upon his spear. "I'll need to know who you are, and what your business is here."

"We've no business here, save the hope of a night's shelter, and of some supplies for our journey. My name's Orisian." That did not sound enough, and he hesitated for only an instant before adding: "I am the Thane of the Lannis-Haig Blood."

The man smiled, and opened his mouth to make some scoffing retort. His certainty faltered as he saw Orisian's expression, and as Torcaill leaned a little closer. He narrowed his eyes.

"You don't have the look of a Thane."

Orisian put a self-conscious hand to the great welt of a wound that disfigured his cheek. The stitches were gone, cut agonisingly out that morning. It was still swollen, though, and tender.

"What's your name, Captain?" Orisian asked him softly.

"Kollen."

"Very well, Kollen. I am Orisian oc Lannis-Haig. And I am tired and cold and hungry. I would be grateful if you could tell us where we can find some food and drink and a fire to warm ourselves at."

They were ushered into a wide, circular hut and settled around the open fire burning in its centre. There were animal hides stretched across the stone walls, picks and hammers leaning against them. The wind gusted across the smoke-hole in the roof, but the air within was hot and close.

Kollen remained doubtful. He said nothing to challenge Orisian's claim, but he and a few of his Guard stood there, wary, while villagers brought food. Children clustered in the doorway, staring curiously at these newcomers; wide-eyed and murmuring at the sight of two Kyrinin sitting cross-legged in the gloom.

"What news is there?" Orisian asked between mouthfuls of stew. "Have you heard whether the fighting's done, in the north?"

"No, the fighting's not done," said Kollen. "Not last we heard. We don't hear much up here, and what we do hear's not much sense. Got a message to arm two dozen fighting men and send them to Kolkyre, then two days later a message saying not. Then rumour is that the army's gathering after all . . ." He waved his hands helplessly. "Who can say?"

"If the fighting's not done, your men should march," Orisian said. "You have to wait to be told to march against the Black Road?" It took so little now to wake his anger. The slightest breath upon its glowing embers could summon up a small flame.

Out of the corner of his eye, he saw Torcaill stiffen.

"You shouldn't let others do the dying on your behalf," Orisian muttered. Then, faintly: "You shouldn't stand aside. That's all."

"I do as my Thane commands me," the Captain growled darkly.

"Yes. I'd not question Lheanor's—"

"Roaric, now," Kollen interrupted him. "Lheanor's dead."

Orisian set down his bowl. "How?"

"Black Road, they say. Inside the Tower of Thrones."

"I'm sorry. We did not now. Was there . . . do you know if anyone else was killed? Hurt?"

Kollen shook his head. On the far side of the fire, K'rina groaned a little. She was hunched up, wrapped in a shawl that Eshenna had found in a corner. Kollen looked sharply at the *na'kyrim*.

"Is she sick? If she's sick . . ."

"It's nothing," said Orisian. "Nothing she can pass to anyone else, at least. We only want a place to sleep. We'll be gone in the morning."

Kollen stared at him. He scratched his chin, fingers raking through his beard. The gesture reminded Orisian of Rothe.

"What's the Thane of the Lannis Blood doing wandering around the Karkyre Peaks, then?" Kollen asked.

Orisian took up the steaming bowl of stew again, and frowned down into it. "Just trying to get home. That's all."

In the morning there was a dusting of snow across Stone. The wind had swept it from the exposed stretches of ground and packed it up against walls and into crevices. The village came alive before dawn. Orisian was already out, sitting on a huge square-cut slab of rock, when the eastern sky began to lighten behind the Peaks. He watched a pair of young boys drive a little flock of goats, vague shapes in the half-light, out across the mountainside, and wondered what pasture they could possibly find in this bare place. Some of the animals wore little bells at their necks. They rang and clattered their way through the village.

A little way further down towards the bridge, Torcaill and his men were gathered, talking quietly, preparing for the renewal of their march. Kollen had given them two men to act as guides, down through the foothills until they reached the road between Ive and Kolkyre. He had done it grudgingly, and Orisian blamed himself for that fact. He had spoken without thought, and without care.

The valley of the Kyre ran away, seemingly endless, into the north and west, sinking all the time. At the outermost limit of his sight, Orisian could see sunlight on summits. They shone. Here in Stone, though, the greatest heights of the Peaks still stood between him and the sun. A woman emerged in the doorway of a nearby hut, shaking out a blanket. It was an action that belonged so wholly and utterly to the mundane world of daily life that it transfixed Orisian. He stared at the woman's blunt outline, the snapping flurry of the blanket, as if seeing something wondrous, something he had never before witnessed. She looked up at him. He could not make out her features in the gloom. She turned and disappeared into the hut.

And Orisian sobbed. Just once: an abrupt, convulsive sob that burst up from within him and shook his shoulders and squeezed water from his eyes. He sniffed and blinked and pressed his sleeve against his eyes, drew it across his nose. His jaw ached, and he feared for a moment that he might have split open his cheek.

Ess'yr was there, on the fringe's of Torcaill's huddle of warriors. Beside those burly figures, she was lean and lithe, standing straight, and looking up at Orisian. He wanted to hide in that moment, wanted to take his terrible smallness and fragility and burrow it down into some safe cranny where he could close his eyes and sleep away this bitter winter. But he returned her gaze; held it for what felt like an age. When at last she turned away, he rose and went down to join them.

III

The Inkallim came to Hommen out of fog. On such heavy air there was no sound to warn of their coming. They emerged, a dark mass, silently; scores of them. Hundreds, perhaps. Fiallic the Banner-captain rode at the head of the long column. Amongst the marching warriors were small groups of captive children, stumbling along in tight, frightened knots, herded by Hunt Inkallim and their dogs. Even those beasts were silent, their baleful presence alone enough to cow the children into terrified obedience.

Kanin oc Horin-Gyre was bitterly disappointed to see them

come, for he was planning slaughter, and feared that their arrival
would deprive him of it. He had his whole little army ready for
battle, taut like a drawn bowstring. The battle he hoped for was
not with the Haig Bloods, though. His spears and shields faced
not south or west, but east. The enemy approaching was Aeglyss
and those – hundreds, by all accounts – who marched with him.

Kanin had been ready to march himself within hours of hearing of Wain's death. He meant, in the towering, agonised fury
that mastered him then, to sweep up the coast and on to Kan
Avor, and to turn that ruined city into a slaughterhouse. The
orders for assembly had been given, the plans made. But word
came that Aeglyss was on the move himself, descending the Glas
valley, marching to join the army of the Black Road, beyond
Hommen. As soon as he heard that news, Kanin thought he
glimpsed an inevitable future: fate would deliver Aeglyss into his
arms, onto his swords. He need only wait, and ready himself, and
brood, rehearsing endlessly in his imagination the death of the
halfbreed.

That hope was snatched away by the emergence of the Inkallim
from the wintry mists. Fiallic and Goedellin of the Lore came to
him, but he already knew what they would say. He could read the
denial of his desires in the old man's hobble, and in the warrior's
grave face.

"Word reached us of your sister's death," Goedellin said.
"Killed in the struggle against Temegrin's company, when the
Eagle assailed Kan Avor in pursuit of Gryvan's Shadowhand. Such
is the tale that reached us."

"I heard the same. I do not believe it."

"No," Goedellin said. "I did not expect that you would. We
doubt it ourselves, though the truth remains obscure. It has
proved . . . difficult to obtain reliable information on what has
taken place at Kan Avor. Even Cannek has not been able to sift
fact from rumour."

"I don't need the Hunt to tell me what happened," Kanin

growled. "My sister is dead. The Eagle is dead. Whose hand wielded the blade does not matter. Aeglyss is responsible."

"And what do you intend to do about it?"

"I mean to destroy the halfbreed, and any who stand at his side."

Goedellin nodded. He smiled. Kanin saw sympathy in that smile, but he was beyond its reach.

"You burn, Thane. The fires of grief burn in you, to be quenched only by blood. Hold fast to your faith, though. Your sister has passed from this world, and now awaits her birth in another, better one. She feels no sorrow, or pain, and must no longer suffer the miseries that we who remain are subject to. The grief you feel is not for her, but for yourself, deprived of her company."

For the first time in his life, Kanin felt the urge to decry such pieties, even those uttered by an Inner Servant of the Lore himself. No, he thought. No, this is not a selfish grief, and it is not a deluded one. Wain was betrayed, and it is not fate that bears the responsibility, but one man. If the creed would deny that, I choose what my own heart tells me over the creed. As soon as that thought was in his mind, he was shamed by it. Nothing he had been taught by his father, his mother, or even Wain herself would condone such arrogance. He could be shamed by it, though, and still know – in his gut, and his heart – that it was true.

"There is a great battle waiting to be fought," Goedellin said. "Just ahead of us, a few more paces, a few more days, down the Black Road. If we are its victors, this world will be changed. And if we are to be worthy of any victory that fate might offer, we must be united. Of one mind, clean and humble. The Banner-captain of the Battle is to be the one who leads us, who bears all our hopes."

Kanin looked towards Fiallic. The Inkallim was a silent and still observer, a model of respect. Everything in his expression and his posture suggested deference to the old, hunched man who was speaking. Speaking platitudes, Kanin's seething mind insisted.

Goedellin stirred the snow at his feet with the butt of his walking stick. "The Children of the Hundred believe the *na'kyrim* can be of no further service to our cause. His part in this is done."

"You mean that you now fear him," Kanin muttered. "You see, too late, that he is a poison, who won't be controlled any more than . . ."

"Enough," Goedellin said. "His presence no longer serves the creed. Satisfy yourself with that. But we will end his service, Thane. Not you. If it comforts you, think thus: your heart will have its desire, for the halfbreed will die. But not by your hand." His beady eyes narrowed. "You would be better served by taking comfort in your faith. Fate has its plan for us all and, no matter how fierce the passions that burn in our breast, it cannot be gainsaid. If it's bloodshed you crave, seek it on the field of battle, on the road to Kolkyre. The world waits to be subdued, Thane. That's the cause in which to spend your anger now."

"I will try to remember your guidance," Kanin said. He was curt, unable to pretend to any enthusiasm. Goedellin appeared satisfied.

"There is often benefit concealed in the cruellest cuts," the old Inkallim said. "We all serve a higher purpose. We are working for the deliverance of the world, of all humankind, out of shadow and into light. The *na'kyrim* has served that purpose, as he was fated to do. Your sister's death was unlooked for – I dared to hope she would be a faithful servant of the creed in this world for years to come – but that of Temegrin is a boon, even if it brings with it much uncertainty and risk. It removes an obstacle upon our path, for he sought too often to pull against the current of fate.

"And if it is true, as rumour testifies, and as Temegrin believed, that the halfbreed has somehow brought the Chancellor of the Haig Blood within our grasp, we will look back on these as days when fate truly smiled upon our endeavours."

Kanin turned away. He could not stand and listen to this, for fear that his innermost thoughts would burst free and condemn him in the eyes of the Lore. Walking away, he had never been so alone. All that had surrounded him throughout his life – his Blood, his faith, his sister – was gone, burned off like a mist consumed by the sun's unforgiving gaze. He moved through an empty landscape, one he did not recognise, populated by people whose language he no longer understood.

The straggling host that came to Hommen the next day was as strange as any that Kanin had ever seen. He could see no order in it, no columns or ranks. It came down the coast road from Kolglas like a huge, leaderless herd of cattle. Standing with Fiallic and Goedellin, amidst the assembled might of the Battle Inkall and his own Blood's warriors, he looked out through softly falling snow and saw Kyrinin – scores of them – coming along the higher ground on the landward side of the road. He saw Tarbains milling about on the flanks of the moving mass; standards and pennants of his own Blood, and Gyre and Fane, lurching along in its dark heart. And Shraeve at the forefront, her ravens around her. Aeglyss rode beside her, small in the saddle; limp.

Something else came with this ragged army. Something that Kanin could not see, or hear, but that stole across his skin and shadowed his mind. This host drove a bow wave of foreboding before it, and Kanin felt it wash over him, felt the idea take root in his mind that this was more than a mere assembly of warriors; that it was somehow fate itself, given form. He doubted all his certainties in that moment. He saw his loathing for Aeglyss clearly for what it was: the futile, foolish ravings of a child standing in the path of one of the Tan Dihrin's grinding glaciers, commanding it to turn aside from its chosen path.

It was the thought of Wain that drew him back. The clear memory of her, riding away from him that last time they had spoken, was handhold enough for him to keep his grip upon his self. Aeglyss was only a man, his resilient hatred insisted. He would die like any other.

The whole eastern side of Hommen, from the crumbling watchtower all the way down to the sea, was defended. A thicket of spears and shields and swords barred the way. Kanin heard the uncertain murmuring that rippled through the ranks as Aeglyss drew near. He even saw a few of his own warriors shuffling backwards, looking around with hunted, fearful eyes. He shouted at them. Most, but not all, obediently resumed their places in the line.

Aeglyss dismounted. He moved like an old man whose brittle bones might snap under his own weight, Kanin thought. When the halfbreed walked slowly forwards, Shraeve flanked him on one side, a powerfully built Kyrinin warrior on the other. Kanin had eyes only for Aeglyss, though. He stared, and knew his hatred would be shining, obvious. He could not have concealed it, even had he wished to.

Aeglyss lifted his arms and spread his hands. Shraeve and the woodwight stopped, letting him take a few paces beyond them. The *na'kyrim* faced Fiallic, but the Inkallim ignored him; looked beyond him, and spoke to his fellow raven.

"This man is to be surrendered to the Hunt," he said to Shraeve. "He goes no further than this."

"No," Aeglyss said.

Fiallic continued to address Shraeve. "And the Shadowhand, as well, if you have him here."

The *na'kyrim* grimaced. "We have him. He is bound for Vaymouth. Nowhere else. He carries a message from me to the Thane of Thanes."

At last Fiallic turned his gaze upon Aeglyss.

"You will be sending messages to no one. We require the Shadowhand. And you. It is not a matter of choice."

"Nothing is about choice to you, is it? Your miserable, gloomy little creed does not . . . ah." He flicked a dismissive hand at the Banner-captain and turned, began to walk away.

Now he dies, thought Kanin, with both a shiver of anticipation and a twist of regret. It would not be his own hand that took the halfbreed's life, but the fact of his death was the most important thing.

"Where is my sister?" he shouted after Aeglyss.

He thought he saw the *na'kyrim*'s head lift a little at his call, but Aeglyss did not look around or slow his stride. Fiallic stepped forwards after the halfbreed, and set his hand on the hilt of his sword.

Aeglyss paused at Shraeve's side, leaning on her shoulder. It looked like a moment of feebleness. He stretched his head up and whispered something to her. She was watching Fiallic, and did not seem to react to the *na'kyrim*'s words. Fiallic came on. And Shraeve blocked his path, putting Aeglyss at her back.

The two Inkallim faced each other, snowflakes tumbling about them. Kanin frowned. He had a sudden, lurching sense of disorientation, as of a man poised on the brink of a precipice. But this was not the dizziness of height; it was an imbalance of the world, a twisting away, out of reach, of possibilities and hopes.

"Stand aside," Fiallic said quietly.

Shraeve only shook her head, stirring little accumulations of snow from her shoulders.

Aeglyss was still walking away, stoop-shouldered, frail. "She sees what you cannot, raven," he said. He turned, amongst his woodwights once more. "You think it is the sun of your power, your authority, that still illuminates the clouds, but your eyes deceive you. It is only afterlight, Fiallic: the fading echo of a day that's already passed. Shraeve has set her face towards the new dawn."

"With regret," Shraeve said, "I challenge you, Banner-captain. I make a claim to your rank and your standing in the Battle. I ask that we reveal fate's intent, in this matter that comes between us."

"No," Kanin heard Goedellin saying behind him. The old Lore Inkallim pushed forwards, stabbing his crooked stick into the soft snow. His hooked back held his head no higher than Kanin's chest, but Goedellin's voice was clear, with all the vigour of his authority. "This is not a fit time for such an issue to be tested, Shraeve. Later, if you must, but first this half-wight is to be—"

"This is a matter for the Battle," Shraeve said levelly. "The fitness of the time is no concern for the Lore, or for any of us. I have seen things . . . I believe that this *na'kyrim* is here because he has a great purpose to serve, a great fate to live out. I have seen enough to leave me without doubts in this. If you mean to kill him, I must oppose you. I am entitled."

Fiallic shifted sideways. Shraeve matched his movement. Beyond them, Aeglyss was watching. There was such contemptuous confidence on his inhuman face that Kanin felt a flicker of alarm.

"I make a claim on the place of Banner-captain," Shraeve insisted. "Fate's judgement is infallible. Let us face it together, Fiallic. There is nothing improper in my challenge." She bowed low, bending from the waist, her head almost brushing Fiallic's chest in its descent.

Again Goedellin thumped the butt of his walking stick down, punching a hole into the snow. Fiallic looked round to the Lore Inkallim, and in the raven's expression Kanin saw the betrayal of everything he had hoped for from this day.

"She is entitled," the Banner-captain said. "The rule of the Battle permits it."

"No," Kanin said before he could help himself, but no one paid him any heed. Shraeve was still bent over, perfectly poised and still. Fat snowflakes dotted her back.

"It will be no service to the creed for either of you to die today," Goedellin growled.

"Do you fear to let fate play itself out, old man?" Aeglyss shouted. "I do not. Let the ravens dance their dance. If she fails, you can have my life, and welcome to it."

Fiallic was already backing away. He settled himself a spear's reach from Shraeve, and slowly bowed down. Goedellin gave an irate snort and stamped away. Shraeve straightened.

"Choose the field, Banner-captain," she said.

There was, on bare, rising ground beyond Hommen's southern-most dwelling, a great sheep pen: a low stone wall that described a perfect circle across the slope. Snow had piled up against the wall: and laid itself into every crevice between the stones. Outside that circle, another assembled itself, Battle Inkallim ringing the killing ground within. They stood in single rank, thirty of them, widely spaced. Each one of them took position and then set their own weapons down on the snow behind them. Beyond that ring of swords and knives the crowds assembled.

Hundreds were there, of many Bloods, of many callings. Warriors and commoners, Inkallim and Kyrinin. And one Thane. Kanin stood above the pen. The snow blew into his face, carried on a sharp wind, but he barely felt it. The flakes were coming down thickly enough now to almost obscure the village below them. The old watchtower was an indistinct hulking mass, the cottages spread around it blurred into a single grey-black shape. The harbour and the sea beyond were gone, sunk away into the winter. Kanin spared none of it more than a moment's glance.

His attention was upon the two figures alone in the centre of the stone enclosure, facing each other in the heart of the white circle that it contained.

Fiallic had sword and shield, Shraeve her twin blades. Neither of them moved for what seemed an interminable time. Snow spun between them, caught in eddies of the air.

"My feet are on the Road," Shraeve said.

"My feet are on the Road," Fiallic replied.

They began to circle one another, taking small, tight steps. Each was as graceful and balanced as the other. There was not a sound from all the great throng gathered to witness the trial between these two warriors. Kanin could hear the soft crunch of snow beneath their precise feet, and the threnodic calling of a crow somewhere far off to the south, and nothing else. The tension was acute, stiffening his back and drying his mouth.

Fiallic, he knew by reputation. It was said he had only ever been defeated once, by Nyve himself, in a wrestling match. That had been many, many years ago, when Fiallic was a teenager and Nyve not yet First, and the loss had, supposedly, cost the future Banner-captain a dislocated shoulder and a broken jaw. Shraeve, Kanin had seen for himself, dealing out slaughter on the battlefield at Grive, and at Glasbridge. She was as ferocious a warrior as he had ever shared a field with, but single combat was – should be – different. Kanin had to believe that Fiallic was more than a match for her in this narrow, snowy arena. The alternative was too bitter a prospect to contemplate.

They were like fighting dogs, he thought, taking the measure of one another. Round and round they circled, their eyes locked and almost unblinking, blades steady. Kanin brushed snow from the crown of his head.

Shraeve moved so completely without warning that he lost track of her for an instant, and only heard rather than saw the clatter of steel on shield, the flurry of quick feet advancing and retreating. Fiallic spun out of her path, cutting at her flank as he went. She blocked the blow with one sword, stabbed in over it with the other. But Fiallic was gone already, gliding over the snow. Neither of them was breathing hard, Kanin could see. Neither looked as though they were engaged in anything more serious or strenuous than a casual training exercise. Shraeve shook her arms, shifted her weight from one foot to another and back again, and rushed in once more.

They battled their way around that walled killing ground, and the patterns they described with bodies and blades were as intricate as any dance. There was, indeed, a certain intimacy, a certain isolation, to the intensity with which the two of them engaged.

They were shaping something, together, alone, that belonged to them and to no one else.

Fiallic deflected an assault, then countered with the shield itself, slashing with its rim at Shraeve's face. It was as smooth and fast a movement as Kanin had ever seen in combat, but not quite fast enough to catch Shraeve. She ducked aside. For just that one fraction of a heartbeat, her balance was less than perfect, and Fiallic's sword came hacking down on her weight-bearing leg. Kanin broadened his shoulders, ready to cry out in acclamation of the victory. Shraeve sprang, drove herself up off that leg, twisting in the air to swing it out of the path of Fiallic's blade. The blow still caught her, but it was only glancing, skidding off her calf. Still, it tumbled her. She landed on fists and knees in a spray of snow. There was blood on her leg.

Fiallic darted in. Shraeve spiralled up and away, like an acrobat, and was on her feet, flicking his attack aside. He has her, though, Kanin thought. He has the tiniest fragment of greater speed, the minutely sharper eye that is required of the victor. He will kill her. And then Aeglyss.

At the thought of the *na'kyrim*, Kanin tore his eyes away from the furious struggle within the enclosure, searching for him. Aeglyss was there, further down the slope, some way round the perimeter of the crowd. He was amongst his Kyrinin, thirty or forty of them. One of them was supporting him. Look at him, Kanin thought. Unable to even stand straight. Any eye can see the man's sick; dying already, perhaps. Why would Shraeve sacrifice herself in such a perverse cause? What hold is it that this creature exerts?

The ringing of blades snapped his attention back to the sheep pen. Fiallic was rushing Shraeve, driving her backwards in a blindingly fast flurry of blows and blocks and feints. He forced her to the wall of their arena, pinning her against its rough stone surface. His shield pushed back one sword, he parried her second with his own blade, and butted her across the bridge of her nose.

Kanin saw the blood bloom, and smear down her face, and once again he thought she must be finished now. But Shraeve ducked down, put her shoulder into Fiallic's armpit and heaved him, by sheer strength, backwards and away from her. Blood dripped from her chin.

Kanin glanced back towards Aeglyss, wondering whether he would see fear there; whether the halfbreed could see his own death, coming down the track towards him. Instead, what he saw was Aeglyss swaying, his head twitching as if fending off flies. Even at this distance, Kanin could see a sheen of sweat on the halfbreed's forehead. There was a faint ringing in Kanin's ears, so faint he could not be sure he heard it.

He saw Fiallic falter, taking a hesitant half-step and giving his head a sharp shake. Shraeve closed on him. Kanin stared at Aeglyss, fury rising in him. The *na'kyrim*'s lips were drawn back from his teeth in a coarse grin of pain or pleasure. His mouth slowly opened. His inhuman eyes were following Fiallic's every movement. No, Kanin thought. No. His skin was tingling.

Fiallic blocked an attack, but he was slow. Shraeve got a cut in at his shoulder, putting a deep wound there. She had blood across her eyes. She should have been barely able to see. Fiallic staggered. He was blinking furiously. There was a look of strained surprise on his face. Inexplicably, he made no attempt to put his shield between himself and Shraeve. She squatted, bringing both blades flashing round in a flat sweep, one above the other, and a fraction behind. The first took Fiallic in the back of the knee, cutting one leg from under him. The second opened his hamstring.

He fell in the snow. Shraeve straightened, slow and considered now. She wiped one sleeve across her eyes, smudging a track through the blood. She walked towards Fiallic. He was rising unsteadily to his feet. Neither leg could take his full weight. He levered himself up with his sword, its point driven into the ground. Shraeve steadied both her blades, one low, one high, and ran at him.

Kanin was moving before Fiallic hit the ground. Intent and purpose had hold of him, and he was pushing his way through the crowd, elbowing people aside blindly. He could see Aeglyss, amongst his wight guards, could see his satisfaction. Kanin had his sword halfway from its scabbard. He heard Igris coming behind, shouting at people to move aside. They could reach the halfbreed, Kanin thought, surprised at the detached clarity of his mind. With his Shield at his side, he could cut through to Aeglyss. Kill him.

A firm hand on his arm twisted him aside. People were scattering, opening up a space of trampled, dirty snow. He was staring at Cannek, hearing the heavy breathing of one of the Inkallim's great dogs. Kanin pulled his arm free, but Cannek reached out and seized it again.

"Not now, Thane," he said softly. "Not now. He has his White Owls, and the Battle will defend him, if Shraeve commands it. And she will."

"Release me," Kanin hissed. The dog growled at the threat in his voice, but he did not care.

"How many swords do you have, Thane?" Cannek asked. He took his hand from Kanin's arm, but did not release his eyes. "Not enough. Not today."

Kanin stared at the Inkallim. The hard, insistent beat of anger was still there in his chest, but its mastery of him was broken for a moment. He looked down, over the heads of the crowd milling between them, and saw Aeglyss. The *na'kyrim* was watching him, a dead smile on his lips. Clouds of snowflakes swept between them.

"It was him," Kanin said. "Fiallic should have won. Would have done, but for him."

"There will be another time," Cannek whispered. "He has mastered the Battle today, but not the Lore. Not the Hunt. Do you hear me? You are Thane of your Blood. If you die today there is none to follow you."

Kanin let his blade slide back into its sheath. It was heavy on his hips, its presence still urging him to release it; use it. But Cannek was right. Fate favoured courage, but not always stupidity. He would die, with all his Shield, if he set himself against the White Owls and the Battle here and now. That did not matter in itself. What mattered was whether he could achieve the half-breed's death before his own. There would surely be another time, soon, when he could be more certain of that.

"The Haig army awaits us now. After that – if there is anything for us after that – we should talk, away from curious eyes and ears," Cannek said. Kanin was no longer listening to him, though.

The crowd was dispersing. There was laughter, here and there; excited voices raised. The tramp of feet across the snow-clad hillside, clouds of breath pluming up. And from the Inkallim, only silence, and obedience. As the others drifted away, they closed in, like black birds thickening on carrion, around the killing pen. Shraeve, Banner-captain of the Battle, climbed out and limped towards Aeglyss. Two of the Inkallim who had ringed the stone enclosure vaulted in and moved towards Fiallic's corpse. This was not how it was meant to be, Kanin was thinking. None of it. This is not fate, but ruin. The corruption of everything we desired. All our hopes. All shaking themselves to dust.

IV

Taim Narran watched Anyara's departure from a distance, for his captors would not permit him to approach her. The sister of his own Thane, and he was denied the chance to bid her farewell, or to comfort her. She bore it well, he could see, and gave no sign of needing his comfort: straight-backed on her horse, looking about her openly and without faltering. But how could she not be feeling vulnerable, beset? She was being carried off to Vaymouth by those whose professed friendship had become the thinnest of skins across the meat of their contempt. They did not call her a prisoner, and she did not comport herself as one, but the distinction between that and hostage was slender; and hostage she surely was. Hostage and shield, for Aewult clearly meant to use her – and Taim himself, and Orisian even – to deflect, or to absorb, his father's anger. Anger that might be savage, now that a battle had been lost, an army battered, a Chancellor mislaid.

Anyara left the camp of the Haig army in the midst of a long column of wagons, carrying the wounded and the sickly off towards Donnish. Taim stood and watched her go until the haze that lay along the coast swallowed her up. He had demanded of Aewult that he be allowed to accompany her, and the Bloodheir had smirked.

"No, Captain. I don't want you and her hatching plots together, the way you and your Thane did. Anyway, I want you to see the end of this. I want you here with me. Your reckoning will come after I'm done with the Black Road."

To Taim, Aewult reeked of fear. The Bloodheir might not even recognise that as what he was feeling, but Taim had no doubt. Aewult was afraid. And he was angry. Those were his reactions to defeat, and those were his reasons for his treatment of Anyara and Taim himself.

The entire army had the same stench. Like a stockman, granted by long familiarity the ability to read the mood of his animals, Taim could gather all the little signs and shape them into an instinctive understanding of the men around him. Everything – the downcast eyes, the bluff, forced laughter, the men staggering drunkenly about after dark – all of it spoke eloquently to him of trepidation. This army had the splinter of defeat lodged in its heart, and it would remain there, and fester, unless and until a cleansing victory was won. The men, the individual threads within the weave of the army, promised one another that they would be clambering over drifts of Black Road dead soon; they muttered around their campfires, painting word pictures of the terrible slaughter that they would visit upon their enemies. But it was lies; hopeful lies they told one another to stave off the doubts within.

New companies were coming up from the south. The grim mood opened its arms as they arrived and drew them in. Every man here on the plain outside Kolkyre knew that there was a terrible battle moving towards them. As surely as the turning seasons, violence was coming. It was like a dark, roiling storm approaching from the horizon. None could see beyond it. That the army of the Black Road had mysteriously slowed to a crawl, lingering in the empty lands along the north coast of Kilkry territory, only made the waiting harder and gave the foreboding more time to sink its roots deep.

Whenever Taim's gaze fell upon Kolkyre, with its ever-present seagulls circling above, and the Tower of Thrones defiantly punctuating its skyline, he feared that the future might be even bleaker than most imagined. The gates of the city were closed. Haig warriors were posted on each of the roads outside them. Nothing, and no one, came or went from Kolkyre save by sea. So, Aewult had pledged, it would remain, until Roaric oc Kilkry-Haig recovered his proper humility and complied with the demands made of him. And so, Roaric seemed to indicate by his mute refusal, he was content for it to remain. Neither man would earn respect or credit from this, Taim thought, but while he felt contempt for Aewult, he felt only pity for Roaric. The young Kilkry Thane had come into his power in evil times, and by evil circumstance, and his nature made him unsuited to facing the challenges of this moment. Perhaps he would learn, in time; perhaps, by the time he learned, it would be too late.

Taim wandered through the outskirts of the encampment, listless and dispirited. The men Aewult had set to watch him – surly, uncommunicative swordsmen – shadowed him at a few paces' distance. Taim paused to watch a gang of camp followers slaughtering a pair of pigs. The animals screamed and struggled. They were scrawny, and not likely to make good eating, but fresh meat was growing rare and precious. A youth held one of the pigs down while a woman cut its throat and it bled.

The morning after Anyara's departure, Taim discovered what her presence had meant to him personally. The whole camp was submerged beneath a miasma of steam and mist and smoke, through which sunlight shone in fragmentary rays, lighting frosted grass and iced puddles in the mud. Guards came to him and unceremoniously removed him from the tent in which he slept, herding him across the crunching ground.

There was a pile of barrels, some of them broken, and behind that a lopsided wagon that had lost a wheel and rested on the stub of its axle. Scattered around the wagon were a dozen or more men, sullen and gaunt. Each one of them was seated, or curled up, on the ground, wrapped in a blanket, and with a shackle running from his ankle to a spike hammered into the frozen soil. A pair of guards were sitting precariously on the elevated end of the wagon, muttering to each other.

As Taim silently allowed them to chain him down, and hobble his legs with cords, one of the guards leered at him from his lofty perch.

"The first time you try to pull up the spike, it's a beating," the man barked. "The second time it's a killing."

They gave him a blanket that smelled musty and old, and a platter of unidentifiable food. He pulled the blanket tight about his shoulders, closed his eyes and waited. And that was how he spent most of each day that followed.

Taim made no complaint to his guards, sought no gentler treatment, no finer food, no warmer cloak. He asked nothing of them, save one thing, and that one thing he requested every morning, every afternoon, every evening: he asked to be allowed to see his wife and his daughter.

There was no privation he could be subjected to that would disturb him, for he had been a warrior all his life, learned long ago that hunger, or cold, or discomfort could be set aside. But he was afraid now, acutely afraid, that he might die without seeing Jaen or Maira again, and that fear was almost intolerable. So he asked, every day, that they should be brought out from the city, and every day he was refused. And with each refusal, hatred for Aewult nan Haig and all his Blood gathered a little more of Taim's heart within its ambit.

He became more and more acutely aware of a contradiction in his hopes. He wanted – needed – Aewult to emerge triumphant from the great confrontation with the Black Road that must now be imminent; at the same time, he longed for the Bloodheir to be humbled, sent scurrying back to Vaymouth with shame swarming about his head. It was a bitter, resentful strand in his thoughts that felt uncomfortable and unfamiliar. He was dismayed that it so preoccupied him.

One night, it snowed. Taim pulled his blanket over his head. He felt the snow piling up on it. He lay there shivering and wondered if the Haig Blood had so lost its collective mind that it would allow him to die here.

He heard footsteps coming over the hard ground. Someone kicked him in the back, and when he sat up, spilling snow, one of the guards thrust another, thicker blanket into his hands. A small fire was built, and the prisoners shuffled into a circle around it, as close as their chains would allow. One man did not stir. He remained curled up like a snow-covered boulder. The guards kicked him once, twice, before they realised he was dead. They levered up the spike securing his chain to the ground and carried the body away.

In the morning, Aewult nan Haig came and squatted down on his haunches in front of Taim. He stayed out of reach.

"Time to get you back on horseback, Captain," the Bloodheir said, smiling.

Taim said nothing. Aewult stood up. He tapped the heel of one boot against the toe of the other to loosen snow from the sole.

"The Black Road is moving again. Seems they've found the courage to face us."

"Let me go back to my men," Taim said. He sat up straight, shrugging the blanket off his shoulders.

Aewult shook his head. "They'll be fighting under Haig command this time. What's left of them will, anyway. I've attached them to one of my father's best companies, from Vaymouth. I'll be keeping you as far away from them — as far away from everything of consequence — as possible. Oh, don't look so disappointed. You can't have expected me to do anything else, surely?"

"Despite everything, I will fight for you, Bloodheir. Against the Black Road, I will always fight. I only ask that you let me do that."

"No." The refusal was emphatic. "You stay a prisoner until this is done. Afterwards, we'll see what's to be done with you, but this is one battle you will watch with bound hands."

Taim struggled to his feet. He was painfully stiff.

"What of Kilkry-Haig?" he asked. "You need Roaric's strength at your side for this."

Aewult's face darkened, and he glared at Taim before spinning about and striding away.

"I'll not ask that prideful whelp for anything," he shouted over his shoulder. "If he chooses to come out and fight, all the better. But he'll do it under my command, or not at all."

* * *

Theor, First of the Lore, had spent a long and tedious day with his officials, seeing to the mundane trifles that kept the Inkall alive and functioning. Appointing tutors to see to the care of the Lore's youngest recruits; agreeing the names of those to be sent amongst the Tarbains once winter was done, to ensure the survival of the creed in their savage hearts; deciding the process of interrogation and examination for those seeking elevation to the ranks of the Inner Servants.

Theor found it difficult to concentrate on such matters. They did not bore him – they were the stitches that held the Inkall together, and he valued them as such – but he was weary and distracted. At dusk he trudged across the snow-filled compound, pausing only to listen to the hooting of an owl somewhere amongst the pine trees. He was not in the mood for company and conversation, so ordered that he be brought food in his own chambers. He ate there alone.

A message had come from Nyve that morning. The First of the Battle had received word from Fiallic, reporting the death of Temegrin the Eagle, in circumstances that remained unclear. It was news both encouraging and disquieting. Ragnor oc Gyre had conspired with the enemies of the creed to protect his own earthly power, and the Eagle was his mouthpiece, hampering every effort to pursue the conflict with the Haig Bloods to its necessary conclusion. His death was a sign that fate might, on this occasion, side with the Inkallim. Yet Wain nan Horin-Gyre had died, too. That was a sore loss. And the Thane of Thanes would not take the death of his Third Captain lightly. Theor anticipated difficulties in convincing Ragnor that the Children of the Hundred had no part in the deed.

The First set aside his half-eaten meal. His appetite was meagre these days. He reclined on his bed, staring up at the ceiling. According to Nyve, there was talk, far away beyond the Stone Vale, that the Horin Blood's tame *na'kyrim* had had a hand in Temegrin's death. That was a disconcerting thought. The very existence of such halfbreeds was an aspect of the hubris that had provoked the Gods into departure. Five races had been created, distinct and self-contained. *Na'kyrim* symbolised the inability of Huanin and Kyrinin to accept the boundaries laid down by the

Gods. To have one playing a role in matters of such import to the creed was . . . unexpected. Puzzling.

Theor rolled onto his side and reached down to the carved box on the floor. He removed a fragment of seerstem, slipped it into his mouth and lay back. He worked it gently between his teeth, feeling its black juices thicken his saliva. A cold tingling stole across his tongue and his cheeks, leaving numbness in its wake. It was a familiar sensation, and one that in years gone by he had always greeted with vague pleasure. Now, though, he felt an undeniable sense of trepidation. His seerstem dreams had been less than comforting of late. It was something all his schooling had not prepared him for. There was, to his knowledge, no precedent in the Lore's history for the powerful and unsettling visions that now came in seerstem's wake.

He was not alone in his experiences. Every one of the few senior Lore Inkallim permitted the use of the herb had been suffering similar disturbance of their meditation. There was much inconclusive debate about what it signified. Theor was himself uncertain, though he had his suspicions. Might it not be possible that they were caught up in the turbulence caused by a fateful convergence of great events? Might this even be the result of thousands upon thousands of lives being channelled into a single, unified path that would carry them all to the Kall itself, and to the ultimate realisation of the Black Road's entire purpose? He hardly dared to hope, and had taken care not to voice such thoughts.

Numbing tendrils spread across his skin, creeping over his scalp towards the back of his skull. He could feel his very thoughts slowing and retreating, leaving space behind them for other things to enter his mind. He closed his eyes.

Much could be gained from seerstem: a sense of the intricate immensity of life and mind, spread out across the world, the scale of the Gods' creation; a humbling awareness of the insignificance of any individual within that pattern. Sometimes it was even possible to glimpse fate's roots, the chains of events and deeds

stretching back from the present into the distant past. Such had
been the case until recently, at least. Theor did not expect what
awaited him now to be quite so soothing.

He felt as if he was sinking into the mattress, as if he himself
was a dwindling spark of light, fading. Anger flickered across the
surface of his mind: not anger to be felt, but anger as a wind that
blew upon him, anger that he tasted and heard. It was a rage
without cause and without object, like a fire that burned without
any fuel. After it came the sickening sense of a tumbling, plummeting fall. He was dimly aware that his hands were clutching
the bed sheet on which his distant body lay.

And then he was adrift in a dark and howling waste; suspended
in a limitless void, with titanic shapes moving far beneath him,
rolling as they hunted through the emptiness. Then flashes: he
was one amongst thousands, running along a hard road; he was
spun through treetops, carried on a vast and monstrous con-
sciousness; he was alone in darkness, where the very fabric of the
air was made of loneliness.

There was the figure of a man, an indistinct outline that spread
and broadened until it filled his field of view and shut out everything else. That figure's head turned, great planes of darkness
sliding over one another. Eyes opened – eyes that were first grey
then black then nothing, voids – and their gaze was a writhing,
piercing thing that burned its way in through Theor's own eyes
and his mouth and his nose and filled him and scoured away the
last shreds of his own awareness.

He heard a voice, deep in his bones: "Who are you? This is not
your place. You do not belong here."

And he woke, crying out. Drenched in cold sweat. Shaking.

Theor struggled upright in his bed. As he fumbled to pour
water from the beaker at his bedside, it was all he could do not to
vomit. It had been worse, this time. Much worse. He wanted to
believe, with all his heart, that these things which the seerstem
was showing him were the signs of the world twisting itself into

a new shape; that they presaged the delivery of all humankind out of its long solitude. And he did feel a powerful sense of great change, an anticipation as if the world was poised upon the brink of a wholly new season, unlike anything it had seen before. But if that was so, why did he feel so unclean, so run through with sickness and corruption? Why was it fear that lay like a stone in the pit of his stomach, not hope?

V

From his vantage point atop a low hillock at the eastern end of the Haig lines, Taim Narran watched arrows climb and then descend like rain upon the ranks of the Black Road army. They were too distant for him to see any bodies falling. The host of the Gyre Bloods was a great grey lake into which the arrows fell and disappeared. He knew what it would be like down there, amongst the torrential shafts. He could imagine the sound of arrowheads thudding into shields and the earth and flesh.

Since first light, the two armies had faced one another, each strung out across the road that led down towards Kolkyre. The great city was only an hour or two's march south of them. If Aewult failed today, the Kilkry Blood would be besieged by the next dawn. The Haig Bloodheir had more than ten thousand men arrayed to block the approach to Kolkyre, his losses at Glasbridge and since more than made good by the fresh companies that had come up from the south. It was as great a host as any the True Bloods had fielded since Gryvan came to power. And it was matched – exceeded, Taim's experienced eye suggested – by the forces of the Black Road.

The northerners were coming forwards now, along their whole line. The grassy expanse between the two armies gradually disappeared beneath the slow and ominous advance. The air was full of arrows, their flight constant, their effect negligible.

Taim was behind a triple line of Haig warriors. His hands were bound, his horse's reins securely held by one of his half-dozen guards. The scabbard at his side remained empty. He was only a spectator, brought here to witness, not to fight. Taim feared what he might witness, though. He mistrusted this day, and what it might bring. There were a hundred or more Taral-Haig riders close behind him, scattered across the top of the little hill, and he could hear them talking. They sounded almost eager for the bloodshed to begin. Most of them had young voices; callow.

The centre of the Black Road army halted. Its wings came on, closing on the higher ground that flanked the road. Taim stretched up out of his saddle, gazing across towards the low ridge to the west where Aewult had stationed himself. He could make out no detail save a thicket of pennants, and the pale glimmer of Palace Shield breastplates. The first blows would fall there, Taim thought, and here where he himself was trapped. The enemy chose to test itself on rising ground, against prepared defenders. It was foolish, but typical of the Black Road: a charge across the low ground where the road pierced the centre of the Haig lines would have been easier, but offered less reward for success, so they chose the harder course, in the hope of a greater prize. They would not care what price they had to pay.

"They'll learn a hard lesson today," he heard one of his guards say.

He could see over the heads of the warriors lined up to the meet the assault. The companies coming rushing up towards them were incoherent, lightly armed. Yet here and there amongst the disordered mass, Taim could see Inkallim, and there were clusters of more disciplined warriors. The Black Road roared with a single voice as it came boiling up the north face of the hillock and crashed into the Haig lines. Taim tugged instinctively against his bonds. They were secure, he already knew, but his body cried out for freedom of movement, now that battle was joined so close. For all his weariness with the brutal business of

the warrior's craft, still it was his calling and his life, and it was
not in his nature to stand by while others died at the hands of his
Blood's oldest enemies.

The Taral-Haig horsemen were caught up in the moment too,
and they closed up into a tighter formation. Some of them were
shouting out. Other voices crowded the air: cries of the wounded
and dying. Taim saw a single Inkallim burst through the ranks of
Haig spearmen. Isolated, she blurred into flashing movement as
she was surrounded. She shattered spears and ducked and rolled;
took the legs from under one man, cut up into the armpit of a
second. An axe came down on her shoulder blade. She staggered,
spun and landed a fatal blow. Her shield turned aside another
attack, her sword stove in the side of a helmet. They killed her
eventually, but not before she had slain or crippled six.

The struggle along the hilltop burned fierce and furious and
then faltered. The Black Road flood receded. Their warriors fell
back, running and tumbling and slipping down the slope. Cheers
rang out, and spears were shaken aloft and rattled against shields.
A rider came cantering up and called the company of Taral-Haig
horsemen off down the line to where battle was still joined. They
went gladly. Too gladly, Taim thought, too hopeful of a speedy
end to a struggle that had not yet run its course.

The dead and injured were dragged out from the front line.
Men shifted themselves, closing up gaps. Taim looked westward.
The far flank of the Haig army was still intact too. Aewult held
the ridge beyond the road, and there was a dense speckling of the
fallen strewn across the grass before and beneath it.

"They're coming again," someone said, and Taim turned back
to the still-living enemy closer at hand.

A dark line, tight-packed, was forming across the front rank of
the Black Road at the foot of the hill. It came fragment by fragment, out from amongst the mass, flecks of charcoal drifting to
the fore and thickening into a wall. It was a soundless thing, and
its silence spread, quieting the field, quieting even, it seemed to

Taim, the Haig warriors arrayed before him. They were bloodied but undefeated, these spearmen from Nar Vay and the woods of Dramain, yet they grew soft and still. Like a black fog clinging to the ground that line was coming on, far away and thus slow, across the trampled grass; hundreds of warriors, moving at a steady trot. The sound of their feet on the slope swelled, it rumbled. But still no cry came from a single throat. There was only the building, deep, rhythmic roar of their footfalls.

"Send to get your horsemen back," Taim hissed at the nearest of his guards.

The man turned reluctantly, his eyes lingering upon the scene unfolding before him.

"Don't try to give any orders here," he snapped.

Taim too found himself unable to look away from the approaching storm. They were close enough now that he could make out individual figures, all of them smooth and flowing in their movements, not one of them breaking rank, falling behind. He was filled with a kind of awe, and a numb surprise that he should be here, on this day, to see this.

"If you can't put horses on their flank, you're done." he persisted. "Your line's too thin."

The guard snorted in disgust. "Maybe if it was Lannis men in it. Three's deep enough when it's Haig."

Three ranks: shield-bearers with short stabbing spears kneeling, and behind them a second row brandishing longer pole-spears; then fierce moorsmen from the high ground between Dramain and Dun Aygll, with axes and hammers and short swords. It was a spiny nut for any attacker to seek to grasp. But not enough, Taim knew in the pit of his stomach. He knew it with the certainty of every year he had spent in the warrior's craft, and every winter he had spent upon his Blood's northern border, staring out across the Vale of Stones and knowing what kind of enemy might one day come across it.

"They're Inkallim, you fool," he said, wearily, knowing it was too late. "All of them. Six might not be deep enough, let alone three."

The guard glared at him, then snapped his gaze back to the mass of warriors now pounding up the slope, only a few shallow breaths from impact. They wore dark leather breastplates, or studded jerkins, leggings with black greaves, shields with carved ravens, and black hair streaming out. Taim heard the guard's sudden intake of breath.

"So many?" the man murmured.

The moment elongated itself, as if the whole world shared in that sucking-in of breath, holding it, poised, as the rolling thunder of the charge resounded through the earth and shook the roots of the hill and built and built until the Inkallim plunged in amongst the spears and there was nothing save the vast crashing clamour of slaughter. The air above the two meeting lines was suddenly full: blood and fragments of broken spears, mud and grass and splinters from shields. Taim wanted to look away, but could not. The front rank of defenders was already gone, consumed in that first fierce impact, nothing more than a long heap of the dead, wounded and fallen. The ravens came over it, trampling their own as willingly as they trampled their foes, unpausing, and danced their way on into the second and the third.

Out to the west, down the long sweep of ground to the road and across it, the rest of the Haig line was shifting, drawn as if by invisible cords towards the murderous chaos enveloping the hillock. Already, though, the whole host of the Black Road was surging into motion, pressing forwards. Taim experienced a twist of horrified disgust at what he was witnessing: thousands upon thousands of men and women, flinging themselves into full, unrestrained battle. More would surely die this day than had fallen on any since that of Kan Avor Field, when the Gyre Blood was driven into exile, over two centuries ago. A terrible decision would be made, through carnage.

He looked for any sign of the men he had led to An Caman and
back, to Kolglas and Glasbridge, but the armies had become
great beasts in which all the warriors were only sinews and scales,
no longer recognisable. The two hosts seethed across the plain,
flung limbs made of horsemen against one another, tore at each
other with claws built from swordsmen. A soft, misty cloud rose
from the heaving masses: the steam of breath and sweat rising as
from the back of a huge, labouring monster.

The smell reached Taim then, of blood and opened guts and
broken earth. He knew it too well. He saw a man staggering back
from the slaughter, unarmed, with one cheek and ear cut away
and his left shoulder and chest drenched in blood, a great thick
coating of it. The man reached out as he stumbled, straining with
his hands to grasp something only he could see, or imagine. Taim
lost track of him as a wedge of spearmen came running up and
swept past to throw themselves into the riot of death.

"Cut my bonds," he shouted at his guard. "I can fight."

The man did not reply. Taim could see in his wide eyes and
open mouth that he was lost in shock.

As anyone might be, on seeing for the first time Inkallim go
about their bloody business. The ravens carved holes in the Haig
lines with obscene ease. It was more massacre than battle. There
was no order in this, no rock for anyone caught in this flood to
cling to. There was only the deafening single noise of battle, a
constantly changing, constantly identical surging bellow. Men
killed and were killed, and it was brutal and brief and mind-
numbing.

Taim's horse stirred beneath him, disturbed by the screams of
other animals dying somewhere out in the carnage. He looked
around. His guards had gathered themselves, and were muttering
together. Men were running now, braving the abuse and even the
blades of their own captains; preferring flight to another moment
facing the Inkallim. Down where the road ran between the two
hillocks, the Haig lines were buckling too. Taim looked the other

way, out across the undulating fields to the east. He could see a body of riders, cutting across the face of a long green slope. They were coming from the north, and therefore had to be of the Black Road.

He had guessed that the battle was lost as soon as he saw the Inkallim massing. Now he knew it beyond doubting. As if summoned by that certainty, a black hand of fear descended upon his heart. It was unlike anything he had felt before. The Inkallim came flowing over the hilltop, and he saw in their approach his own doom, the snuffing-out of all hope. It was a potent, almost overwhelming, despair, like a smothering, ill-fitting cloak thrown over him, closing out the light.

Taim looked at his guards and saw in them the perfect reflection of the terror running unchecked through him. They led him away, heading down the reverse slope of the hill at a steady trot. The roar of the battle filled the air behind and above them. Taim could see figures streaming away from the field, down the road back towards Kolkyre: scores, hundreds, of fragments blown free of the army and sent tumbling southwards. And why not? What other response could there be, save flight?

Even as he thought it, Taim felt his own fear receding. As a cloud might uncover the sun, so the veil of horror parted and he glimpsed his true feelings. Whatever the source of that all-embracing fear, it had not been his own heart. It had been a foreign thing, imposed from outwith his mind, and at the slackening of its grip upon him his anger rose up.

"Turn us back," he cried at his guards. "Rally the lines."

But they were still beneath the shadow, bereft of all courage. They rode on and took him with them. The horses broke into a canter, bounding on over grassy fields. Everywhere, men were running. Glancing back over his shoulder, Taim could see the hill, dark against the grey sky. The Black Road held the summit now, but they were not content with that. They were coming on, in amongst the fleeing Haig men.

An alarmed shout from one of his escort turned Taim's head eastward. The company of horsemen that he had seen before, far out on a distant slope, was arrowing in now. Like a falcon stooping for its prey, it came sweeping down upon the flank of the rout. Riders surged through the crowds, stabbing down with spears or simply trampling men under the horses. Two of Taim's guards peeled away, kicking their mounts into a full gallop and making for safety.

The man who held the reins of Taim's horse hesitated.

"Give me a blade," Taim shouted at him, but he saw no comprehension in the warrior's eyes, only panic. The reins fell loose, and suddenly Taim was alone, carried impotently through the mass of running men by his wild horse.

He seized the animal's mane with both hands and hauled at it. They barged through a crowd of running spearmen, knocking several of them to the ground. Taim could hear the rumble of approaching hoofs, but did not dare to look around as he wrestled with his recalcitrant mount. A deep ditch yawned before and beneath them at the edge of a field. The horse veered sharply to the right rather than make the leap. Taim lurched sideways, but kept his seat. He saw Haig warriors scrambling across the reed-choked ditch, flailing through black water, clawing at the muddy bank. Everywhere, for as far as could see, the ground was thick with the remnants of Aewult's army, in full, frantic flight.

He heard the Black Road rider coming, and his body was reacting before his mind had even registered the fact. He kicked himself free of the saddle, twisting in the air to get his arms in front of his face as he arced into the ditch. He crashed down into water and weed, plunging into mud with such force that he was momentarily breathless and lost. He rolled, and water flooded his mouth. He tried to rise, but his feet slid from under him and his bonds made his hands clumsy. When he did manage to haul himself erect, coughing, shedding muddy water and countless fragments of broken reeds, he saw the Black Roader turning her mount, coming back with spear descending slowly. She was hacking at her horse's flanks with her heels, shouting. She was desperate for his death.

Taim did not trust his footing. Mud had him about his ankles. He stood quite still, and waited for her. She came faster than was wise, leaning out and down, extending her spear to reach him. He twisted sideways. The spearpoint cut a nick into his shoulder, but he got both hands onto its shaft and held on with all the strength he could summon. The horse bore the woman on along the edge of the ditch, and Taim was pulled violently off his feet, thrown forwards into the steep bank. But he did not lose his grip on the spear.

She should, by rights, have been unhorsed, but she was a skilled rider. As the spear twisted in her hand, it almost threw her from her saddle. She swayed wildly. At the last possible moment, she released the spear. She hauled herself upright on the reins. Her horse came to a skidding halt and reared. Taim scrambled up the bank. The sodden earth gave beneath his feet. The spear tangled with his legs and threatened to trip him. Too slow, he thought. Too slow. She was drawing a short sword, wrestling her horse around. Taim had a knee atop the bank. He knew he was too late.

But the horse stole a few precious moments from its rider. It stamped and tossed its head, stepping sideways for a couple of paces before she managed to kick it into another charge. It was not much; just enough for Taim to clamber onto level ground. The spear was the wrong way round in his hands, and with bound wrists he had no chance to turn it. He stabbed its point into the ground and dropped the butt into the horse's chest just as it thundered down upon him. He heard the horse scream, felt shards of the shattered spear striking his face, saw the horse's shoulder rushing into his face. The great animal smashed him aside and plunged on into the ditch.

Taim was not sure at first whether he would be able to rise

again. He rolled onto his stomach and crawled towards the ditch's edge. He could hear the horse thrashing down there amongst the reeds. When he looked down, he saw the woman there too, on her hands and knees in the water, dazed and spitting out soil. The sight was enough to put a last flicker of strength into his legs.

He threw himself down onto her and hammered her into the water. He got his legs clasped about her waist, and his hands together on the back of her neck. The fall had shaken her and robbed her of her sword; otherwise it might have been Taim who died. He held her face under the water. She writhed and beat at his arms and legs, but he did not yield. Her horse was still kicking and struggling on its side a little way up the ditch, tearing great chunks out of the banks with its hoofs. After a time, the woman stopped struggling.

Taim groped about in the mud, warily watching the horse's flailing legs, and soon found her sword. He cut his bonds on it, sheathed it in his own scabbard, climbed out of the ditch and jogged away southwards.

VI

Taim's first thought was to make for Kolkyre, but that was impossible. Chaos seemed to have risen up and taken hold of the world, and now shook it as if to break it apart. The army of the Black Road quickly spread itself across the whole plain, its every element rushing in disordered, hungry pursuit of its defeated prey. Every time he sought to turn towards Kolkyre, he found some obstacle in his path: a mob of Tarbains swarming over a couple of Aewult's supply wagons on a farm track; Gyre riders quartering fields and chasing down Haig warriors who had tried to hide amongst the grass and ditches; a farmhouse burning, with a hundred Black Roaders herding cattle together amidst the smoke.

Taim ran, sometimes alone, sometimes amongst others fleeing from the battle. He kept a steady pace, wary of tiring himself. Others had not been so cautious, and he passed many solitary men who had fallen, exhausted or overcome by wounds. In a tiny copse of lean trees, he found two dozen Taral-Haig spearmen gathered, arguing over what to do. He stayed only long enough to beg a drink of water from one of them. They were full of fear and anger, and leaderless. They shouted at one another. Some wanted to fight their way through to Kolkyre, others to keep running all the way back to Drandar. He left them, and pressed on across the treeless ridges and shallow dales of Kolkyre's hinterland.

Late on the day of the battle, when the scattered clouds out over the sea were already burning orange with the sun's setting light, he paused at an abandoned farmstead that stood on a low finger of ground reaching out from the eastern hills. The valley of the River Kyre lay to the south of him, broad and open. He thought he could see movement on the road that followed the river's course, but could not tell whether it was friend or foe. He could see Kolkyre, too: dark and distant down at the river mouth. Companies of men were moving back and forth across the plain around it, most of them streaming southwards. There was, though, order amidst the turmoil. He could just make out a great column forming up, outside the city walls. Kilkry-Haig, he guessed; Roaric attempting, too late, to limit the disaster that had befallen the True Bloods.

"What Blood are you?" someone asked behind him, and Taim spun around.

There were three men, smeared in dirt and blood, watching him with wary, hostile eyes. They must have been hiding somewhere amongst the outbuildings. Taim cursed himself for his carelessness. The one who had spoken did not, at least, have the accent of a northerner.

"Lannis," Taim said flatly.

One of the men grunted and looked away northwards, no longer interested. Another sneered, "Can hardly call yourself a Blood any more, can you? As good as masterless."

Taim shrugged, making himself meek. He was reasonably confident he could kill these men if he had to, but he had no intention of picking a fight when there were so many more dangerous opponents abroad.

"We've no food to spare, if that's what you're looking for," the third man muttered.

"I'm not hungry. I only wanted to rest for a time."

The men remained suspicious, but seemed to conclude that he was not worth any further time or trouble. They disappeared into the farmhouse. Taim moved a little further away and leaned on the wall of a cattle pen. He could hear crashing from within the house. They would take whatever of value they could find, of course. The sound of that ransacking was in his ears as he watched the day's second, brief battle.

The Black Road came out of the north in fragments. There was no line drawn up, no structure. First in a trickle, then a flood, warriors threw themselves against the Kilkry-Haig army assembling within sight of Kolkyre's northern gate. There was little wind, and no sound reached Taim above the noise of wreckage being created in the farmhouse behind him. The companies of warriors were too far away to be anything more in his sight than smudges drifting up and against each other, merging and mixing. He watched the stain of their struggle swell and spread. Like thickening smoke from some far-off fire, more and more Black Road warriors flowed down the road and into the battle.

Taim turned away. He could guess the outcome and had no desire to witness it.

Twilight was descending. If there were White Owls, or even Hunt Inkallim, amongst the host spreading itself over Kilkry lands, darkness would offer more threat than protection. He meant to move on through the night.

He glanced up at the farmhouse, and saw a face at a window: one of the looters, staring out at him. Taim recognised the danger in that attention, and trotted off down into the valley of the Kyre.

Taim reached the river around the middle of the night. There was no moonlight. He had slowed to a walk, picking his careful way across the empty pastures of the valley floor. He heard the road that hugged the Kyre's northern bank long before he saw any sign of it: the trundling of wheels on cobbles, the fraught voices of frightened, lost men.

As he drew closer, just as he began to hear the river itself, he almost walked into a group of men lying in the wet grass, wrapped in dark cloaks that rendered them all but invisible. One sprang up in his path, crying out and lunging at him. Taim knocked the man down and ran on before his comrades could rouse themselves.

The confusion on the road was dangerous. All but blind in the darkness, warriors and farmers and villagers were milling about. Almost all were heading upriver, away from Kolkyre, but many strayed from the road, stumbling into fields and the clumps of trees along the riverside. A great wagon, hauled by long-horned cattle, nearly crushed Taim when he had to duck into its path to avoid a horseman cantering recklessly along. He found himself caught up in a great throng of country folk who had fled their village. Some of them grasped at him, reaching out in hope or desperation, asking for news. He had none to give, and shrugged off their hands.

He left the road, and went tentatively onto a marshy bit of ground by the river. Water closed over his booted feet, but there was a huge tree stump and he sat there for a time, thinking. There was no crossing of the Kyre downstream, he knew, save the bridge at Kolkyre itself. That would be in Black Road hands by now. The only other bridge he had heard of was the one that led to Ive, and that must be the best part of a day's walk up the valley. There would be ferry boats somewhere, but he did not know where. He briefly considered attempting to swim the river, but it was broad, and sounded to him powerful and fast. He had never been a strong swimmer. Reluctantly, he made his way along the riverside until he found a tree strong enough to hold his weight, and he wedged himself into the fork of a low branch to wait for dawn, and the clarity of daylight.

In the morning, Taim found more than he could have hoped for: forty or so Lannis men riding up the road. Only then, filled with relief at the sight of them, did he recognise how deeply he had slipped into despondency and uncertainty. Like a man tasting clean water for the first time in days, he embraced their leader, and went from man to man clasping hands and laughing. And they were as glad, to have the Captain of Anduran returned to them. They had no spare horses, but one man climbed up behind another and gave his own mount to Taim.

"Do you know where the rest of us are? What became of them?" Taim asked.

There were only shaken heads and downcast eyes in response. He had not expected more.

"Did you feel it, in the battle?" someone asked him. "There was a shadow across us, across every man's spirit. Nothing of our own making."

"I felt it," Taim grunted. "It passed, though, didn't it? You're men still. You've swords still, and horses."

"We do."

"Good. We'll make for Ive. Everyone will gather there, or at Donnish."

"We're to submit ourselves to the Bloodheir again, then?" grumbled one of the men.

Taim cowed him with a single fierce glare. "We're to find another chance to face the Black Road, that's what we're to do. There'll be no way in or out of Kolkyre by now. Whether we like it or not, it'll be Haig that decides this war, so if you want to be a part of the decision that's where we go." And, he thought, it'll be to Haig that Orisian must go, if he can. There was nowhere else now. If their Thane still lived, he must find his way to the Haig army sooner or later. And if he was no longer alive . . . Taim did not know the answer to that.

They followed the river up into the hills. Behind them, beyond obscuring ridges, pillars of smoke climbed into grey skies. There were fewer people on the road now. Those who did share it with them were mostly the slow ones: whole families, the sick and the aged.

There was a young girl, no more than eight or nine years old, sitting on the grass, holding a wailing baby in her arms. She watched them pass by. Tears had run streaks down through the dirt on her cheeks, but now she was silent; just watching, in defeated resignation. Taim reined in his horse and stared down at the girl. She looked back at him, without fear or hope, without any sign of emotion.

"Come," he called down to her, bending down and holding out a hand.

She shuffled backwards across the grass. The baby was screaming, a sound of such undiluted distress that it cut Taim to the quick.

"We can carry you, if you're too tired to walk," he said.

The little girl shook her head and hugged the babe tighter against her chest.

"You shouldn't stay here." Taim's men had passed him by now, riding on. "It might not be safe."

"I'm waiting," she said, so soft and shy that he barely caught it.

"Who for?" he asked. But she did not reply. She would not look at him any more. Taim left her, not knowing what else to do. Thinking of Jaen, and of Maira their daughter.

The river grew more turbulent. The rich pastures bordering it gave way to sparser, poorer grasslands and stretches of bare rock.

The hills bulged up ever higher, and colder air blew around their haunches.

In the afternoon, the silhouettes of riders appeared above and behind Taim's band. They kept pace for a time, paralleling the course of the road. A group of villagers trudging along a little way ahead saw them too, and began to run.

"Haig or Black Road?" one of the warriors near Taim wondered.

"I don't know. Black Road, if I had to guess."

The distant figures fell away beneath the ridgeline after a while. Taim picked up his pace. He looked back down the road. It wound its way off towards the coastal plain. There was bad weather out there, coming in from the sea: fat clouds and a wall of rain or sleet that hung like a curtain from the sky. All down the road's winding path people were scattered, crawling their way up the valley. It could not be long, Taim knew, before the wolves of the Black Road descended upon this straggling flock.

At the place where the road to Ive forked off southwards, the Kyre was narrow, funnelled between two rock buttresses. A single-arched stone bridge spanned the channel. On the north side of the river, the hillside was steep and bleak. The road to Highfast was cut into its face. Taim looked that way for a while, thinking of Orisian, but turned his men south and led them clattering across the bridge.

There was a little village there, at the south end of the bridge, perched above the river on a huge flat platform of bare ground: squat stone huts, some roofed with turf, some with slate. There was a miserable-looking inn, a blacksmith, and some stables and sheds. And scores of people, perhaps hundreds. They were crowded around every building, sheltering against the walls. Many were curled up, with cloaks or blankets pulled over their heads – sleeping or sick. Families were clustered around tiny fires they had made from whatever meagre pile of wood they could assemble. Some Haig warriors were handing out flatbreads from a barrow, beating back those who tried to grab an extra portion.

"Find some feed and water for the horses," Taim instructed.

He went in search of anyone of authority, anyone who could tell him something of how things stood. He found no one. A listless despair had settled over the village, brought perhaps by the hundreds who had already fled this way. The warriors here were without captains; half of the place's original inhabitants had already left, making for Ive. It was obvious that many of those now encamped here would not be going further soon, if ever. Few had set out upon their journey with adequate preparation, and all had been on the move for too long without rest. The sky was already darkening towards dusk, and foul weather gathering further down the valley, threatening to come surging up towards the Karkyre Peaks.

"Black Road!"

The shout sped through the village, taken up by one voice after another. Taim ran back to the bridge. Riders were on the road across the valley, still some way further downriver but moving fast. Ahead of them a few desperate figures were running, striving to reach the bridge before they were cut down. Taim could see some of them flinging aside their belongings. They had no chance, though. He saw first one, then two, caught and killed by their pursuers.

"Block the bridge," Taim shouted at the nearest of his men as he ran for his horse. "A shield line across this end."

He slapped a Haig warrior on the shoulder as he sprinted by, shouting, "Get your men together. If we don't hold the bridge, we're all done."

He did not wait to see if the man did as he was told. People — those who could — were already running, gathering their families, rushing for the road south. Taim could hear children crying. He leaped up into the saddle. Ten or twelve of his horsemen were at his side. Most of the rest were on foot, arraying themselves across the roadway, blocking off the near end of the bridge. They squatted down behind their round shields. Few had the spears that were needed to meet a charge.

A young man came staggering across the bridge. The wall of shields parted to let him through. He was the last. The Black Road riders were close. Taim could see the dull texture of their mail shirts as they pounded up. He could hear the snorting breath of the lead horse as it swung towards the bridge.

A knot of Haig spearmen appeared at his side. He looked down at them and saw their fear.

"Wait here with me," he muttered. "There's been enough running for now, don't you think? These are people of the True Bloods we're fighting for. They'll die if the Black Road crosses this bridge, so fight well."

The first horseman came across the bridge at the gallop. The valley rang to the sound of hoof on stone, every rock face reflecting the sound. There were flecks of foam at the mouth of his great bay horse. He crashed down upon the shield line at full pace, as if he had not even seen it. Horse and rider went plunging through, both tumbling, and took three or four men with them. More came close behind, and they hesitated no more than the first had. They fell like hammer blows on kindling, ploughing through the thin Lannis ranks. Horses went down. Men were crushed, and knocked flying.

Taim turned to the little wedge of Haig men drawn up beside him. There was no sense in waiting. There was to be no subtlety to this; it would be won and lost quickly, in the first savage moments when men must choose between courage and fear.

"Go," Taim shouted at the Haig men. For an instant, he was not sure they would do as he commanded. But then they were running, and crying out, and driving their way to the heart of the fight.

"Us too," Taim called to his companions, and they charged in. The battleground was constricted, the slaughter compressed into the small open space where the bridge disgorged the road between huts. Taim's horse stamped on someone as it lunged forwards. It barged through and took him up against a woman who was laying about her from horseback with a long thin-bladed sword. She cut at Taim's arm. He blocked the blow and swung for her flank. Her horse lurched sideways and carried her out of his reach. A spear stabbed into her stomach from below, and he turned away, seeking another opponent. More warriors were still coming across the bridge. Taim saw one of his men battered to the ground and trampled. A horse reared beside him, and twisted and crashed down on its side. He urged his own mount on, closer and closer to the bridge. He killed one man, and another.

He glimpsed villagers rushing up to the edge of the fray, falling on injured or unwary Black Roaders, clubbing them and jabbing at them with knives. He hacked and slashed until his arm ached. And, quite suddenly, it was done, and the enemy were all dead or downed, and the bridge still belonged to Taim and his men.

Sleet was falling, and the day's light was almost done. Taim could hear people cheering. He sat on his horse at the mouth of the bridge and stared off down the valley. There were other companies of warriors on the road, out there in the gloom, drawing closer.

He sheathed his sword and turned back towards the village. One of the Haig warriors grinned up at him.

"It's not done yet," Taim said wearily before the man could speak. "Is there a ford across the river anywhere near here? Another bridge?"

The spearman shook his head, his brief joy dispelled by Taim's grave expression.

"Get whatever you can find out of the houses, then," Taim said. "Benches, tables. Anything. We need to put a wall across the bridge."

VII

The Black Road came across the bridge only once in the night: a single, wild rush not of warriors but of commonfolk, who came pouring out of the darkness brandishing staffs and axes and looted swords. They swarmed over the half-built barricade and spilled on into the village, howling with a delirious glee. The fight spread quickly, tumbling itself into side streets and across the inn's yard, into doorways.

In the almost moonless dark, it was hard to tell friend from foe. Villagers fought alongside Taim and his men, and the killing was frenzied and frenetic. A youth clad in a mail hauberk far too big for him came at Taim, lunging clumsily with a short sword. Taim knocked him down. The boy – no more than fourteen or fifteen, Taim guessed – sprawled at his feet, stunned. He lay groaning in a pool of yellow light cast from the window of a hut. Taim stared at him as he struggled to rise.

"Don't," he muttered, too softly for anyone to hear.

Someone came running and drove a spear into the small of the boy's back. He wailed and writhed. Like a fish, Taim thought as he backed away. He ran towards the barricade, stepping over bodies. Figures rushed at him and he cut them down. At the bridge, the struggle was intimate. Men were on the ground, wrestling and stabbing with knives. Some had climbed atop the heap of timber and furniture and were swinging staffs at every head that came within reach. Taim ducked low and cut their legs from under them. More came scrambling over the barricade, and he killed them as they came.

Eventually, the night's quiet descended once more, punctuated only by the groans and cries of the wounded, who lay amidst slush and puddles. Taim went to the inn and slumped in a chair before the fire. He was foggy from lack of sleep, dull-eyed and heavy-limbed. He stared into the flames.

Someone brought him a bowl of broth. Someone else set a

beaker of ale down on the table beside him. No one was talking. There was coughing, thick and liquid; mutters of pain from the wounded who were scattered around the room. A child was curled up on the floor in front of the fire, asleep. Taim's head nodded. His face slackened.

A hand on his shoulder startled him back to wakefulness.

"There's beds upstairs," someone was saying to him. "We'll find you if you're needed."

Taim climbed the stairs, and found a bed with a coarse blanket and a hard mattress. He stretched out on it and was instantly asleep.

Dawn lit the village in muted greys. There were still corpses strewn across the road and slumped against the walls of huts. A torpid silence hung over the little collection of buildings. Those who moved did so quietly and carefully, as if fearing to draw even the slightest attention to themselves. Some were readying themselves to walk southwards: folding a few possessions into packs, searching out the last few scraps of food they could find.

There would soon be no one left here save those without any choice in the matter, Taim knew as he looked out from the doorway of the inn. Behind him, laid out on tables and on the floor, were the sick and the injured. They could not walk away from here. Nor would the old woman he'd seen sitting on a stool in the inn's kitchen. She was too frail for the long road to Ive.

He could see the barricade across the bridge. All through the night, huts had been stripped of their contents to build it higher. Twenty or so Lannis and Haig warriors were sitting in its shelter now, talking softly amongst themselves, sharing water from their skins. Taim lifted his gaze, followed the rise and fall of the bridge across to the far side of the river. There was movement on the tall, steep slope above the road: shapes shifting amongst the rocks. A lot of them. And he thought he could make out a long line of riders snaking its way up the valley. He wondered dispassionately how long the bridge could be held; how many dead it would take before the Black Road could overwhelm them. How much time could be bought for those struggling southwards. And whether he had any choice in any of this. Did he want to sacrifice his men – himself – in this cause?

Something flashed out from the high ground north of the river. His first, instant thought was that it was a bird, but it darted down and skittered across the surface of the road not twenty paces from where he stood: a crossbow bolt. Another followed it. He heard its dry, muffled impact in the turf roof of one of the cottages.

Someone was behind him, peering over his shoulder.

"What's this place called, anyway?" Taim asked.

"Ive Bridge."

Taim nodded. "Ive Bridge. Yes, I suppose it would be."

* * *

"At the bridge. Ive Bridge," the old woman said.

Orisian moved closer, coming up to Torcaill's shoulder.

"You're sure?" the warrior asked the woman.

She grimaced at him. "I'm old, not stupid. I can tell the difference."

"Lannis men?" Orisian said.

She fixed him with a look that bordered on the contemptuous. "Is it that you're all deaf, is that it? Yes, Lannis men. Fighting on the bridge. Black Road all over the place, other side of the river, apparently. Not this side yet, though."

"How far is it?" asked Orisian.

She considered her answer for a few moments longer than he would have liked. "Half a day, I should think. Not more. Probably less."

They watched her shuffle off down the road. She moved steadily, for a woman of such age. They had seen others, on this road, less strong and more desperate. The long trail down from Stone had been all but empty. Only a handful of goatherds and hunters had shared it with them. That mountain track had brought them to the Ive road now, though, and they had found themselves caught up in a steady trickle of people trudging southwards. All of them told the same tale of defeat and destruction, and testified to the truth of it with their bent backs and fretful faces. Every one of them – men, women, children – looked lost, cast adrift; hounded by fears and grim memories.

"See who's coming here," Torcaill murmured, nodding up the road.

Three warriors were trotting along. They carried nothing save spears and shields. Orisian moved into the centre of the road.

"Have you come from Ive Bridge?" he shouted at them as they drew near.

The lead warrior slowed a fraction, glared at Orisian. And dismissed him. Orisian saw the decision in the man's eyes. He shifted sideways to block his path, and stretched out an arm. Torcaill's men, scattered along the roadside, were rising to their feet.

"What's happening at Ive Bridge?" Orisian asked.

"Nothing any more," the first of the warriors muttered. The three of them fell into a walk, but showed no inclination to stop. They made to pass Orisian by. He took hold of an arm and pulled at the man.

"Are there Lannis men there?"

The warrior jerked his arm free and glared at Orisian. His lips drew back in a nascent snarl, only to loosen as he saw Torcaill and his men crowding up. He was suddenly uneasy.

"Might be," he grunted. "Their luck's run out, though. Too few of them to hold the bridge."

"You left them. Is that it? You're Haig, aren't you?"

"What of it?"

"Perhaps you don't think Lannis men are good enough to die beside."

The warrior snorted and brushed past Orisian.

"I don't mean to die beside anyone today, or any day soon."

Torcaill gently pulled Orisian aside.

"Sire . . ." he said.

Orisian stared after the three Haig men as they hurried on. They quickly overhauled the old woman, and disappeared around a dipping turn in the road. A pair of buzzards were spiralling up, Orisian saw, higher and higher into the sky like dancers to some silent tune.

"You know where we're going," he said to Torcaill, still watching the birds.

* * *

They were moving too slowly. Taim Narran knew that. All his men must know it, though no one spoke of it. They spoke of nothing, walking in steadfast silence behind the dishevelled flock of survivors from Ive Bridge. There were half a dozen wounded there, carried on makeshift litters; a little gang of lost children, who never strayed more than few paces from one another; the last few stubborn villagers who had left their homes only after long argument; a sick woman, swaying on the back of a sullen donkey. It was not much to salvage, but it was the best that Taim had been able to do.

Ive Bridge was gone. Anyone they had left behind – and there had been some, too sick or frightened or infirm to move – was in the hands of the Black Road now. Dead, or enslaved. Taim had left most of his warriors there, too: corpses in the streets of a village they had never heard of until the time came for them to die in it. He still did not know whether he could justify their deaths to their families, should he ever be asked. He did not know whether he could justify his own death, which he thought was likely to come before the end of this cold day.

Once already he and his handful of men had turned to stand

against the pursuit. They chose a place where the road narrowed between two rocky spurs. The stretch leading up to the gap was steep, weaving its way between boulders. The Black Road warriors were panting and distracted by the time they finished the ascent, and had perhaps not known that there were still fighting men amongst those they hunted. Taim had led the rush down upon them. He rode the tide of reckless abandon that was in him, surrendered himself to it. He almost paid a heavy price. A sword got under his guard and slammed across his side. Had its wielder been more deft or skilled, it would have been a crippling wound, but the blade came at an acute angle. It cut him, possibly broke a rib, to judge by the stabbing pain that now accompanied each breath. His own countering cut was more sure and more telling. It opened his assailant's shoulder joint and sent him slithering away down a scree of loose rock.

They had won a little time there. Only a little, though. The brief satisfaction of seeing the Black Roaders fleeing back down the trail was soon succeeded by resignation. There were forty or more warriors within sight, scattered all along the road's sweeping curves. Some were mounted. One, distant, was standing up in his stirrups, hammering the shaft of a spear against his shield, howling defiance up at the figures on the heights. Taim had heard his own death in that shout.

One of the children was crying, and some of the others were beginning to sniff and murmur in sympathy. They were exhausted and bewildered. There would be no chance to rest, though, Taim knew. The Black Road might come more slowly, more cautiously, having been bloodied once, but they would come.

He found himself strangely calm as he trudged along. His one regret was that he had not seen Jaen or Maira. That would break his heart if he dwelled on it, or upon the thought that they were surely now trapped in Kolkyre with the cruel host of the Black Road all around. Everything else, he could bear. Even the failure of this effort to save these few strangers.

"Rider," one of the men walking at his side said.

Taim turned and walked backwards for a few paces. The road was nearly level, cutting an almost straight path back through rock and spindly bushes. There was a solitary rider there, sharp against a blue sky. He was holding a sword up above his head.

"Doesn't look like he's in a good mood," Taim muttered.

Others came up out of a dip in the road, coalescing around that first horseman, gathering about him, blocking out the blue firmament bit by bit. Taim spun around once more and looked ahead. There was little help on offer from the land. A little further on, the ground humped on either side of the road, a jumble of rocks. That would have to do.

"Tell the rest to hurry on," Taim said quietly. "We'll stand there. Do the best we can."

He set his men amongst boulders on either side of the road: only fifteen or so. Too few, of course, especially now that the enemy had seen their paltry number and would be confident, hungry. Taim waited with his back to stone. The winter sun was on his face, almost warm. There had been a day like this once, very long ago, when he and Jaen were freshly betrothed and they had gone along the banks of the Glas looking for willow sprigs to make a basket. It was the wrong time of year – the withies would not be as soft and pliable as they ought to be for such work – but Jaen had wanted to go, so they had gone. That was what he remembered now, of all things. It made him smile, and made him sad.

He heard the hard crack of a crossbow bolt against rock.

"It'll take them a long time if they mean to finish us off like that," a warrior hunched down beside Taim said.

"The longer the better," Taim murmured. "I doubt they've got the patience for that, though. Black Road's never been famous for patience."

He ventured a snatched glance over the top of the sheltering boulder and saw three or four riders advancing at a walk, many more coming on foot after them. Another quarrel hissed over his head.

"No patience at all," he observed as he ducked back down.

Hoofs on the road, picking up their pace. Cries of bloody intent. Feet running. Taim shifted onto the balls of his feet, crouched down, waiting.

"The horses mustn't get through," he called out. "Take them, if nothing else."

The sun was on his back now. He could feel it through his jerkin. It was almost possible to believe that it was not winter at all.

He surged up, sword already back, two-handed. He cut the lead rider out of his saddle. The jarring impact shivered through his arms and down through his ribcage and he cried out in pain. Another horse flashed past. He tried to cut at its hindquarters but missed. He was out in the road now, and as he steadied himself he saw a score of Black Roaders descending upon him.

The first ran at Taim with a spear. He ducked under it and let the woman tumble over him, then sprang up and knocked another aside with a backhanded stroke against her shield. They came on like a swarm of wolves. One of his warriors, and then two, were at his side, fending off attacks. They hacked and swung. Taim could feel sweat beading across his forehead. He barely saw those he fought, those he killed. Body after body appeared before him and he cut them down, barged them aside, and each of them was only a shape, a danger. The pain in his flank soared but it was nothing that could reach him.

The man on his left went down, speared in the belly. Taim took a glancing blow on his hip that staggered him for a moment. A sword came darting in to pounce on his weakness. He turned it aside, and snapped his own blade round and up fast enough to open a wrist to the bone. He felt almost light, as if his feet could glide weightless over the cobbles of the road.

And then people were running. Fleeing. Someone hit him

from behind and knocked him to his knees. Men came past him and the Black Roaders were falling away, going down beneath swords. He looked up, bleary-eyed, and saw a riderless horse galloping back, pounding down the road. And Torcaill. He saw Torcaill running, and tripping a Black Road warrior, standing on the man's back and driving a swordpoint down into his spine.

Taim did not hear fighting all around him now. It was moving away, fading. Someone had their hand on his elbow and was hauling him up. He was unsteady on his feet. He had to hunch over a little to protect his ribs.

"Taim," said Orisian.

Taim laughed, not wholly certain at that moment whether he could trust his eyes, and not caring.

"Sire. Can I lean on you, sire? I am not sure I can walk too well."

He put his arm around Orisian's shoulder and hobbled to the side of the road, where he could sit on a flat-topped rock. Those Black Roaders still alive were scattering, some back the way they had come, others out over the scrubby ground. Orisian's two Kyrinin were standing in the roadway, methodically sending arrow after arrow skimming out, straight and true. Taim shook his head, trying to rid himself of the strange blurry feeling that was settling inside his skull. He looked at his Thane, and saw a small warrior: shield on one arm, sword in hand, a raw scar across the breadth of his cheek. And hard eyes.

There were bodies thick on the road. A hand was reaching up, opening and closing. Someone was whimpering, like a beaten child. A woman was crawling along on her hands and knees. She spilled blood from her stomach as she went. Torcaill and two of his men moved amongst the human debris. They stood over the woman. She put a hand on Torcaill's boot. He looked over towards Taim and Orisian.

"We can't care for them," Taim heard Orisian say, and was surprised at the coldness of his voice. But he did not watch Torcaill killing the woman, Taim noted. Nor did he flinch at the sound of the blow falling.

"We will have to move on, sire," Taim murmured. "There will be more of them before long."

"I know. Is Aewult beaten, then?"

Taim nodded, wincing and pressing an arm against his chest.

"Where's Anyara? Do you know?"

And Taim had to tell him, and that was perhaps the hardest thing he had done that day.

Epilogue

I

White Owl Kyrinin carried the *na'kyrim* on a litter made of birch saplings. His hand trailed over the side, brushing the grass for a little distance until someone noticed and lifted it and laid it across his stomach. A hundred woodwights walked in procession before and behind the litter. Battle Inkallim rode on either side of it. Like an honour guard, Kanin oc Horin-Gyre thought in disgust. Hundreds of warriors lined the path along which Aeglyss was borne. The silence was heavy.

Kanin watched from a distance, looking down on the scene from higher ground. The skin of the halfbreed's hands and face almost shone, even at that remove. Ivory plaques, of the purest white, shining. It could have been a corpse that was carried with such reverential care through the serried ranks of the Black Road; a Thane being taken to his resting place. But it was not, and Kanin watched with attentive loathing. He wanted Aeglyss to live a little longer. Long enough to ensure that it could be Kanin's own hand that ended his life, and that the ending was fittingly painful and prolonged.

Kolkyre was within sight, a grey bulk far off to the south. It was almost obscured by the greasy smoke of the many pyres burning between here and there: the meat and bone of the fallen smeared across the sky in vast grainy slicks. What breeze there was came from the south, and it carried the smell of the corpse fires on it. It filled Kanin's nostrils with its noisome texture, and he did not find that unfitting. There was a truth in the conjoining of Aeglyss and that vile stench, a coincidental expression of the halfbreed's essential nature. Kanin did not know, and did not care, whether he was the only one to recognise it. That he did was enough. It only took one man to kill another.

His Shield were about him, watching in silence as he did. He could not even be certain of them, he suspected. Their silence might be one of contempt, or fascination, or even awe. He could not tell. The litter and its foul burden drifted on. In its wake, the crowd of warriors closed up. Many stood gazing after it. Fools, one and all, Kanin thought. They think they see a sign of fate's favour, and for that one delusion they'll forgive all sins, any corruption. That was the flaw in the creed. That was the crack in its armour that Aeglyss would hammer his wedge into, and split open.

A movement at his feet caught Kanin's eye. A great black dog loped past him, so close as to almost brush against his leg. It went out onto the grass and sat, its muscular back to him. He could hear it panting.

"They're taking him back to Kan Avor, by all accounts."

Kanin looked round at Cannek. The Inkallim's approach had been soundless, but that was no great surprise for one of the Hunt.

"He's spent, I gather," Cannek continued. "Whatever influence he exerted on the battle has cost him almost his whole strength."

"Influence? We don't know that. Shraeve and her acolytes claim the victory for him, but we can't know the truth of it."

Cannek shrugged. "I saw the Haig lines crumble. I saw their thousands flee, wailing in terror, long before their losses justified it. And I felt . . . I do not know what I felt, Thane. But there was something. Did you feel nothing?"

Kanin frowned and looked away. Of course he had felt something. On the day of the battle there had been a hunger and a fury abroad surpassing anything he had seen before. He had

witnessed acts of unflinching self-sacrifice and bloody determination beyond all expectation, even by the standards of the Black
Road. The faithful had thrown themselves onto the spears of the
enemy with utter abandon. There had been an almost delirious,
ecstatic embracing of death. But Kanin would acknowledge
nothing. He would deny the presence of the halfbreed in the very
air, and in his heart, on the day of that battle, for if he spoke of it
he would make it real. And how could he hope to oppose someone with such capabilities?

"True or not, the conviction is spreading that he had a hand in
our triumph," Cannek said. "I have heard many speaking of it.
Some are calling him the herald of the Kall. Minon, Orlane,
Dorthyn reborn in the service of the creed. Bloodheir to
Amanath, the Fisherwoman; inheritor of her mantle."

"Bloodheir?" Kanin barked. "Let them call him what they like.
It means nothing. He clouds minds. He makes every thought
deceptive, traitorous to the skull that holds it."

"Indeed. The victory has not convinced you of his right to a
place amongst us, then?"

Kanin scowled at the Inkallim.

"Send your Shield away for a moment, Thane," Cannek said.

Kanin sighed. Trust was no longer an element in his being.
Wain's death had expunged it. Nothing in the world, and no one,
seemed worthy of it to him any more. Not even the creed. Not
fate. And even before that he would have called any man a fool
who claimed that he could trust the Hunt. But still, he had no
enemies save one now. He nodded at Igris, and when the shieldman hesitated, he snapped at him, "Move away. All of you."

Cannek watched them go, with the wry, self-satisfied smile
that so often adorned his features.

"Goedellin is troubled," the Inkallim murmured. "And that
means the Lore is troubled. *I* am troubled, Thane."

"I am sorry to hear that."

"It was always our hope, from the very beginning of this, that your Blood would emerge stronger. The Children of the Hundred have long attached importance to the fidelity that your line has shown for the creed."

"A pity Shraeve did not share your concern, since she was there in Kan Avor when my sister was slain."

There was the slightest flicker of discomfort in Cannek's face at that. Once, Kanin would have drawn some satisfaction from it. Now, he hardly cared.

"Shraeve is a matter for us to consider," the Inkallim grunted. "To deal with, if necessary. You are my greatest concern now, Thane."

"Me?"

"Your Blood dies with you, unless you have an heir you've kept secret from us all."

Kanin snorted and looked back towards the great throng below them. Aeglyss was almost out of sight, passing beyond the edge of the host.

"Nobody would profit from your demise, and that of your Blood, save Ragnor," Cannek said. "And the other Thanes, perhaps, picking over the carcass of your lands. None of which would serve to strengthen the creed. Your people would suffer for your vengeance, if you lose your life in the attempt."

"I was always taught that it was a weakness to fear consequences," Kanin murmured. "The creed would surely say the suffering of my people, my suffering, is of no import. If suffering is written in the Last God's Book, we must embrace it."

"It would be better to talk with Goedellin if you wish to debate such things," Cannek said, "though he is a trifle . . . distracted these days. The Hunt deals in more practical matters, so I'll ask what I came to ask: stay your hand, Thane. For a time, at least. Do not rush into some hasty assault on the halfbreed. We would regret your loss."

"Ha. I am touched by your concern. But I will do as I see fit. Why should I not?"

The huge dog stood up and looked round, its wet eyes on Kanin. It stretched, elongating itself.

"Because the Hunt will accept this burden," hissed Cannek. "We will test what protection fate sees fit to set about the half-wight."

"You will set the Hunt against the Battle?" Kanin asked.

Cannek shrugged and smiled again. "Fate always follows a surprising course, in my experience. We are all striding towards our deaths. The only question is when we will reach the end of the Road."

Kanin stared at the hound. He watched spittle creeping across its jowls.

"Soon, I think," he said. "All of us. Soon."

II

Thirty men from the Nar Vay shore – hard men once, who had been born to fishermen and strand gleaners, grown up with the salt smell of the sea and the feel of a boat beneath them – were huddled together on hard ground. They were shoremen no longer, but warriors, and defeated ones at that. They were cold, for it was night, it had been snowing for some time and their captors would not allow them to make a fire, or even to move around. They sat, wrapped in whatever cloaks or banners or tent canvas they had managed to scavenge from the wasteland of corpses that now surrounded Kolkyre, and the snow built up on their shoulders and their backs. They crowded close together, a hot press of bodies, so close that they breathed on one another's faces. One man, wounded in the battle they had lost, had already died this night, in the midst of that huddle. They had pushed and passed the dead man out to the edge and he lay there still, stiff, disappearing incrementally beneath snowflakes. Their guards showed no more interest in the corpse than they would in a long-fallen tree or a rock.

These Haig men had been taken soon after the battle was done. Fleeing south, racing for Kolkyre even though they knew that city was no friend to their Blood, they were encircled by mounted spearmen, who killed a few of them and herded the rest back northwards, made chattels of them. They expected to die in time, for that was what they had always been told to expect of the Black Road. The lethargic apathy of the humbled kept them docile. They had surrendered much of their pride and their resilience in those moments of panic when they broke and scattered from the battle line, undone by a strange, compulsive terror that none of them now spoke of, for they did not understand it, and were ashamed of it. They spoke of nothing at all. There was nothing to say. They merely waited. They did not know whether it was the cold they waited for, or a spear, or starvation, but they believed it was one of those.

Horses came out of the darkness, soft and slow. One or two of the prisoners looked up. They turned away again at once, hid their faces. Inkallim had come, black-haired, grim, astride huge horses that blew gouts of steam from their noses. Guards drifted from their fires to speak with these newcomers. Few words were exchanged.

One of the Inkallim – a sinewy woman with two swords sheathed across her back – jumped down, thumping into the deepening snow. She walked, limping slightly, to the cluster of captives and stood over them. She surveyed them with contempt. They made themselves small, hoping to avoid her gaze.

"Fate smiles upon you tonight," she said, and her voice made some of them shiver. "A task falls to you that will earn you the gratitude of your Thane. Stand up."

No one moved.

"Stand up!" the Inkallim shouted, and they did, one by one. They rose clumsily. Some had to hold their neighbours to keep them from falling. One man dropped the threadbare cloak from his shoulders and bent to pick it up again.

The Inkallim turned and beckoned someone forwards from amongst the riders. A horse stepped carefully over the snow. It bore a hunched figure, enclosed in a hooded cape. The horse came close. Some of the prisoners shuffled back, intimidated by its dark size.

"Let them see you," the Inkallim said quietly.

The rider straightened a little, not enough to take the bend entirely out of his spine, and slipped back his hood with one hand. The revealed face was pale and angular. He stared down at the Nar Vay men. There was silence and then, haltingly, a few murmurs of surprise, of recognition.

"Some of you know him," the Inkallim said, and smiled bleakly. "Those who do not: this is your High Thane's Chancellor. This is Mordyn Jerain. And you are his escort. We give you your freedom, that you may return this man to Vaymouth, and to his place at the side of Gryvan oc Haig."

The prisoners looked at one another, uncertain and hesitant. This was too out of line with the fatalism that had mastered them, too unexpected. They thought they had misheard her.

"You will be renowned," she said, "as the men who brought back the Shadowhand."

They looked up at the sickly, bent figure on the horse. And Mordyn Jerain smiled down at them. It was an unnerving, lifeless smile.

"Take me to Vaymouth. There are many things I must discuss with the Thane of Thanes. Many things."

To be continued . . .

The Passage of Time

The First Age

Began when the Gods made the world and put the One Race in it to inhabit it.

Ended when the One Race rose up against the Gods and was destroyed.

The Second Age

Began when the Gods made the Five Races: Huanin, Kyrinin, Whreinin, Saolin and Anain.

The Huanin and Kyrinin made war upon the Whreinin and destroyed that race, and were thereafter named the Tainted Races for their sin, and forfeited the love of the Gods.

Ended when the Gods departed from the world.

The Third Age

Began with the absence of the Gods, and with chaos.

Year

280 The Adravane and Aygll Kingships arose

398 Marain the Stonemason began the construction of Highfast, at the behest of the Aygll King

451 The Alsire Kingship arose, and the era of the Three Kingships began

775 The three Huanin Kingships united against the Kyrinin clans and the War of the Tainted began

787 Tarcene, the Aygll King, was bound, his mind enslaved, by the *na'kyrim* Orlane; his own daughter, in despair, killed him

788 Tane, the Kyrinin's Shining City, was captured by the Huanin armies, the Deep Rove was raised by the Anain, and the War of the Tainted ended

792 Morvain's Revolt, a rising against the faltering Aygll Kingship, culminated in a failed siege of Highfast

793 The last Aygll monarch – Lerr, the Boy King – was slain at In'Vay, and the era of the Three Kingships ended; Aygll lands descended into chaos and the Storm Years began

847 The Bloods – Kilkry, Haig, Gyre, Ayth and Taral – were founded in Aygll lands, and Kulkain oc Kilkry became the first Thane of Thanes; the end of the Storm Years

849 Kulkain oc Kilkry bade Lorryn the *na'kyrim* establish at Highfast a library for the preservation of learning and knowledge

852 The last Alsire King was slain, and the first King of the Dornach line took his throne in Evaness

922 The Black Road heresy arose in Kilvale; Amanath the Fisherwoman, its originator, was executed and the creed outlawed by the Bloods

939 Avann oc Gyre-Kilkry, Thane of the Gyre Blood, adopted the creed of the Black Road

940 Civil war broke out amongst the Kilkry Bloods, between the adherents of the Black Road and those opposed to the creed

942 Following their defeat in battle at Kan Avor, the Gyre Blood and all adherents of the Black Road were exiled beyond the

Vale of Stones, and founded there the Bloods of the Black Road: Gyre, Horin, Gaven, Wyn and Fane

945 The Lore and Battle Inkalls were founded by the Bloods of the Black Road

948 The last attempt by the Kilkry Bloods to crush the fledgling Bloods of the Black Road in the north ended in failure; their armies retired south of the Vale of Stones and the fortification of Tanwrye began

959 The Hunt Inkall was founded by the Bloods of the Black Road

973 The Lannis Blood was founded, in reward for Sirian Lannis dar Kilkry's defeat of the invading forces of the Black Road at Kolglas

997 Haig replaced Kilkry as first amongst the True Bloods

1052 The Dargannan Blood was founded

1069 The Lannis-Haig Blood defeated Horin-Gyre in the Battle of the Stone Vale, near Tanwrye

1070 Tavan oc Lannis-Haig died, and his son Croesan succeeded him as Thanc of the Lannis Blood

1097 The Lannis-Haig Blood was afflicted by the Heart Fever, which killed almost one in six

1102 The Dargannan Blood rebelled against the authority of Haig, and Gryvan oc Haig, Thane of Thanes, summoned the armies of the True Bloods to march against them

Cast of Characters

The True Bloods

Haig
Lannis-Haig
Kilkry-Haig
Dargannan-Haig
Ayth-Haig
Taral-Haig

Haig Blood

Gryvan oc Haig	The High Thane, Thane of Thanes
Abeh oc Haig	Gryvan's wife
Aewult nan Haig	Gryvan's first son, the Bloodheir
Ishbel	Aewult's companion
Kale	Gryvan's bodyguard and Captain of his Shield
Mordyn Jerain, the Shadowhand	Chancellor of the Haig Blood, a Tal Dyreen
Tara Jerain	The Chancellor's wife
Torquentine	A man in Vaymouth
Magrayn	A woman in Vaymouth, Torquentine's doorkeeper
Lammain	Craftmaster of the Goldsmiths
Lagair Haldyn	Gryvan's Steward in Kolkyre

Lannis-Haig Blood

Orisian oc Lannis-Haig		The Thane
Anyara nan Lannis-Haig		Orisian's sister
Taim Narran		Captain of Castle Anduran
Jaen		Taim's wife
Rothe		Orisian's shieldman
Coinach		Anyara's shieldman
Torcaill		A warrior
The Dead:	Kennet	Orisian's father, killed at Kolglas
	Lairis	Orisian's mother, died of the Heart Fever
	Fariel	Orisian's elder brother, died of the Heart Fever
	Croesan	The late Thane, Orisian's uncle, killed at Anduran
	Naradin	Croesan's son, killed at Anduran
	Eilan	Naradin's wife, killed at Anduran
	Inurian	Kennet's *na'kyrim* counsellor, killed at Sarn's Leap

Kilkry-Haig Blood

Lheanor oc Kilkry-Haig		The Thane
Ilessa oc Kilkry-Haig		Lheanor's wife
Roaric nan Kilkry-Haig		Lheanor's second son, now the Bloodheir
Cailla		A kitchen maid in Kolkyre
Ochan the Cook		A man in Kolkyre
Ammen Sharp		Ochan's son
Herraic		Lheanor's cousin, Captain of the Highfast garrison
The Dead:	Gerain	Lheanor's first son, killed in battle at Grive

Dargannan-Haig Blood

Igryn oc Dargannan-Haig	Former Thane, now blinded and imprisoned at Vaymouth

The Bloods Of The Black Road

Gyre
Horin-Gyre
Gaven-Gyre
Wyn-Gyre
Fane-Gyre
and The Inkallim

Gyre Blood

Ragnor oc Gyre	The High Thane, Thane of Thanes
Temegrin, the Eagle	Third Captain of the High Thane's armies

Horin-Gyre Blood

Kanin oc Horin-Gyre	The Thane
Wain nan Horin-Gyre	Kanin's sister
Vana oc Horin-Gyre	Mother to Kanin and Wain, widow of Angain
Igris	Kanin's shieldman
The Dead: Angain	The late Thane, died in his bed

Inkallim

Theor	First of the Lore Inkall
Nyve	First of the Battle Inkall
Avenn	First of the Hunt Inkall
Fiallic	Banner-captain and field commander of the Battle Inkall
Goedellin	Inner Servant of the Lore Inkall, emissary of Theor
Shraeve	A captain of the Battle Inkall
Cannek	A Hunt Inkallim

Others

Huanin
Kyrinin
Na'kyrim

Huanin

Alem T'anarch	Ambassador of the Dornach Kingship to the Haig Blood

Kyrinin

Ess'yr	A woman of the Fox clan, now in the company of Orisian
Varryn	Ess'yr's brother, now in the company of Orisian
Mar'athoin	A young warrior of the Heron clan
Hothyn	Son of the White Owl Voice, leader of a spear *a'an*

Na'kyrim

Yvane	A *na'kyrim*, now in the company of Orisian
Hammarn	A *na'kyrim* from Koldihrve, now in the company of Orisian
Cerys	A *na'kyrim*, the Elect of Highfast
Amonyn	A *na'kyrim* in Highfast, lover of Cerys
Olyn	A *na'kyrim* in Highfast, Keeper of Crows
Tyn	A *na'kyrim*, the Dreamer in Highfast
Eshenna	A *na'kyrim* in Highfast, originally from Dyrkyrnon
Bannain	A *na'kyrim* in Highfast, a messenger
K'rina	A *na'kyrim* from Dyrkyrnon, once foster-mother to Aeglyss
Aeglyss	A *na'kyrim* formerly in the service of the Horin-Gyre Blood, survivor of the Breaking Stone of the White Owls